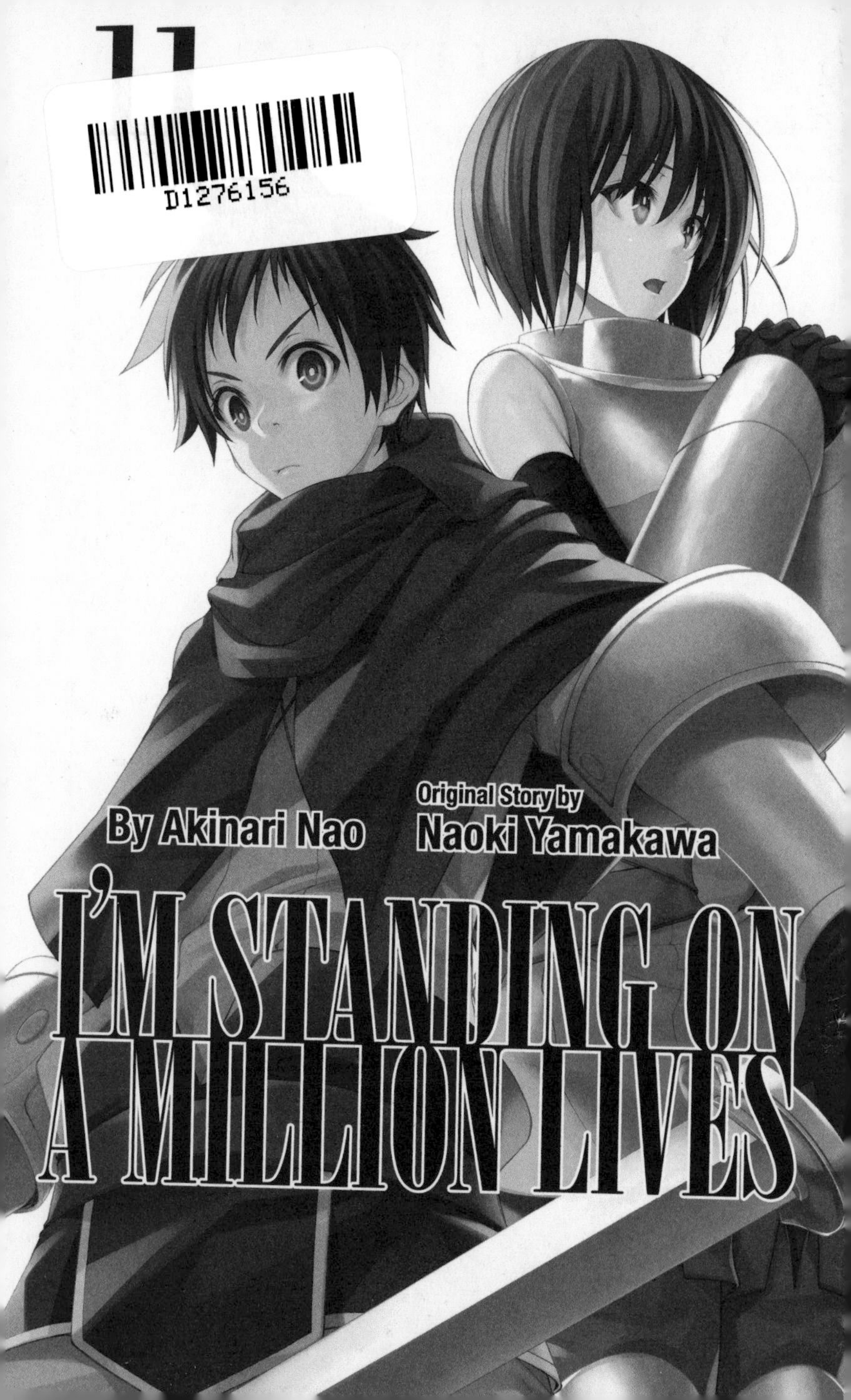

11

By Akinari Nao

Original Story by
Naoki Yamakawa

I'M STANDING ON A MILLION LIVES

⚔ CONTENTS ⚔

#50 The Elephant Content with His Chains

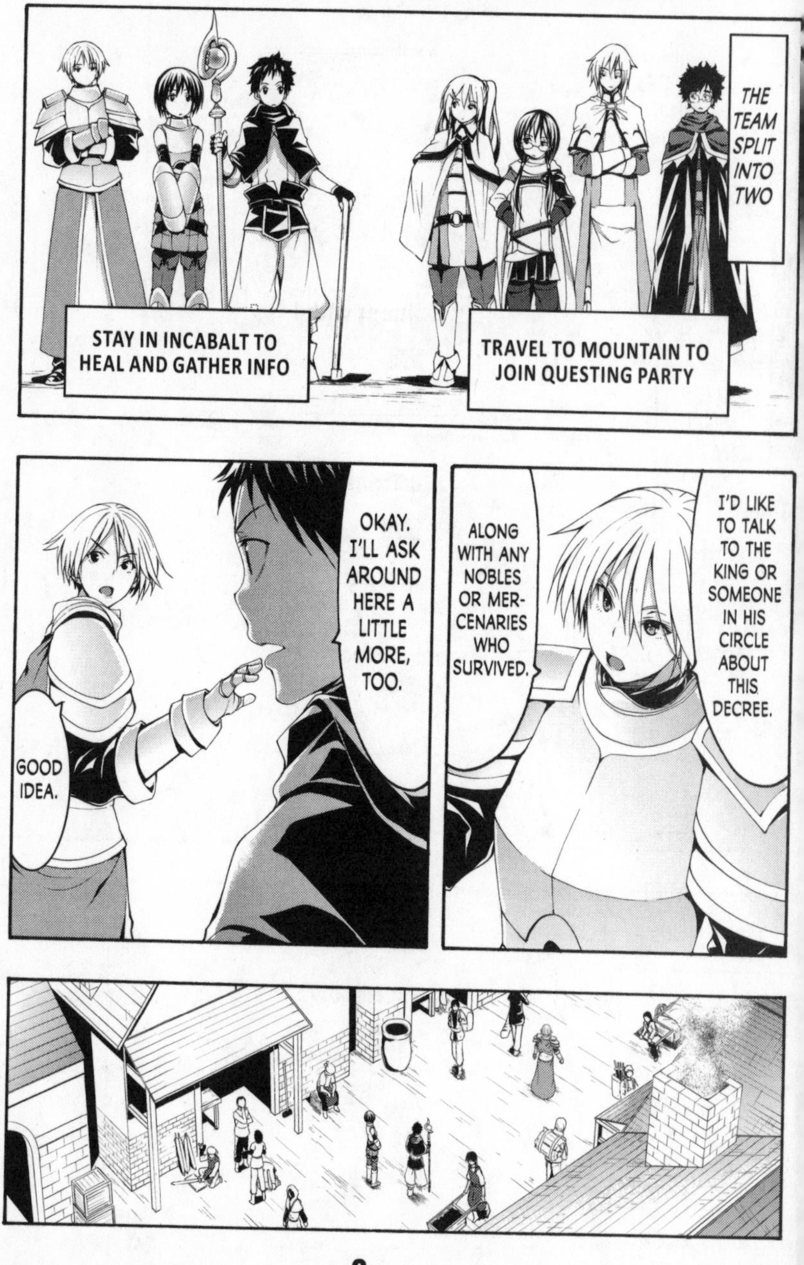
THE TEAM SPLIT INTO TWO
TRAVEL TO MOUNTAIN TO JOIN QUESTING PARTY
STAY IN INCABALT TO HEAL AND GATHER INFO
I'D LIKE TO TALK TO THE KING OR SOMEONE IN HIS CIRCLE ABOUT THIS DECREE.
ALONG WITH ANY NOBLES OR MERCENARIES WHO SURVIVED.
OKAY. I'LL ASK AROUND HERE A LITTLE MORE, TOO.
GOOD IDEA.

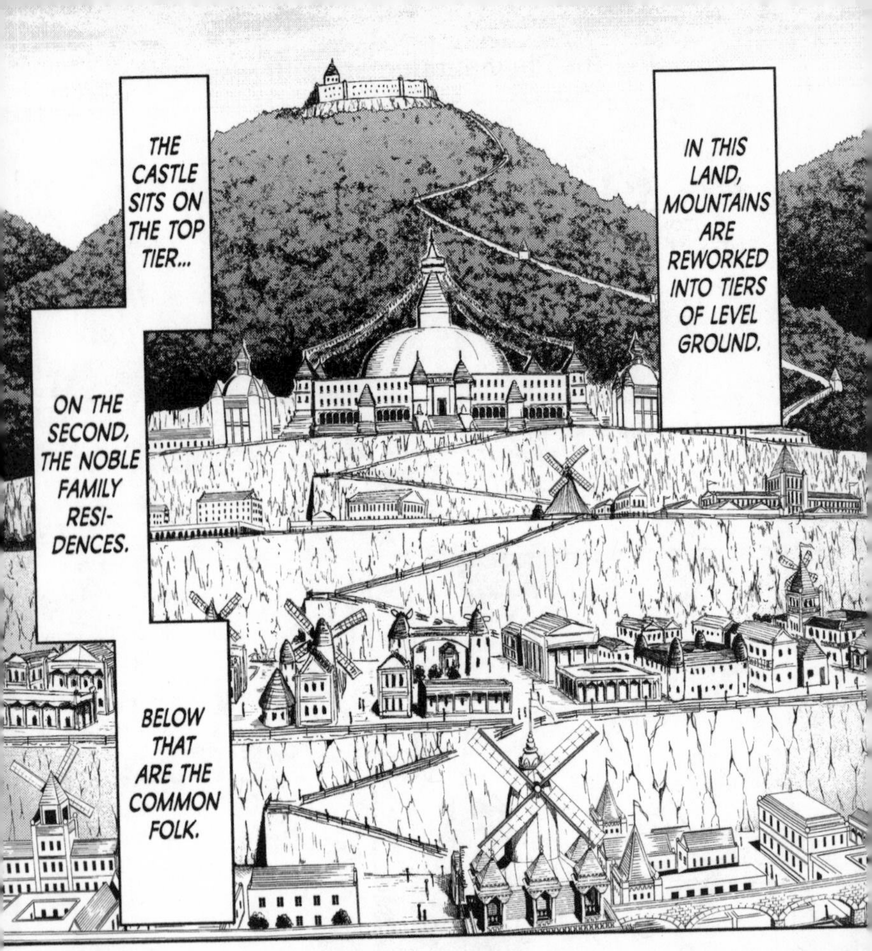
IN THIS LAND, MOUNTAINS ARE REWORKED INTO TIERS OF LEVEL GROUND.
THE CASTLE SITS ON THE TOP TIER...
ON THE SECOND, THE NOBLE FAMILY RESI-DENCES.
BELOW THAT ARE THE COMMON FOLK.

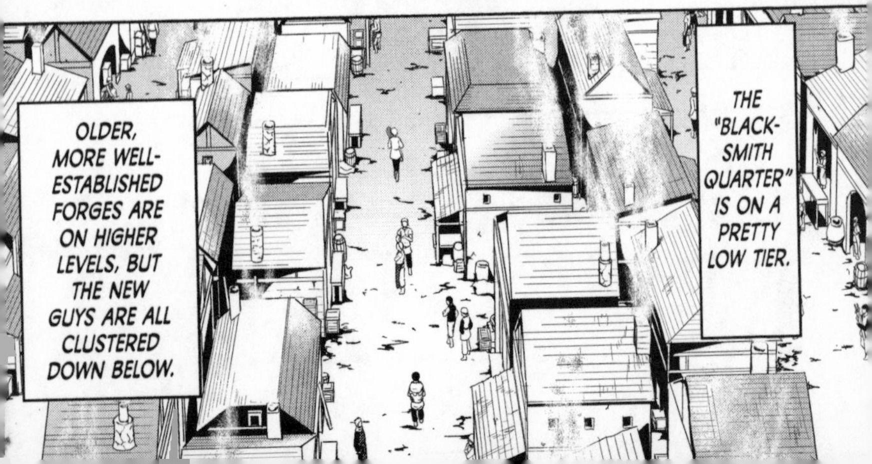
THE "BLACK-SMITH QUARTER" IS ON A PRETTY LOW TIER.
OLDER, MORE WELL-ESTABLISHED FORGES ARE ON HIGHER LEVELS, BUT THE NEW GUYS ARE ALL CLUSTERED DOWN BELOW.

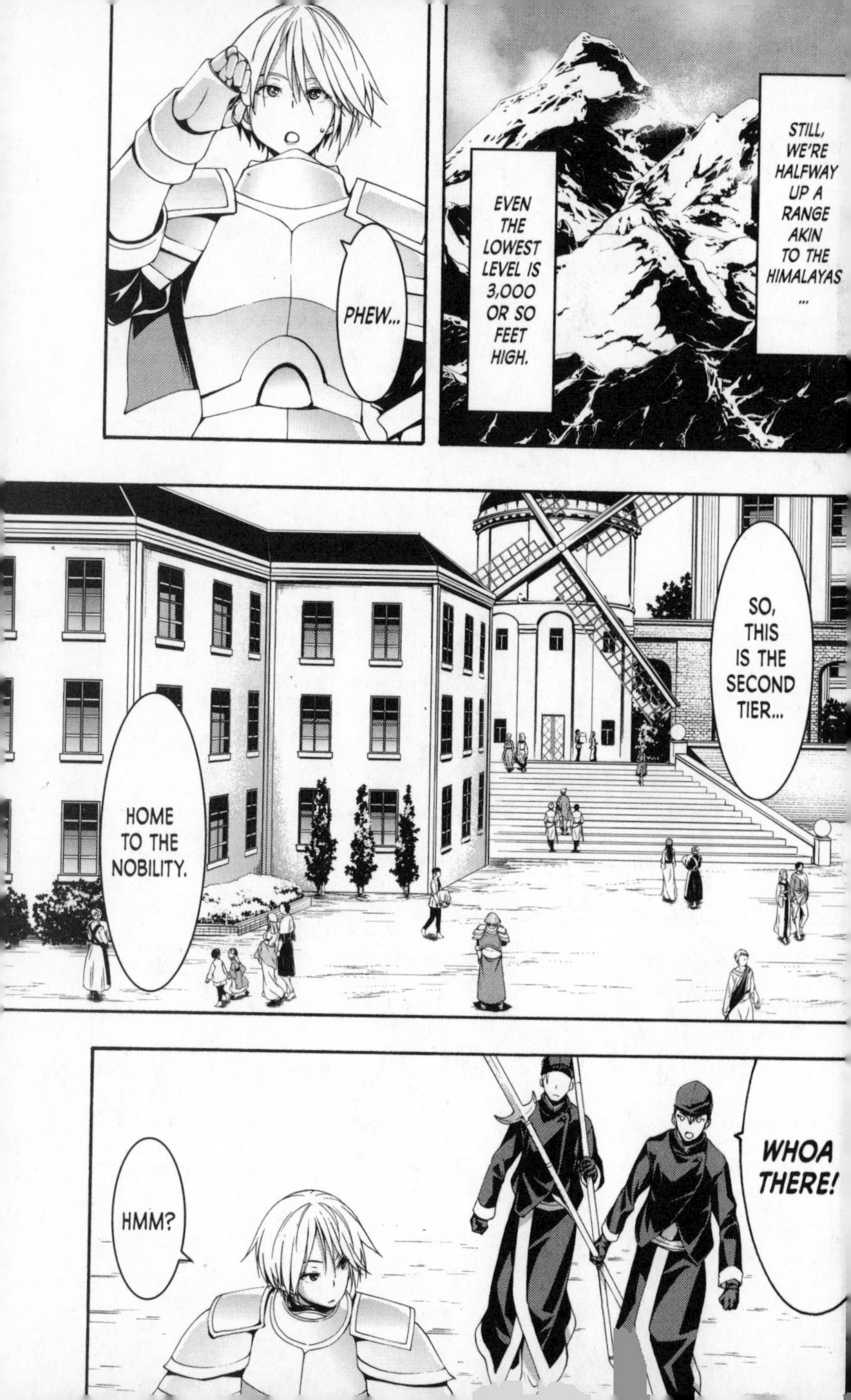
STILL, WE'RE HALFWAY UP A RANGE AKIN TO THE HIMALAYAS...
EVEN THE LOWEST LEVEL IS 3,000 OR SO FEET HIGH.
PHEW...
SO, THIS IS THE SECOND TIER...
HOME TO THE NOBILITY.
WHOA THERE!
HMM?

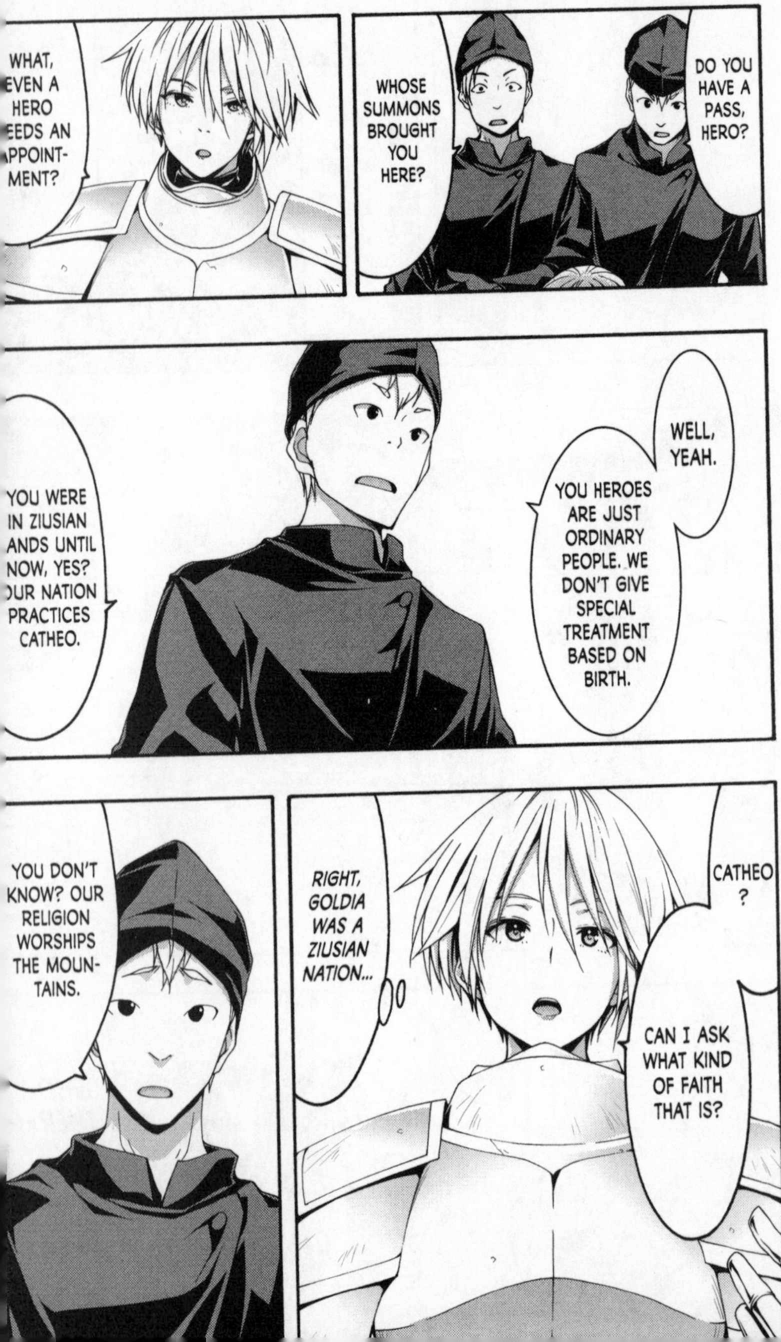
DO YOU HAVE A PASS, HERO?
WHOSE SUMMONS BROUGHT YOU HERE?
WHAT, EVEN A HERO EEDS AN PPOINT- MENT?
WELL, YEAH.
YOU HEROES ARE JUST ORDINARY PEOPLE. WE DON'T GIVE SPECIAL TREATMENT BASED ON BIRTH.
YOU WERE IN ZIUSIAN ANDS UNTIL NOW, YES? UR NATION PRACTICES CATHEO.
CATHEO?
CAN I ASK WHAT KIND OF FAITH THAT IS?
RIGHT, GOLDIA WAS A ZIUSIAN NATION...
YOU DON'T KNOW? OUR RELIGION WORSHIPS THE MOUN- TAINS.

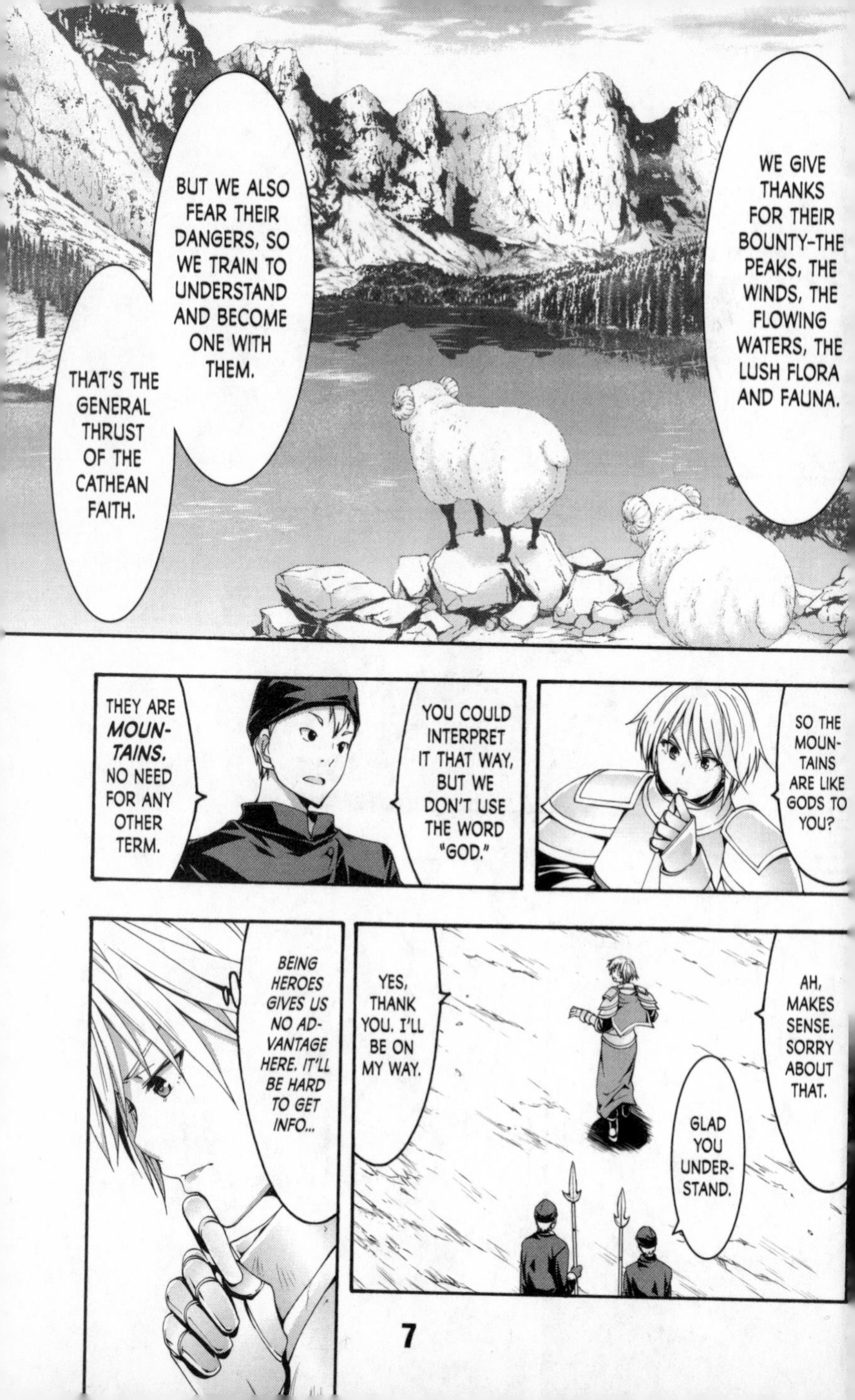
WE GIVE THANKS FOR THEIR BOUNTY—THE PEAKS, THE WINDS, THE FLOWING WATERS, THE LUSH FLORA AND FAUNA.
BUT WE ALSO FEAR THEIR DANGERS, SO WE TRAIN TO UNDERSTAND AND BECOME ONE WITH THEM.
THAT'S THE GENERAL THRUST OF THE CATHEAN FAITH.
SO THE MOUN-TAINS ARE LIKE GODS TO YOU?
YOU COULD INTERPRET IT THAT WAY, BUT WE DON'T USE THE WORD "GOD."
THEY ARE *MOUN-TAINS.* NO NEED FOR ANY OTHER TERM.
AH, MAKES SENSE. SORRY ABOUT THAT.
GLAD YOU UNDER-STAND.
YES, THANK YOU. I'LL BE ON MY WAY.
BEING HEROES GIVES US NO AD-VANTAGE HERE. IT'LL BE HARD TO GET INFO...

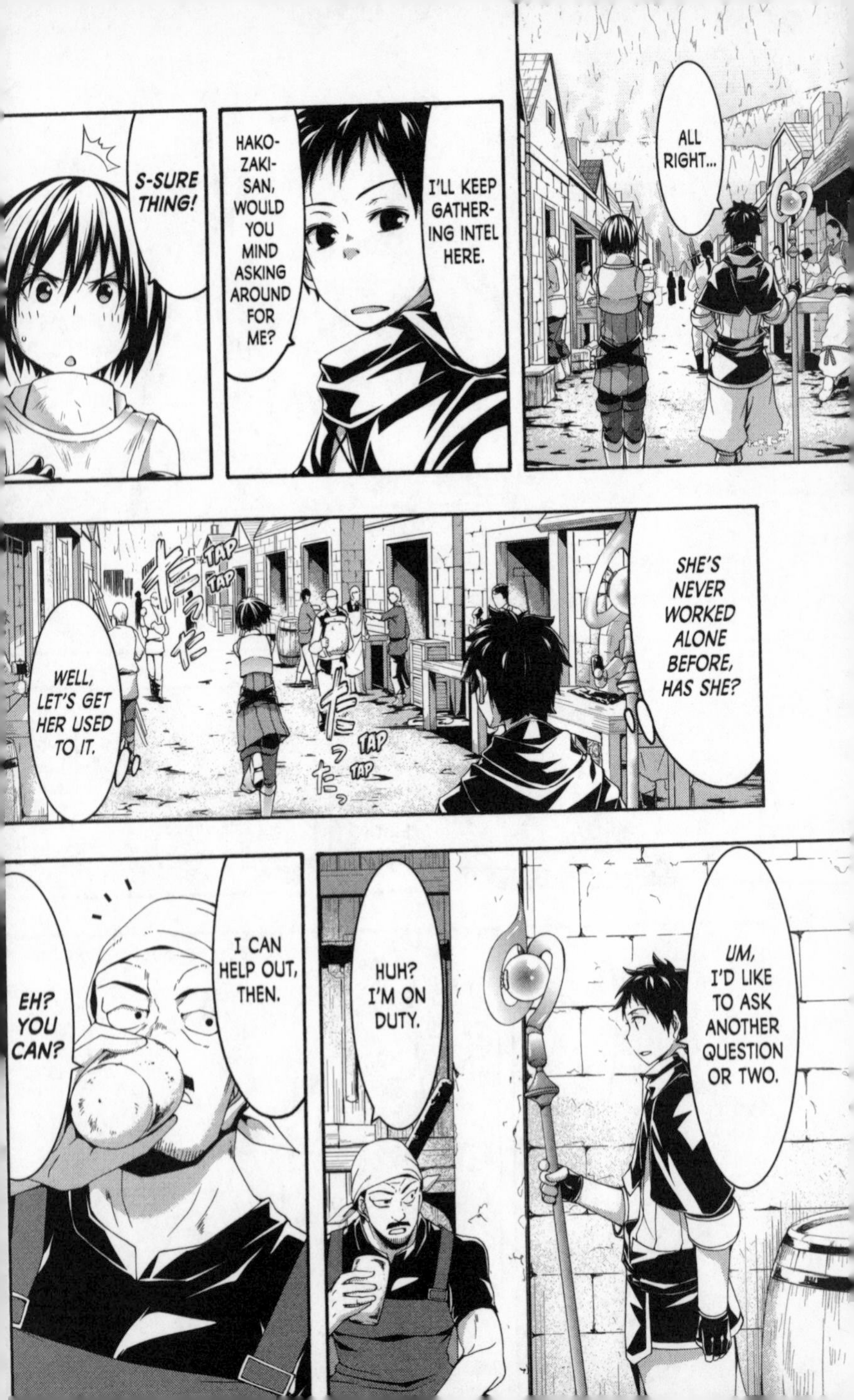
ALL RIGHT...
I'LL KEEP GATHERING INTEL HERE.
HAKOZAKI-SAN, WOULD YOU MIND ASKING AROUND FOR ME?
S-SURE THING!
SHE'S NEVER WORKED ALONE BEFORE, HAS SHE?
TAP TAP
TAP TAP
WELL, LET'S GET HER USED TO IT.
UM, I'D LIKE TO ASK ANOTHER QUESTION OR TWO.
HUH? I'M ON DUTY.
I CAN HELP OUT, THEN.
EH? YOU CAN?

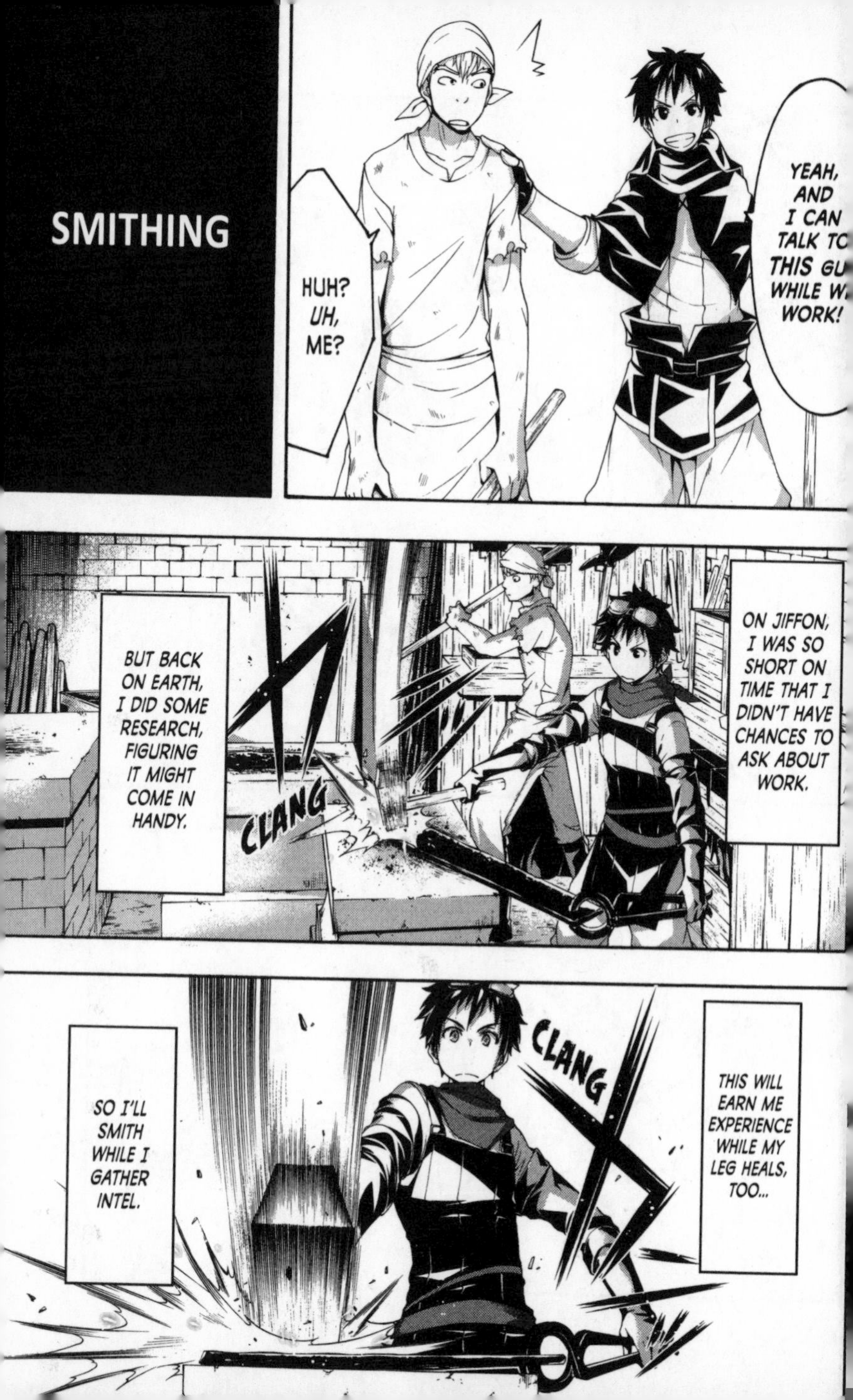
YEAH, AND I CAN TALK TO THIS GU WHILE W WORK!
HUH? UH, ME?
SMITHING
ON JIFFON, I WAS SO SHORT ON TIME THAT I DIDN'T HAVE CHANCES TO ASK ABOUT WORK.
CLANG
BUT BACK ON EARTH, I DID SOME RESEARCH, FIGURING IT MIGHT COME IN HANDY.
THIS WILL EARN ME EXPERIENCE WHILE MY LEG HEALS, TOO...
CLANG
SO I'LL SMITH WHILE I GATHER INTEL.

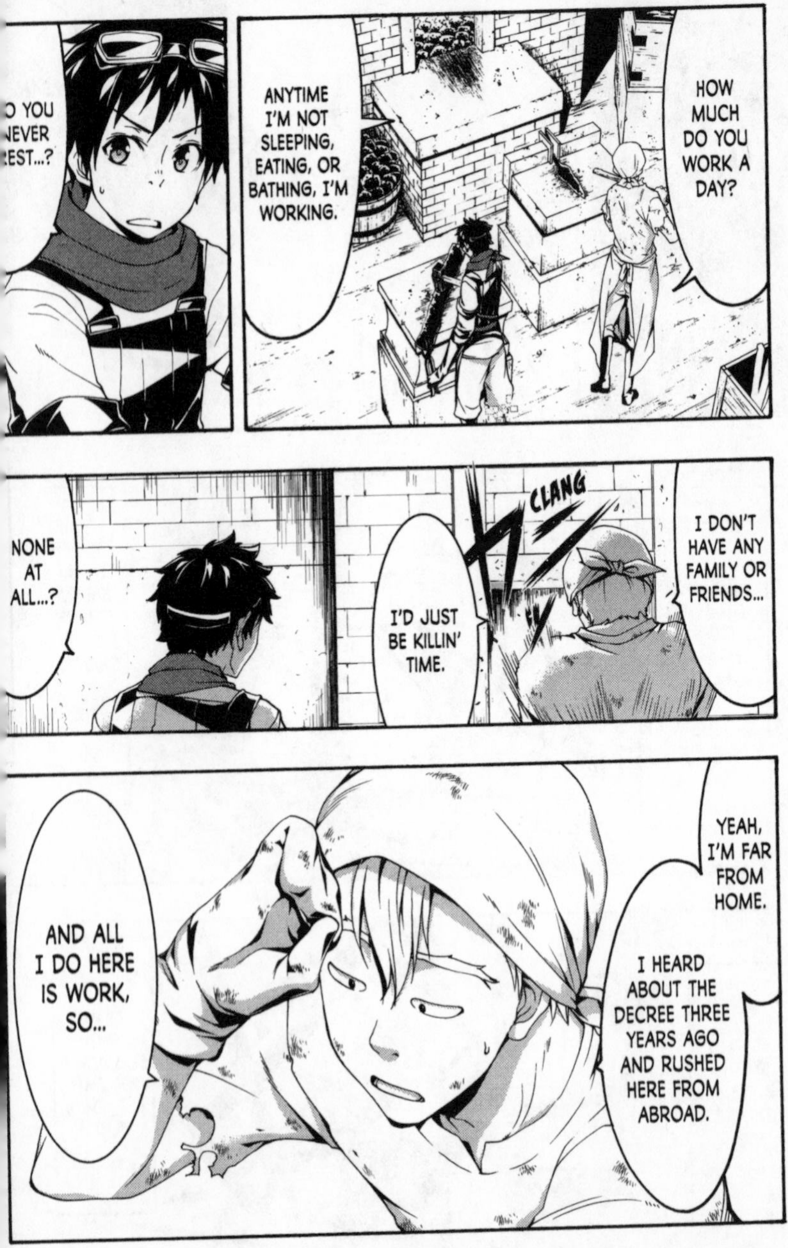
HOW MUCH DO YOU WORK A DAY?
ANYTIME I'M NOT SLEEPING, EATING, OR BATHING, I'M WORKING.
O YOU NEVER EST...?
I DON'T HAVE ANY FAMILY OR FRIENDS...
CLANG
I'D JUST BE KILLIN' TIME.
NONE AT ALL...?
YEAH, I'M FAR FROM HOME.
I HEARD ABOUT THE DECREE THREE YEARS AGO AND RUSHED HERE FROM ABROAD.
AND ALL I DO HERE IS WORK, SO...

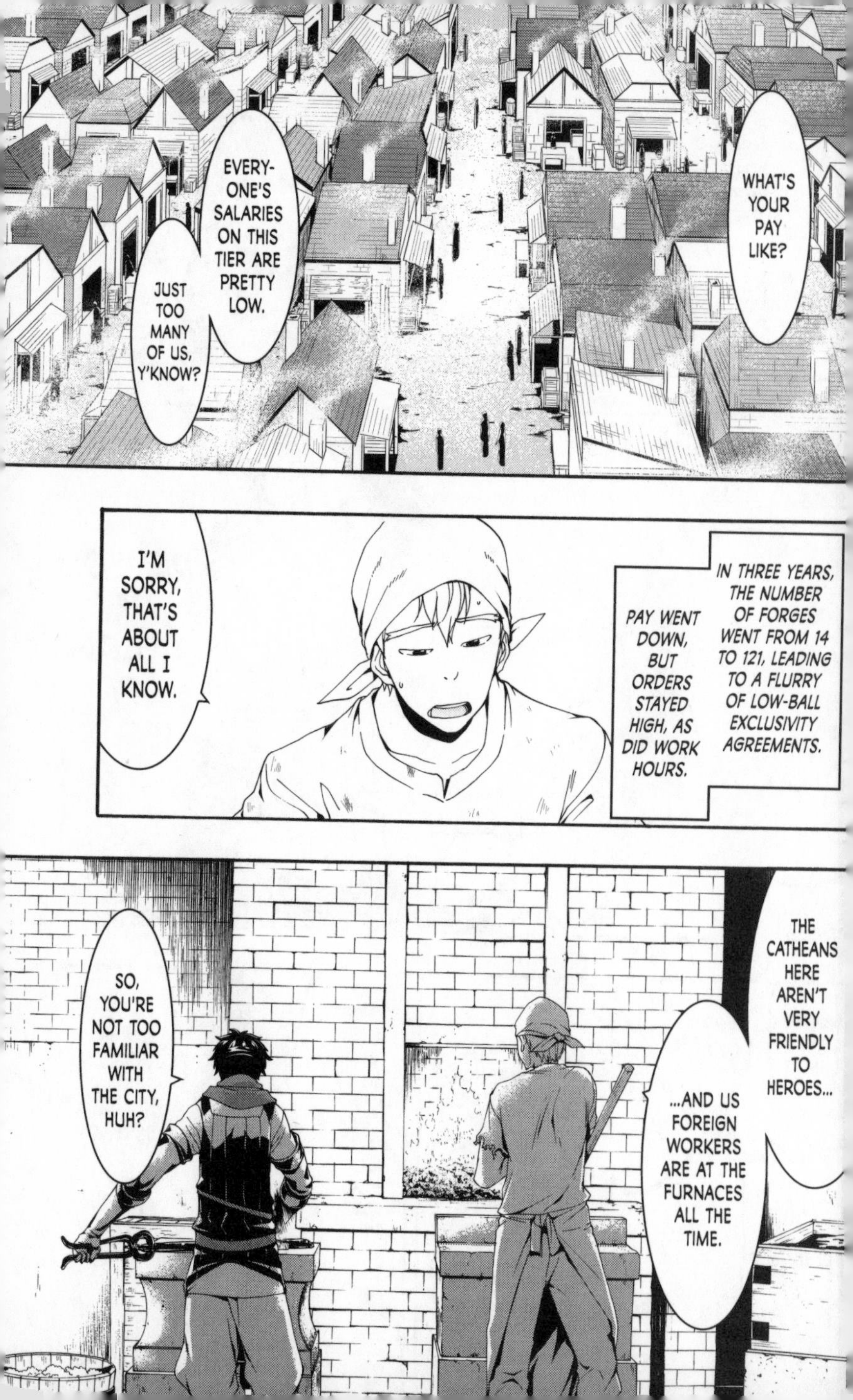
WHAT'S YOUR PAY LIKE?
EVERY-ONE'S SALARIES ON THIS TIER ARE PRETTY LOW.
JUST TOO MANY OF US, Y'KNOW?
IN THREE YEARS, THE NUMBER OF FORGES WENT FROM 14 TO 121, LEADING TO A FLURRY OF LOW-BALL EXCLUSIVITY AGREEMENTS.
PAY WENT DOWN, BUT ORDERS STAYED HIGH, AS DID WORK HOURS.
I'M SORRY, THAT'S ABOUT ALL I KNOW.
THE CATHEANS HERE AREN'T VERY FRIENDLY TO HEROES...
...AND US FOREIGN WORKERS ARE AT THE FURNACES ALL THE TIME.
SO, YOU'RE NOT TOO FAMILIAR WITH THE CITY, HUH?

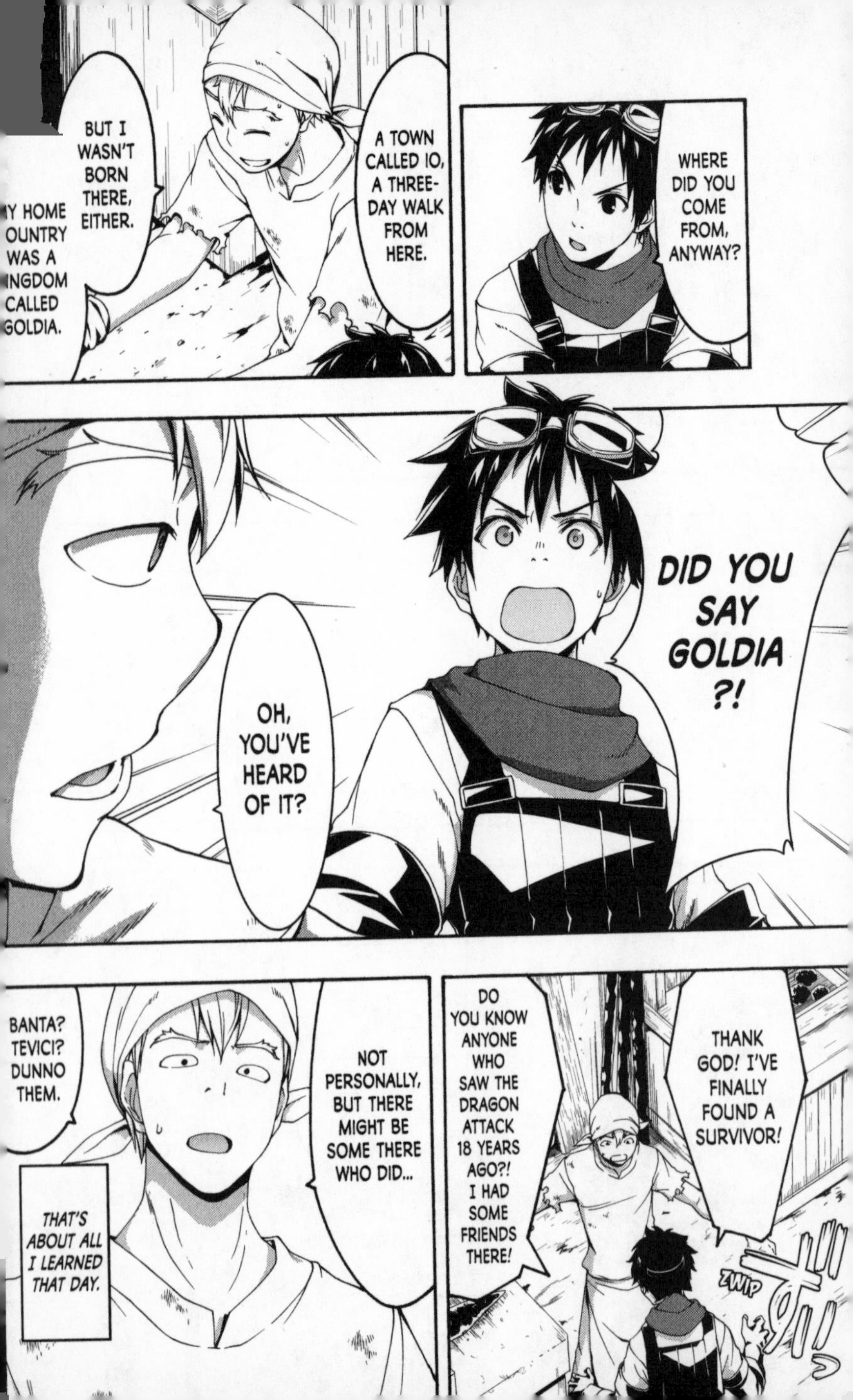
WHERE DID YOU COME FROM, ANYWAY?
A TOWN CALLED IO, A THREE-DAY WALK FROM HERE.
BUT I WASN'T BORN THERE, EITHER.
Y HOME OUNTRY WAS A INGDOM CALLED GOLDIA.
DID YOU SAY GOLDIA ?!
OH, YOU'VE HEARD OF IT?
THANK GOD! I'VE FINALLY FOUND A SURVIVOR!
ZWIP
DO YOU KNOW ANYONE WHO SAW THE DRAGON ATTACK 18 YEARS AGO?! I HAD SOME FRIENDS THERE!
NOT PERSONALLY, BUT THERE MIGHT BE SOME THERE WHO DID...
BANTA? TEVICI? DUNNO THEM.
THAT'S ABOUT ALL I LEARNED THAT DAY.

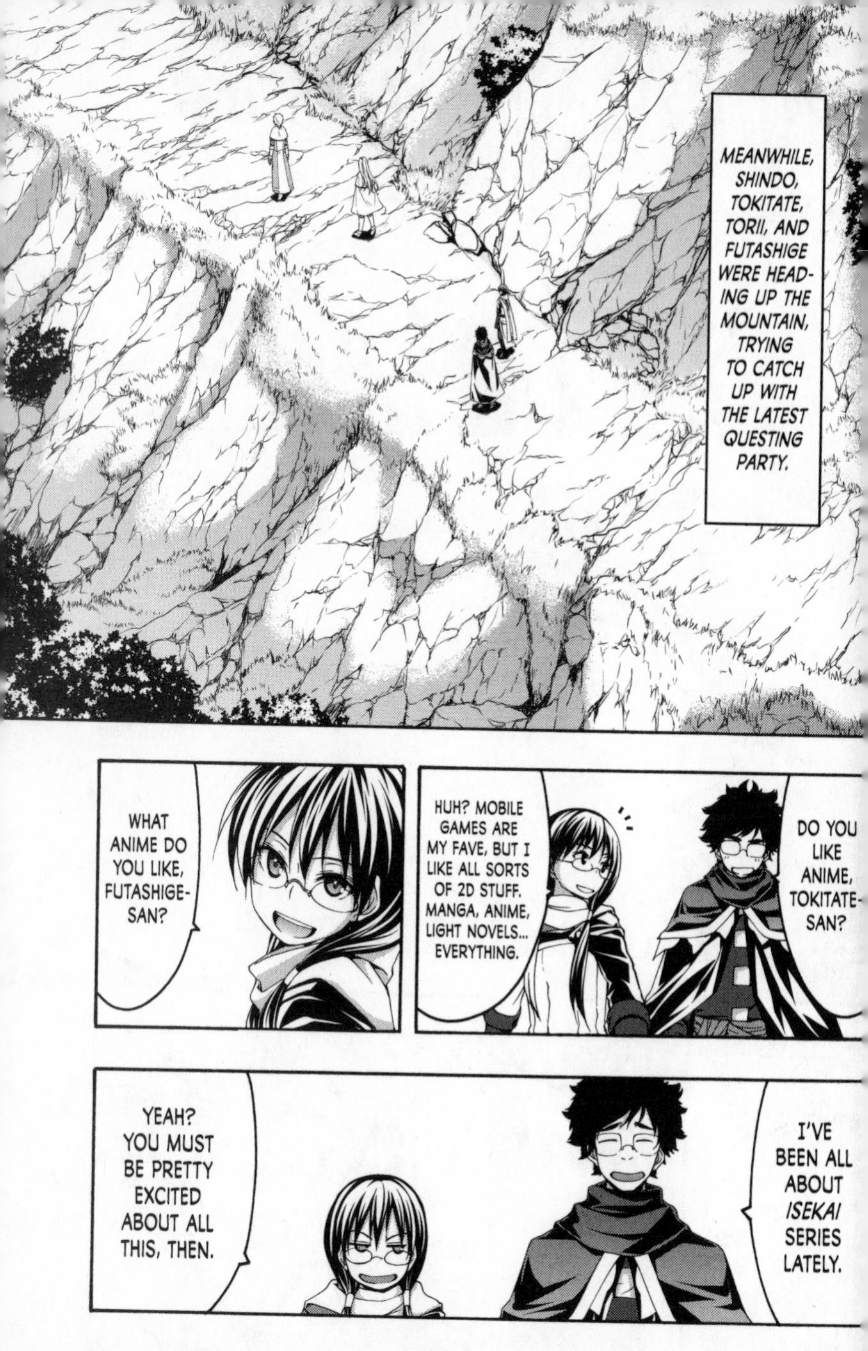
MEANWHILE, SHINDO, TOKITATE, TORII, AND FUTASHIGE WERE HEADING UP THE MOUNTAIN, TRYING TO CATCH UP WITH THE LATEST QUESTING PARTY.
DO YOU LIKE ANIME, TOKITATE-SAN?
HUH? MOBILE GAMES ARE MY FAVE, BUT I LIKE ALL SORTS OF 2D STUFF. MANGA, ANIME, LIGHT NOVELS... EVERYTHING.
WHAT ANIME DO YOU LIKE, FUTASHIGE-SAN?
I'VE BEEN ALL ABOUT *ISEKAI* SERIES LATELY.
YEAH? YOU MUST BE PRETTY EXCITED ABOUT ALL THIS, THEN.

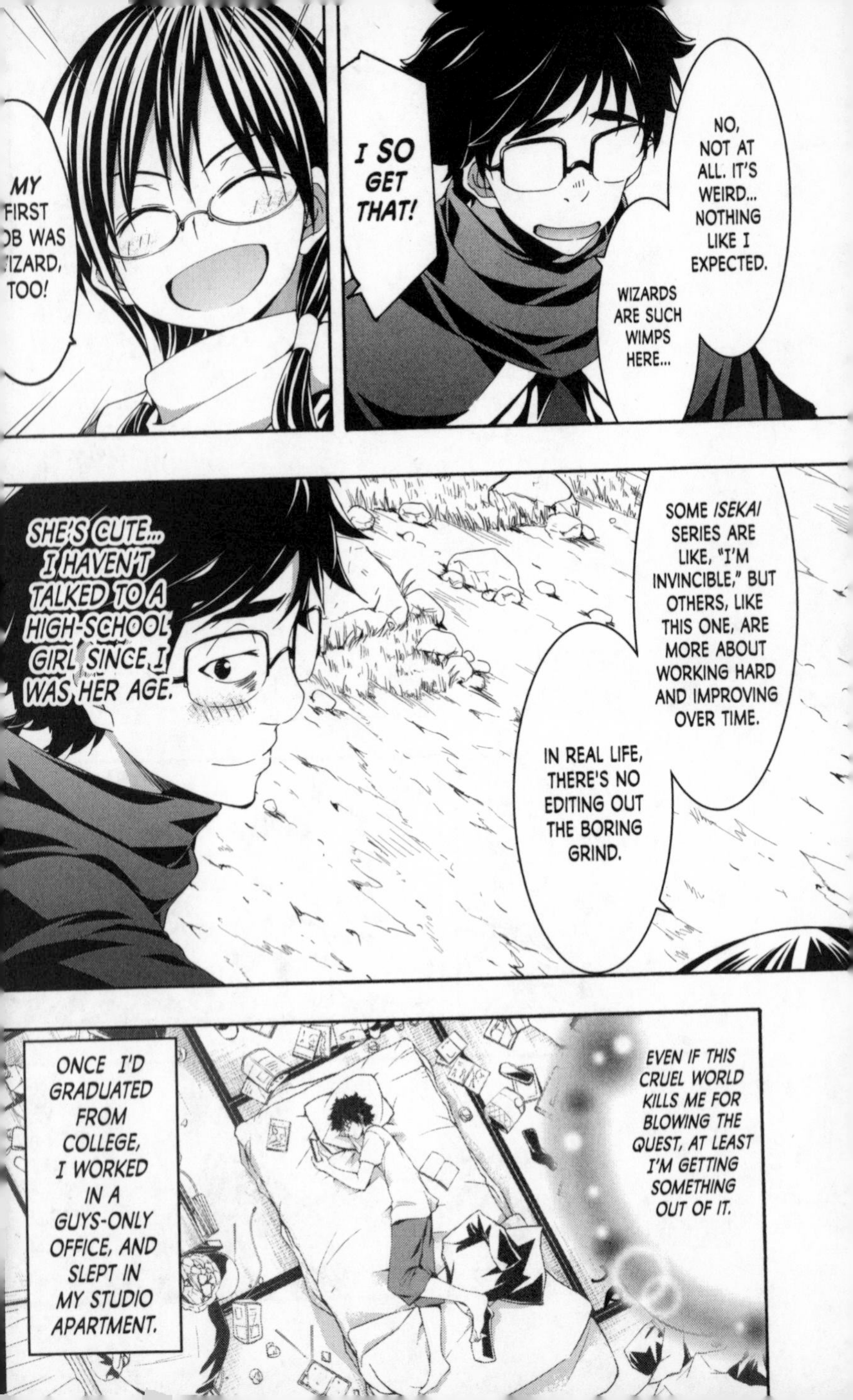
NO, NOT AT ALL. IT'S WEIRD... NOTHING LIKE I EXPECTED.
WIZARDS ARE SUCH WIMPS HERE...
I SO GET THAT!
MY FIRST OB WAS IZARD, TOO!
SOME *ISEKAI* SERIES ARE LIKE, "I'M INVINCIBLE," BUT OTHERS, LIKE THIS ONE, ARE MORE ABOUT WORKING HARD AND IMPROVING OVER TIME.
IN REAL LIFE, THERE'S NO EDITING OUT THE BORING GRIND.
SHE'S CUTE... I HAVEN'T TALKED TO A HIGH-SCHOOL GIRL SINCE I WAS HER AGE.
EVEN IF THIS CRUEL WORLD KILLS ME FOR BLOWING THE QUEST, AT LEAST I'M GETTING SOMETHING OUT OF IT.
ONCE I'D GRADUATED FROM COLLEGE, I WORKED IN A GUYS-ONLY OFFICE, AND SLEPT IN MY STUDIO APARTMENT.

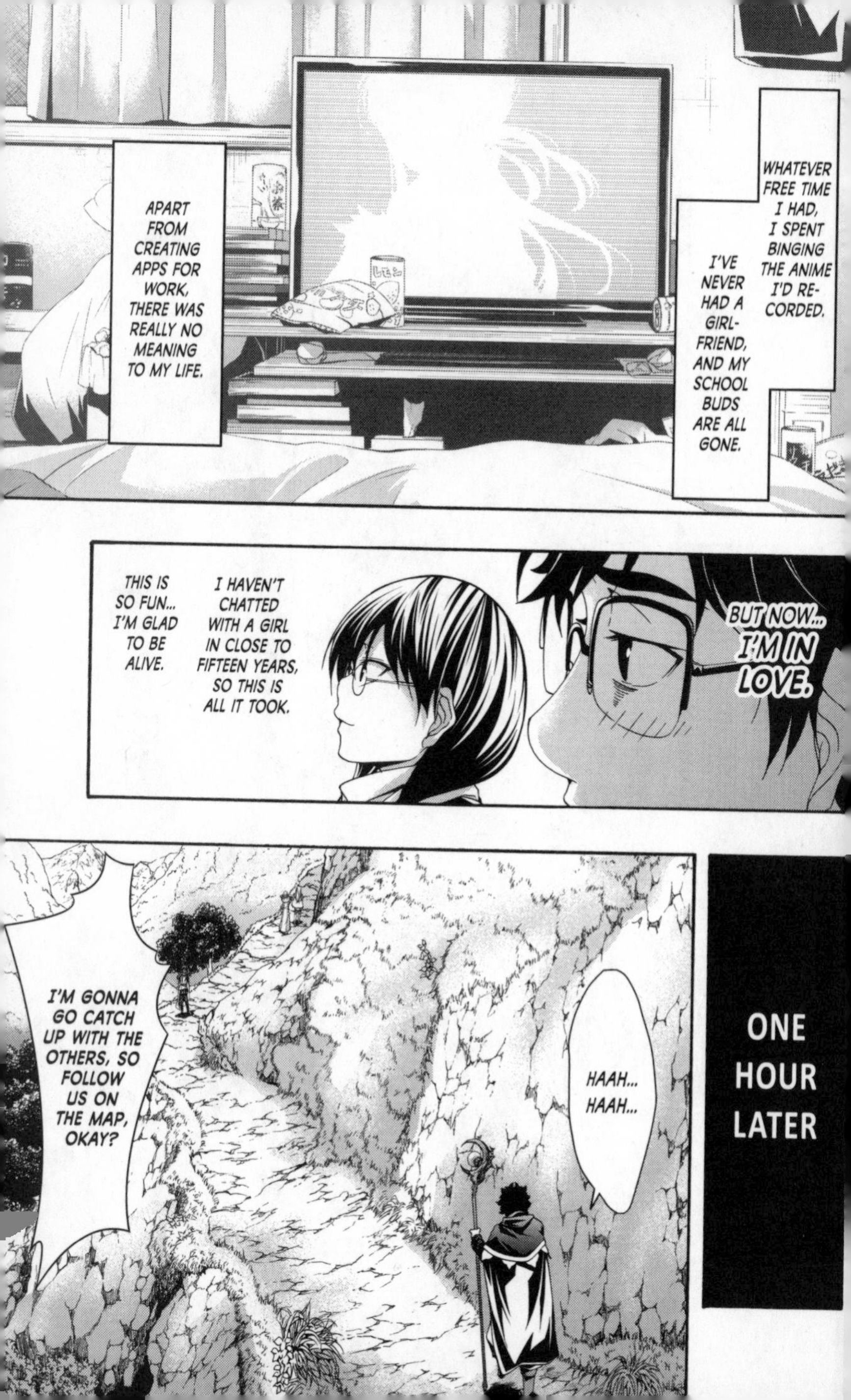
WHATEVER FREE TIME I HAD, I SPENT BINGING THE ANIME I'D RE-CORDED.
I'VE NEVER HAD A GIRL-FRIEND, AND MY SCHOOL BUDS ARE ALL GONE.
APART FROM CREATING APPS FOR WORK, THERE WAS REALLY NO MEANING TO MY LIFE.
BUT NOW... I'M IN LOVE.
I HAVEN'T CHATTED WITH A GIRL IN CLOSE TO FIFTEEN YEARS, SO THIS IS ALL IT TOOK.
THIS IS SO FUN... I'M GLAD TO BE ALIVE.
ONE HOUR LATER
HAAH... HAAH...
I'M GONNA GO CATCH UP WITH THE OTHERS, SO FOLLOW US ON THE MAP, OKAY?

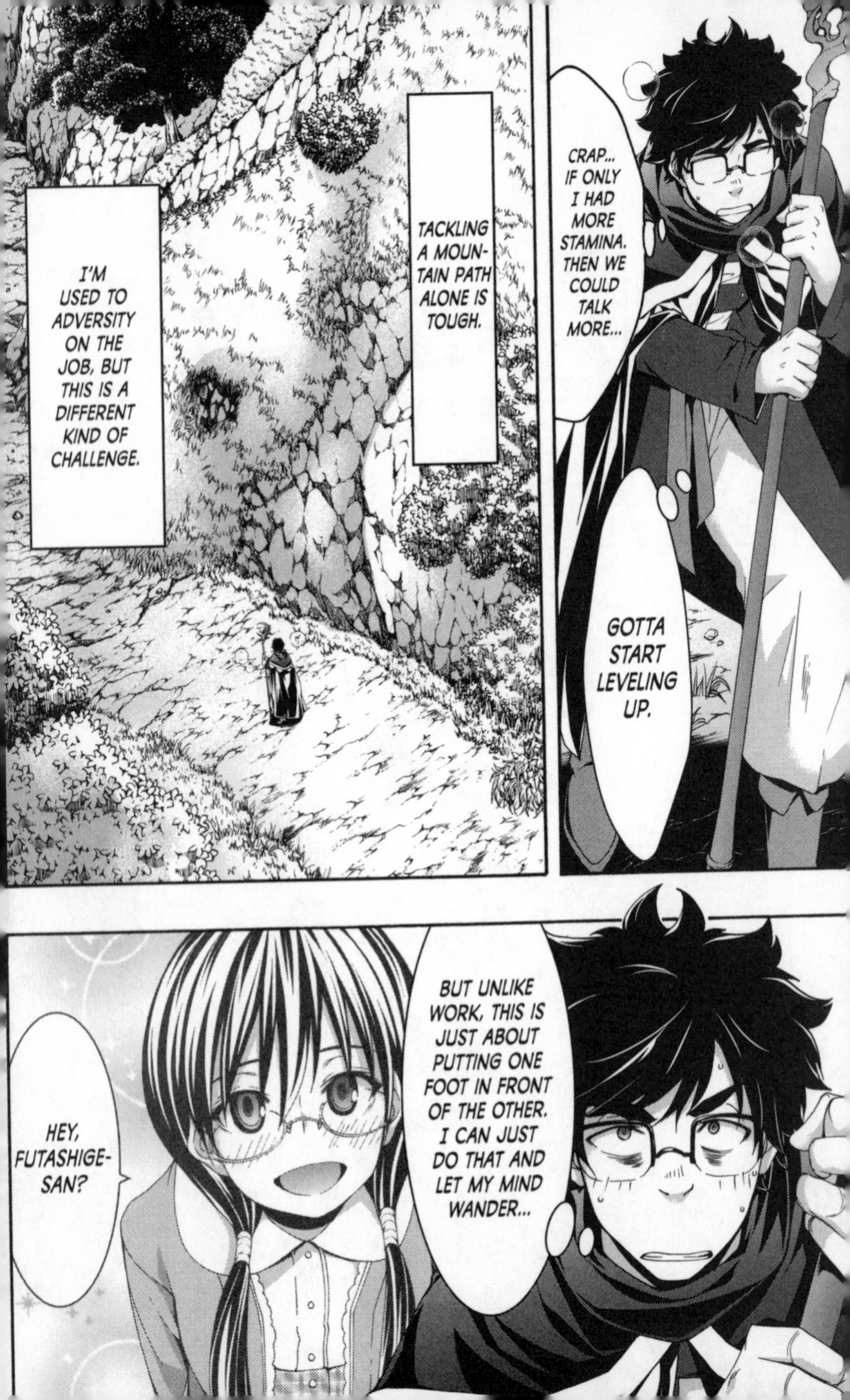
CRAP... IF ONLY I HAD MORE STAMINA. THEN WE COULD TALK MORE...
GOTTA START LEVELING UP.
TACKLING A MOUN-TAIN PATH ALONE IS TOUGH.
I'M USED TO ADVERSITY ON THE JOB, BUT THIS IS A DIFFERENT KIND OF CHALLENGE.
BUT UNLIKE WORK, THIS IS JUST ABOUT PUTTING ONE FOOT IN FRONT OF THE OTHER. I CAN JUST DO THAT AND LET MY MIND WANDER...
HEY, FUTASHIGE-SAN?

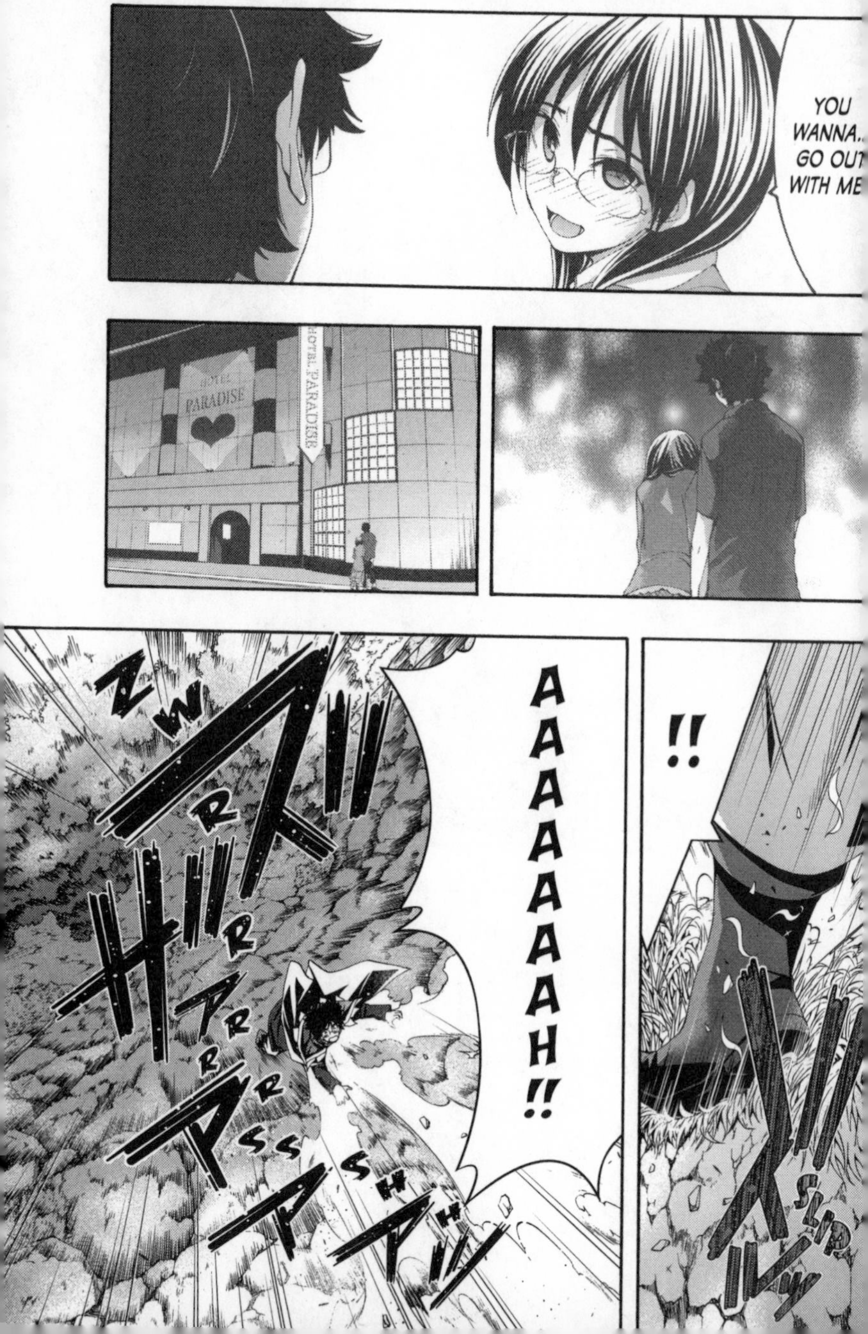
YOU WANNA... GO OUT WITH ME
HOTEL PARADISE
HOTEL PARADISE
!!
SLIP
AAAAAAAAAH!!
ZWRRRRRSSSHH

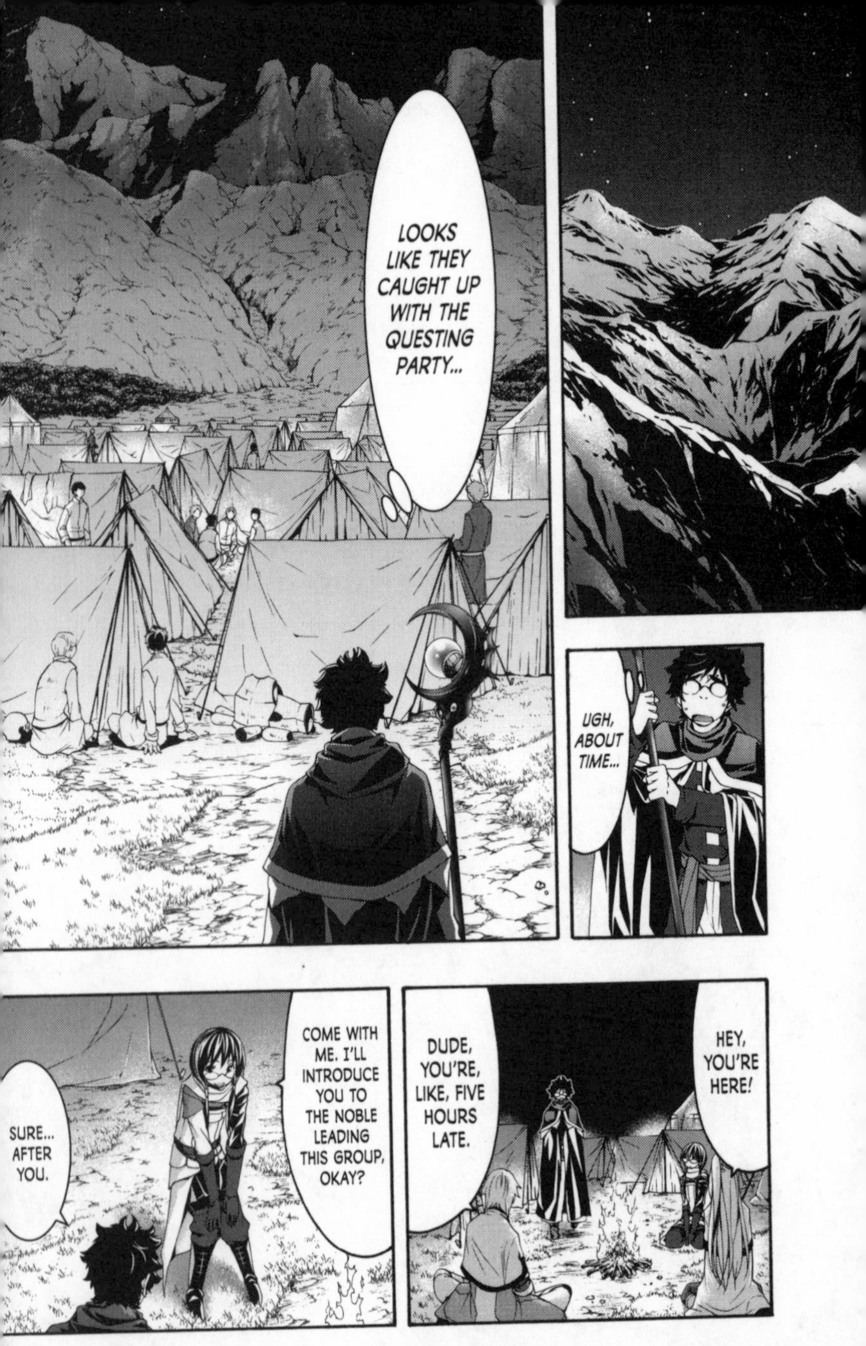
UGH, ABOUT TIME...
LOOKS LIKE THEY CAUGHT UP WITH THE QUESTING PARTY...
HEY, YOU'RE HERE!
DUDE, YOU'RE, LIKE, FIVE HOURS LATE.
COME WITH ME. I'LL INTRODUCE YOU TO THE NOBLE LEADING THIS GROUP, OKAY?
SURE... AFTER YOU.

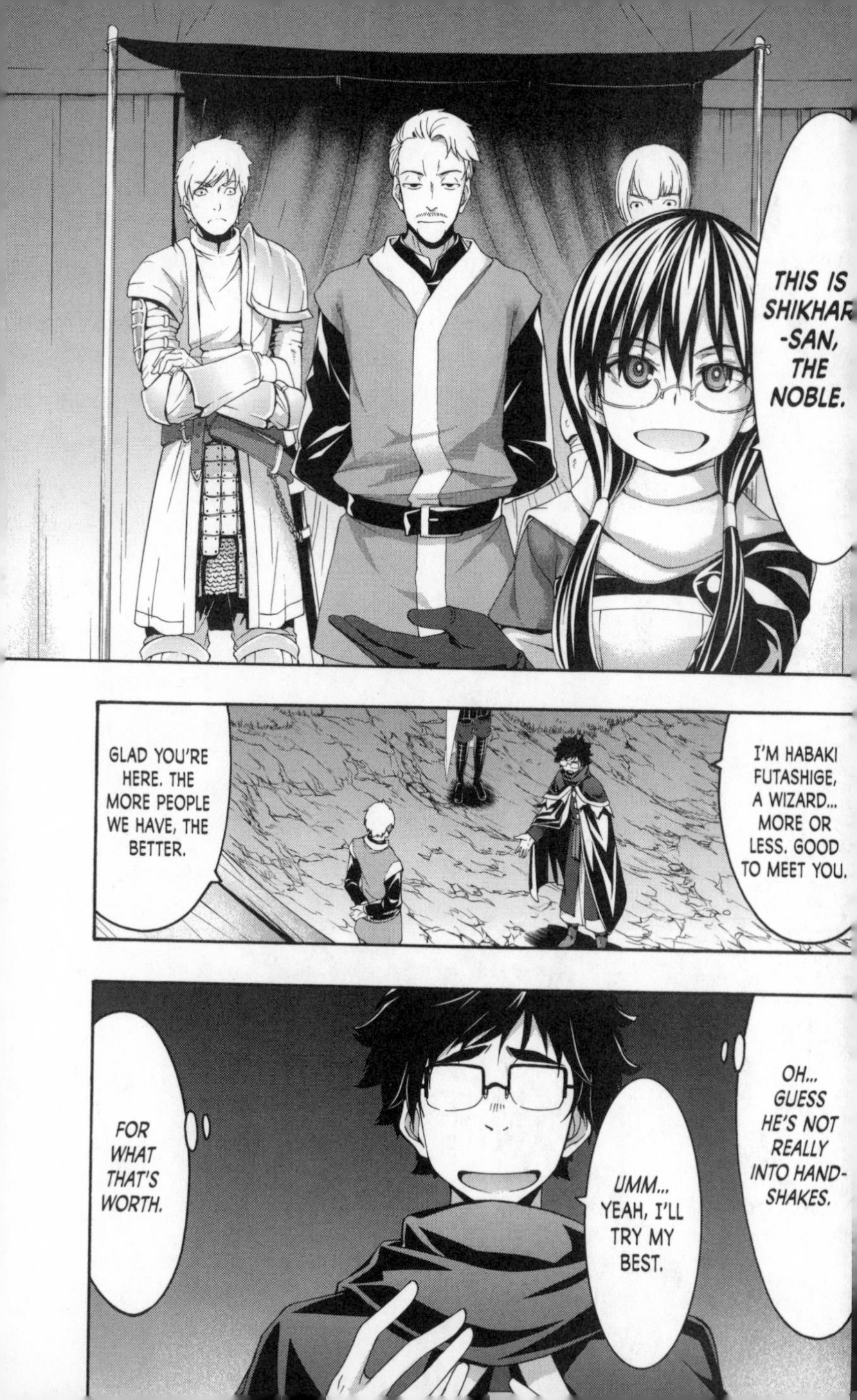
THIS IS SHIKHAR-SAN, THE NOBLE.
I'M HABAKI FUTASHIGE, A WIZARD... MORE OR LESS. GOOD TO MEET YOU.
GLAD YOU'RE HERE. THE MORE PEOPLE WE HAVE, THE BETTER.
OH... GUESS HE'S NOT REALLY INTO HAND-SHAKES.
UMM... YEAH, I'LL TRY MY BEST.
FOR WHAT THAT'S WORTH.

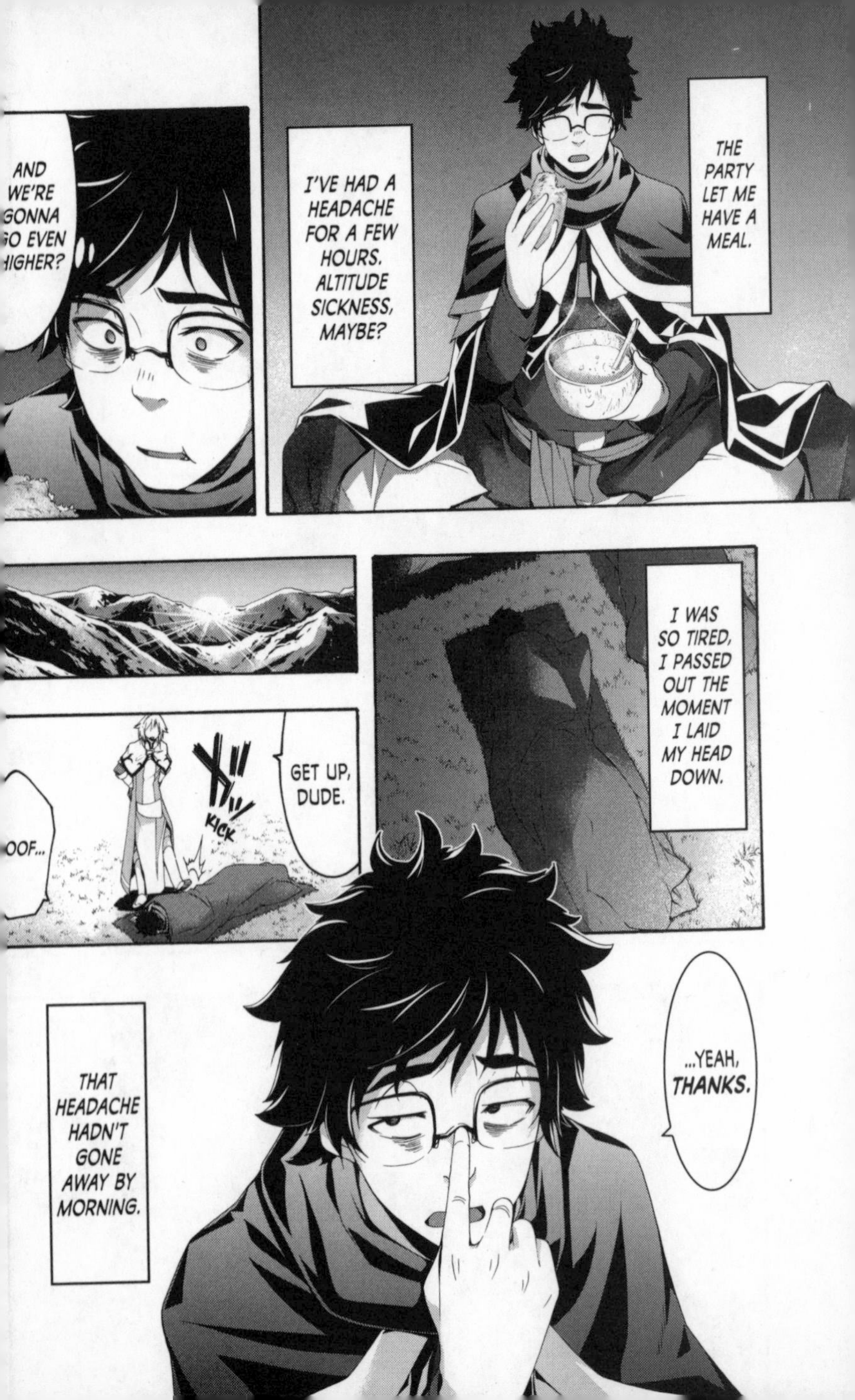
THE PARTY LET ME HAVE A MEAL.
I'VE HAD A HEADACHE FOR A FEW HOURS. ALTITUDE SICKNESS, MAYBE?
AND WE'RE GONNA GO EVEN HIGHER?
I WAS SO TIRED, I PASSED OUT THE MOMENT I LAID MY HEAD DOWN.
GET UP, DUDE.
KICK
OOF...
...YEAH, THANKS.
THAT HEADACHE HADN'T GONE AWAY BY MORNING.

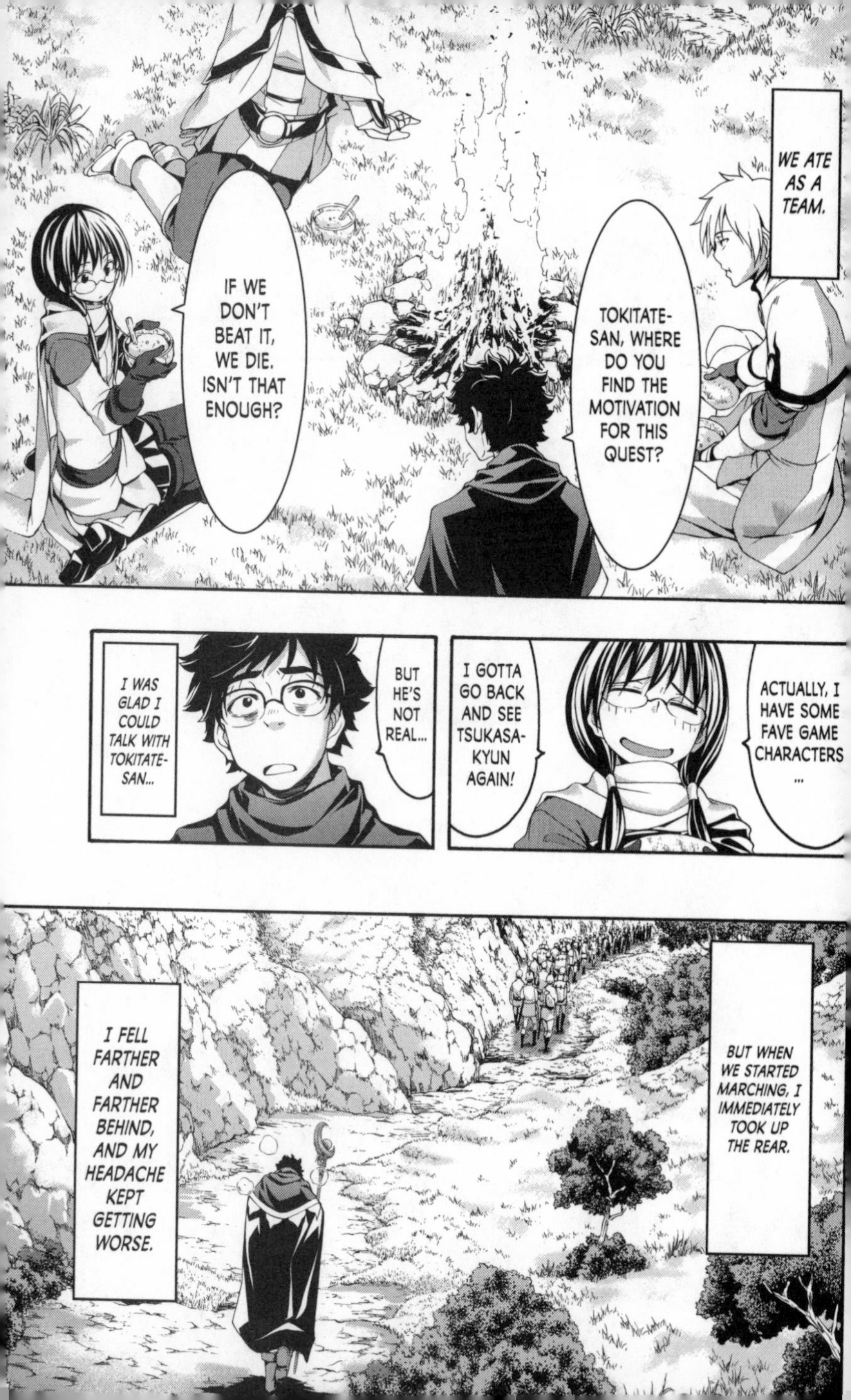
WE ATE AS A TEAM.
TOKITATE-SAN, WHERE DO YOU FIND THE MOTIVATION FOR THIS QUEST?
IF WE DON'T BEAT IT, WE DIE. ISN'T THAT ENOUGH?
ACTUALLY, I HAVE SOME FAVE GAME CHARACTERS...
I GOTTA GO BACK AND SEE TSUKASA-KYUN AGAIN!
BUT HE'S NOT REAL...
I WAS GLAD I COULD TALK WITH TOKITATE-SAN...
BUT WHEN WE STARTED MARCHING, I IMMEDIATELY TOOK UP THE REAR.
I FELL FARTHER AND FARTHER BEHIND, AND MY HEADACHE KEPT GETTING WORSE.

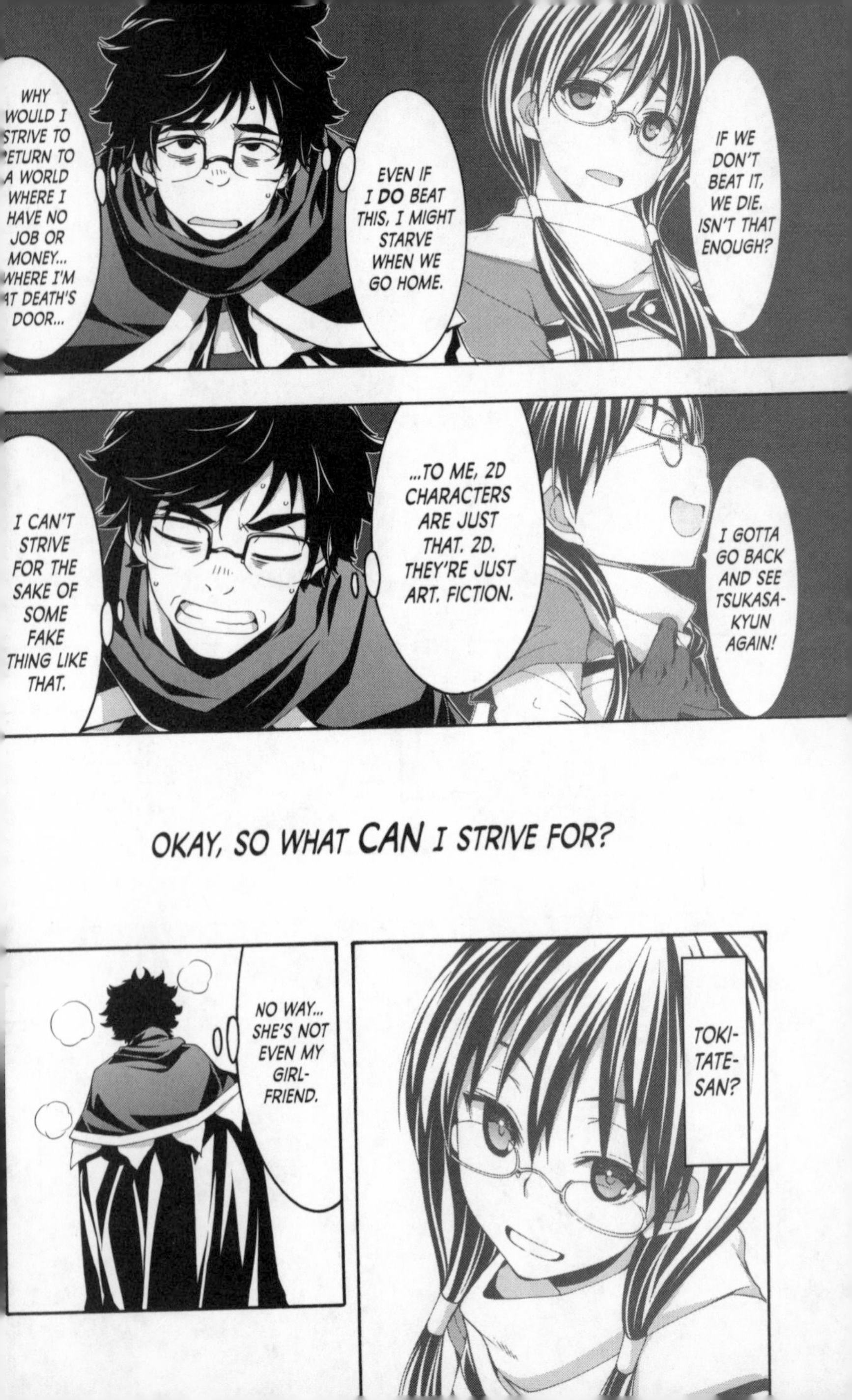
IF WE DON'T BEAT IT, WE DIE. ISN'T THAT ENOUGH?
EVEN IF I DO BEAT THIS, I MIGHT STARVE WHEN WE GO HOME.
WHY WOULD I STRIVE TO RETURN TO A WORLD WHERE I HAVE NO JOB OR MONEY... WHERE I'M AT DEATH'S DOOR...
I GOTTA GO BACK AND SEE TSUKASA-KYUN AGAIN!
...TO ME, 2D CHARACTERS ARE JUST THAT. 2D. THEY'RE JUST ART. FICTION.
I CAN'T STRIVE FOR THE SAKE OF SOME FAKE THING LIKE THAT.
OKAY, SO WHAT CAN I STRIVE FOR?
TOKI-TATE-SAN?
NO WAY... SHE'S NOT EVEN MY GIRL-FRIEND.

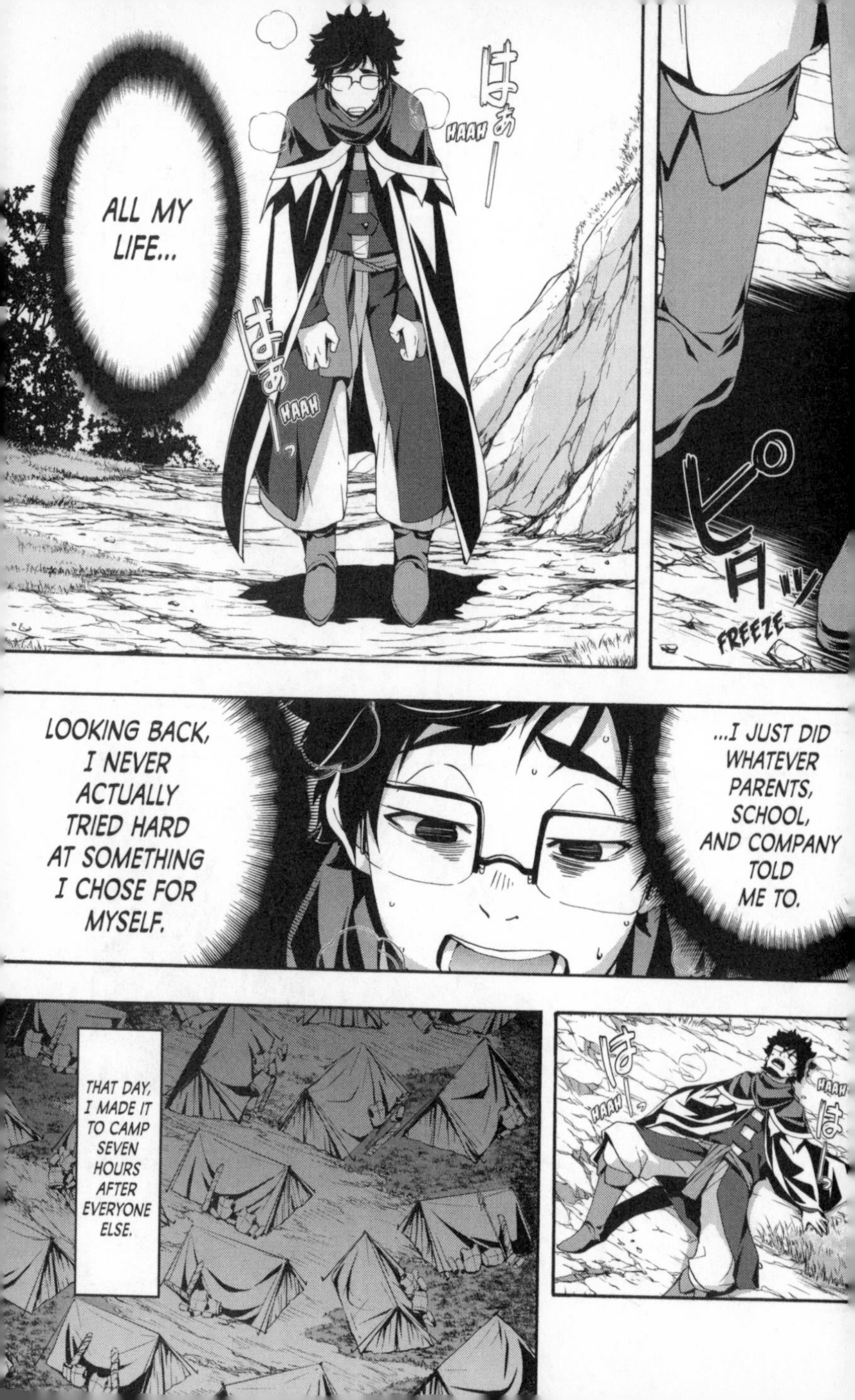
ピタッ
FREEZE
はぁー
HAAH
はぁっ
HAAH
ALL MY LIFE...
LOOKING BACK, I NEVER ACTUALLY TRIED HARD AT SOMETHING I CHOSE FOR MYSELF.
...I JUST DID WHATEVER PARENTS, SCHOOL, AND COMPANY TOLD ME TO.
はっ
HAAH
はっ
HAAH
THAT DAY, I MADE IT TO CAMP SEVEN HOURS AFTER EVERYONE ELSE.

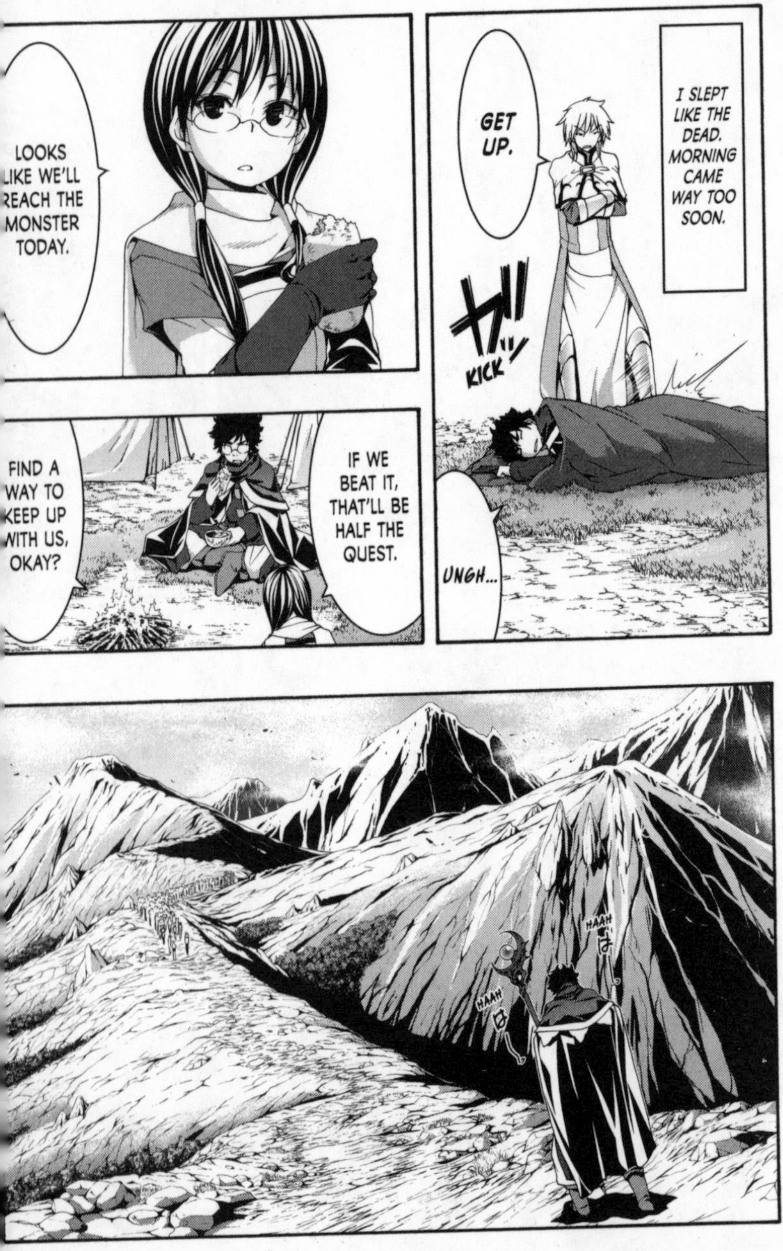
I SLEPT LIKE THE DEAD. MORNING CAME WAY TOO SOON.
GET UP.
KICK
UNGH...
LOOKS LIKE WE'LL REACH THE MONSTER TODAY.
IF WE BEAT IT, THAT'LL BE HALF THE QUEST.
FIND A WAY TO KEEP UP WITH US, OKAY?
HAAH
HAAH

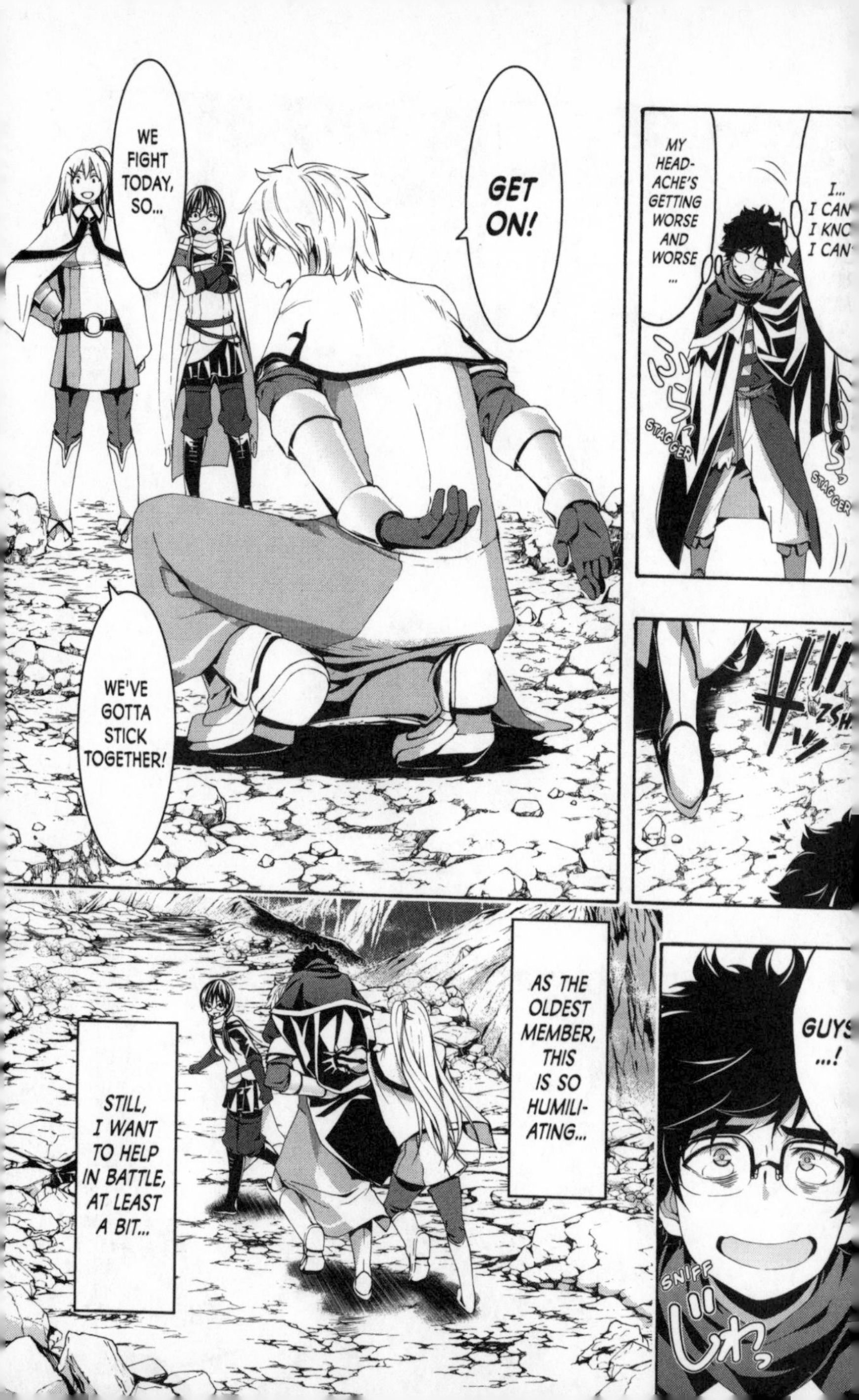
I... I CAN I KNO I CAN
MY HEAD-ACHE'S GETTING WORSE AND WORSE ...
STAGGER
STAGGER
GET ON!
WE FIGHT TODAY, SO...
WE'VE GOTTA STICK TOGETHER!
GUYS ...!
SNIFF
AS THE OLDEST MEMBER, THIS IS SO HUMILI-ATING...
STILL, I WANT TO HELP IN BATTLE, AT LEAST A BIT...

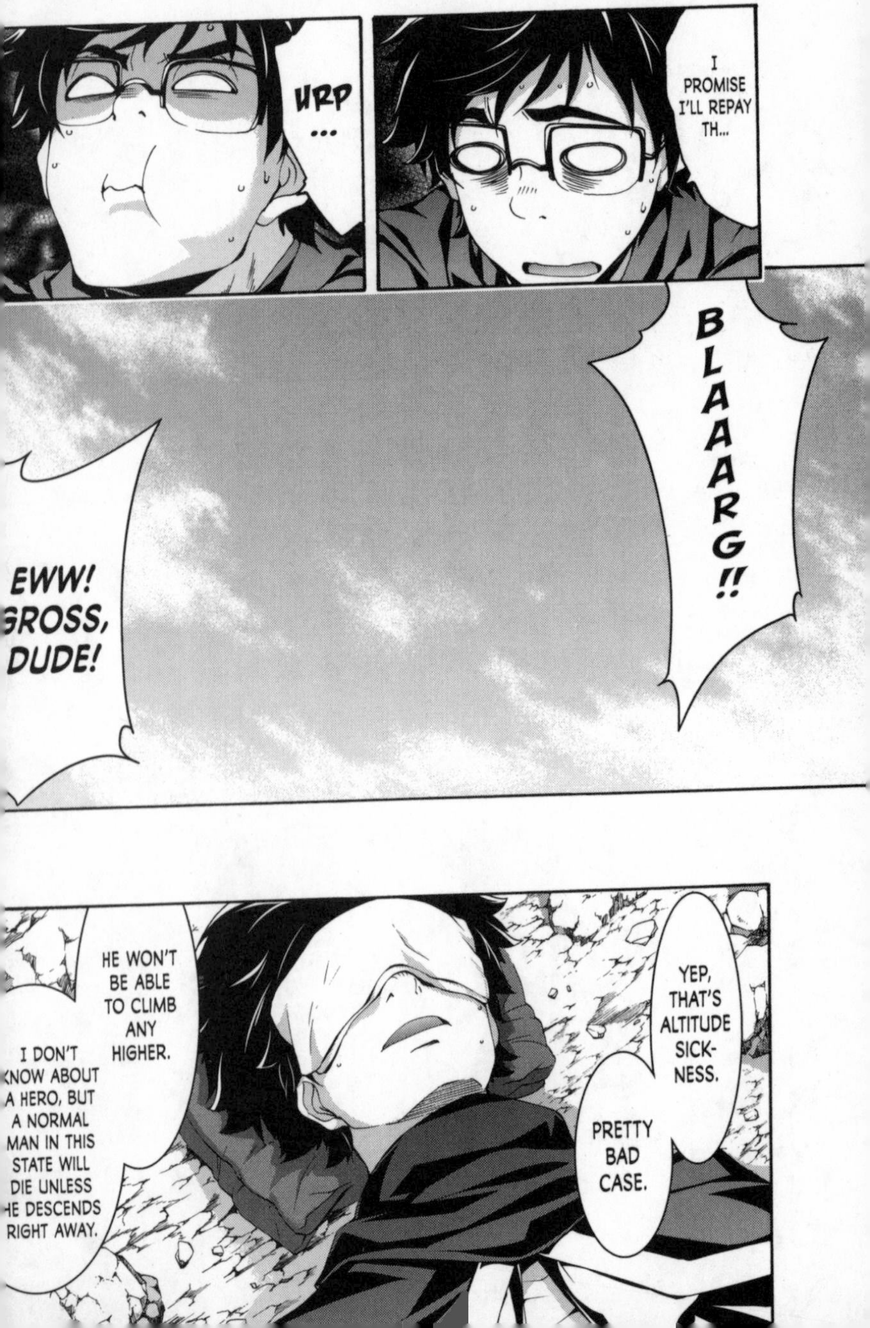
I PROMISE I'LL REPAY TH...
URP ...
BLAAARG!!
EWW! GROSS, DUDE!
YEP, THAT'S ALTITUDE SICK-NESS.
PRETTY BAD CASE.
HE WON'T BE ABLE TO CLIMB ANY HIGHER.
I DON'T KNOW ABOUT A HERO, BUT A NORMAL MAN IN THIS STATE WILL DIE UNLESS HE DESCENDS RIGHT AWAY.

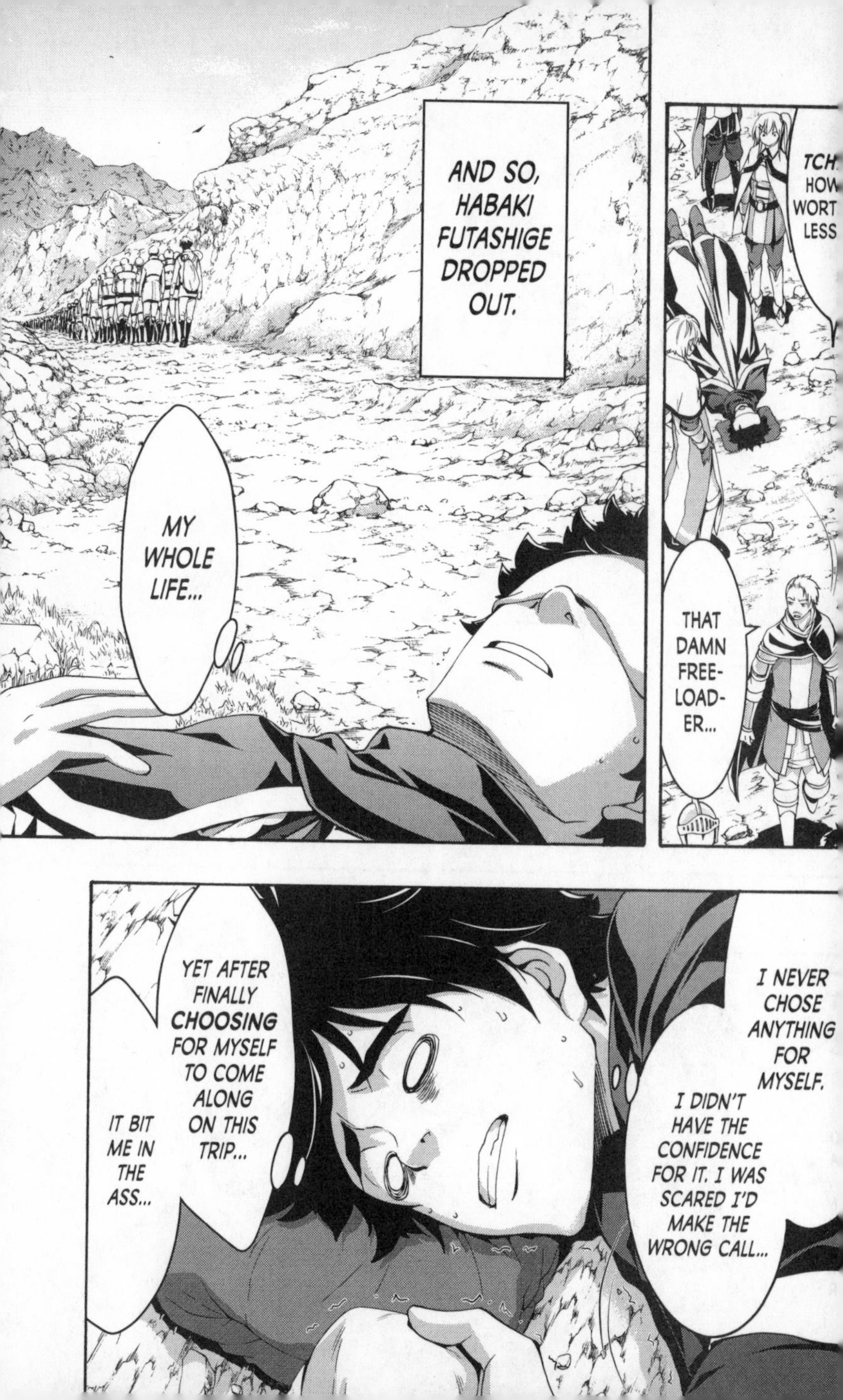
TCH
HOW WORT LESS
THAT DAMN FREE-LOAD-ER...
AND SO, HABAKI FUTASHIGE DROPPED OUT.
MY WHOLE LIFE...
I NEVER CHOSE ANYTHING FOR MYSELF.
I DIDN'T HAVE THE CONFIDENCE FOR IT. I WAS SCARED I'D MAKE THE WRONG CALL...
YET AFTER FINALLY **CHOOSING** FOR MYSELF TO COME ALONG ON THIS TRIP...
IT BIT ME IN THE ASS...

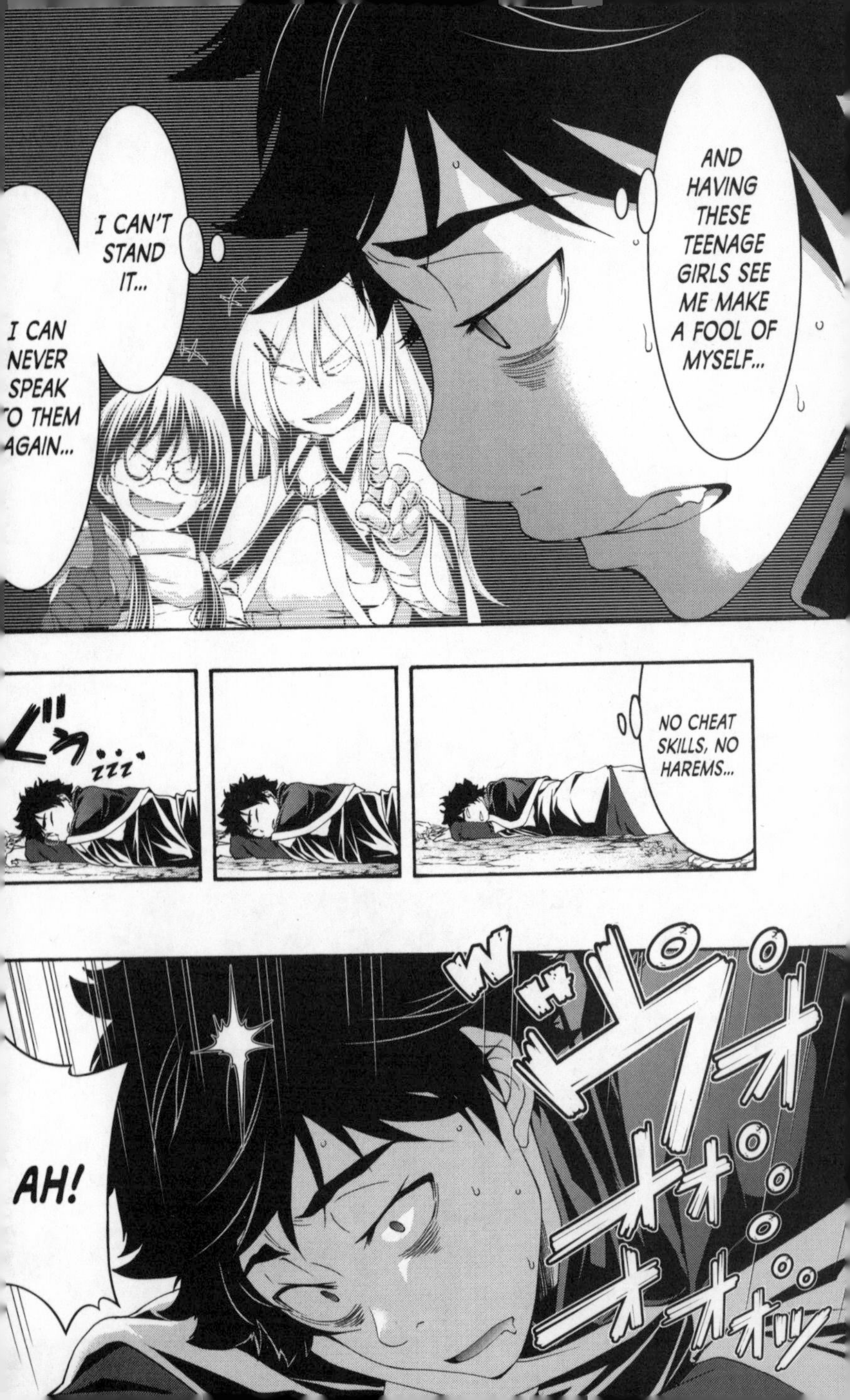
AND HAVING THESE TEENAGE GIRLS SEE ME MAKE A FOOL OF MYSELF...
I CAN'T STAND IT...
I CAN NEVER SPEAK TO THEM AGAIN...
NO CHEAT SKILLS, NO HAREMS...
zzz
AH!

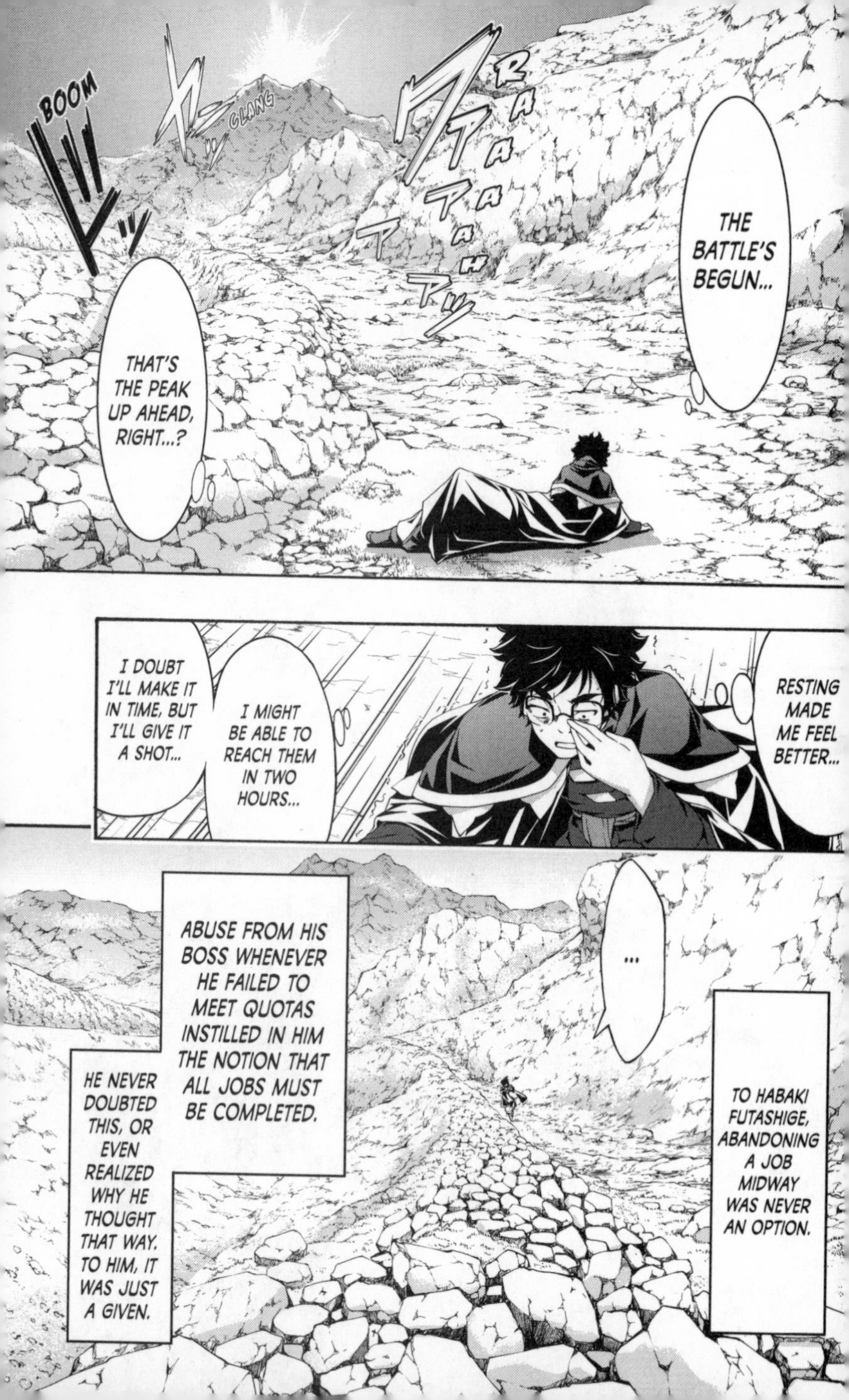
THE BATTLE'S BEGUN...
RAAAH
CLANG
BOOM
THAT'S THE PEAK UP AHEAD, RIGHT...?
RESTING MADE ME FEEL BETTER...
I MIGHT BE ABLE TO REACH THEM IN TWO HOURS...
I DOUBT I'LL MAKE IT IN TIME, BUT I'LL GIVE IT A SHOT...
...
TO HABAKI FUTASHIGE, ABANDONING A JOB MIDWAY WAS NEVER AN OPTION.
ABUSE FROM HIS BOSS WHENEVER HE FAILED TO MEET QUOTAS INSTILLED IN HIM THE NOTION THAT ALL JOBS MUST BE COMPLETED.
HE NEVER DOUBTED THIS, OR EVEN REALIZED WHY HE THOUGHT THAT WAY. TO HIM, IT WAS JUST A GIVEN.

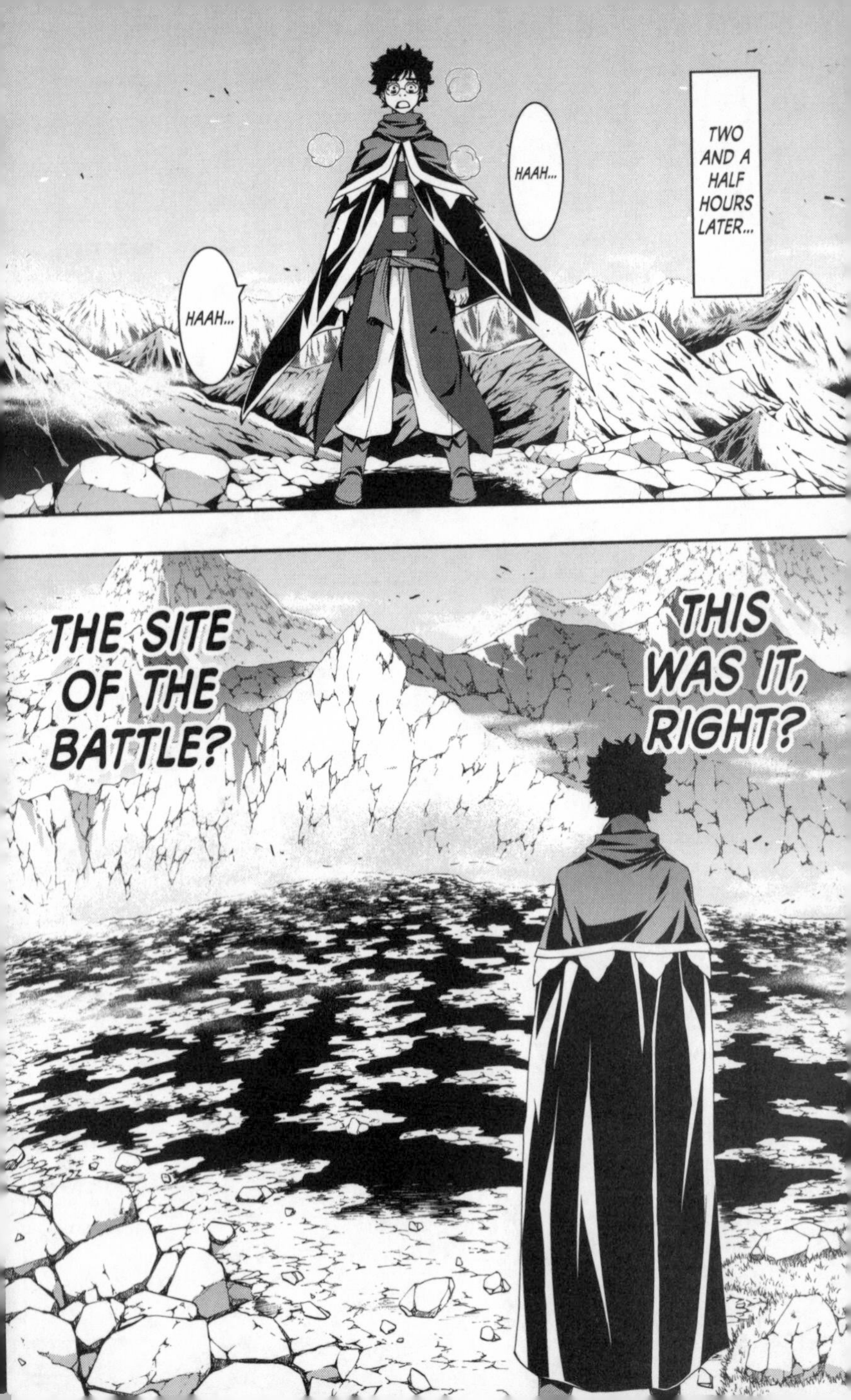
TWO AND A HALF HOURS LATER...
HAAH...
HAAH...
THIS WAS IT, RIGHT?
THE SITE OF THE BATTLE?

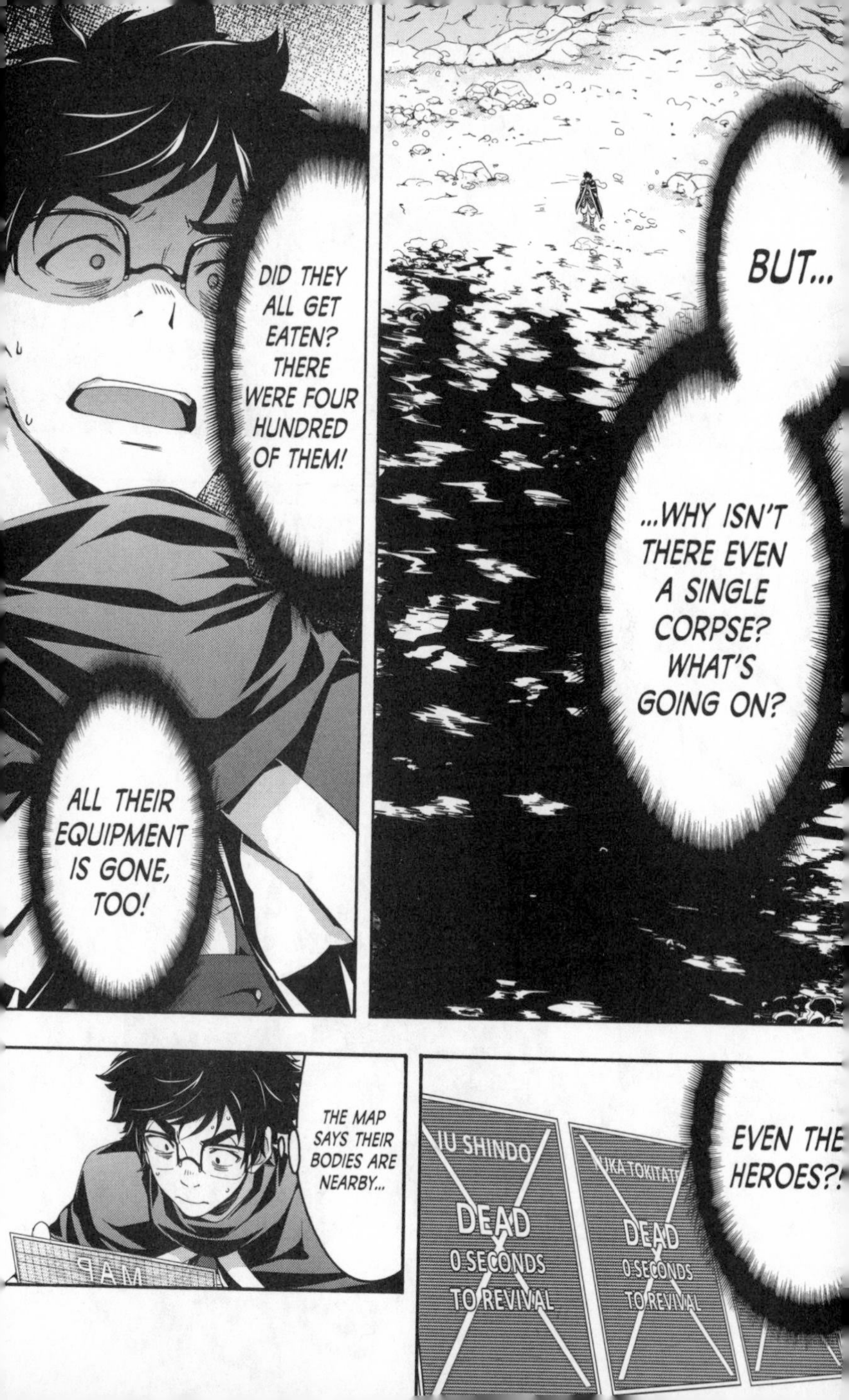
BUT...
...WHY ISN'T THERE EVEN A SINGLE CORPSE? WHAT'S GOING ON?
DID THEY ALL GET EATEN? THERE WERE FOUR HUNDRED OF THEM!
ALL THEIR EQUIPMENT IS GONE, TOO!
EVEN THE HEROES?!
IU SHINDO
DEAD
0 SECONDS TO REVIVAL
DEAD
0 SECONDS TO REVIVAL
THE MAP SAYS THEIR BODIES ARE NEARBY...

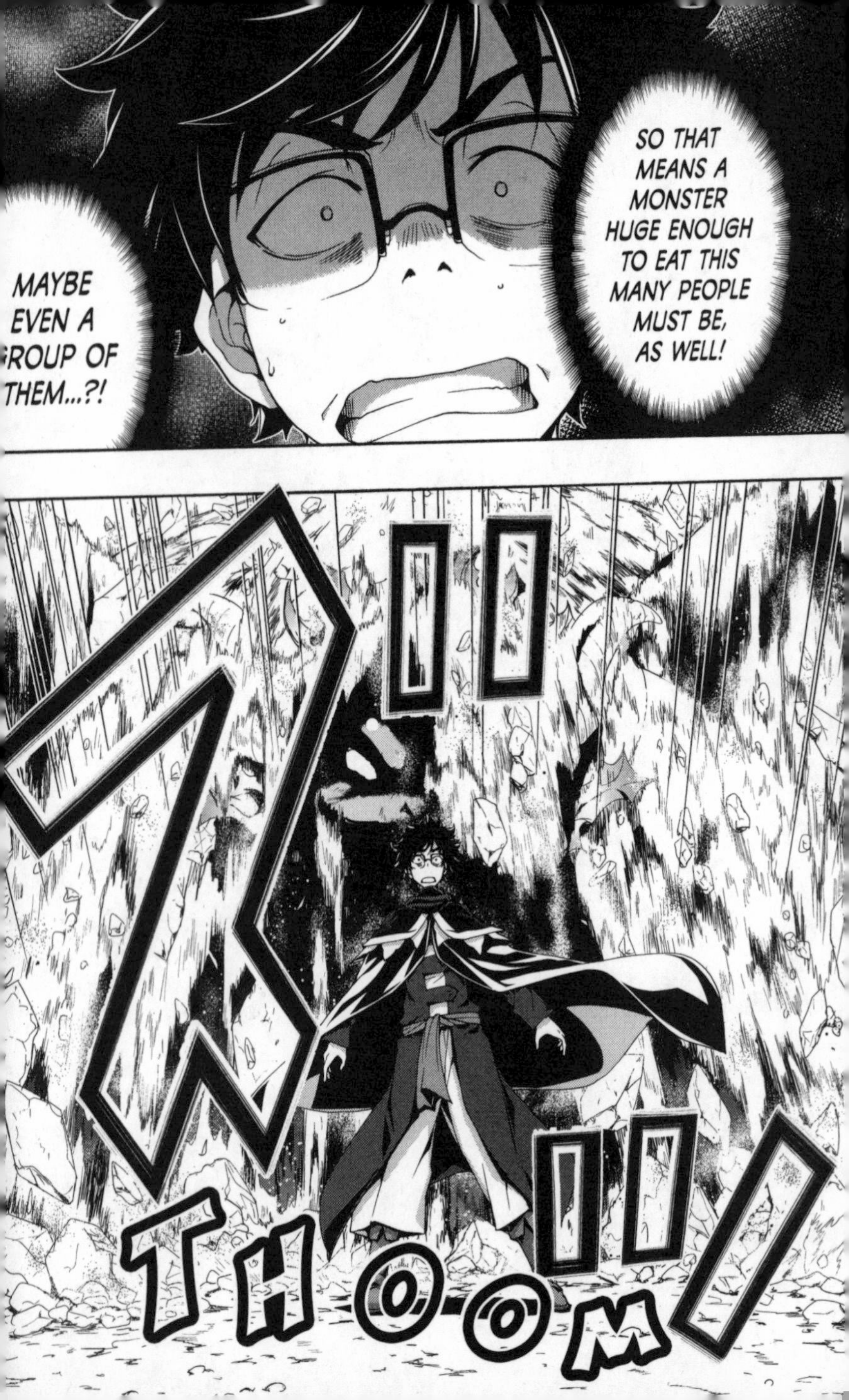
SO THAT MEANS A MONSTER HUGE ENOUGH TO EAT THIS MANY PEOPLE MUST BE, AS WELL!
MAYBE EVEN A ROUP OF THEM...?!
THOOM!!

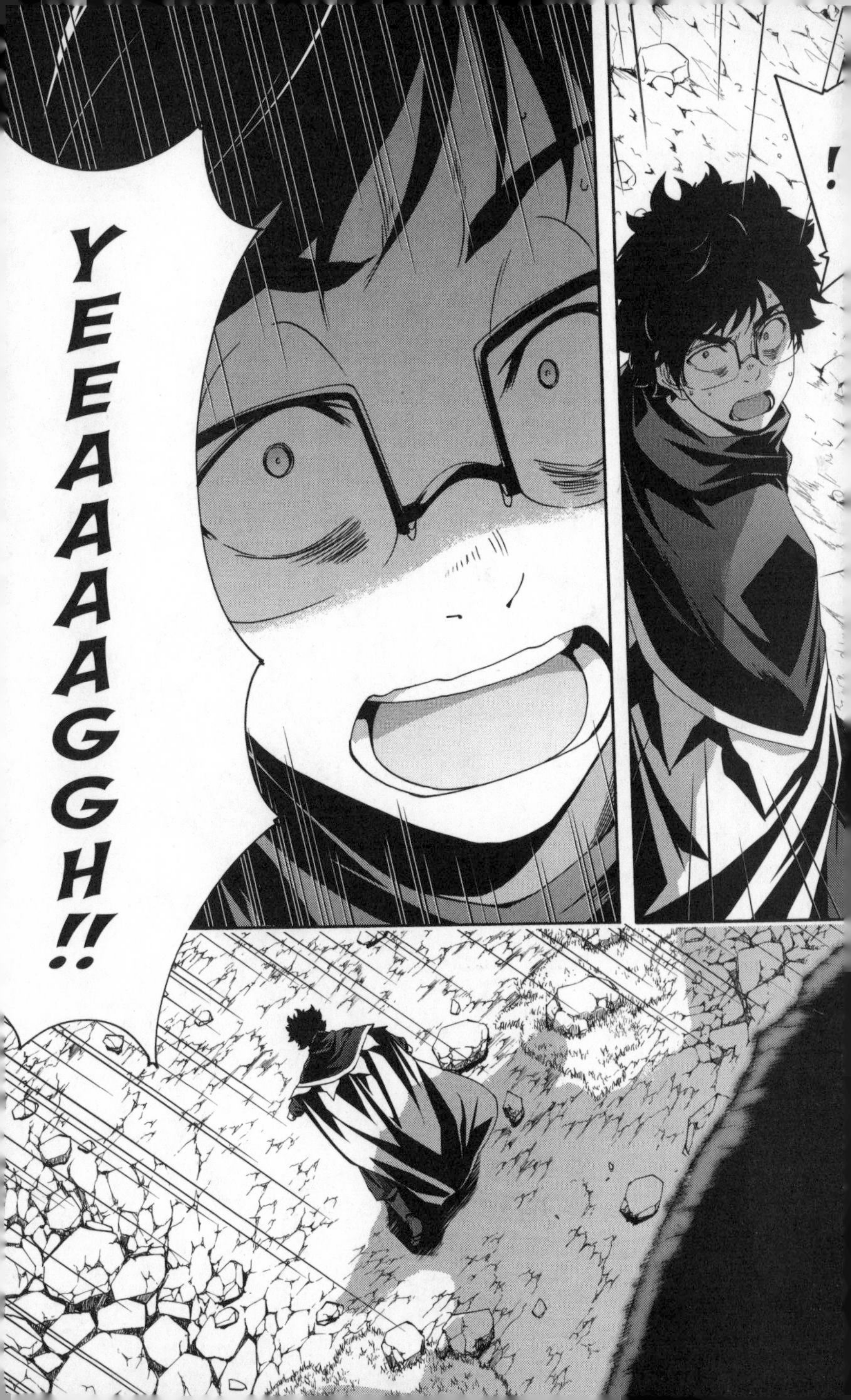
!
YEEAAAAGGH!!

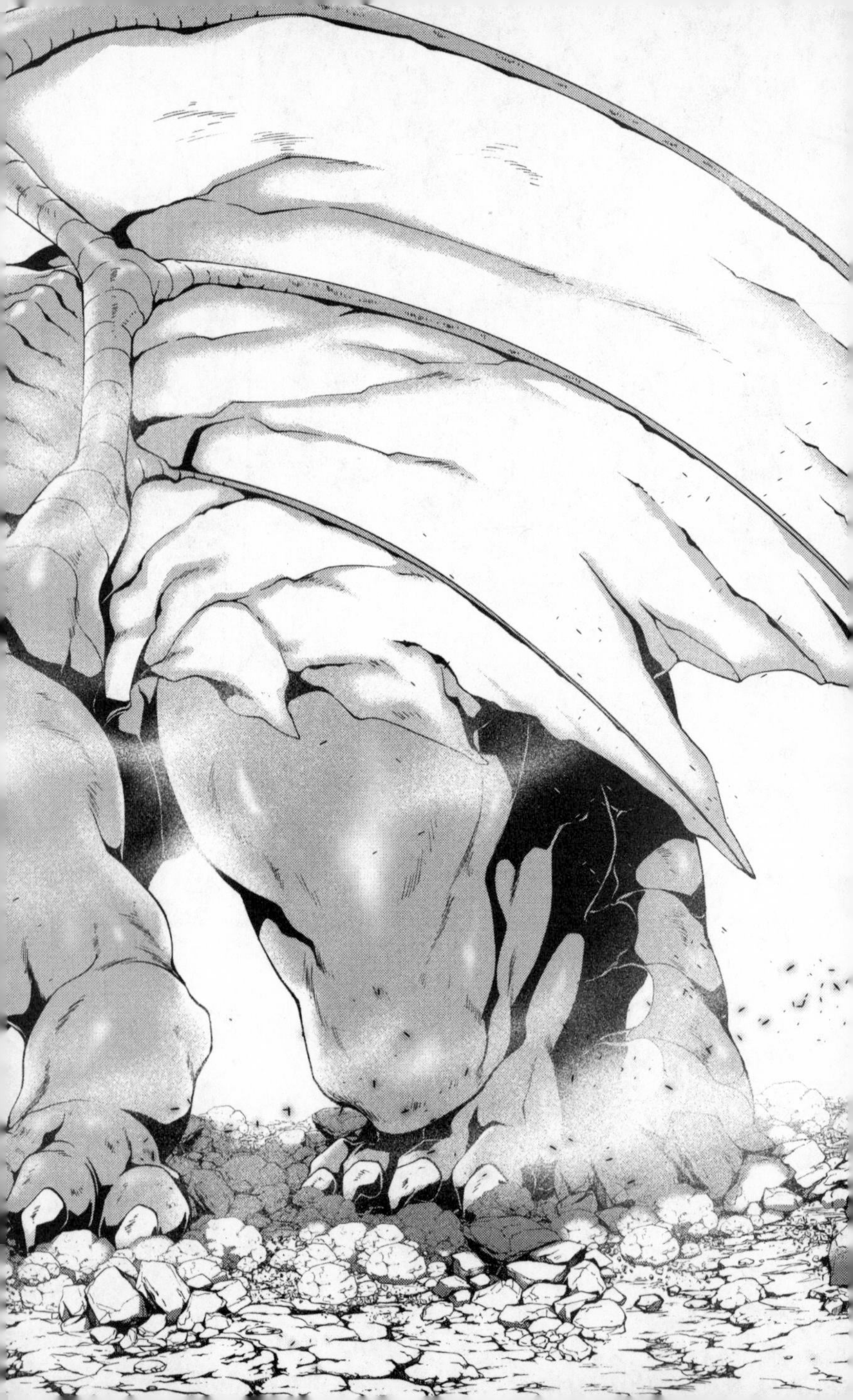

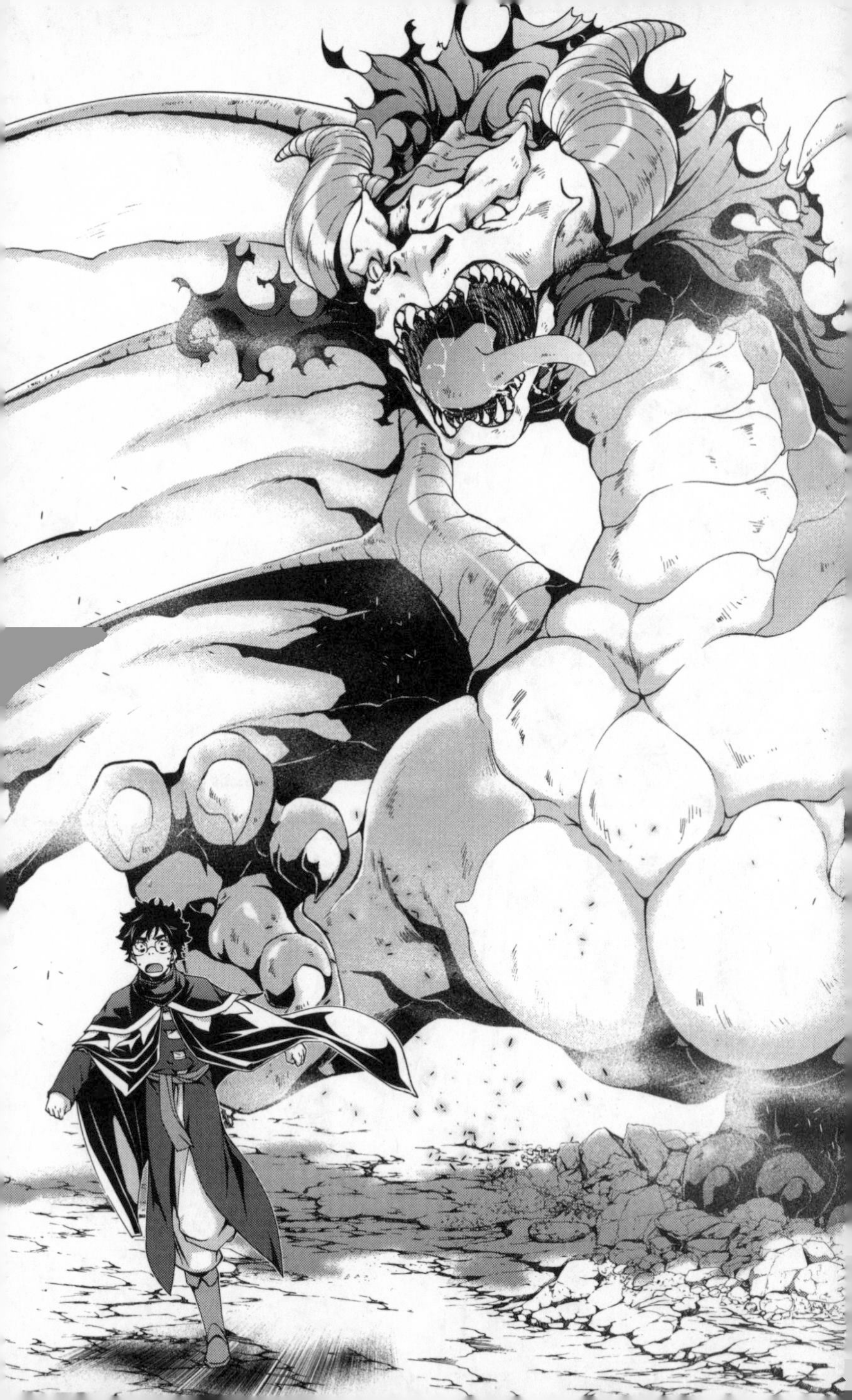

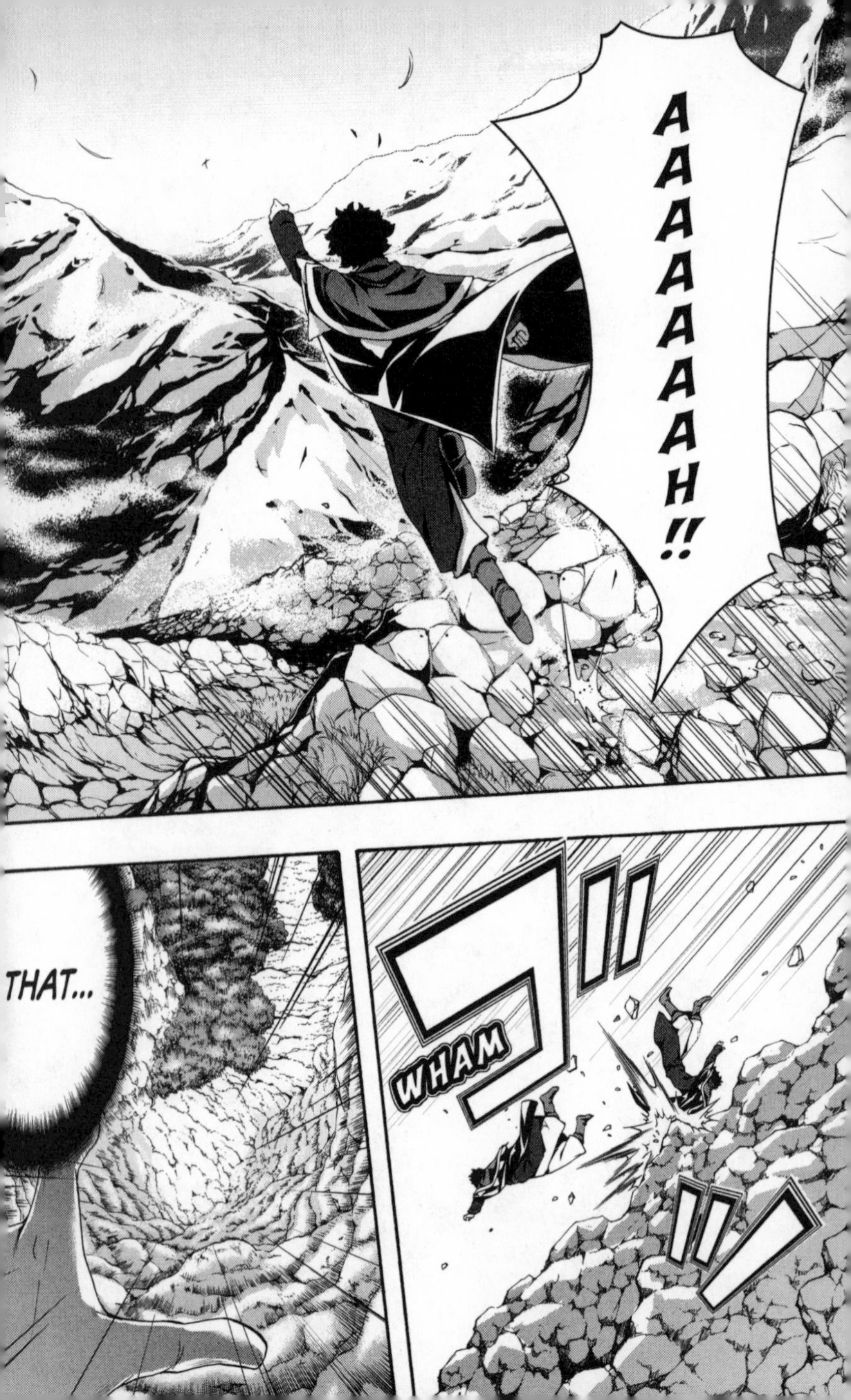

AAAAAAAH!!
WHAM
THAT...

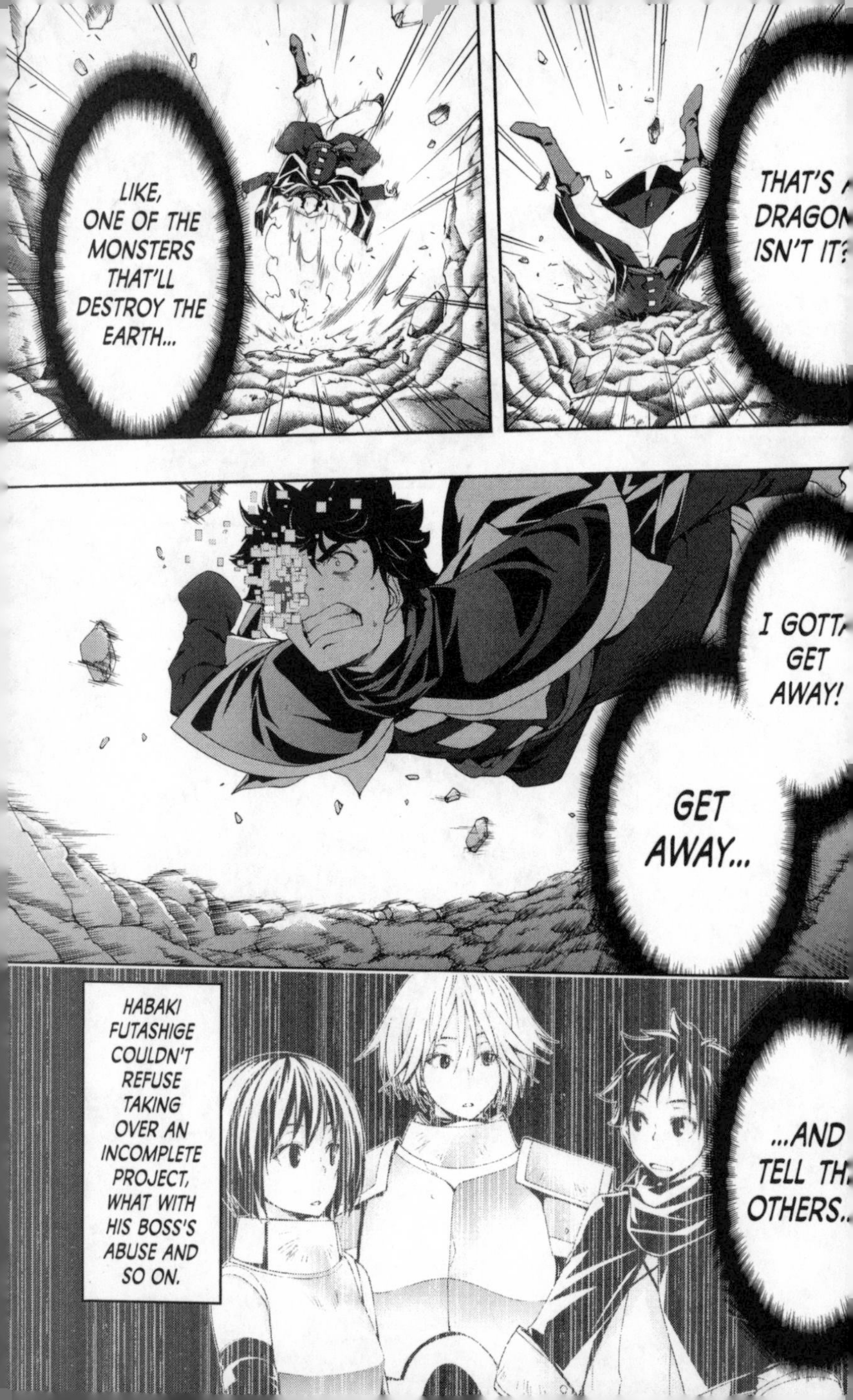
THAT'S A DRAGON ISN'T IT?
LIKE, ONE OF THE MONSTERS THAT'LL DESTROY THE EARTH...
I GOTTA GET AWAY!
GET AWAY...
...AND TELL TH OTHERS..
HABAKI FUTASHIGE COULDN'T REFUSE TAKING OVER AN INCOMPLETE PROJECT, WHAT WITH HIS BOSS'S ABUSE AND SO ON.

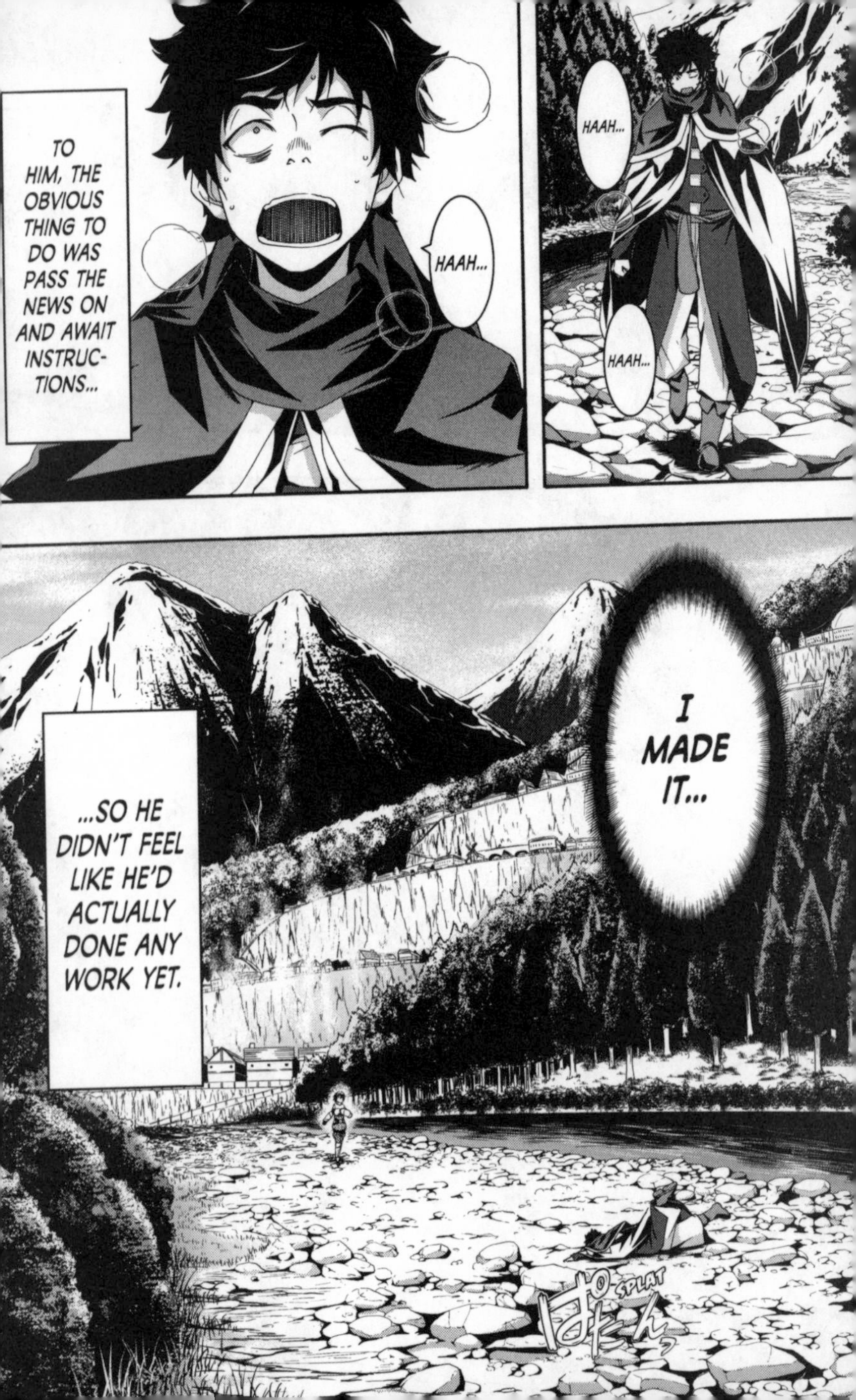
HAAH...
HAAH...
TO HIM, THE OBVIOUS THING TO DO WAS PASS THE NEWS ON AND AWAIT INSTRUC-TIONS...
HAAH...
I MADE IT...
...SO HE DIDN'T FEEL LIKE HE'D ACTUALLY DONE ANY WORK YET.
SPLAT

#51 Money and Transformation

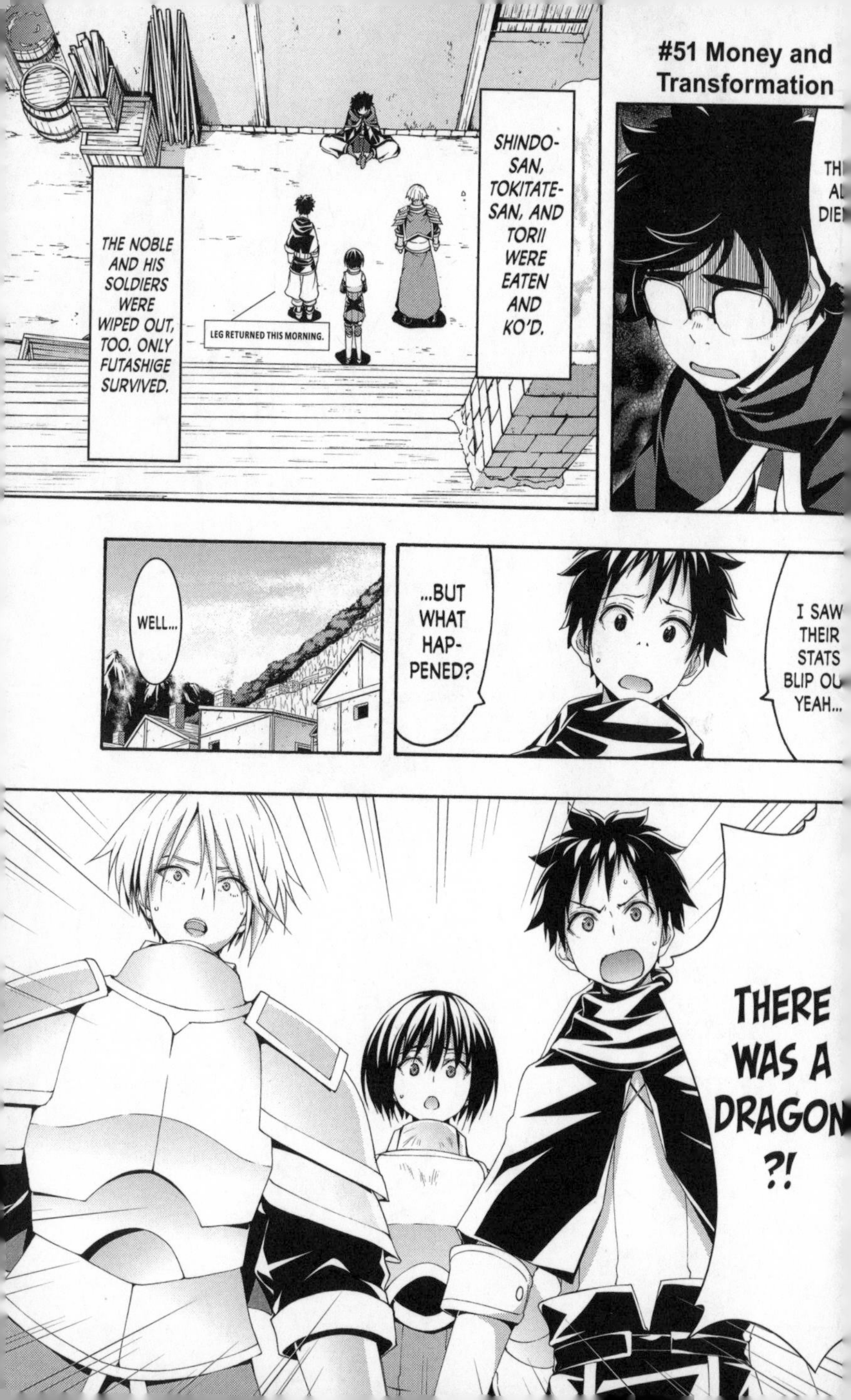
SHINDO-SAN, TOKITATE-SAN, AND TORII WERE EATEN AND KO'D.
THE NOBLE AND HIS SOLDIERS WERE WIPED OUT, TOO. ONLY FUTASHIGE SURVIVED.
LEG RETURNED THIS MORNING.
I SAW THEIR STATS BLIP OU
YEAH...
...BUT WHAT HAP-PENED?
WELL...
THERE WAS A DRAGON ?!

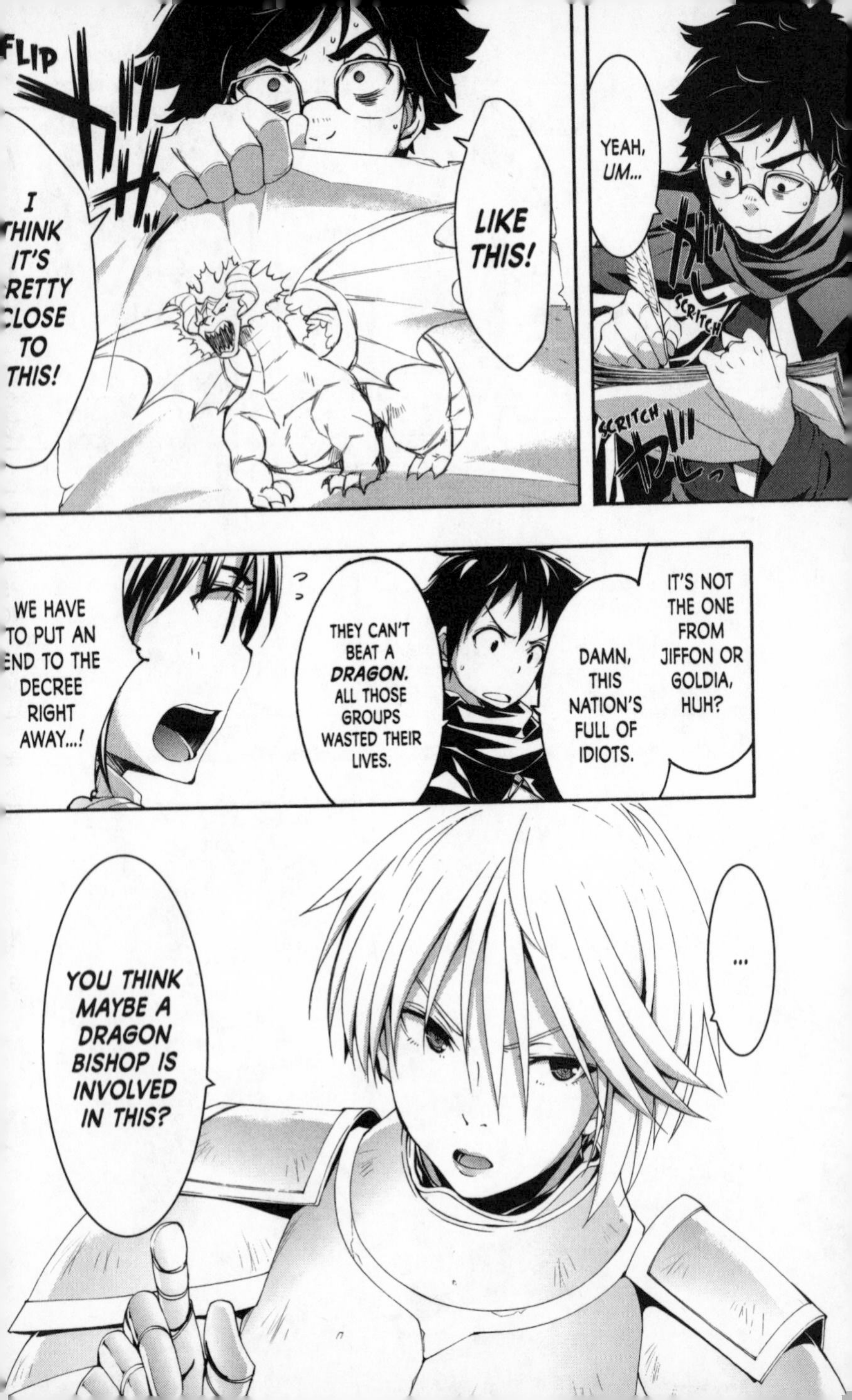
YEAH, UM...
SCRITCH
SCRITCH
LIKE THIS!
FLIP
I THINK IT'S RETTY CLOSE TO THIS!
IT'S NOT THE ONE FROM JIFFON OR GOLDIA, HUH?
DAMN, THIS NATION'S FULL OF IDIOTS.
THEY CAN'T BEAT A *DRAGON.* ALL THOSE GROUPS WASTED THEIR LIVES.
WE HAVE TO PUT AN ND TO THE DECREE RIGHT AWAY...!
...
YOU THINK MAYBE A DRAGON BISHOP IS INVOLVED IN THIS?

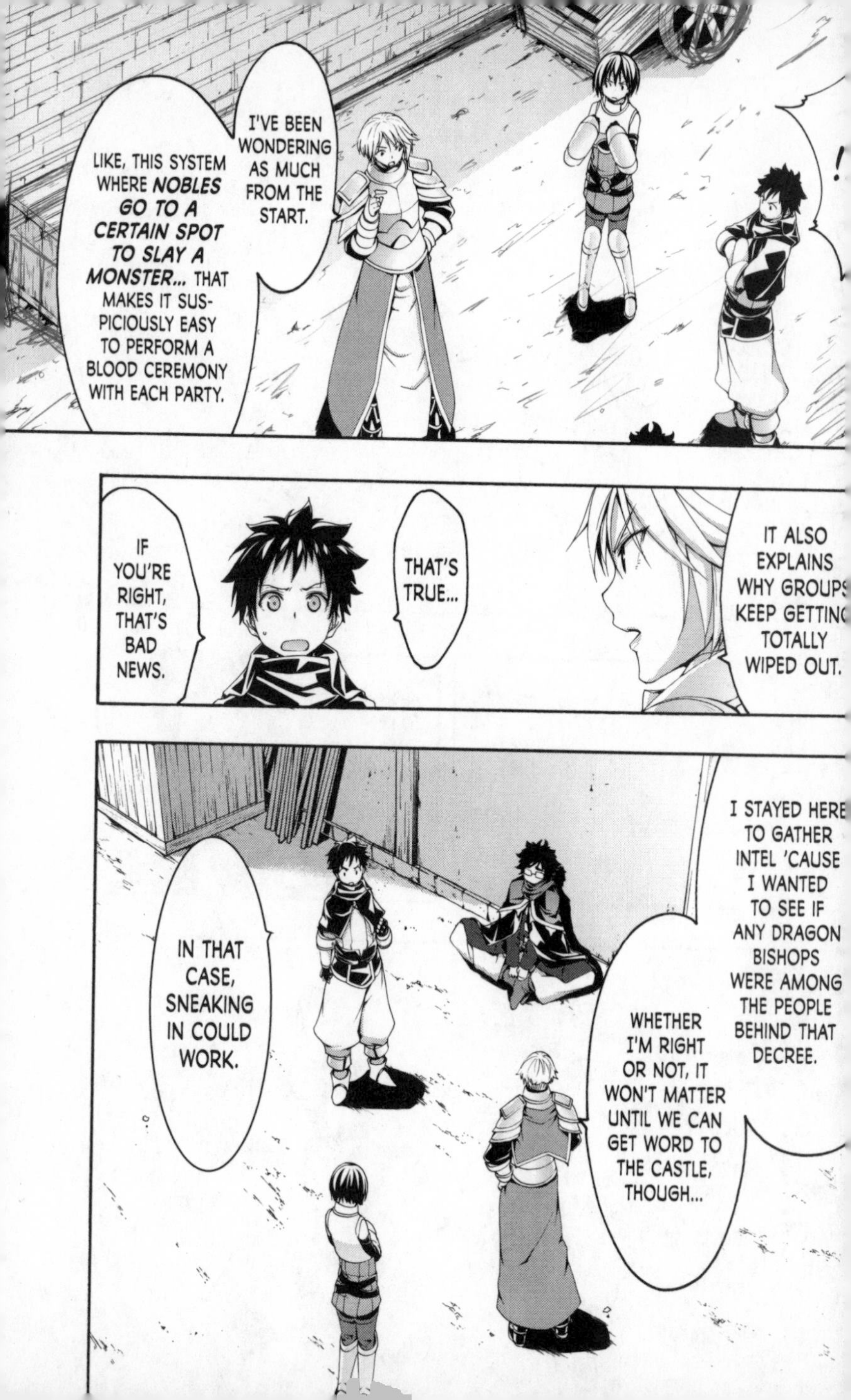
!
I'VE BEEN WONDERING AS MUCH FROM THE START.
LIKE, THIS SYSTEM WHERE ***NOBLES GO TO A CERTAIN SPOT TO SLAY A MONSTER...*** THAT MAKES IT SUSPICIOUSLY EASY TO PERFORM A BLOOD CEREMONY WITH EACH PARTY.
IT ALSO EXPLAINS WHY GROUPS KEEP GETTING TOTALLY WIPED OUT.
THAT'S TRUE...
IF YOU'RE RIGHT, THAT'S BAD NEWS.
I STAYED HERE TO GATHER INTEL 'CAUSE I WANTED TO SEE IF ANY DRAGON BISHOPS WERE AMONG THE PEOPLE BEHIND THAT DECREE.
WHETHER I'M RIGHT OR NOT, IT WON'T MATTER UNTIL WE CAN GET WORD TO THE CASTLE, THOUGH...
IN THAT CASE, SNEAKING IN COULD WORK.

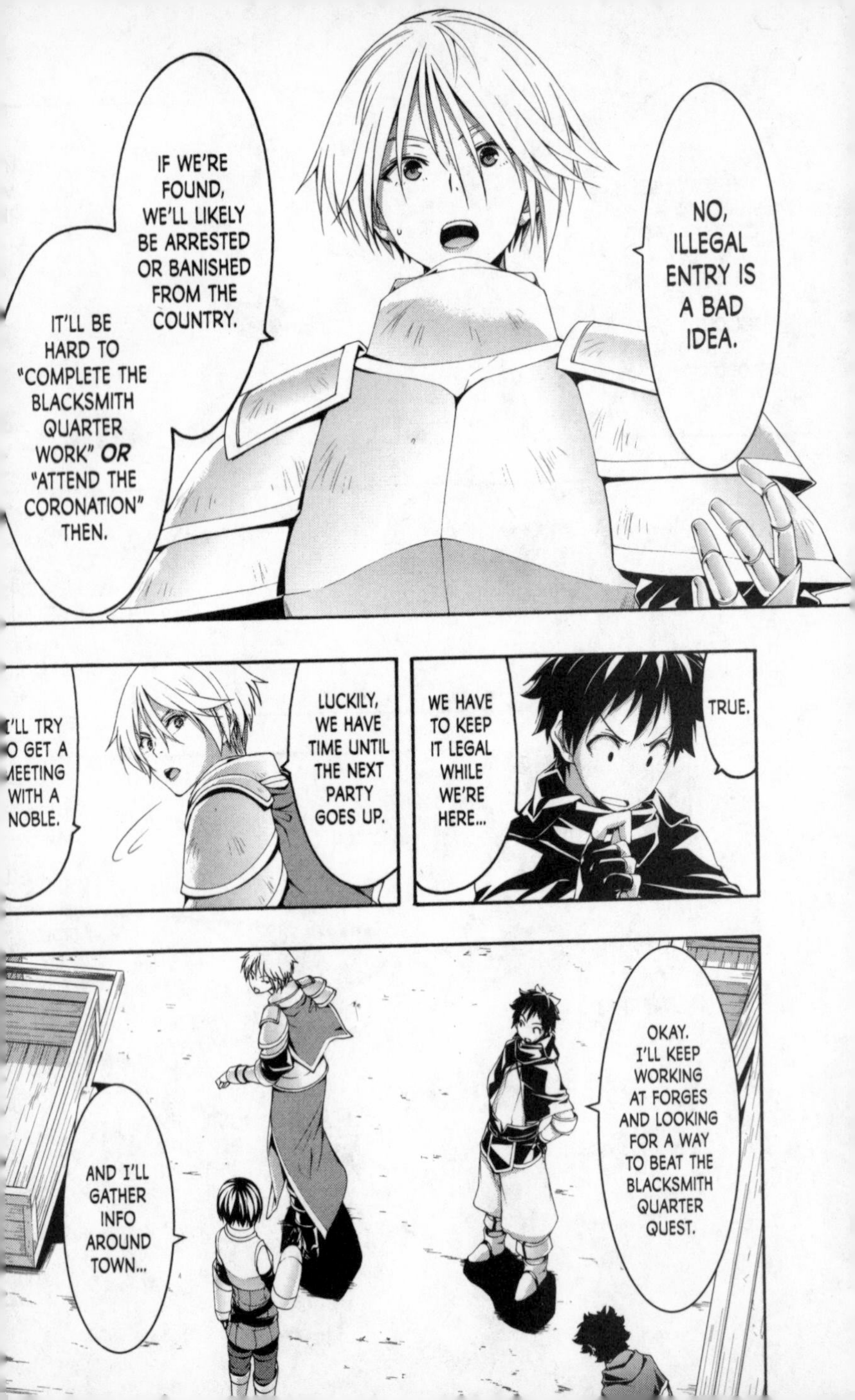
NO, ILLEGAL ENTRY IS A BAD IDEA.
IF WE'RE FOUND, WE'LL LIKELY BE ARRESTED OR BANISHED FROM THE COUNTRY.
IT'LL BE HARD TO "COMPLETE THE BLACKSMITH QUARTER WORK" *OR* "ATTEND THE CORONATION" THEN.
TRUE.
WE HAVE TO KEEP IT LEGAL WHILE WE'RE HERE...
LUCKILY, WE HAVE TIME UNTIL THE NEXT PARTY GOES UP.
'LL TRY O GET A IEETING WITH A NOBLE.
OKAY. I'LL KEEP WORKING AT FORGES AND LOOKING FOR A WAY TO BEAT THE BLACKSMITH QUARTER QUEST.
AND I'LL GATHER INFO AROUND TOWN...

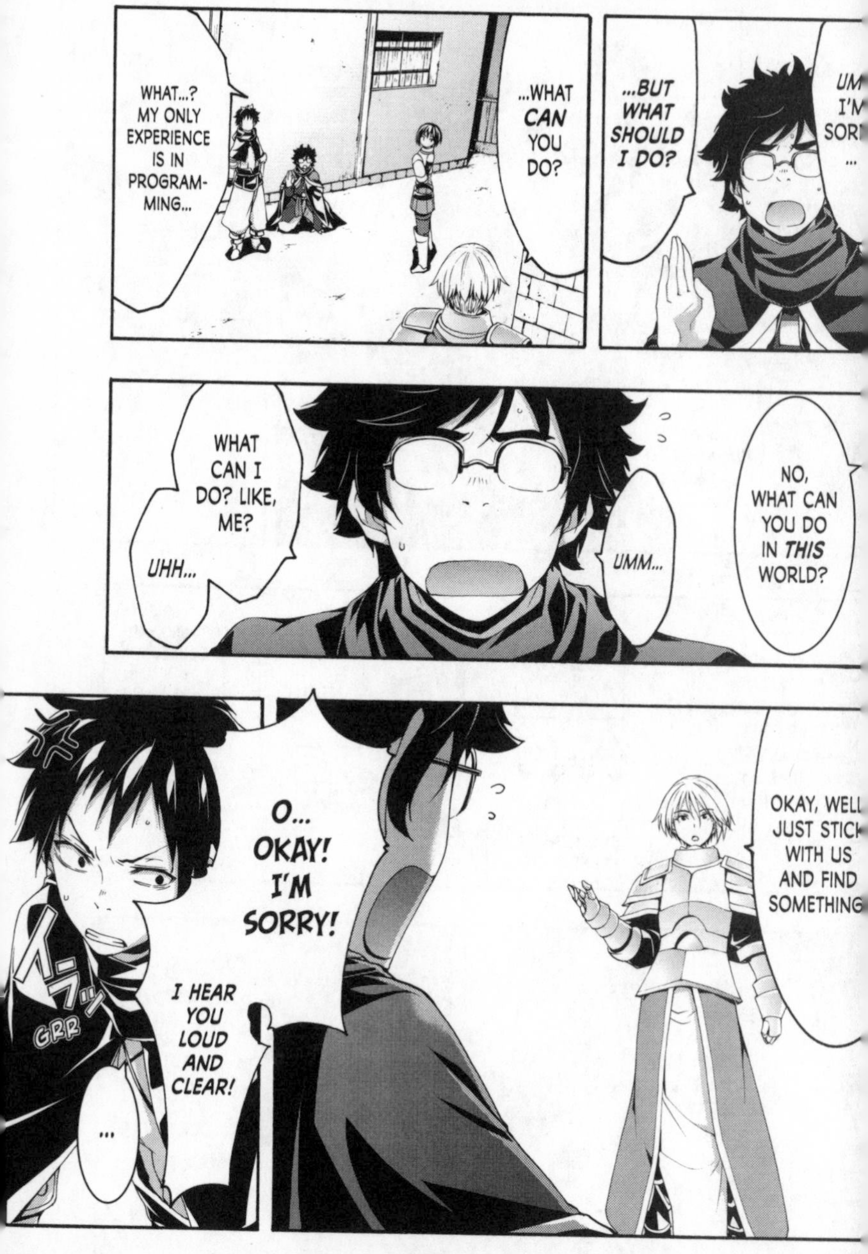
UM I'M SOR ...
...BUT WHAT SHOULD I DO?
...WHAT CAN YOU DO?
WHAT...? MY ONLY EXPERIENCE IS IN PROGRAMMING...
NO, WHAT CAN YOU DO IN THIS WORLD?
UMM...
WHAT CAN I DO? LIKE, ME?
UHH...
OKAY, WELL JUST STICK WITH US AND FIND SOMETHING
O... OKAY! I'M SORRY!
I HEAR YOU LOUD AND CLEAR!
GRR
...

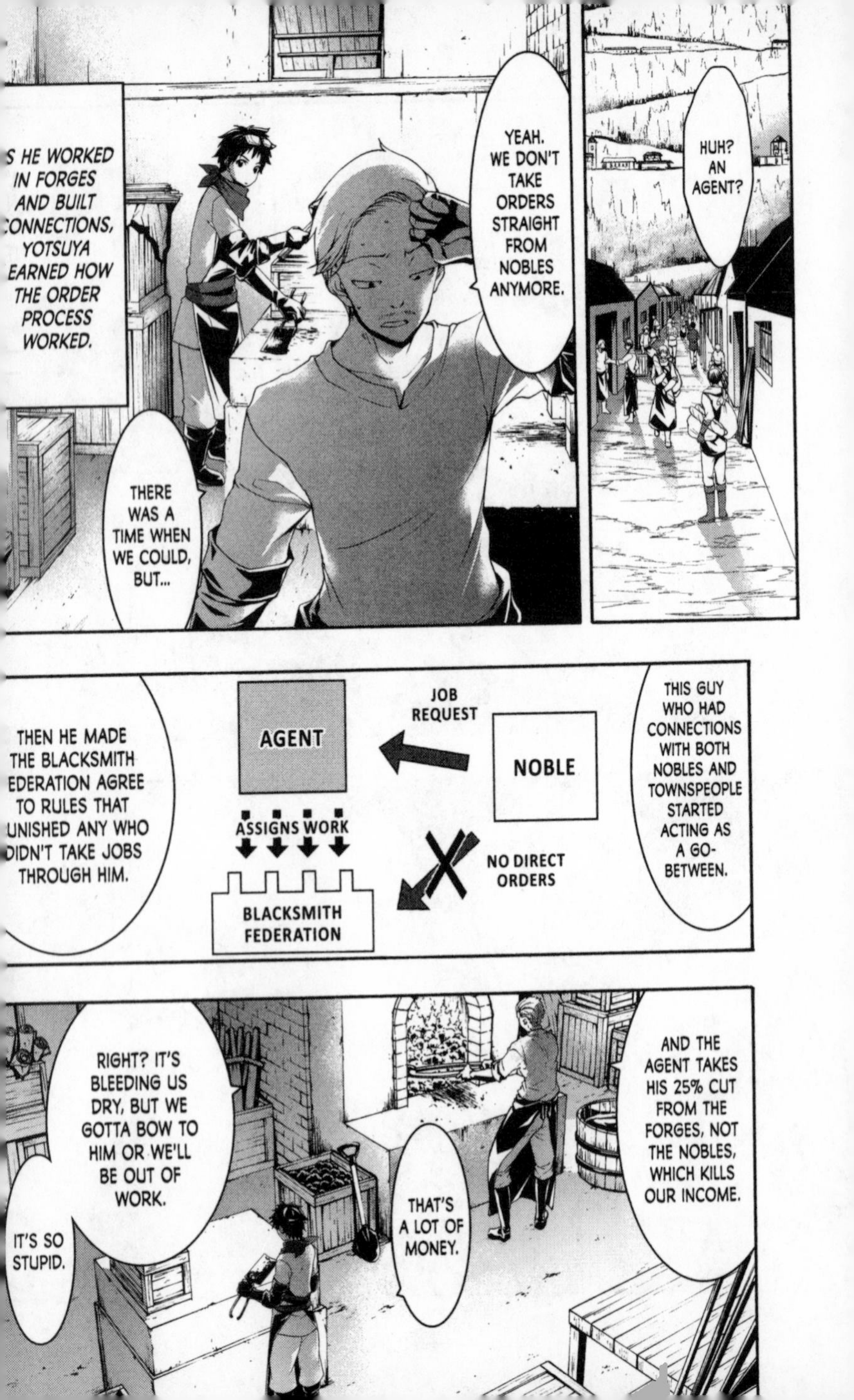
HUH? AN AGENT?
YEAH. WE DON'T TAKE ORDERS STRAIGHT FROM NOBLES ANYMORE.
S HE WORKED IN FORGES AND BUILT ONNECTIONS, YOTSUYA EARNED HOW THE ORDER PROCESS WORKED.
THERE WAS A TIME WHEN WE COULD, BUT...
THIS GUY WHO HAD CONNECTIONS WITH BOTH NOBLES AND TOWNSPEOPLE STARTED ACTING AS A GO-BETWEEN.
JOB REQUEST
NOBLE
AGENT
NO DIRECT ORDERS
ASSIGNS WORK
BLACKSMITH FEDERATION
THEN HE MADE THE BLACKSMITH EDERATION AGREE TO RULES THAT UNISHED ANY WHO DIDN'T TAKE JOBS THROUGH HIM.
AND THE AGENT TAKES HIS 25% CUT FROM THE FORGES, NOT THE NOBLES, WHICH KILLS OUR INCOME.
THAT'S A LOT OF MONEY.
RIGHT? IT'S BLEEDING US DRY, BUT WE GOTTA BOW TO HIM OR WE'LL BE OUT OF WORK.
IT'S SO STUPID.

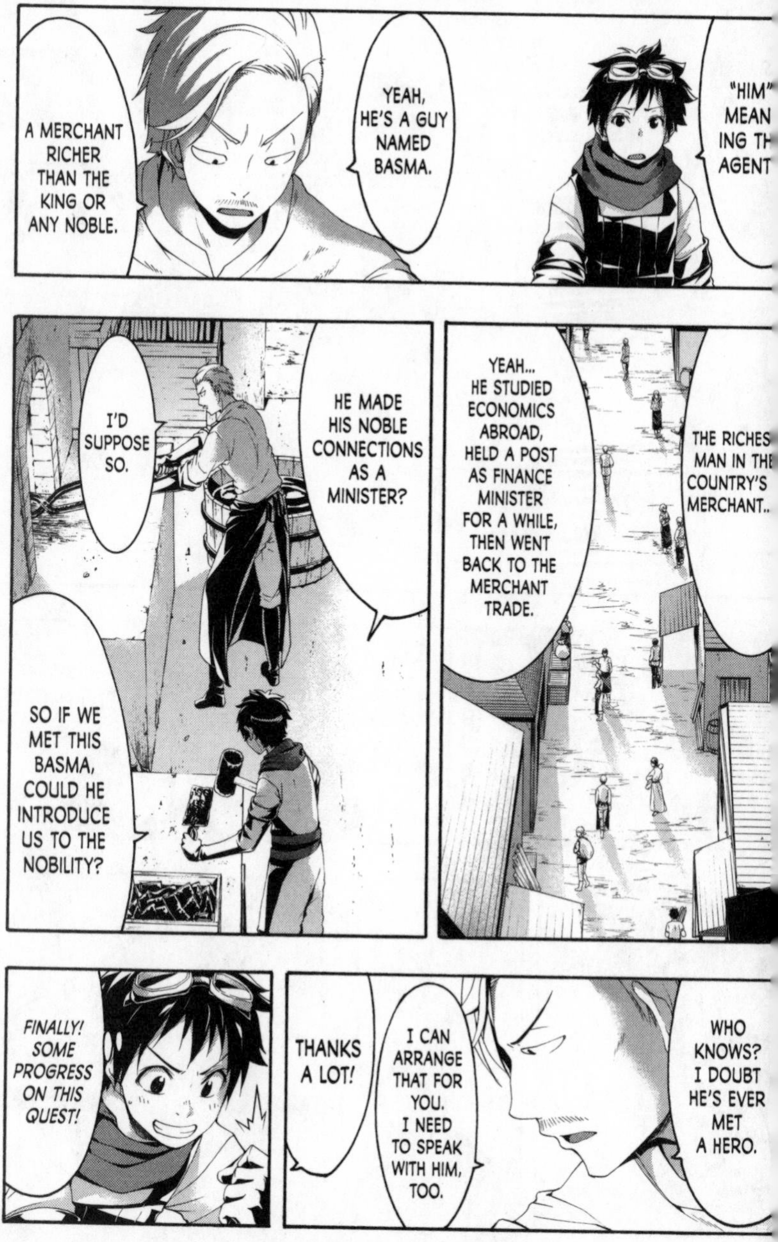
"HIM" MEAN ING TH AGENT
YEAH, HE'S A GUY NAMED BASMA.
A MERCHANT RICHER THAN THE KING OR ANY NOBLE.
THE RICHES MAN IN THE COUNTRY'S MERCHANT..
YEAH... HE STUDIED ECONOMICS ABROAD, HELD A POST AS FINANCE MINISTER FOR A WHILE, THEN WENT BACK TO THE MERCHANT TRADE.
HE MADE HIS NOBLE CONNECTIONS AS A MINISTER?
I'D SUPPOSE SO.
SO IF WE MET THIS BASMA, COULD HE INTRODUCE US TO THE NOBILITY?
WHO KNOWS? I DOUBT HE'S EVER MET A HERO.
I CAN ARRANGE THAT FOR YOU. I NEED TO SPEAK WITH HIM, TOO.
THANKS A LOT!
FINALLY! SOME PROGRESS ON THIS QUEST!

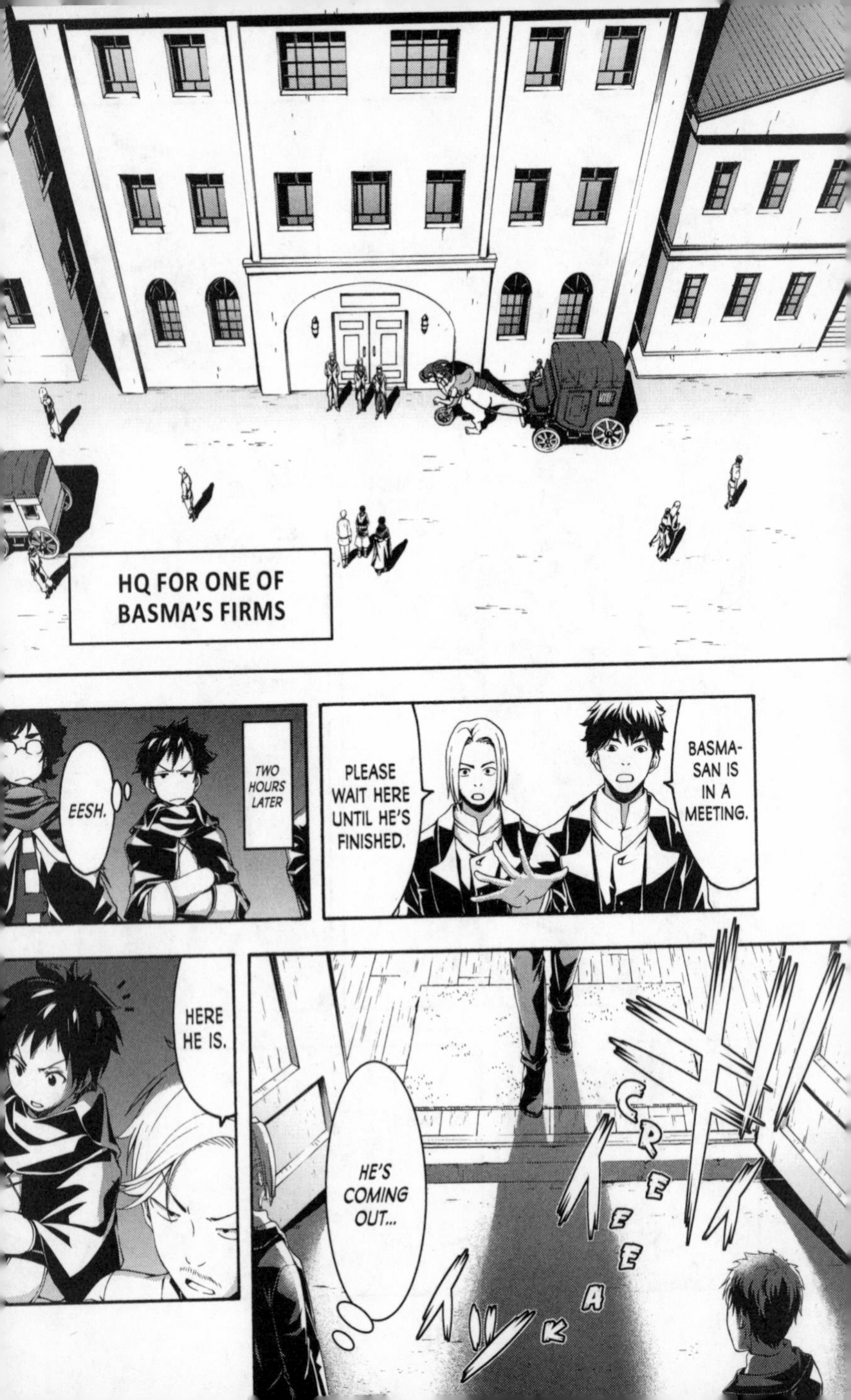
HQ FOR ONE OF BASMA'S FIRMS
BASMA-SAN IS IN A MEETING.
PLEASE WAIT HERE UNTIL HE'S FINISHED.
TWO HOURS LATER
EESH.
CREEEAK
HE'S COMING OUT...
HERE HE IS.

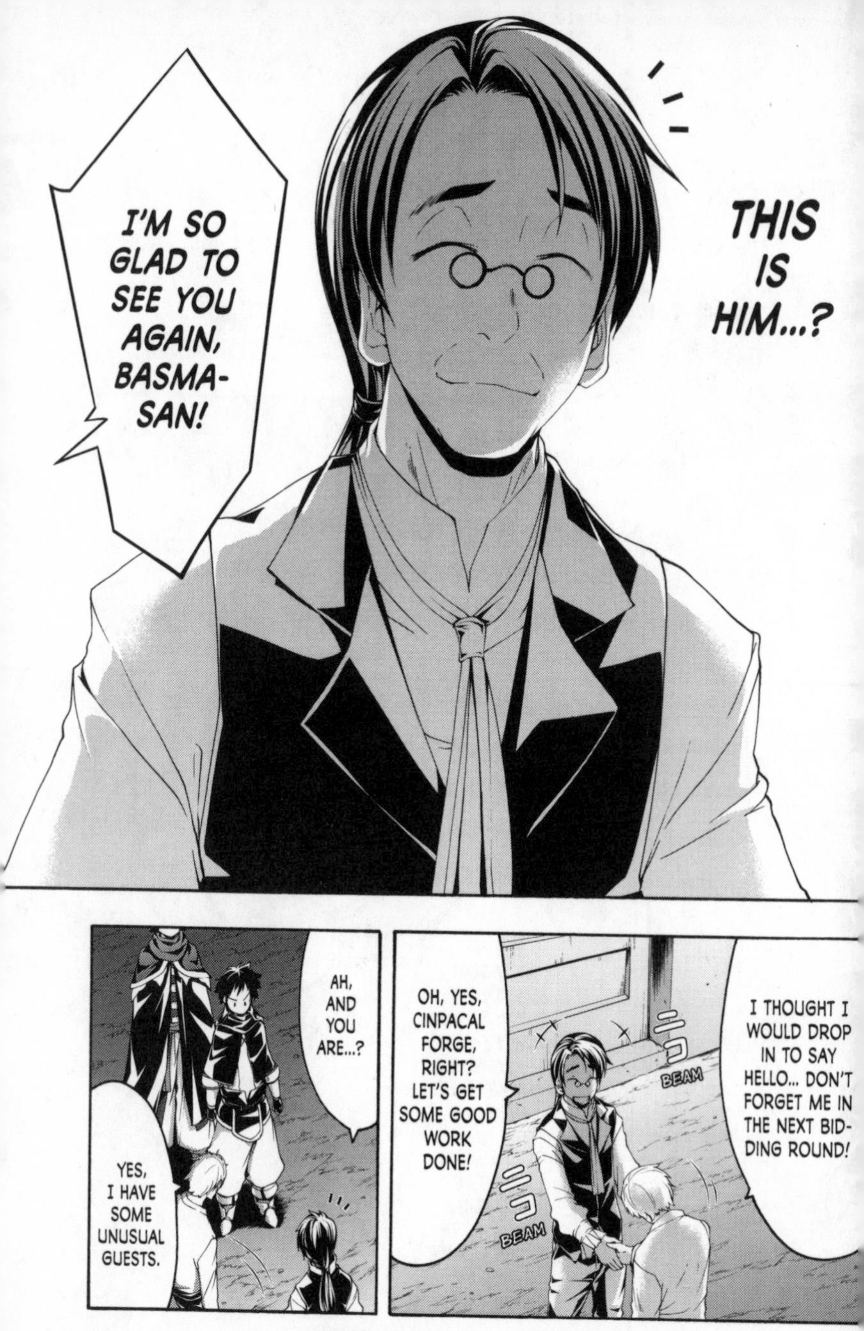
I'M SO GLAD TO SEE YOU AGAIN, BASMA-SAN!
THIS IS HIM...?
I THOUGHT I WOULD DROP IN TO SAY HELLO... DON'T FORGET ME IN THE NEXT BID-DING ROUND!
OH, YES, CINPACAL FORGE, RIGHT? LET'S GET SOME GOOD WORK DONE!
BEAM
BEAM
AH, AND YOU ARE...?
YES, I HAVE SOME UNUSUAL GUESTS.

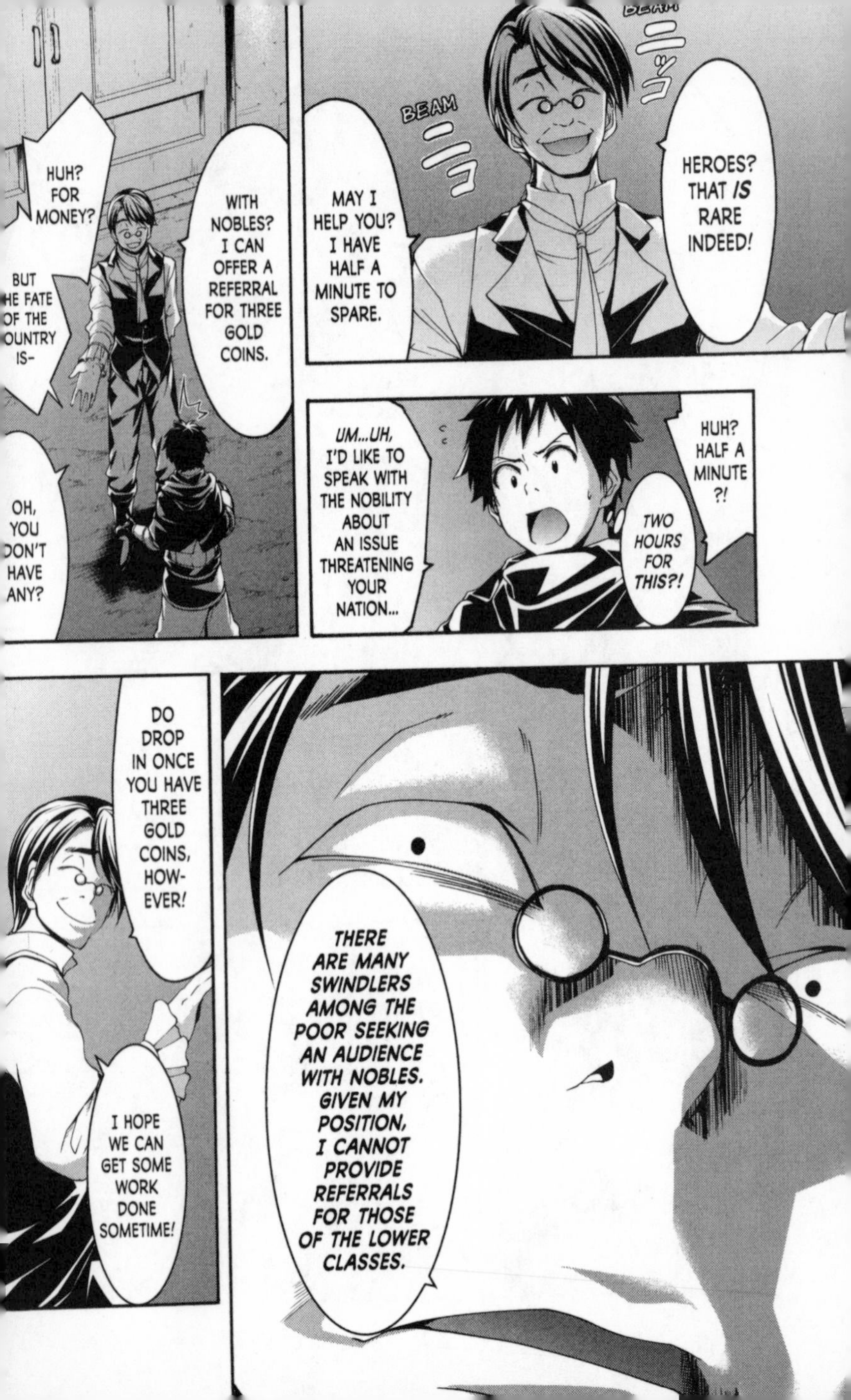
BEAM
ニッコ
BEAM
ニコ
HEROES? THAT IS RARE INDEED!
MAY I HELP YOU? I HAVE HALF A MINUTE TO SPARE.
HUH? HALF A MINUTE?!
TWO HOURS FOR THIS?!
UM...UH, I'D LIKE TO SPEAK WITH THE NOBILITY ABOUT AN ISSUE THREATENING YOUR NATION...
WITH NOBLES? I CAN OFFER A REFERRAL FOR THREE GOLD COINS.
HUH? FOR MONEY?
BUT HE FATE OF THE OUNTRY IS-
OH, YOU DON'T HAVE ANY?
THERE ARE MANY SWINDLERS AMONG THE POOR SEEKING AN AUDIENCE WITH NOBLES. GIVEN MY POSITION, I CANNOT PROVIDE REFERRALS FOR THOSE OF THE LOWER CLASSES.
DO DROP IN ONCE YOU HAVE THREE GOLD COINS, HOW-EVER!
I HOPE WE CAN GET SOME WORK DONE SOMETIME!

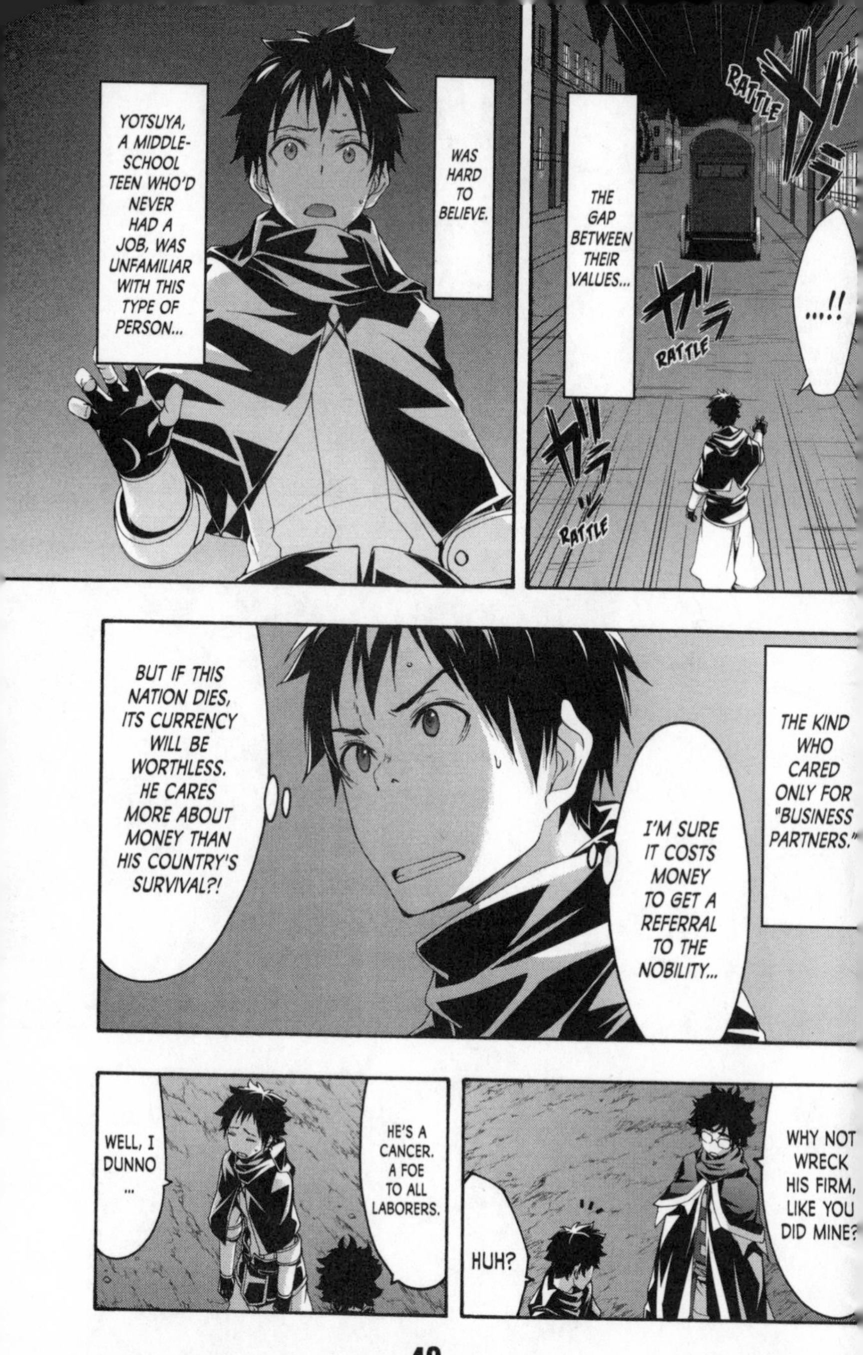
RATTLE
THE GAP BETWEEN THEIR VALUES...
...!!
RATTLE
RATTLE
WAS HARD TO BELIEVE.
YOTSUYA, A MIDDLE-SCHOOL TEEN WHO'D NEVER HAD A JOB, WAS UNFAMILIAR WITH THIS TYPE OF PERSON...
THE KIND WHO CARED ONLY FOR "BUSINESS PARTNERS."
I'M SURE IT COSTS MONEY TO GET A REFERRAL TO THE NOBILITY...
BUT IF THIS NATION DIES, ITS CURRENCY WILL BE WORTHLESS. HE CARES MORE ABOUT MONEY THAN HIS COUNTRY'S SURVIVAL?!
WHY NOT WRECK HIS FIRM, LIKE YOU DID MINE?
HUH?
HE'S A CANCER. A FOE TO ALL LABORERS.
WELL, I DUNNO...

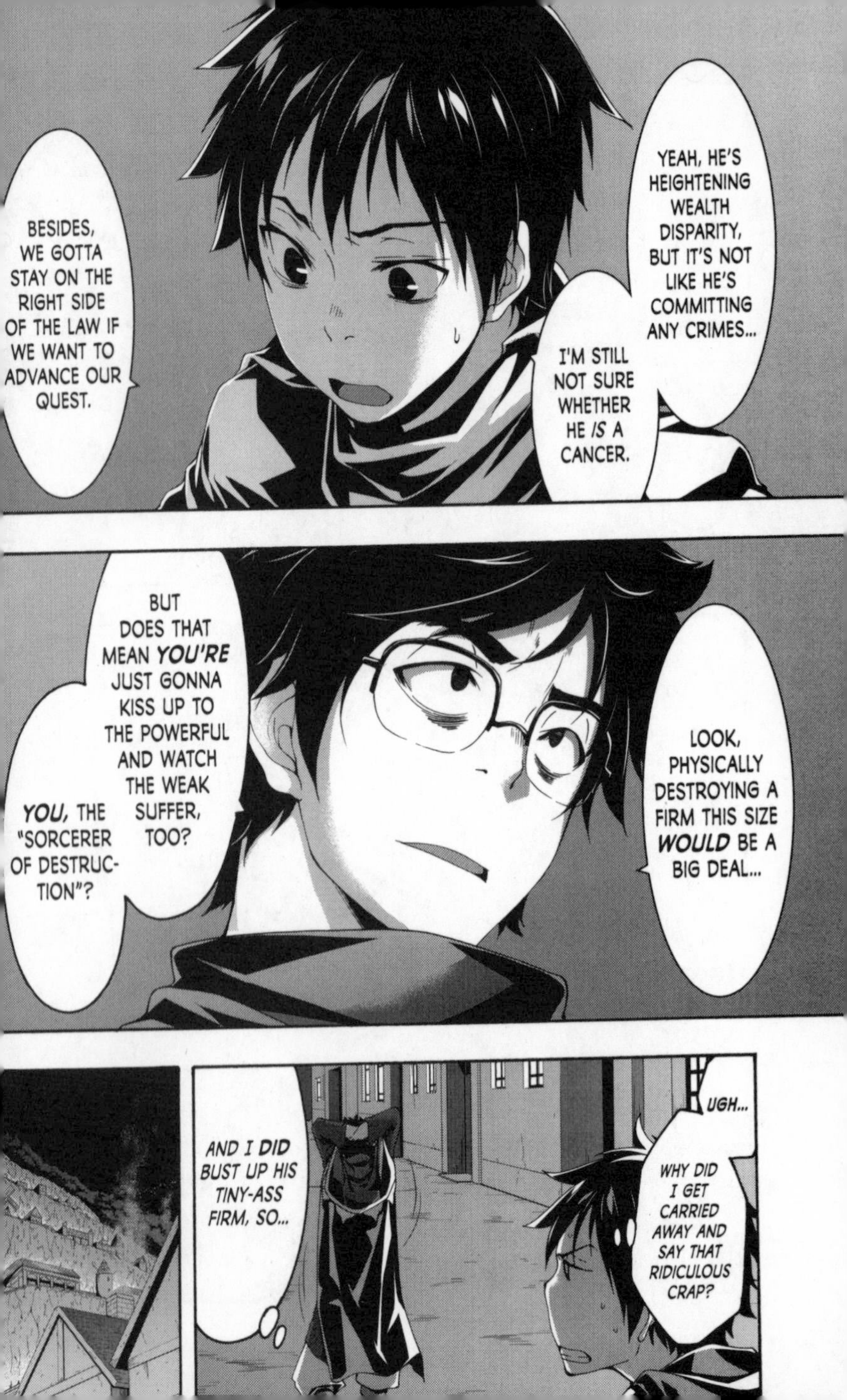
YEAH, HE'S HEIGHTENING WEALTH DISPARITY, BUT IT'S NOT LIKE HE'S COMMITTING ANY CRIMES...
I'M STILL NOT SURE WHETHER HE *IS* A CANCER.
BESIDES, WE GOTTA STAY ON THE RIGHT SIDE OF THE LAW IF WE WANT TO ADVANCE OUR QUEST.
LOOK, PHYSICALLY DESTROYING A FIRM THIS SIZE ***WOULD*** BE A BIG DEAL...
BUT DOES THAT MEAN ***YOU'RE*** JUST GONNA KISS UP TO THE POWERFUL AND WATCH THE WEAK SUFFER, TOO?
YOU, THE "SORCERER OF DESTRUCTION"?
UGH...
WHY DID I GET CARRIED AWAY AND SAY THAT RIDICULOUS CRAP?
*AND I **DID** BUST UP HIS TINY-ASS FIRM, SO...*

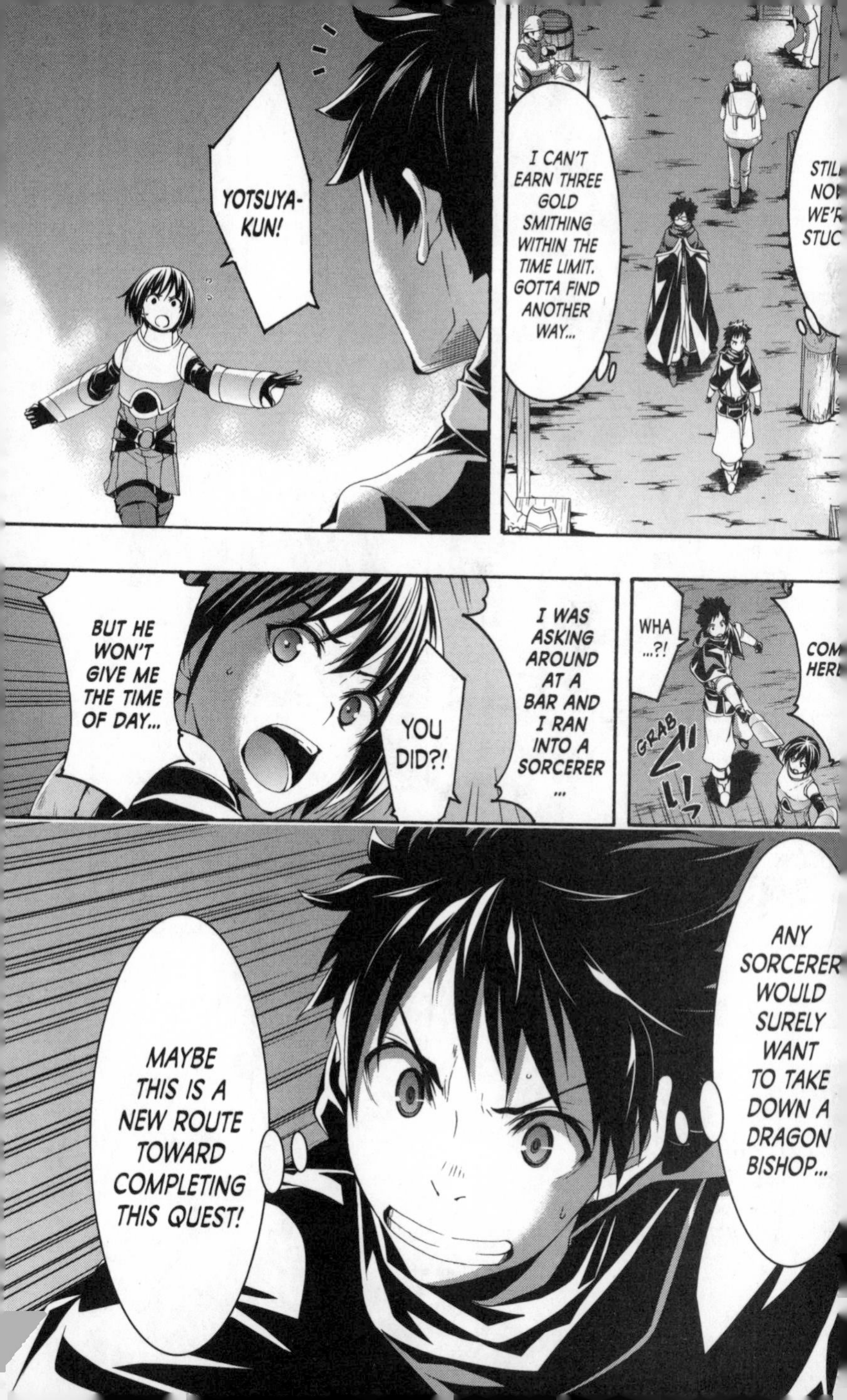

STIL NO WE'R STUC
I CAN'T EARN THREE GOLD SMITHING WITHIN THE TIME LIMIT. GOTTA FIND ANOTHER WAY...
YOTSUYA-KUN!
COM HER
WHA ...?!
GRAB
I WAS ASKING AROUND AT A BAR AND I RAN INTO A SORCERER ...
YOU DID?!
BUT HE WON'T GIVE ME THE TIME OF DAY...
ANY SORCERER WOULD SURELY WANT TO TAKE DOWN A DRAGON BISHOP...
MAYBE THIS IS A NEW ROUTE TOWARD COMPLETING THIS QUEST!

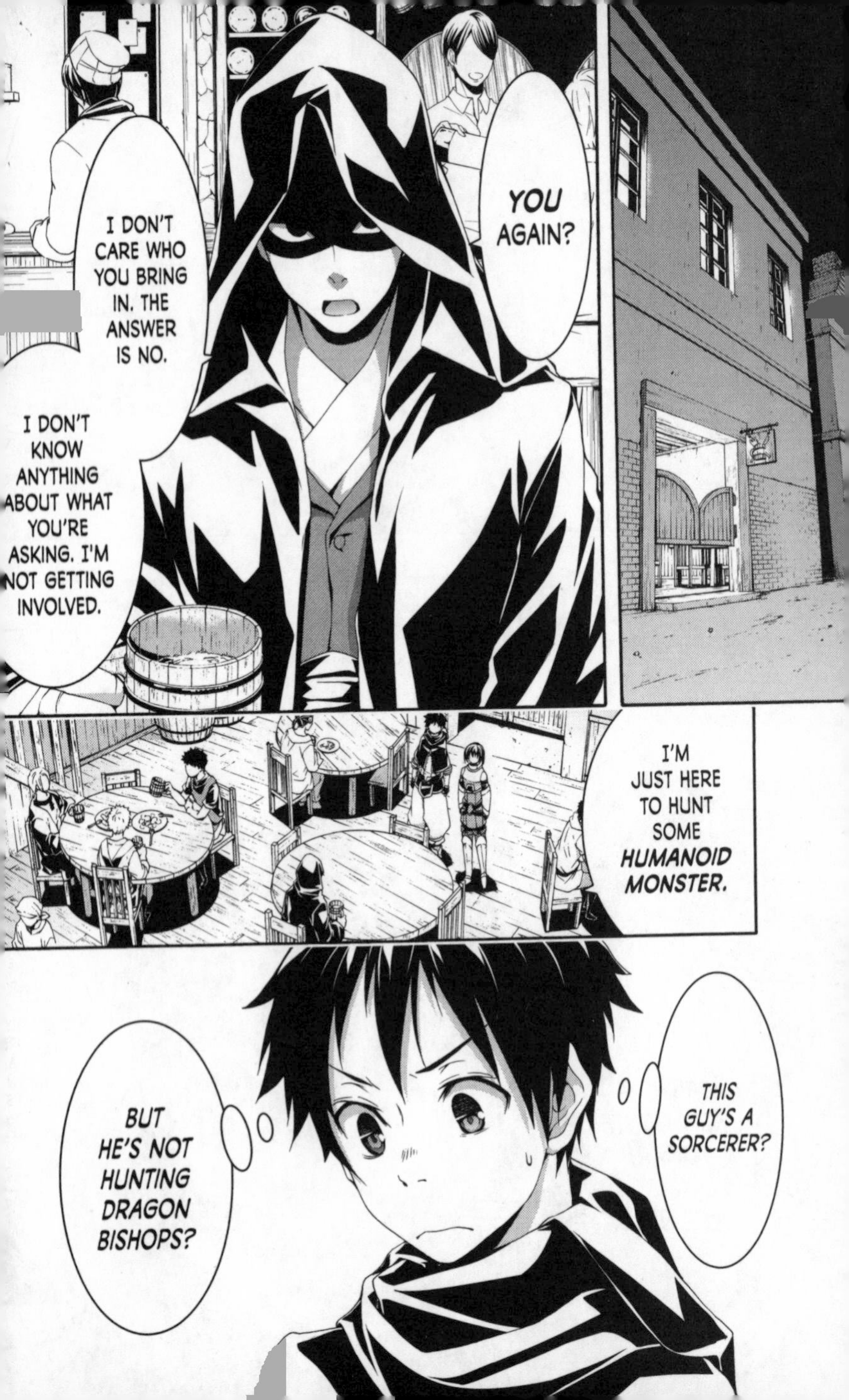
YOU AGAIN?
I DON'T CARE WHO YOU BRING IN. THE ANSWER IS NO.
I DON'T KNOW ANYTHING ABOUT WHAT YOU'RE ASKING. I'M NOT GETTING INVOLVED.
I'M JUST HERE TO HUNT SOME *HUMANOID MONSTER.*
THIS GUY'S A SORCERER?
BUT HE'S NOT HUNTING DRAGON BISHOPS?

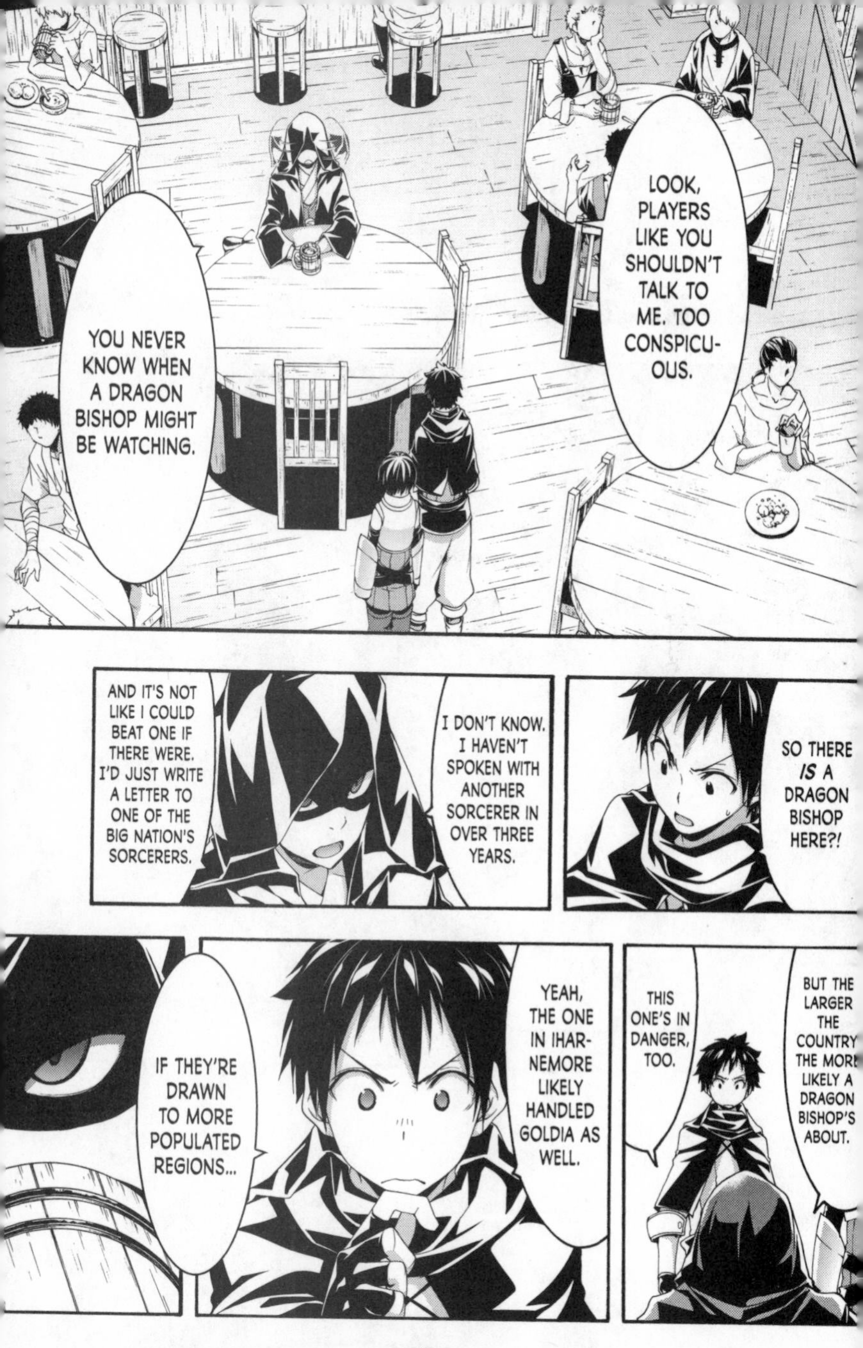
LOOK, PLAYERS LIKE YOU SHOULDN'T TALK TO ME. TOO CONSPICU-OUS.
YOU NEVER KNOW WHEN A DRAGON BISHOP MIGHT BE WATCHING.
SO THERE *IS* A DRAGON BISHOP HERE?!
I DON'T KNOW. I HAVEN'T SPOKEN WITH ANOTHER SORCERER IN OVER THREE YEARS.
AND IT'S NOT LIKE I COULD BEAT ONE IF THERE WERE. I'D JUST WRITE A LETTER TO ONE OF THE BIG NATION'S SORCERERS.
BUT THE LARGER THE COUNTRY THE MORE LIKELY A DRAGON BISHOP'S ABOUT.
THIS ONE'S IN DANGER, TOO.
YEAH, THE ONE IN IHAR-NEMORE LIKELY HANDLED GOLDIA AS WELL.
IF THEY'RE DRAWN TO MORE POPULATED REGIONS...

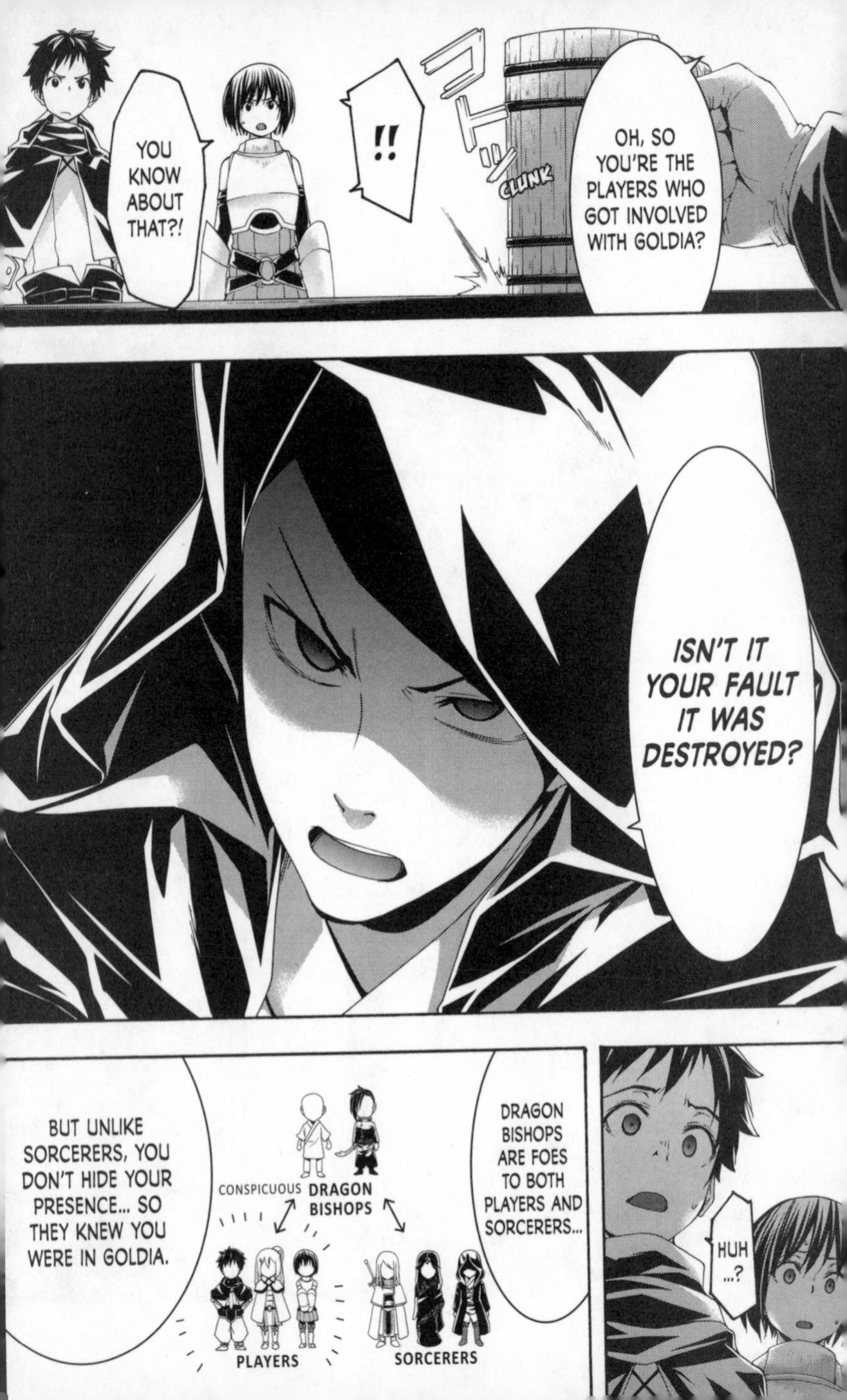
OH, SO YOU'RE THE PLAYERS WHO GOT INVOLVED WITH GOLDIA?
CLUNK
!!
YOU KNOW ABOUT THAT?!
ISN'T IT YOUR FAULT IT WAS DESTROYED?
HUH ...?
DRAGON BISHOPS ARE FOES TO BOTH PLAYERS AND SORCERERS...
DRAGON BISHOPS
CONSPICUOUS
PLAYERS
SORCERERS
BUT UNLIKE SORCERERS, YOU DON'T HIDE YOUR PRESENCE... SO THEY KNEW YOU WERE IN GOLDIA.

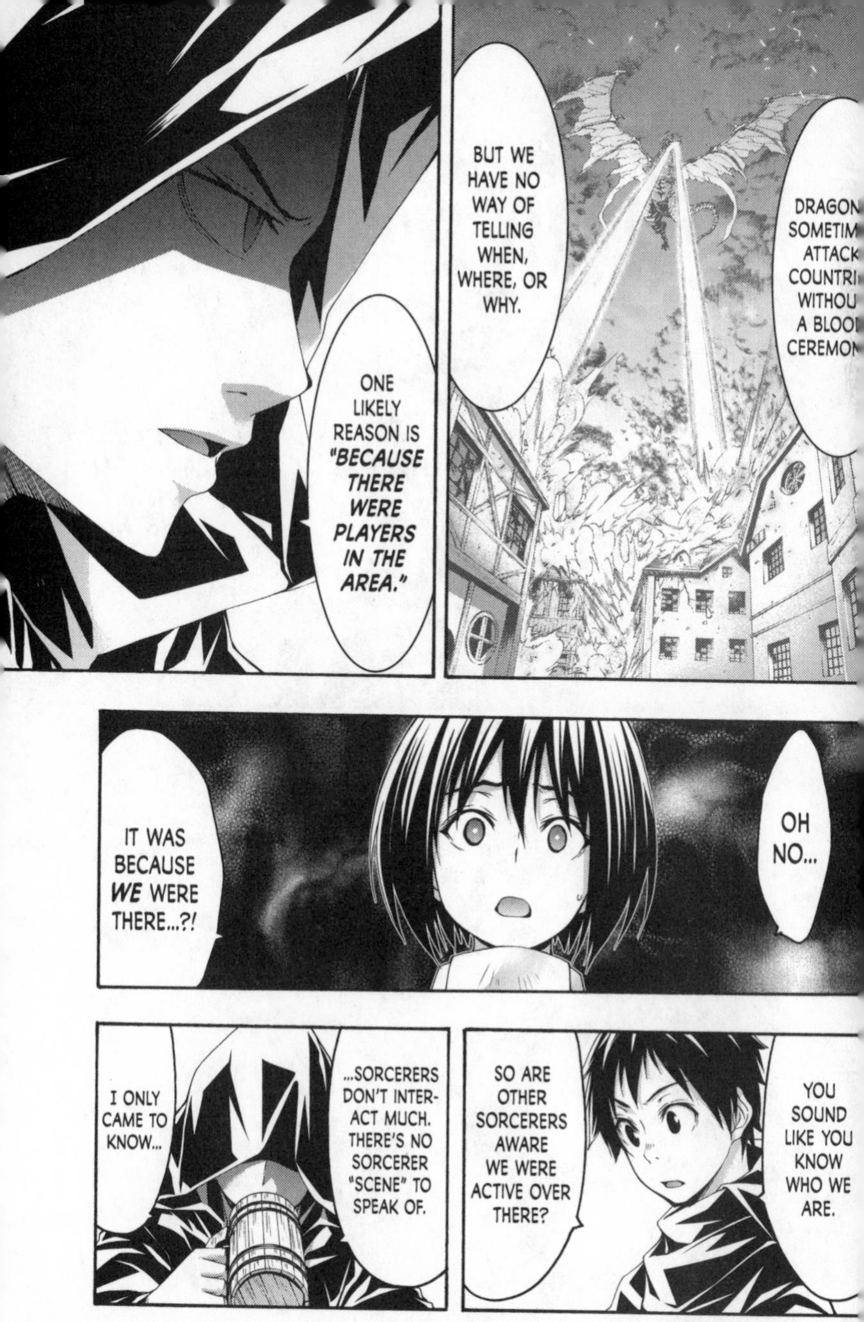
DRAGON SOMETIM ATTACK COUNTRI WITHOU A BLOO CEREMON
BUT WE HAVE NO WAY OF TELLING WHEN, WHERE, OR WHY.
ONE LIKELY REASON IS "BECAUSE THERE WERE PLAYERS IN THE AREA."
OH NO...
IT WAS BECAUSE WE WERE THERE...?!
YOU SOUND LIKE YOU KNOW WHO WE ARE.
SO ARE OTHER SORCERERS AWARE WE WERE ACTIVE OVER THERE?
...SORCERERS DON'T INTER-ACT MUCH. THERE'S NO SORCERER "SCENE" TO SPEAK OF.
I ONLY CAME TO KNOW...

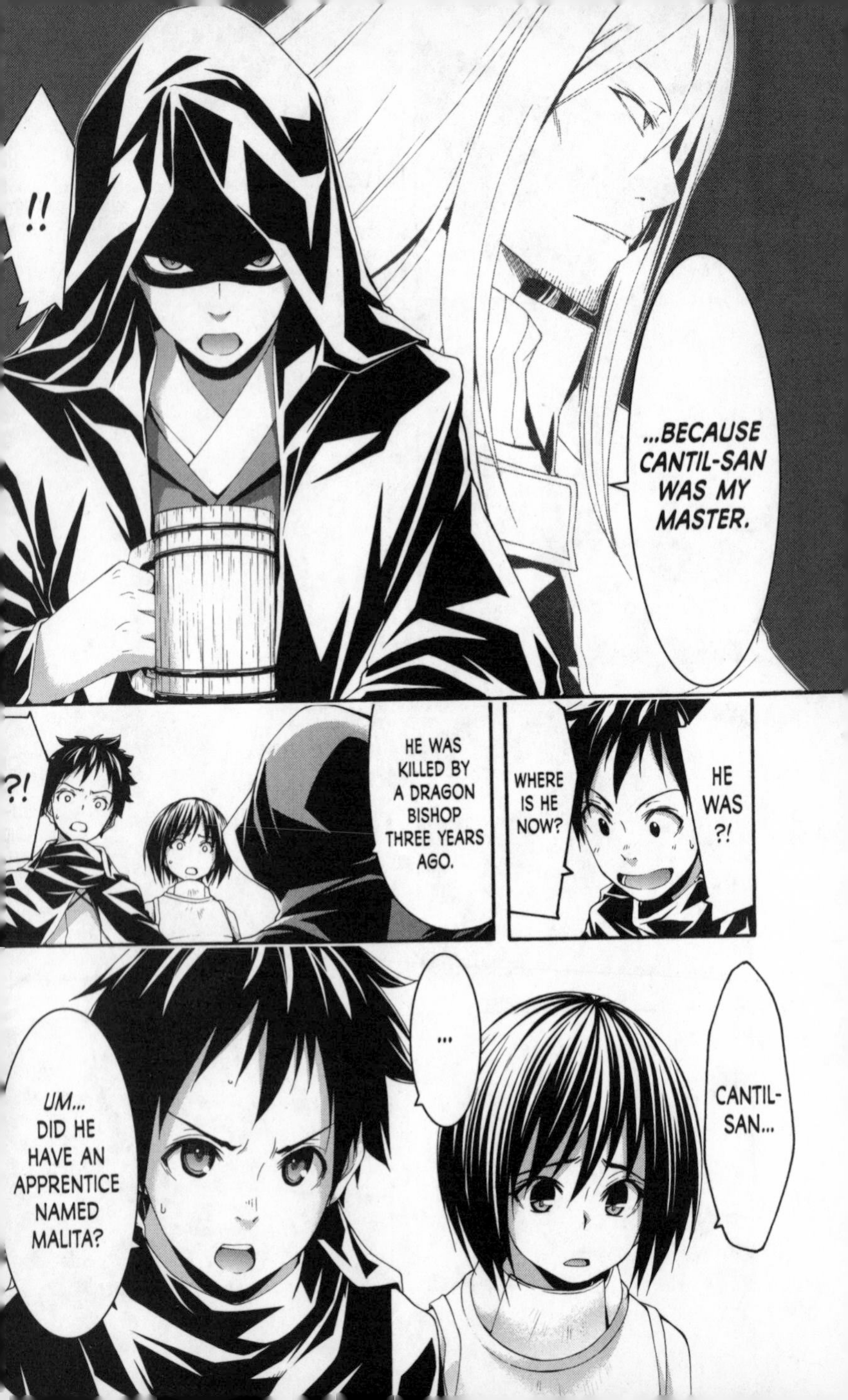
...BECAUSE CANTIL-SAN WAS MY MASTER.
!!
HE WAS ?!
WHERE IS HE NOW?
HE WAS KILLED BY A DRAGON BISHOP THREE YEARS AGO.
?!
CANTIL-SAN...
...
UM... DID HE HAVE AN APPRENTICE NAMED MALITA?

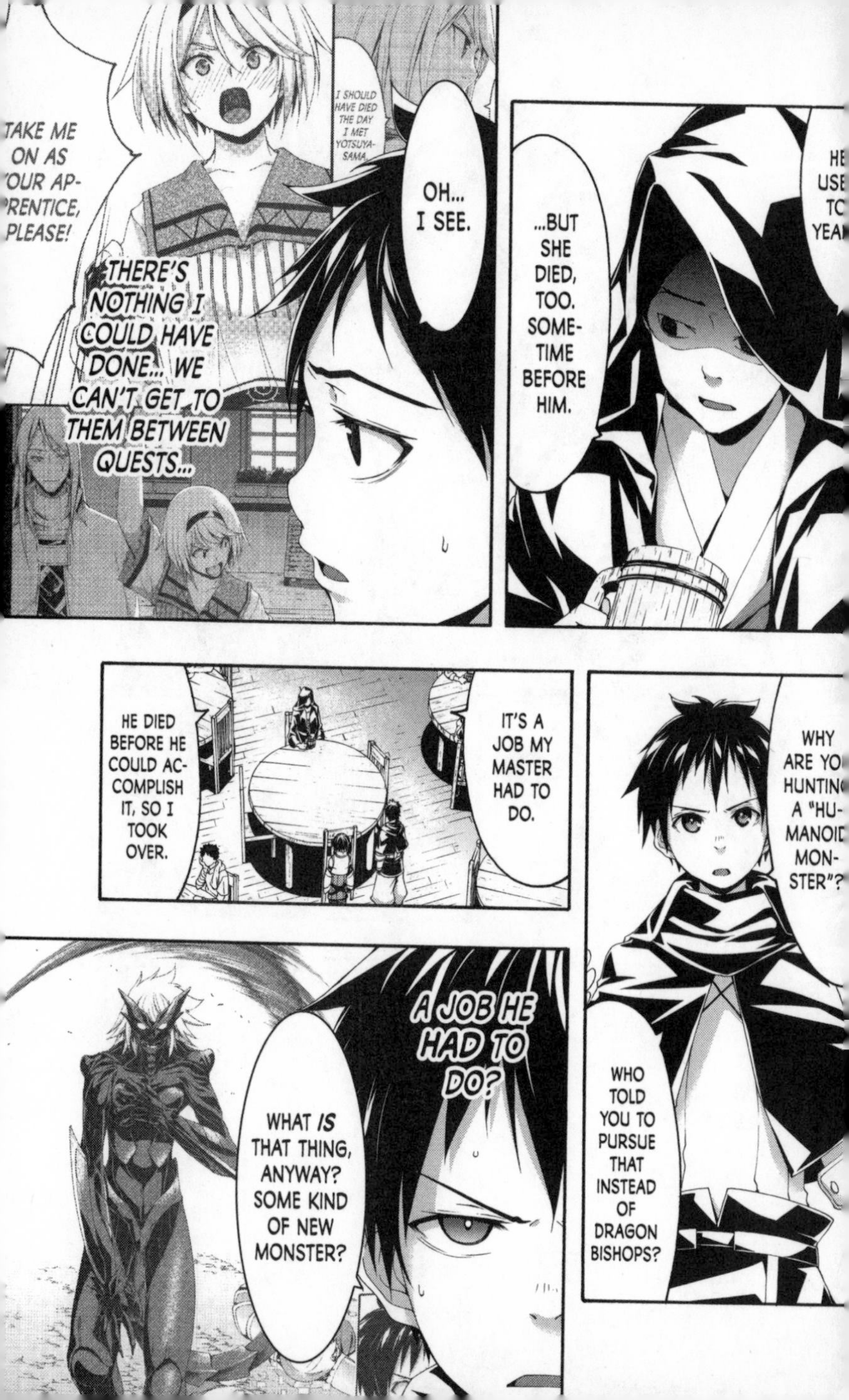
HE USE TO YEA
...BUT SHE DIED, TOO. SOME-TIME BEFORE HIM.
OH... I SEE.
I SHOULD HAVE DIED THE DAY I MET YOTSUYA-SAMA.
TAKE ME ON AS 'OUR AP-'RENTICE, PLEASE!
THERE'S NOTHING I COULD HAVE DONE... WE CAN'T GET TO THEM BETWEEN QUESTS...
WHY ARE YO HUNTIN A "HU-MANOID MON-STER"?
IT'S A JOB MY MASTER HAD TO DO.
HE DIED BEFORE HE COULD AC-COMPLISH IT, SO I TOOK OVER.
WHO TOLD YOU TO PURSUE THAT INSTEAD OF DRAGON BISHOPS?
A JOB HE HAD TO DO?
WHAT *IS* THAT THING, ANYWAY? SOME KIND OF NEW MONSTER?

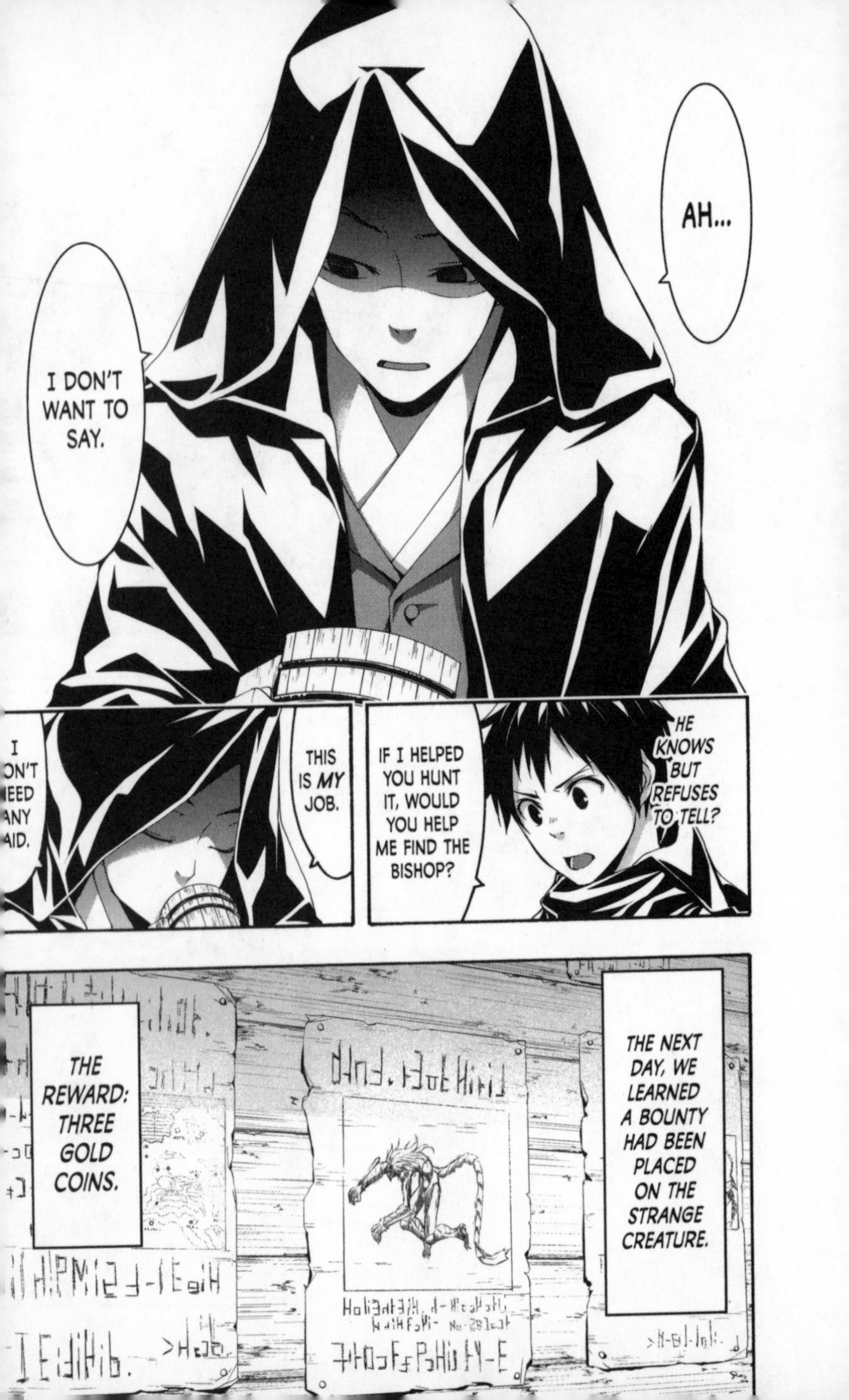
AH...
I DON'T WANT TO SAY.
HE KNOWS BUT REFUSES TO TELL?
IF I HELPED YOU HUNT IT, WOULD YOU HELP ME FIND THE BISHOP?
THIS IS *MY* JOB.
I ON'T IEED ANY AID.
THE NEXT DAY, WE LEARNED A BOUNTY HAD BEEN PLACED ON THE STRANGE CREATURE.
THE REWARD: THREE GOLD COINS.

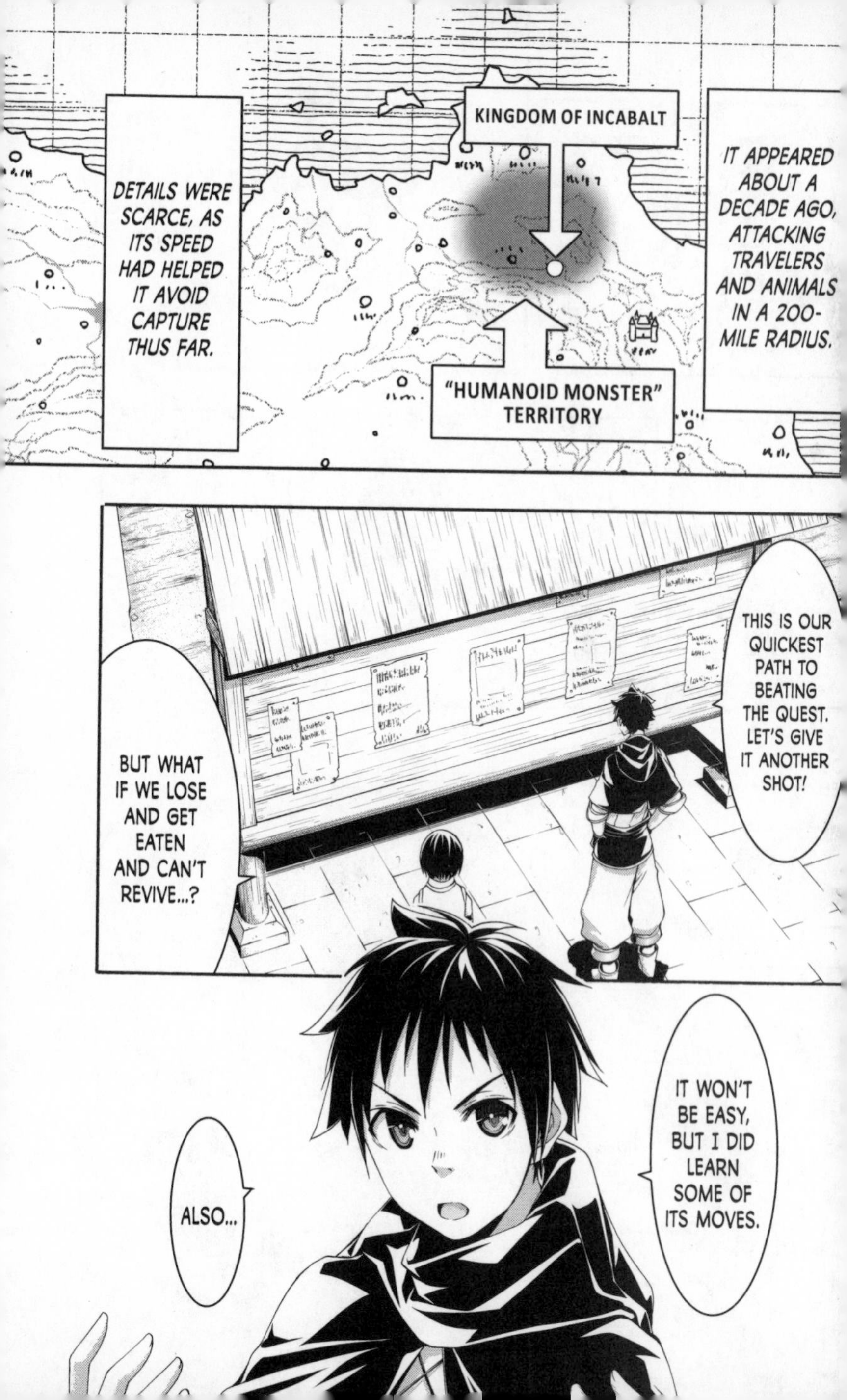
IT APPEARED ABOUT A DECADE AGO, ATTACKING TRAVELERS AND ANIMALS IN A 200-MILE RADIUS.
KINGDOM OF INCABALT
"HUMANOID MONSTER" TERRITORY
DETAILS WERE SCARCE, AS ITS SPEED HAD HELPED IT AVOID CAPTURE THUS FAR.
THIS IS OUR QUICKEST PATH TO BEATING THE QUEST. LET'S GIVE IT ANOTHER SHOT!
BUT WHAT IF WE LOSE AND GET EATEN AND CAN'T REVIVE...?
IT WON'T BE EASY, BUT I DID LEARN SOME OF ITS MOVES.
ALSO...

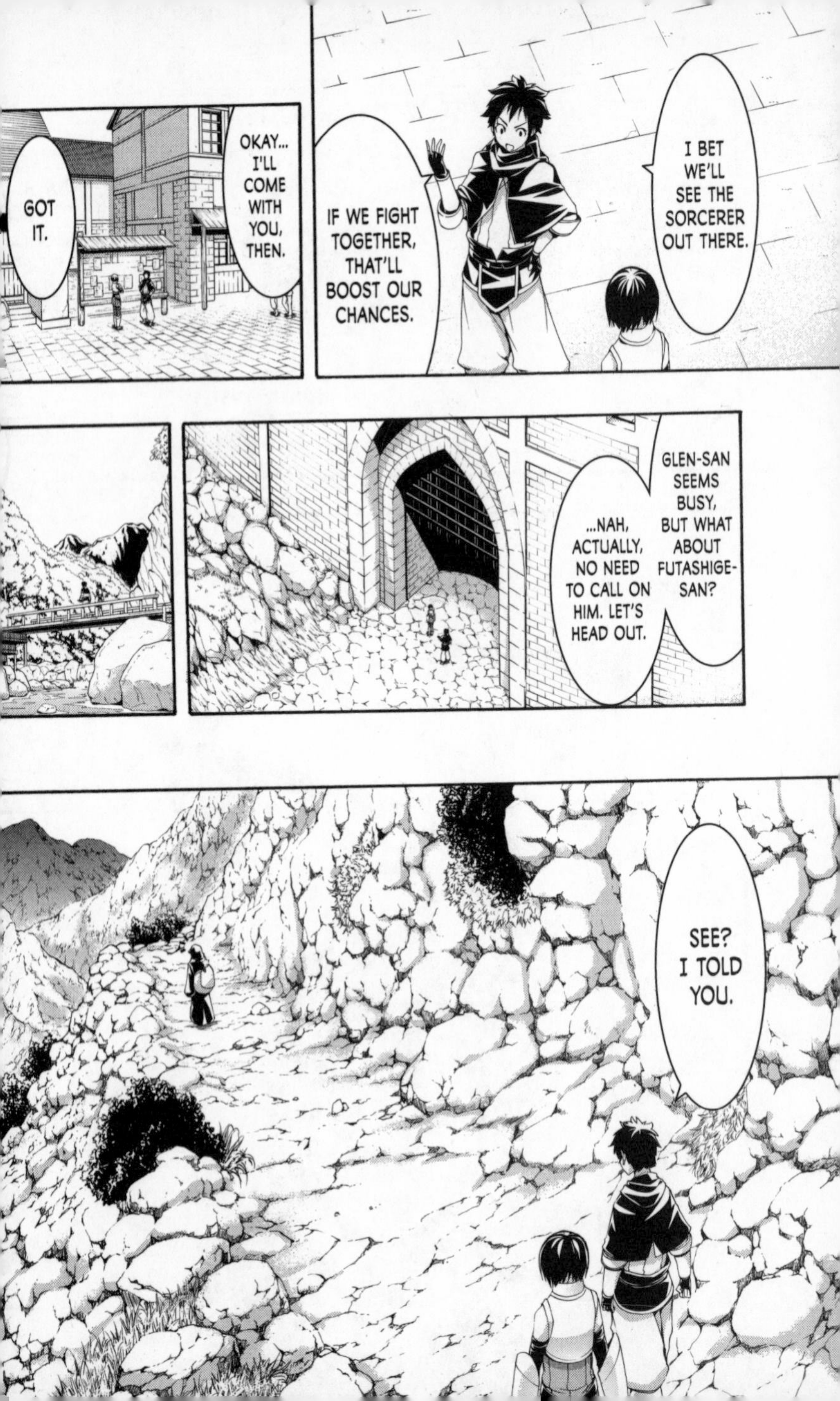
I BET WE'LL SEE THE SORCERER OUT THERE.
IF WE FIGHT TOGETHER, THAT'LL BOOST OUR CHANCES.
OKAY... I'LL COME WITH YOU, THEN.
GOT IT.
GLEN-SAN SEEMS BUSY, BUT WHAT ABOUT FUTASHIGE-SAN?
...NAH, ACTUALLY, NO NEED TO CALL ON HIM. LET'S HEAD OUT.
SEE? I TOLD YOU.

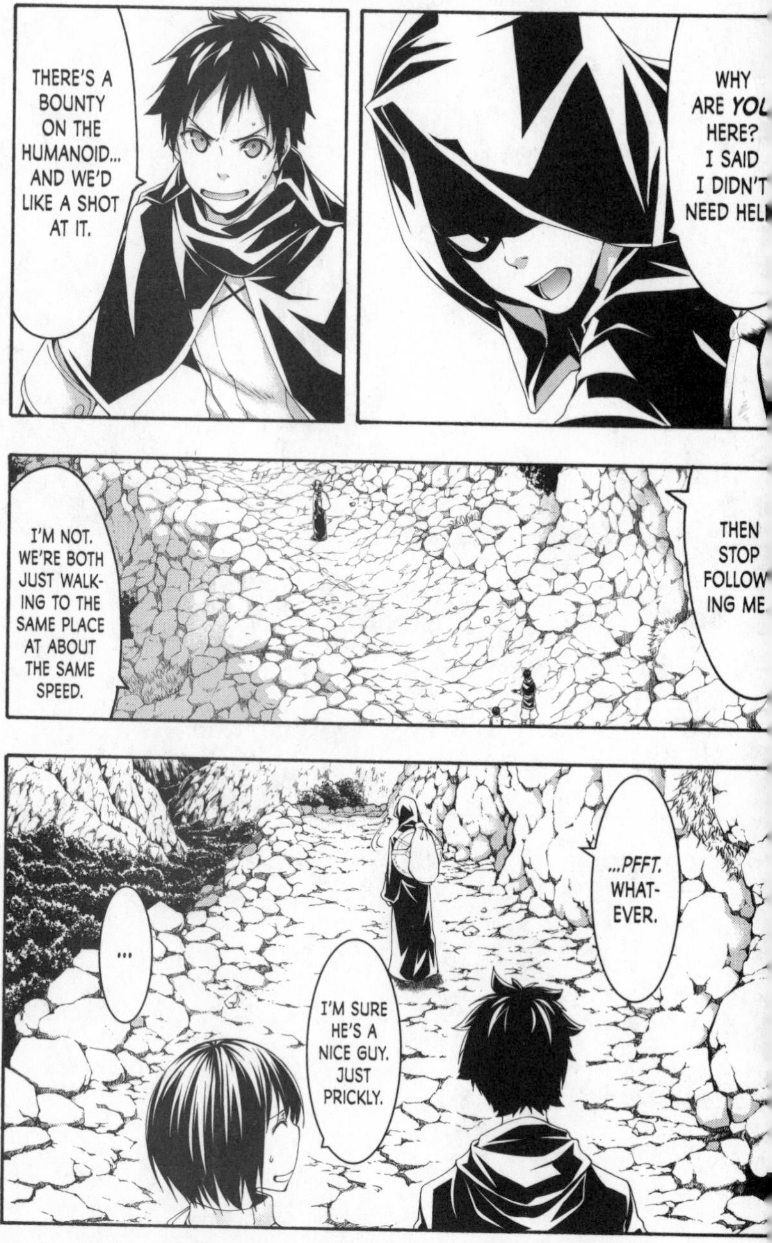
WHY ARE YOU HERE? I SAID I DIDN'T NEED HEL
THERE'S A BOUNTY ON THE HUMANOID... AND WE'D LIKE A SHOT AT IT.
THEN STOP FOLLOWING ME
I'M NOT. WE'RE BOTH JUST WALKING TO THE SAME PLACE AT ABOUT THE SAME SPEED.
...PFFT. WHATEVER.
...
I'M SURE HE'S A NICE GUY. JUST PRICKLY.

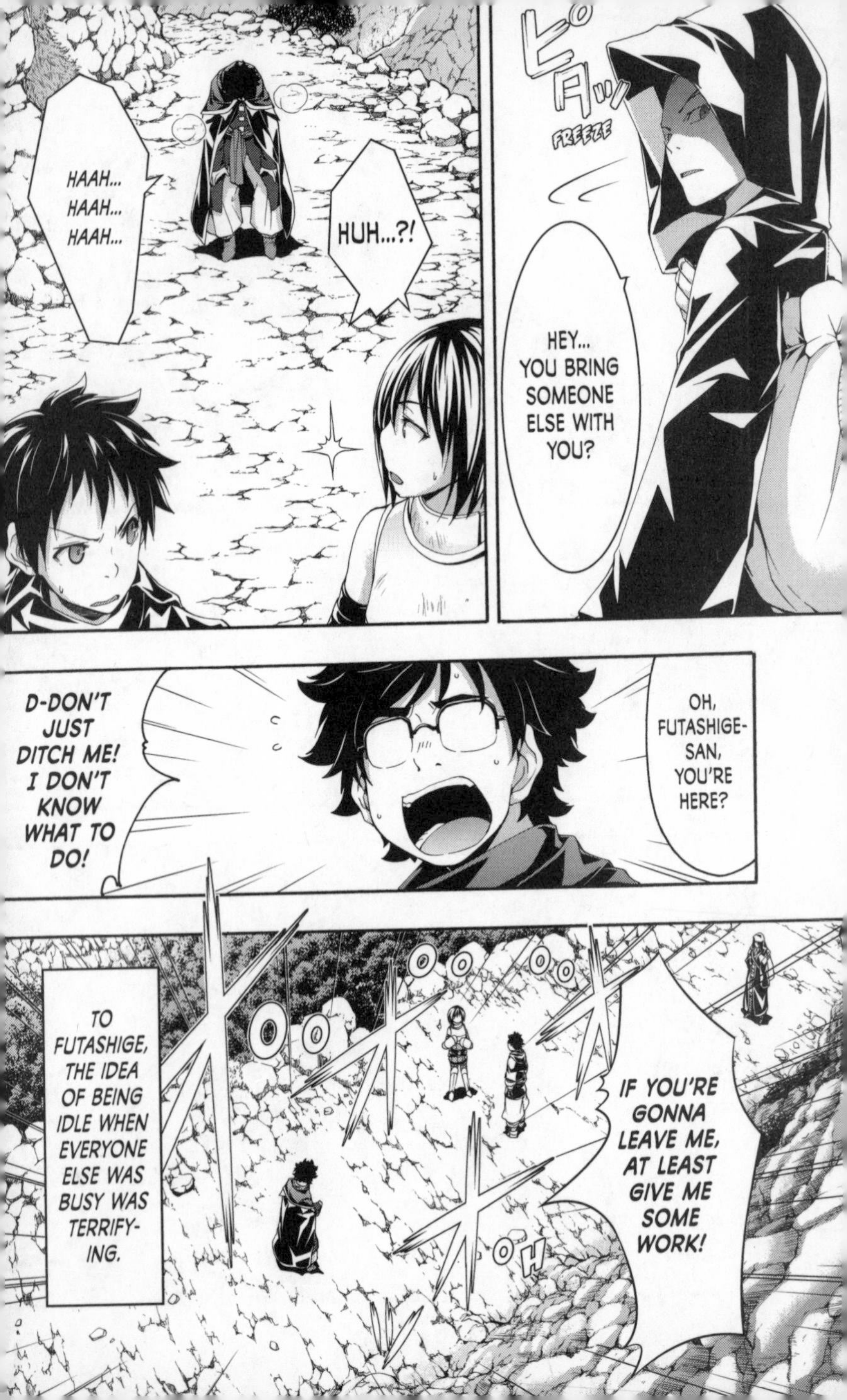
FREEZE
HEY... YOU BRING SOMEONE ELSE WITH YOU?
HAAH... HAAH... HAAH...
HUH...?!
OH, FUTASHIGE-SAN, YOU'RE HERE?
D-DON'T JUST DITCH ME! I DON'T KNOW WHAT TO DO!
IF YOU'RE GONNA LEAVE ME, AT LEAST GIVE ME SOME WORK!
TO FUTASHIGE, THE IDEA OF BEING IDLE WHEN EVERYONE ELSE WAS BUSY WAS TERRIFY-ING.

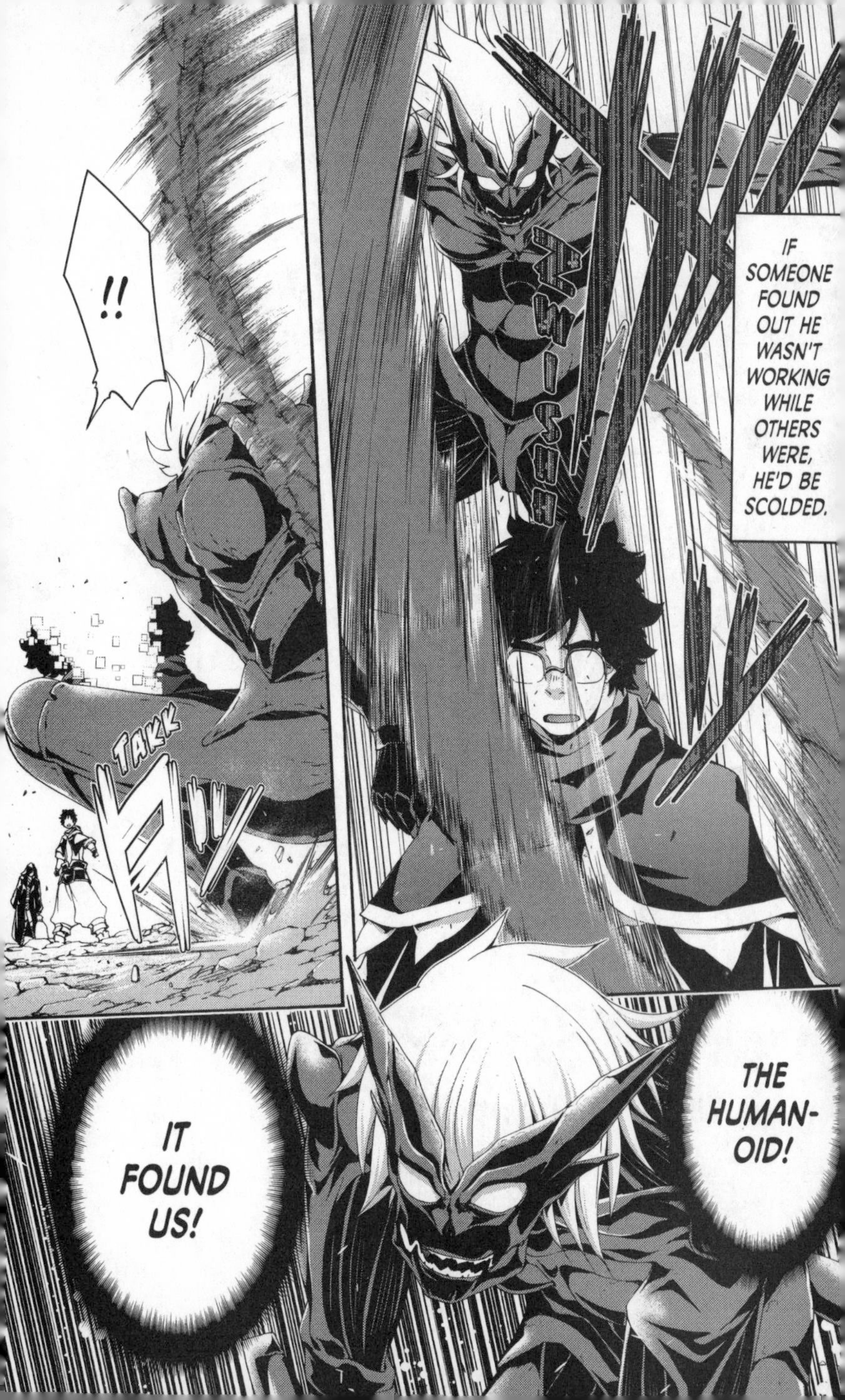
IF SOMEONE FOUND OUT HE WASN'T WORKING WHILE OTHERS WERE, HE'D BE SCOLDED.
!!
TAKK
THE HUMAN-OID!
IT FOUND US!

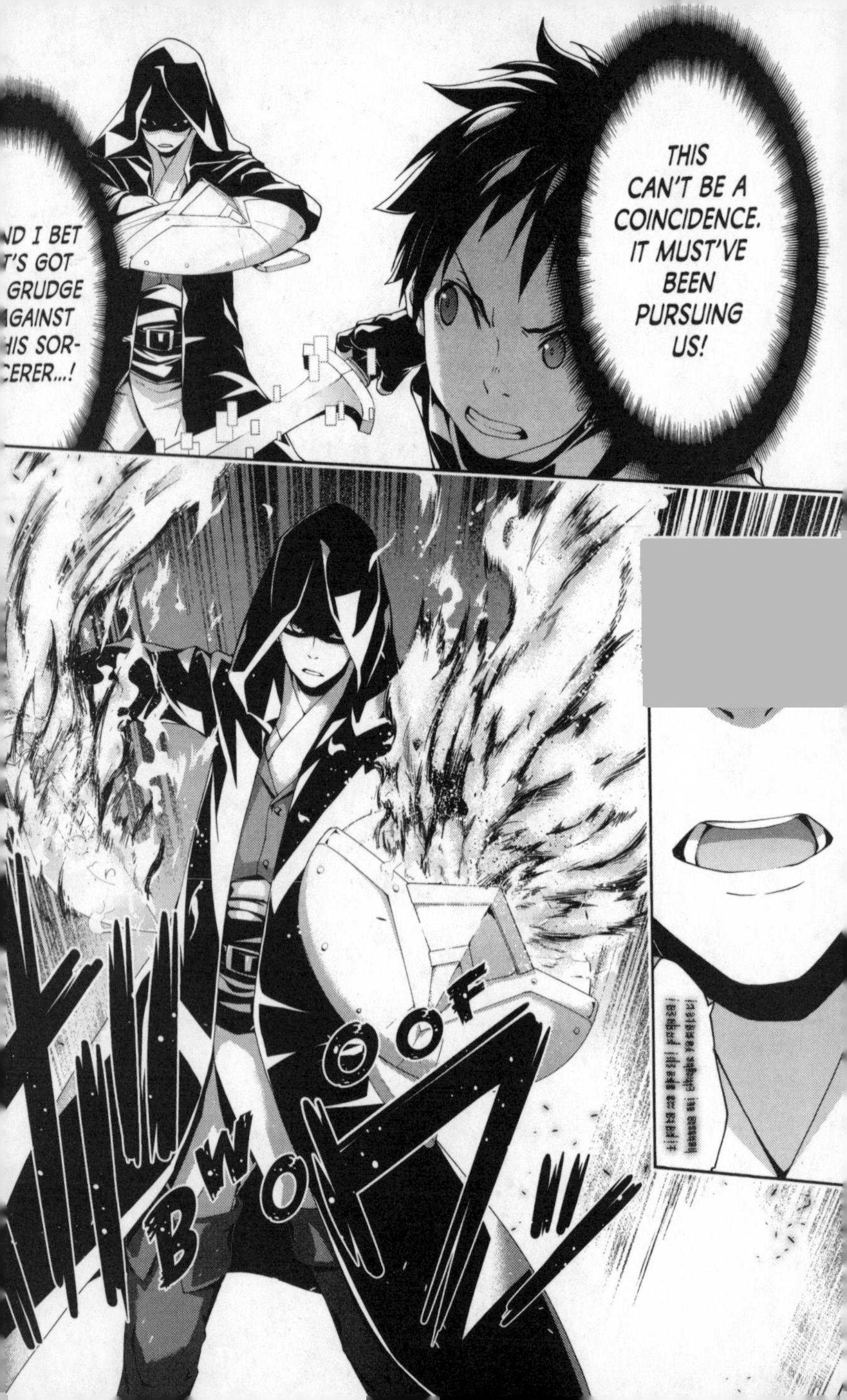
THIS CAN'T BE A COINCIDENCE. IT MUST'VE BEEN PURSUING US!
ND I BET T'S GOT GRUDGE GAINST HIS SOR-CERER...!
BWOOOOF!!

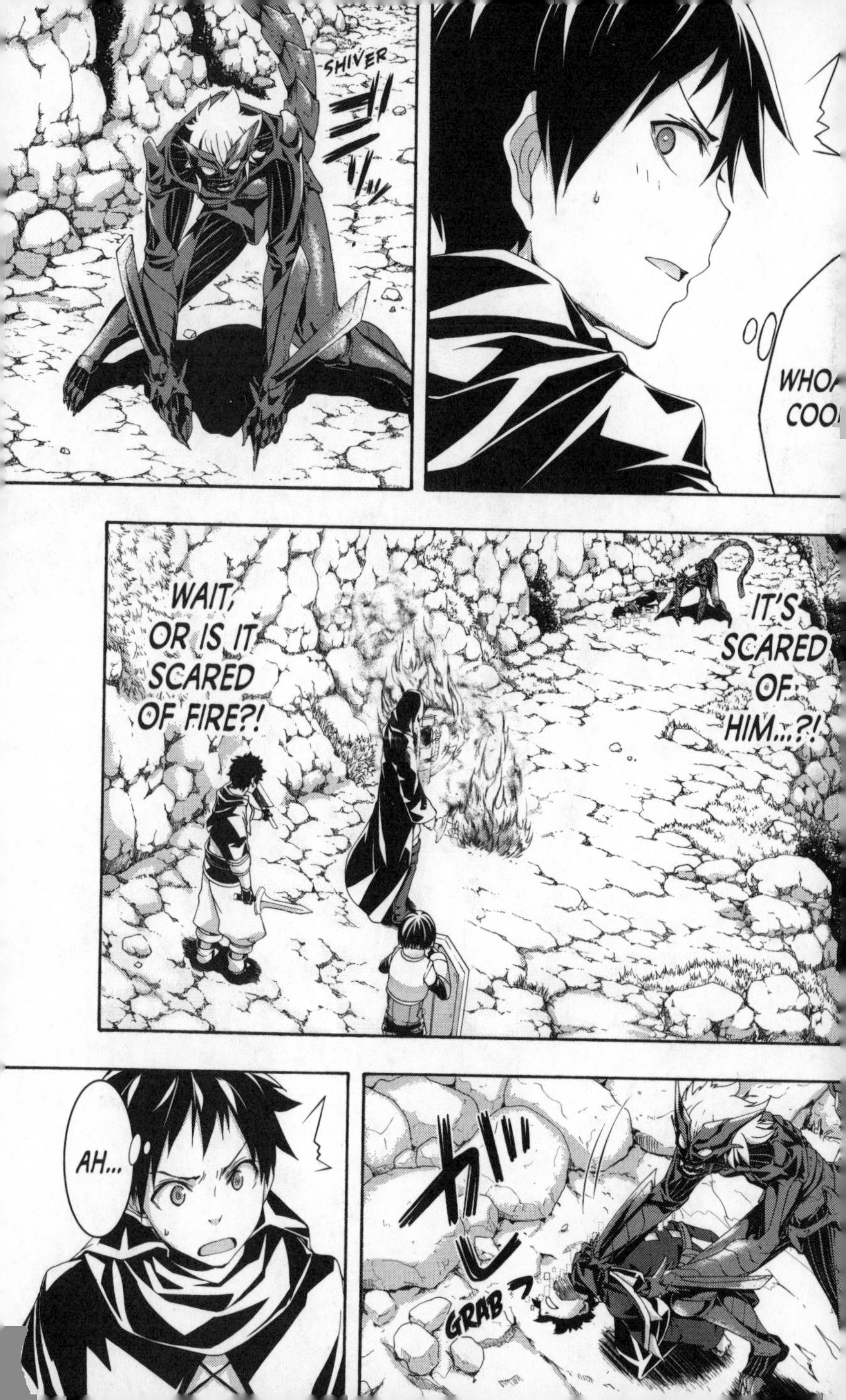
WHOA COO
SHIVER
IT'S SCARED OF HIM...?!
WAIT, OR IS IT SCARED OF FIRE?!
GRAB
AH...

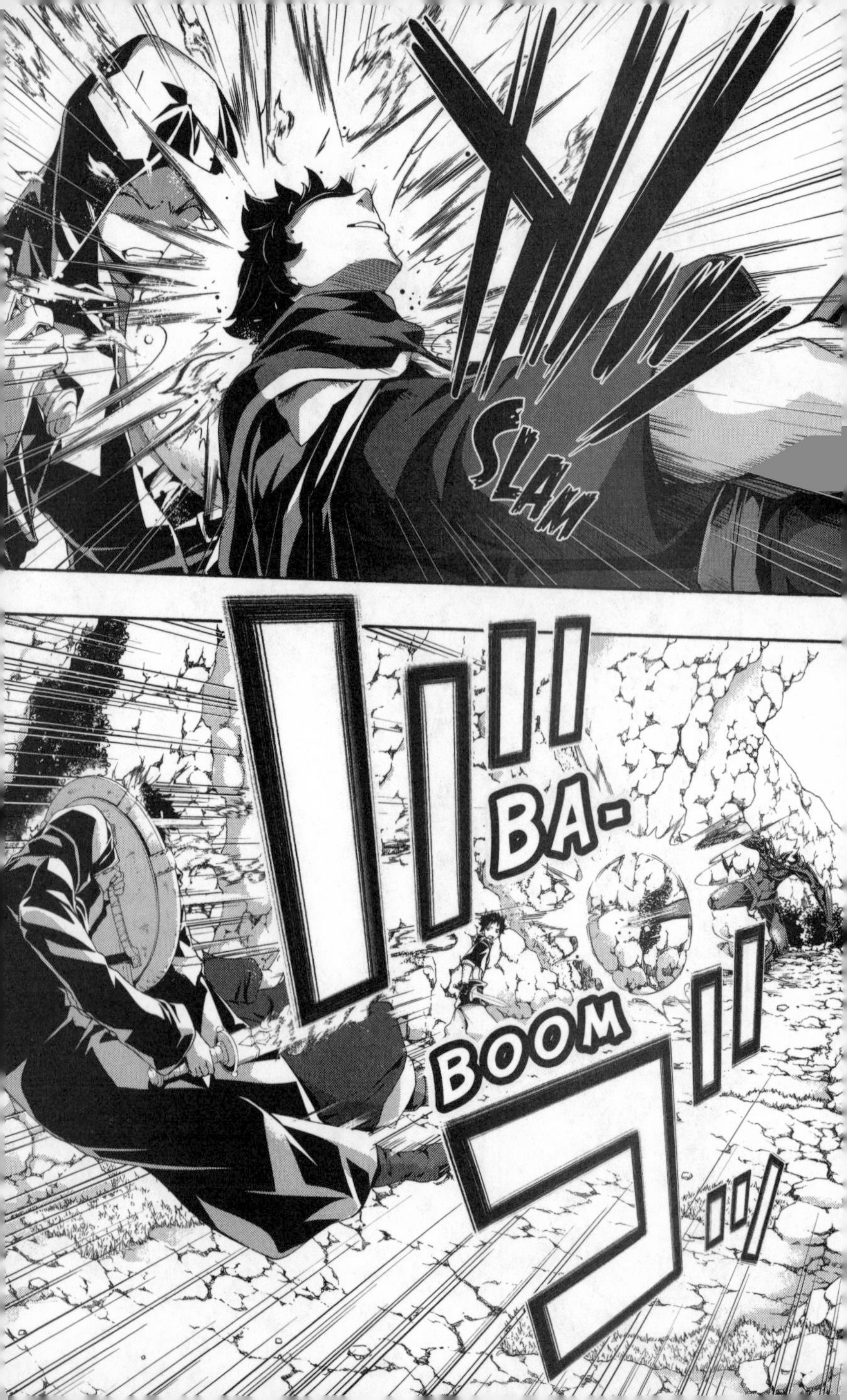
SLAM
BA-
BOOM

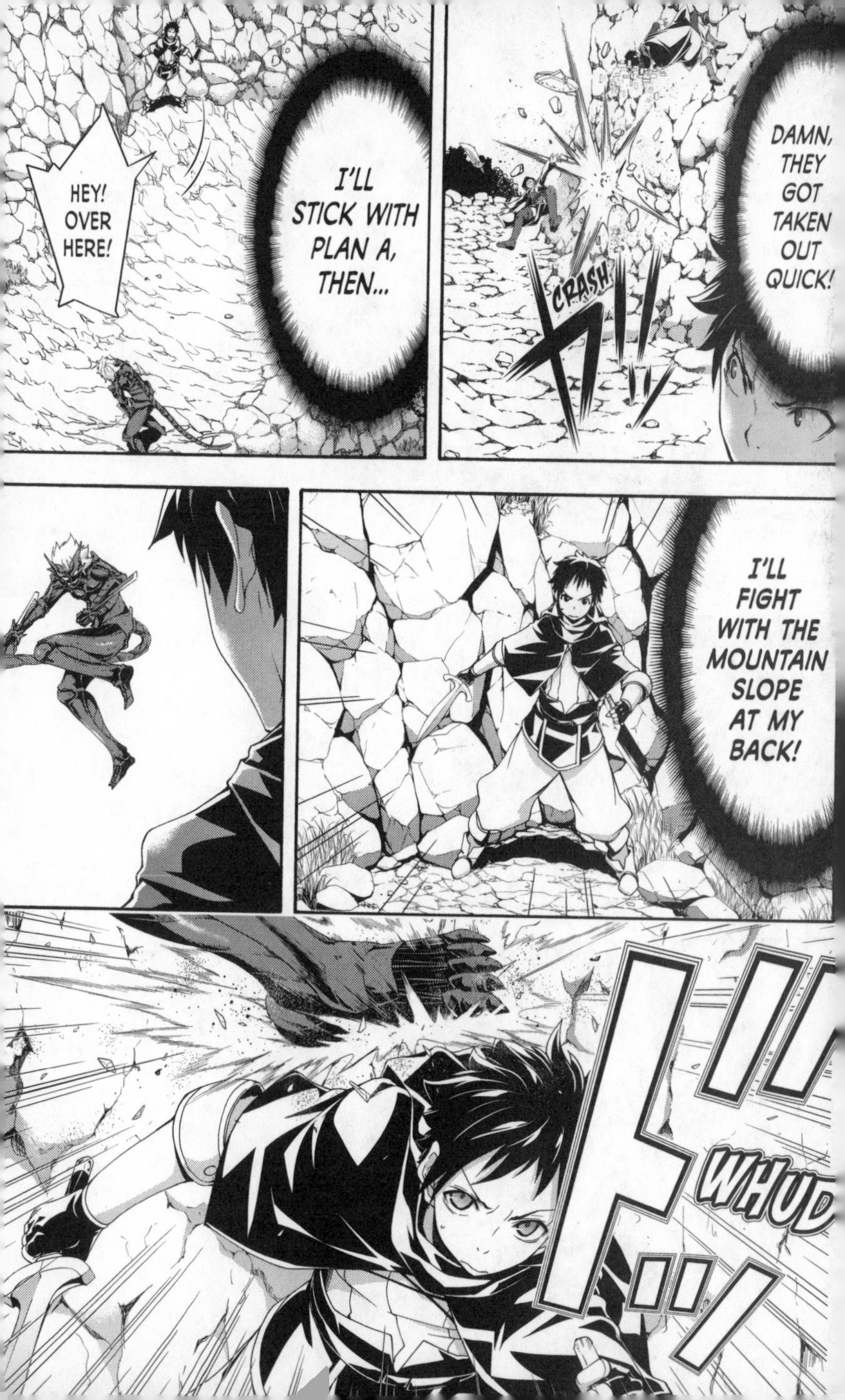
DAMN, THEY GOT TAKEN OUT QUICK!
CRASH
I'LL STICK WITH PLAN A, THEN...
HEY! OVER HERE!
I'LL FIGHT WITH THE MOUNTAIN SLOPE AT MY BACK!
WHUD

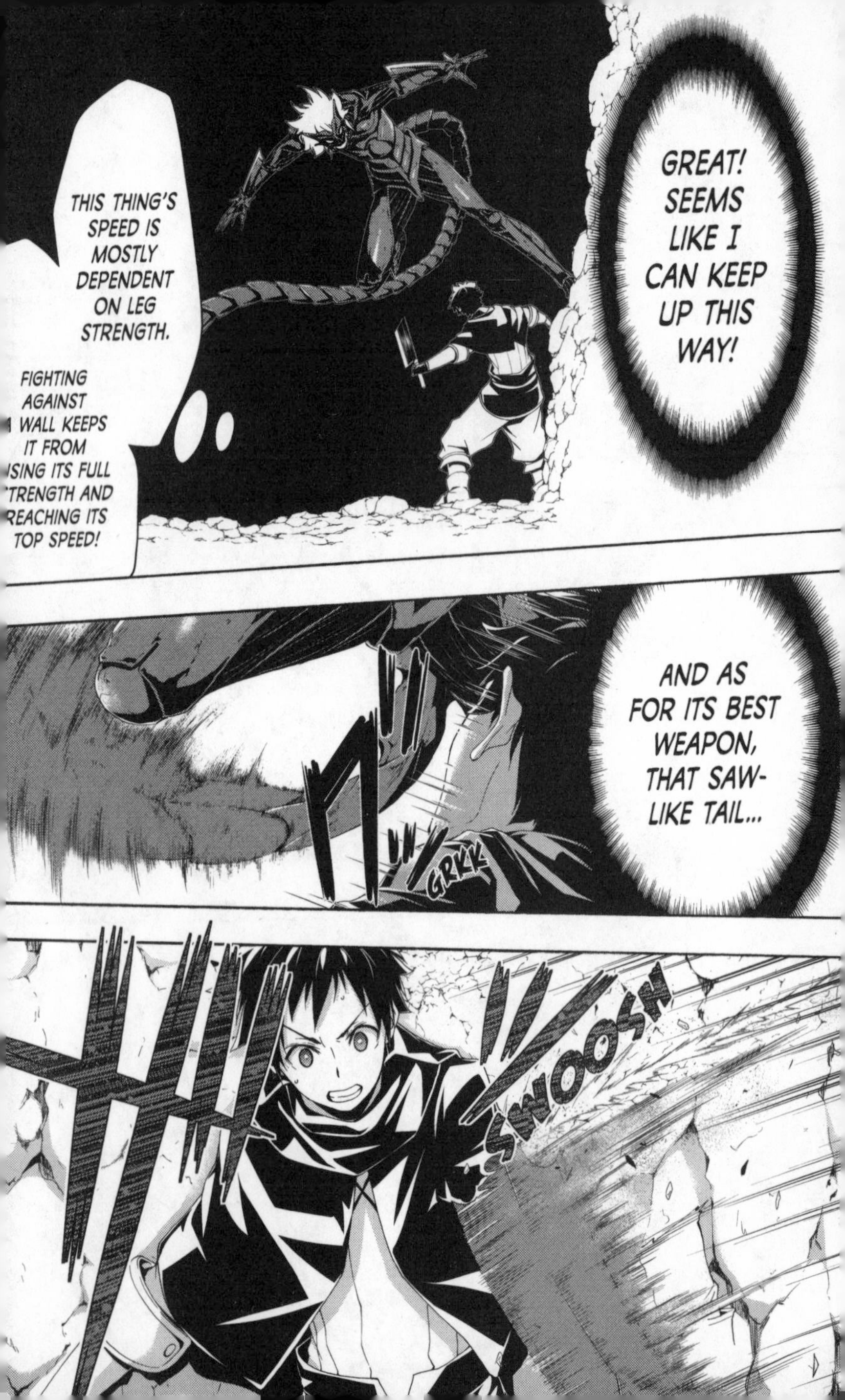
GREAT! SEEMS LIKE I CAN KEEP UP THIS WAY!
THIS THING'S SPEED IS MOSTLY DEPENDENT ON LEG STRENGTH.
FIGHTING AGAINST WALL KEEPS IT FROM SING ITS FULL TRENGTH AND EACHING ITS TOP SPEED!
AND AS FOR ITS BEST WEAPON, THAT SAW-LIKE TAIL...
GRKK
SWOOSH

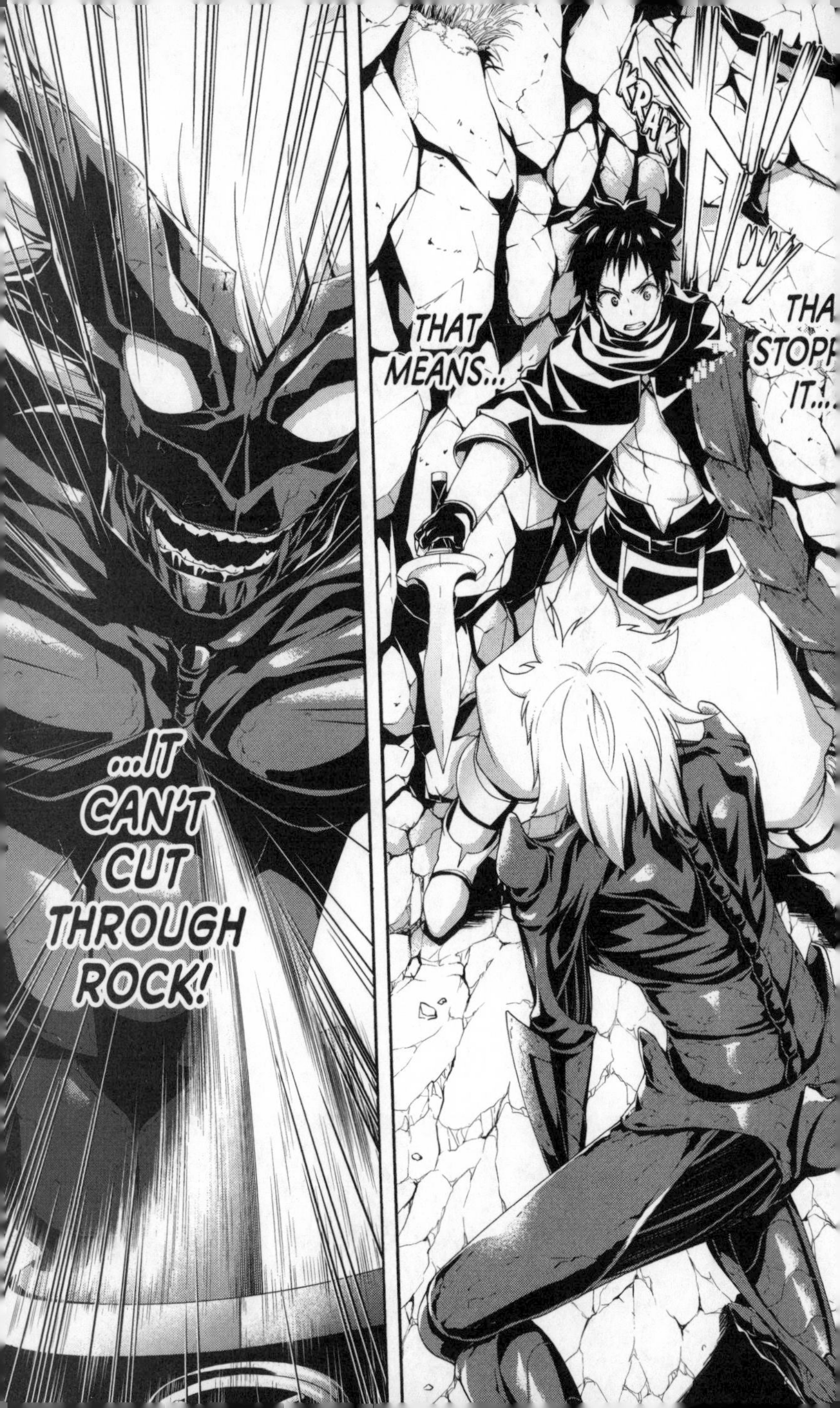
KRAK
THA STOPP IT...
THAT MEANS...
...IT CAN'T CUT THROUGH ROCK!

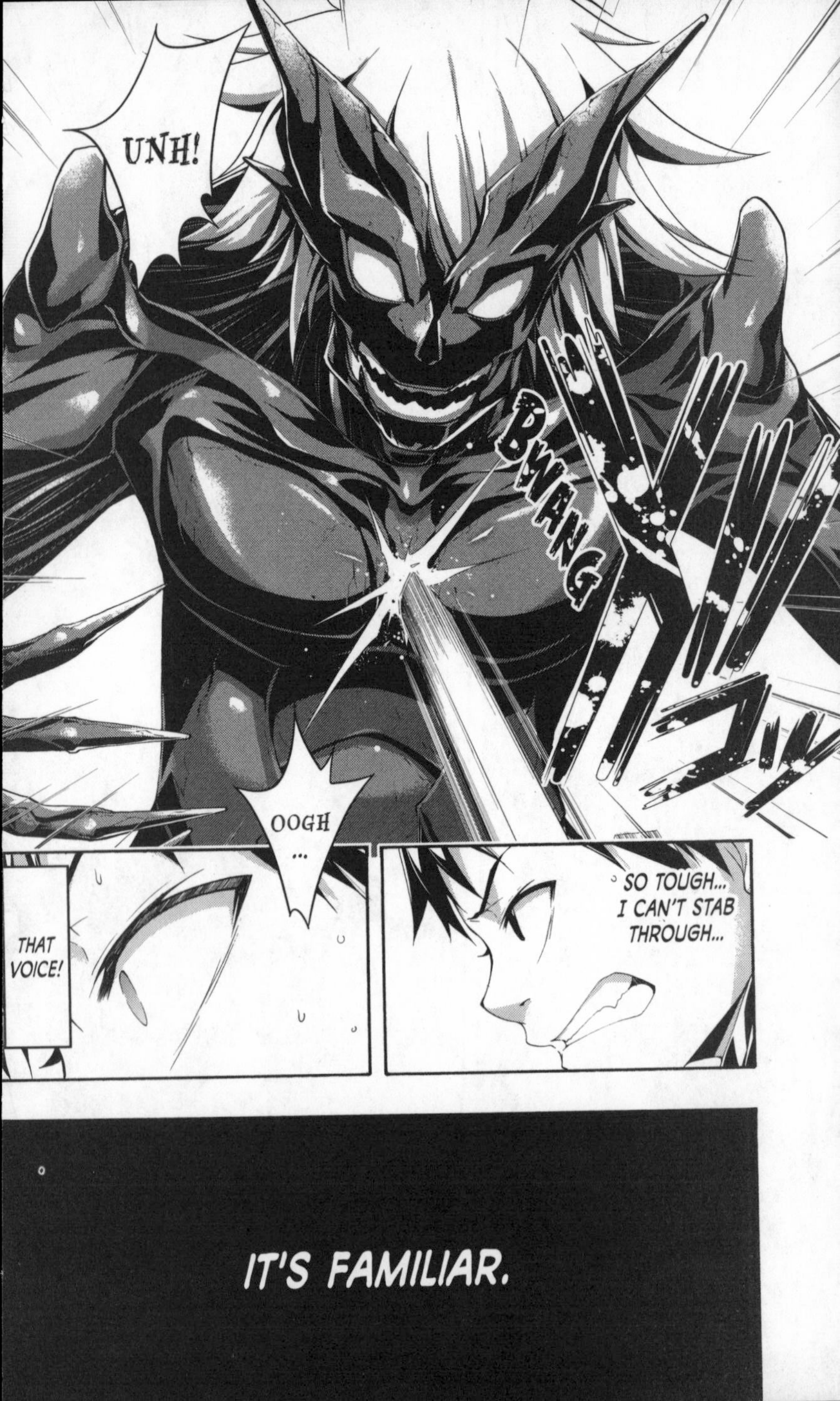
UNH!
BWANG
OOGH...
SO TOUGH... I CAN'T STAB THROUGH...
THAT VOICE!
IT'S FAMILIAR.

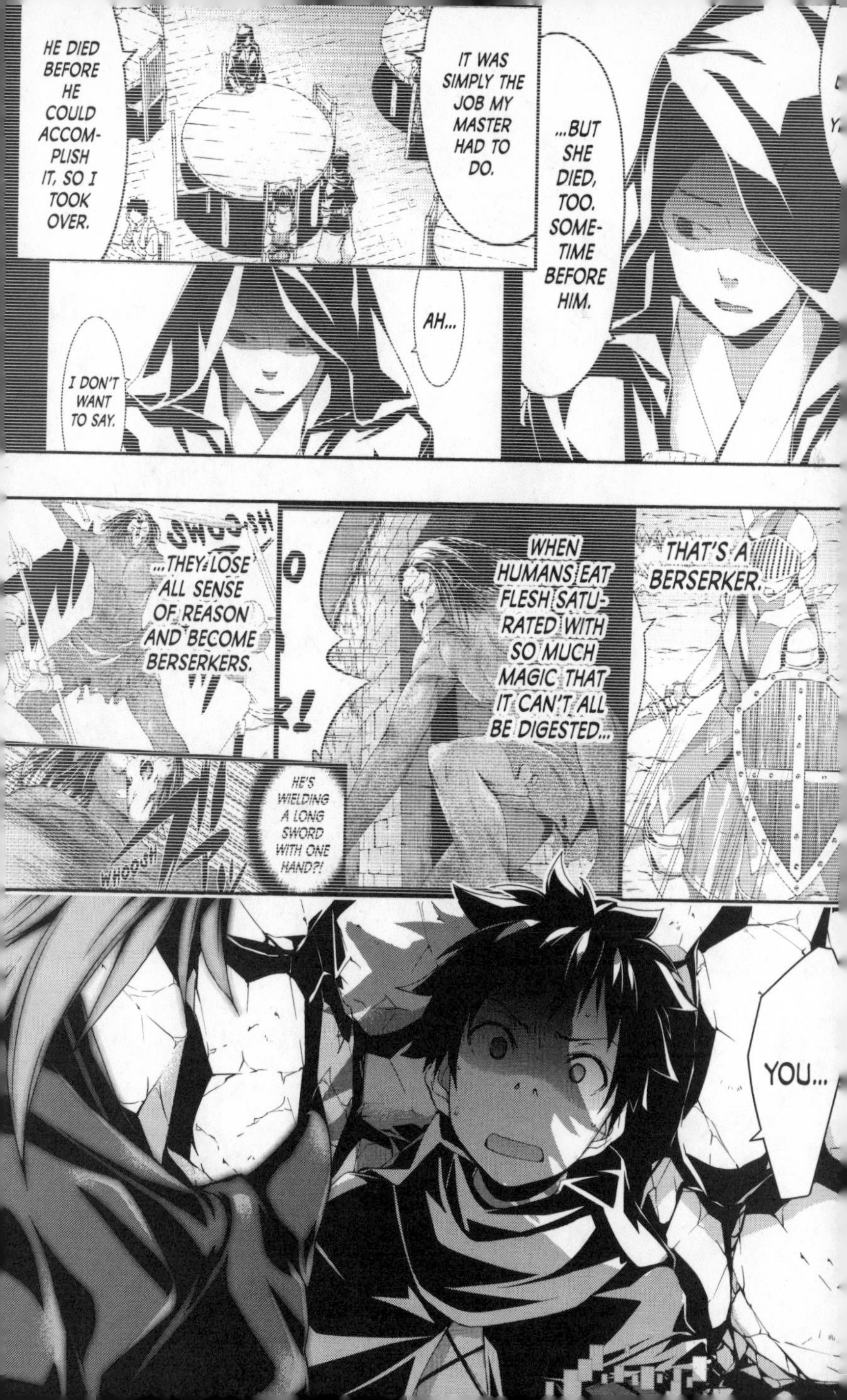
IT WAS SIMPLY THE JOB MY MASTER HAD TO DO.
HE DIED BEFORE HE COULD ACCOMPLISH IT, SO I TOOK OVER.
...BUT SHE DIED, TOO. SOMETIME BEFORE HIM.
AH...
I DON'T WANT TO SAY.
THAT'S A BERSERKER.
WHEN HUMANS EAT FLESH SATURATED WITH SO MUCH MAGIC THAT IT CAN'T ALL BE DIGESTED...
SWOOSH
...THEY LOSE ALL SENSE OF REASON AND BECOME BERSERKERS.
HE'S WIELDING A LONG SWORD WITH ONE HAND?!
WHOOSH
YOU...

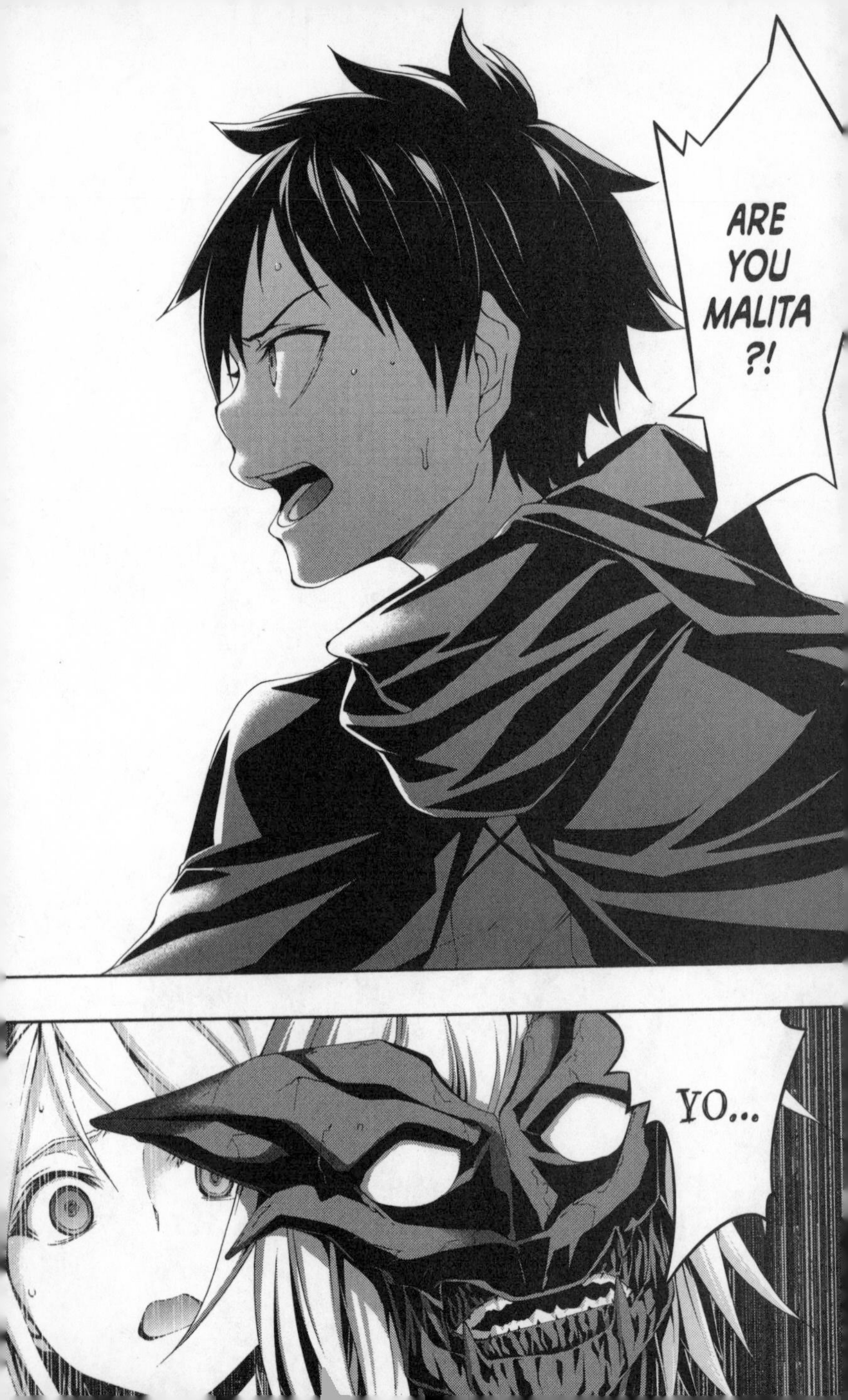
ARE YOU MALITA ?!
YO...

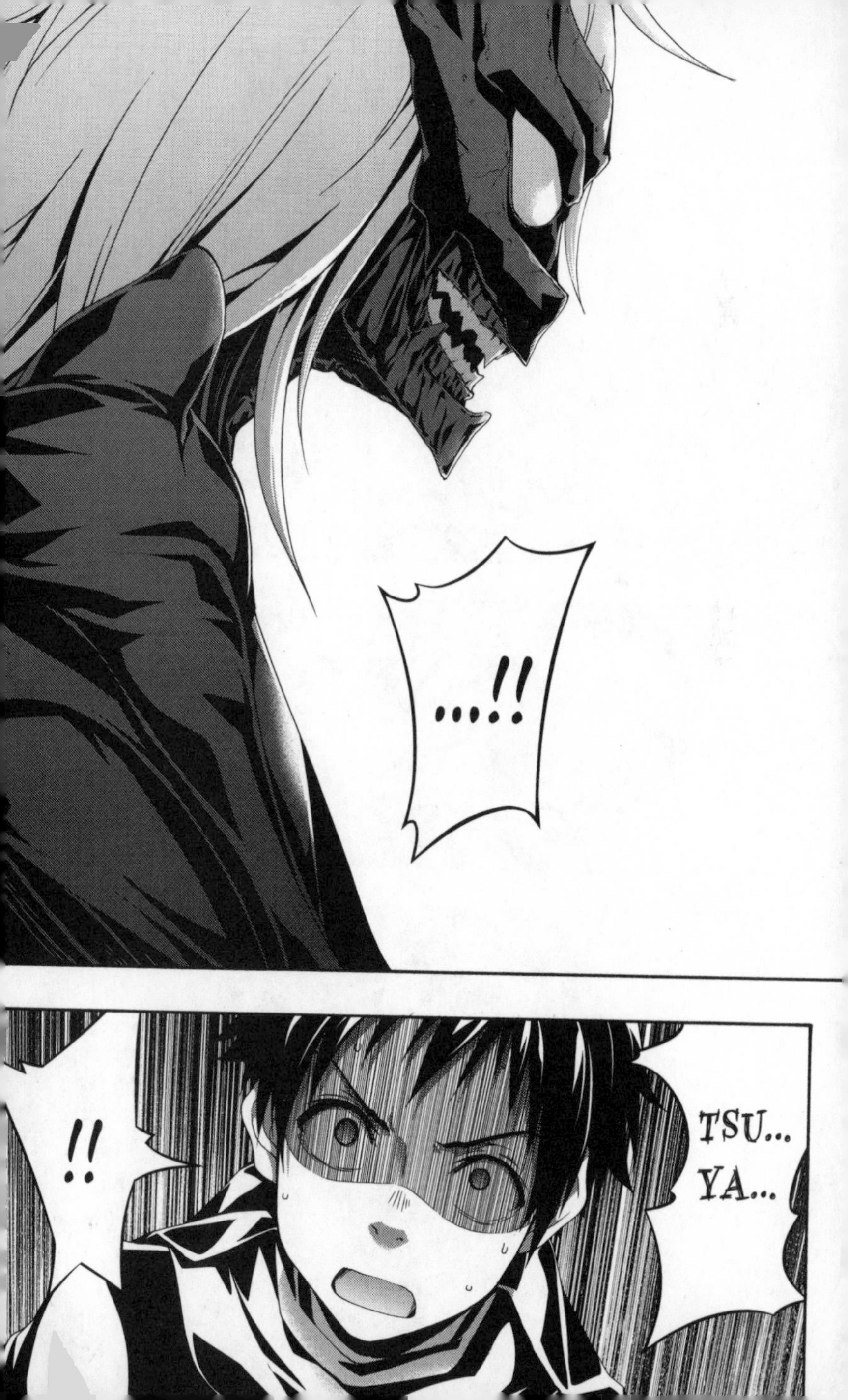
...!!
TSU... YA...
!!

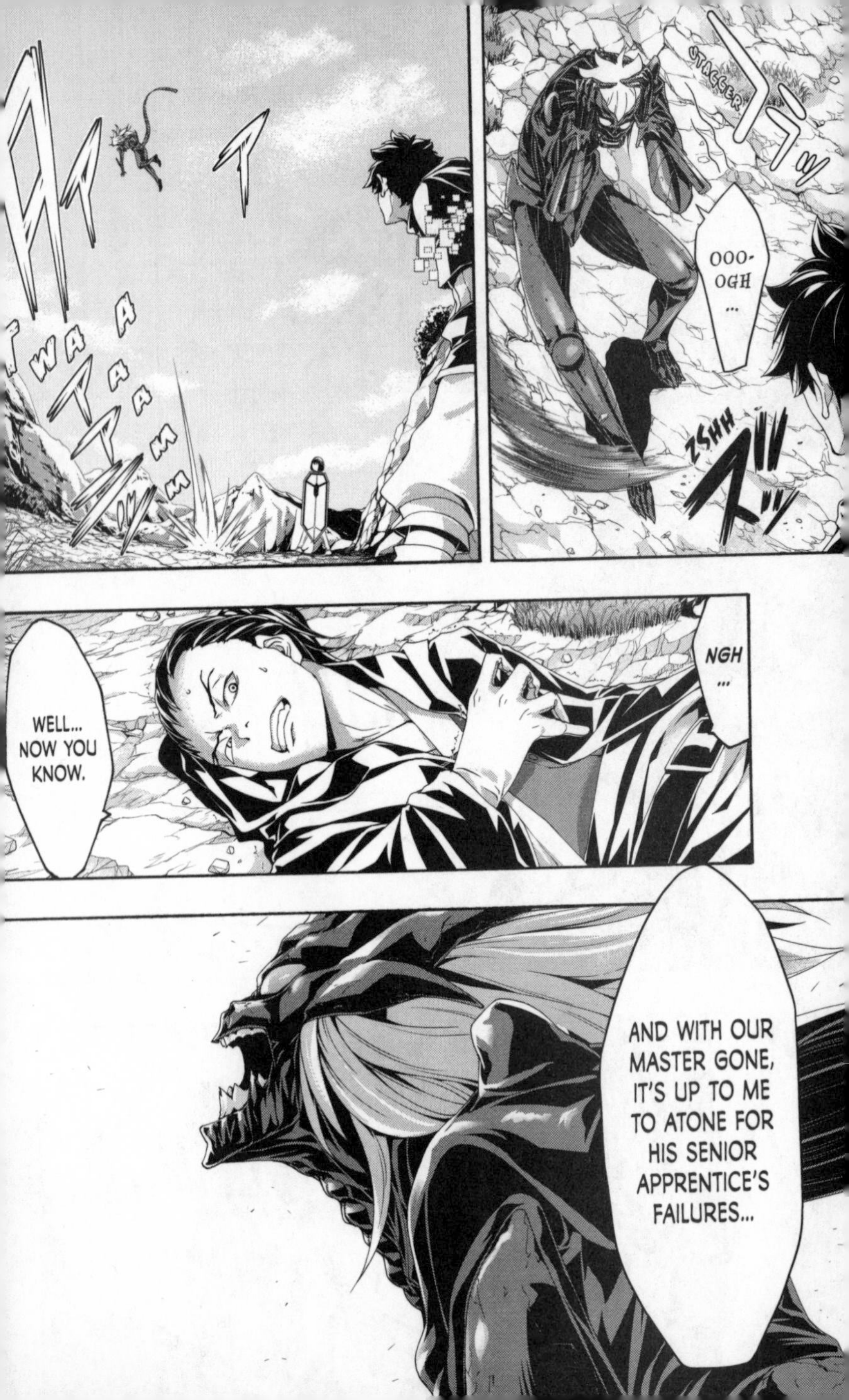
STAGGER
OOO-OGH...
ZSHH
FWAAAAMM
NGH...
WELL... NOW YOU KNOW.
AND WITH OUR MASTER GONE, IT'S UP TO ME TO ATONE FOR HIS SENIOR APPRENTICE'S FAILURES...

#52 Jangani, Cathean Mon

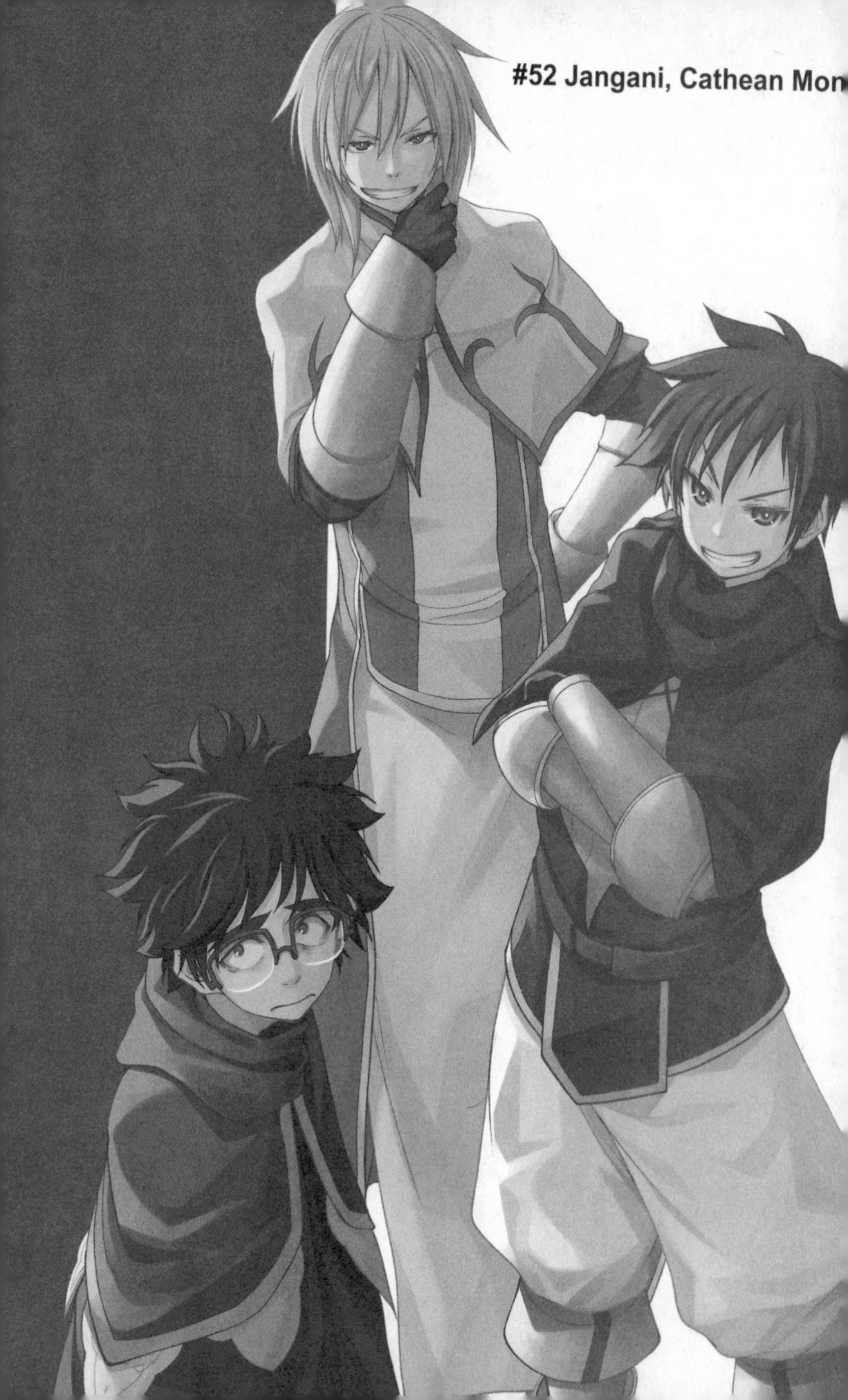

I'M STANDING ON A MILLION LIVES

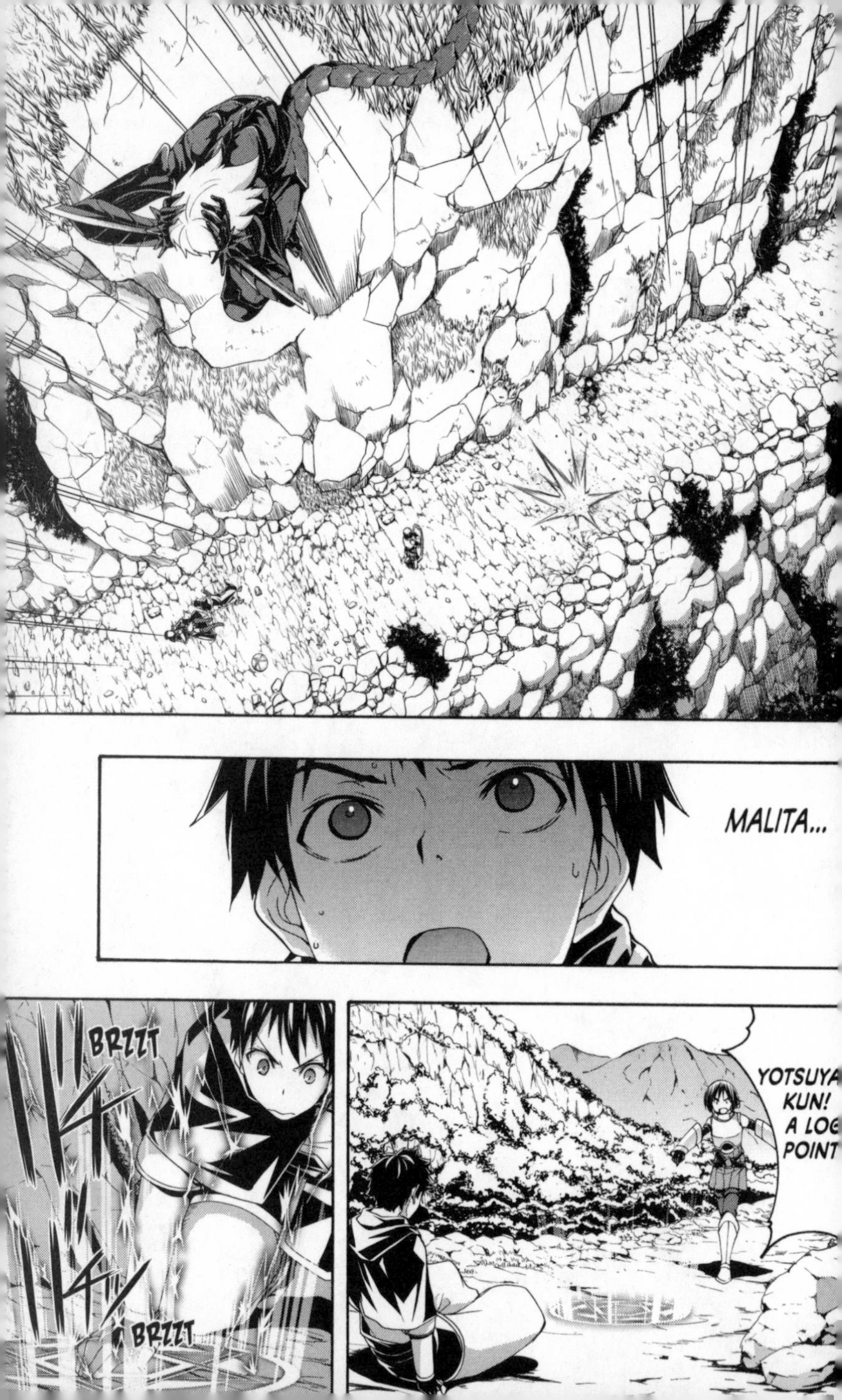
MALITA...
YOTSUYA KUN! A LOG POINT
BRZZT
BRZZT

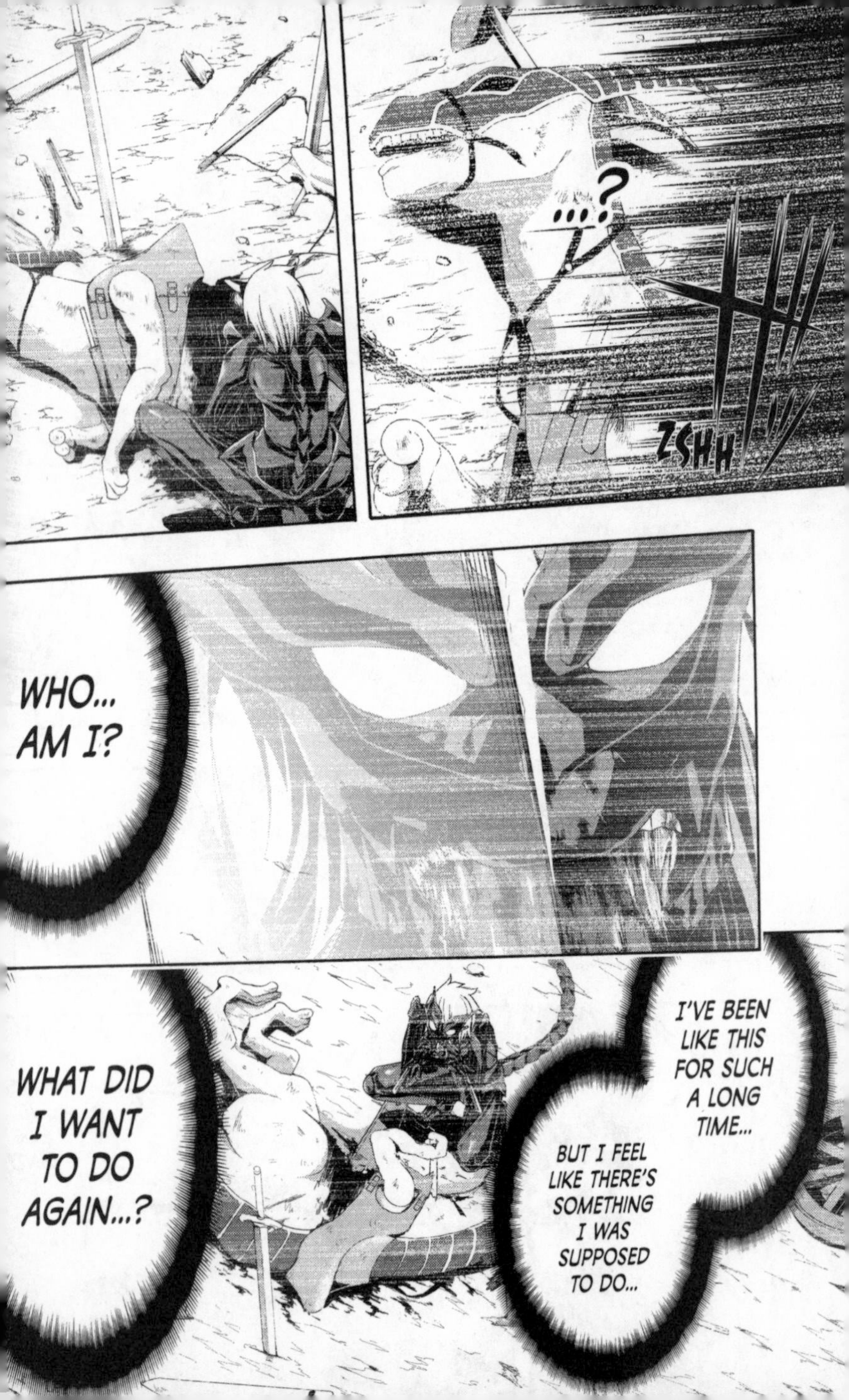
...?
ZSHH
WHO... AM I?
I'VE BEEN LIKE THIS FOR SUCH A LONG TIME...
BUT I FEEL LIKE THERE'S SOMETHING I WAS SUPPOSED TO DO...
WHAT DID I WANT TO DO AGAIN...?

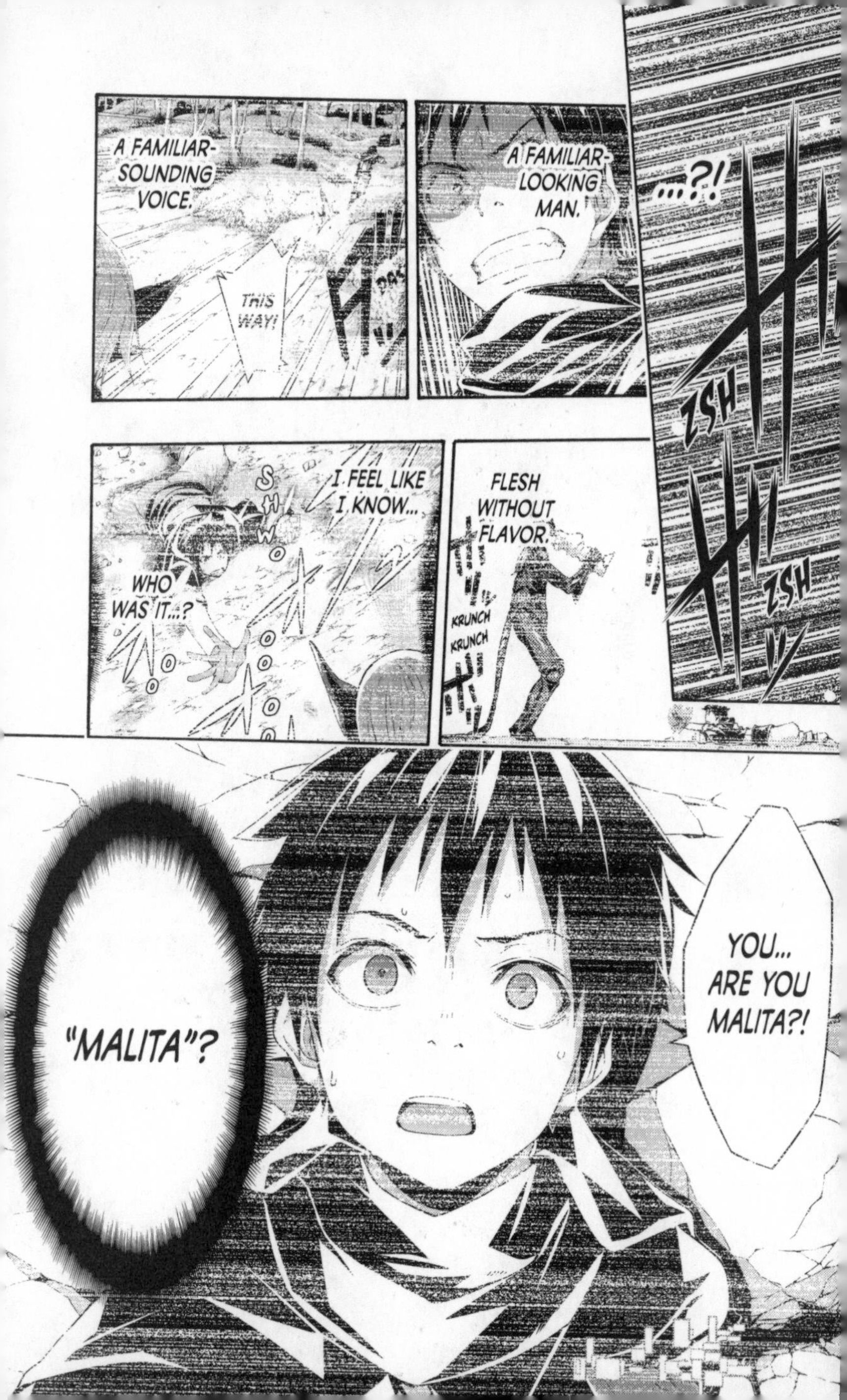
...?!
ZSH
ZSH
A FAMILIAR-LOOKING MAN.
A FAMILIAR-SOUNDING VOICE.
THIS WAY!
FLESH WITHOUT FLAVOR.
KRUNCH KRUNCH
I FEEL LIKE I KNOW...
WHO WAS IT...?
YOU... ARE YOU MALITA?!
"MALITA"?

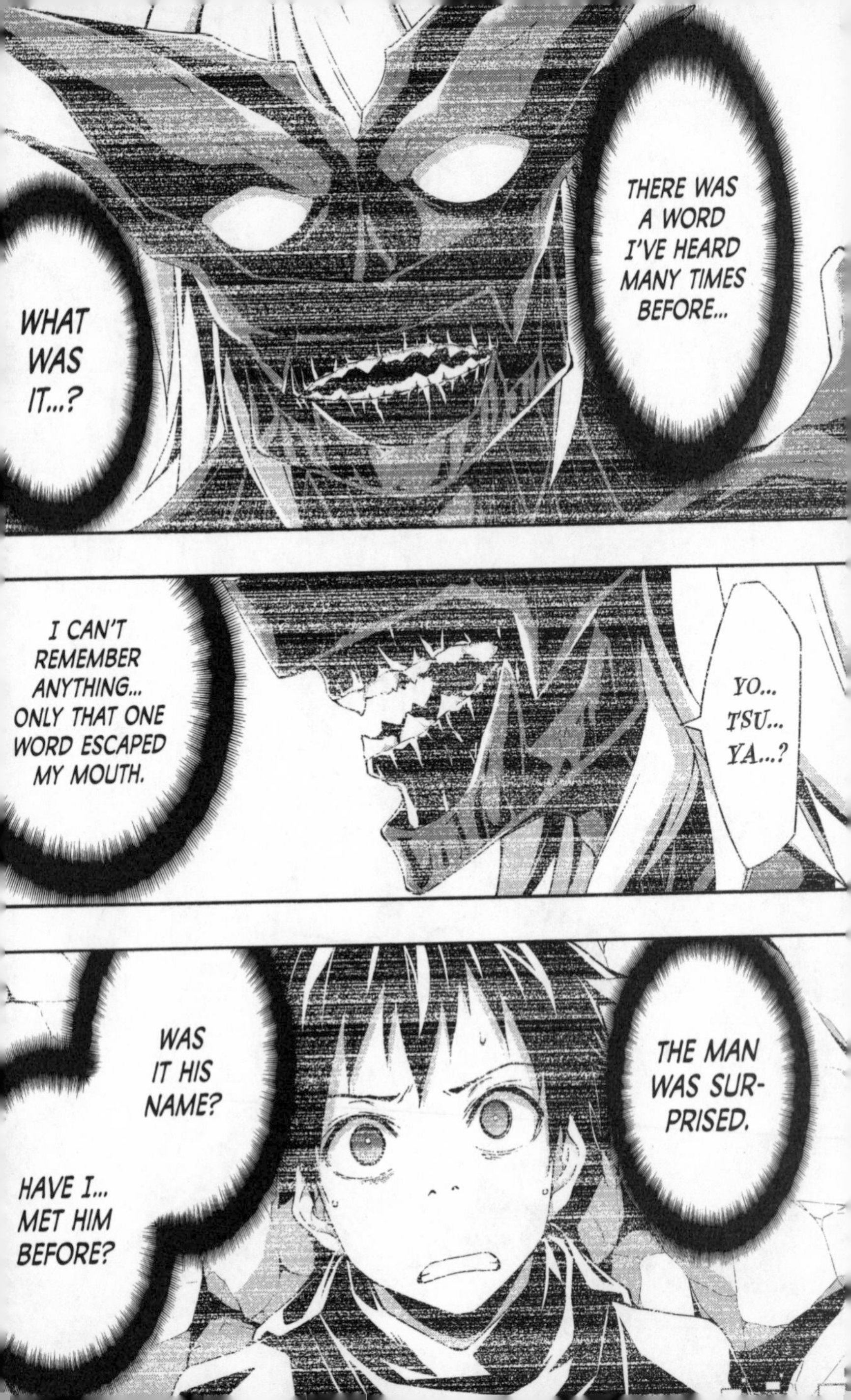
THERE WAS A WORD I'VE HEARD MANY TIMES BEFORE...
WHAT WAS IT...?
YO... TSU... YA...?
I CAN'T REMEMBER ANYTHING... ONLY THAT ONE WORD ESCAPED MY MOUTH.
THE MAN WAS SUR-PRISED.
WAS IT HIS NAME?
HAVE I... MET HIM BEFORE?

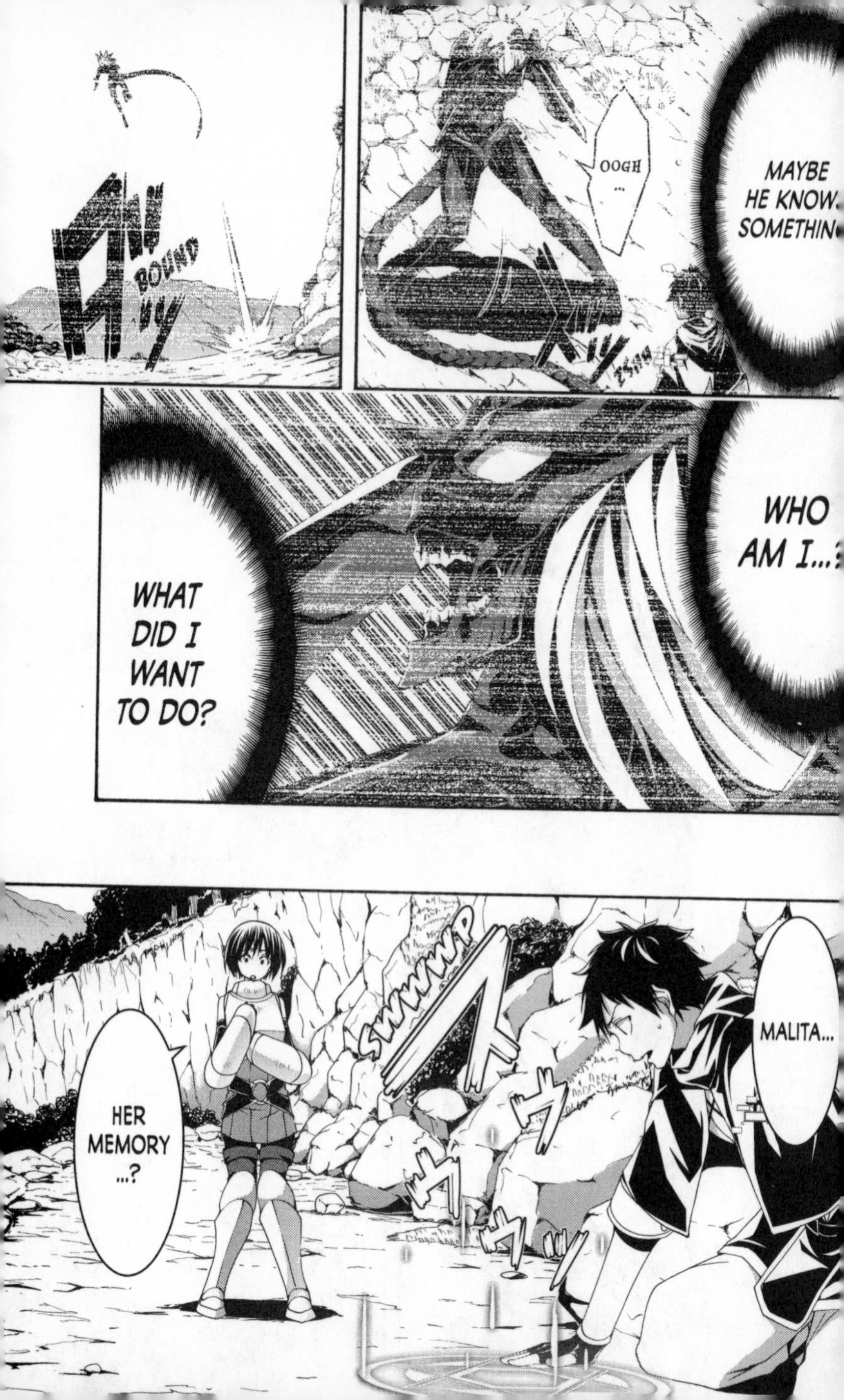
MAYBE HE KNOW SOMETHIN
OOGH ...
BOUND
WHO AM I...?
WHAT DID I WANT TO DO?
MALITA...
SWWWP
HER MEMORY ...?

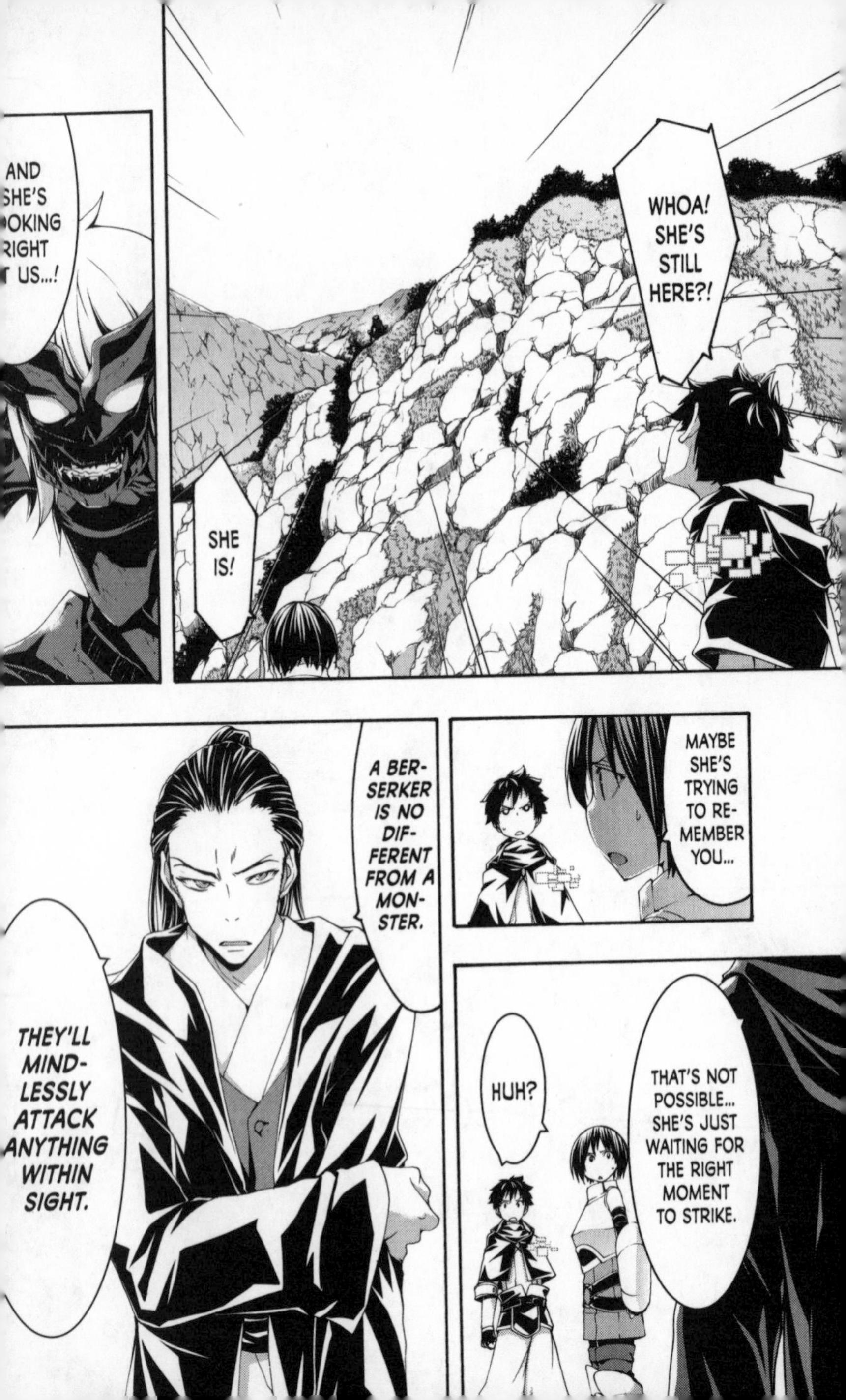

WHOA! SHE'S STILL HERE?!
SHE IS!
AND SHE'S OOKING RIGHT T US...!
MAYBE SHE'S TRYING TO REMEMBER YOU...
THAT'S NOT POSSIBLE... SHE'S JUST WAITING FOR THE RIGHT MOMENT TO STRIKE.
HUH?
A BERSERKER IS NO DIFFERENT FROM A MONSTER.
THEY'LL MINDLESSLY ATTACK ANYTHING WITHIN SIGHT.

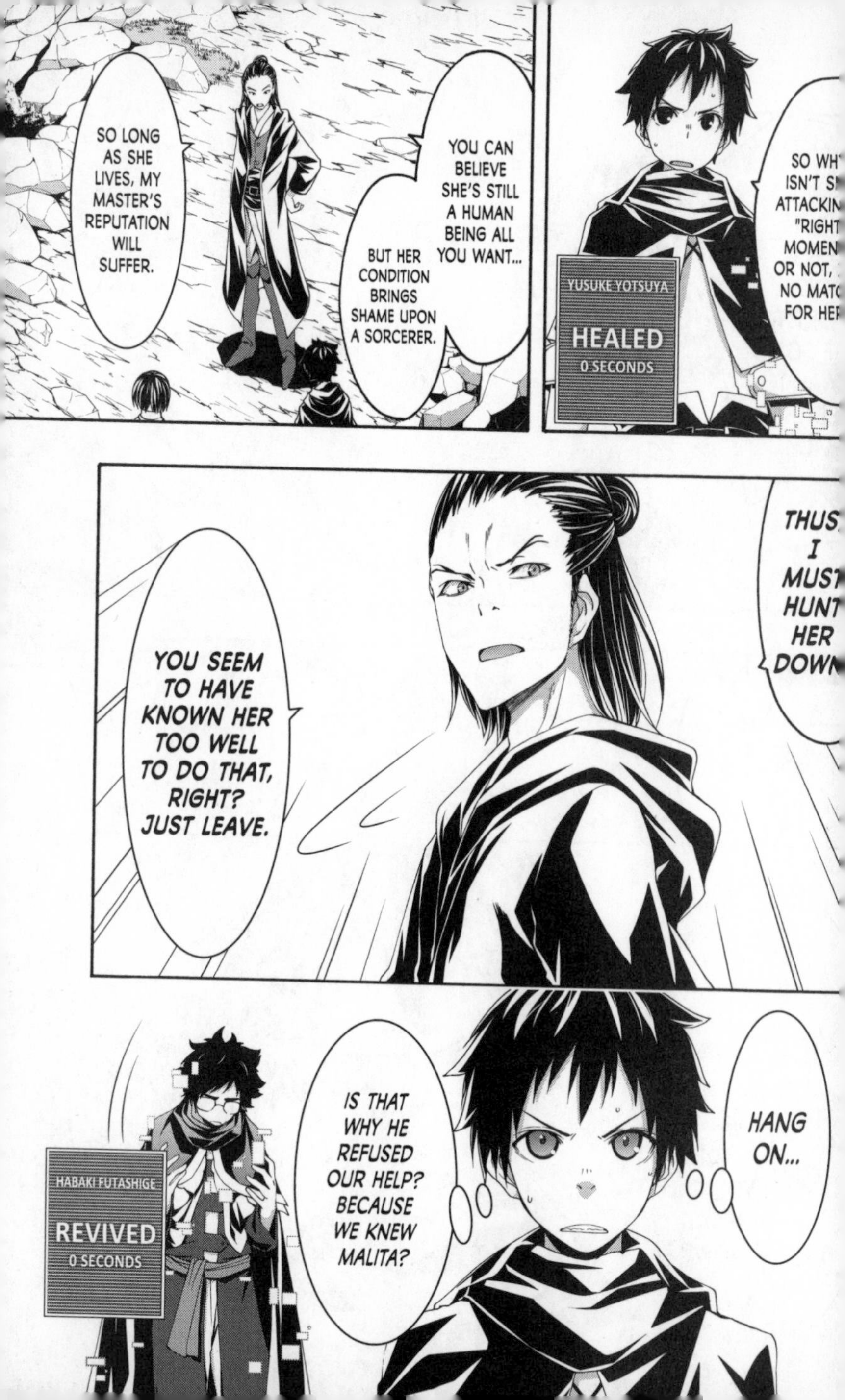
SO WH ISN'T S ATTACKIN "RIGHT MOMEN OR NOT, NO MATC FOR HE
YUSUKE YOTSUYA
HEALED
0 SECONDS
YOU CAN BELIEVE SHE'S STILL A HUMAN BEING ALL YOU WANT...
BUT HER CONDITION BRINGS SHAME UPON A SORCERER.
SO LONG AS SHE LIVES, MY MASTER'S REPUTATION WILL SUFFER.
THUS, I MUST HUNT HER DOWN
YOU SEEM TO HAVE KNOWN HER TOO WELL TO DO THAT, RIGHT? JUST LEAVE.
HANG ON...
IS THAT WHY HE REFUSED OUR HELP? BECAUSE WE KNEW MALITA?
HABAKI FUTASHIGE
REVIVED
0 SECONDS

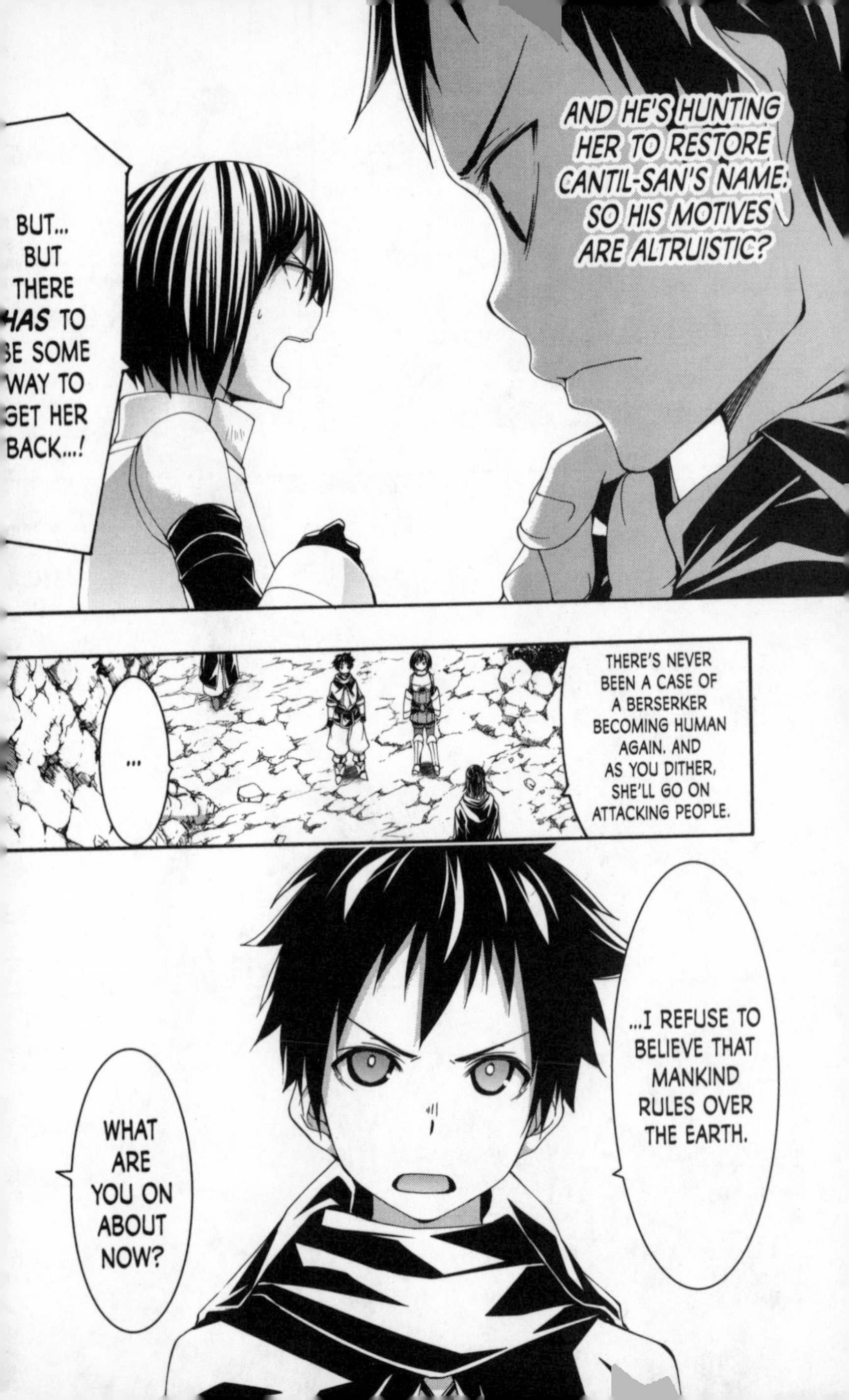
AND HE'S HUNTING HER TO RESTORE CANTIL-SAN'S NAME. SO HIS MOTIVES ARE ALTRUISTIC?
BUT... BUT THERE *HAS* TO BE SOME WAY TO GET HER BACK...!
THERE'S NEVER BEEN A CASE OF A BERSERKER BECOMING HUMAN AGAIN. AND AS YOU DITHER, SHE'LL GO ON ATTACKING PEOPLE.
...
...I REFUSE TO BELIEVE THAT MANKIND RULES OVER THE EARTH.
WHAT ARE YOU ON ABOUT NOW?

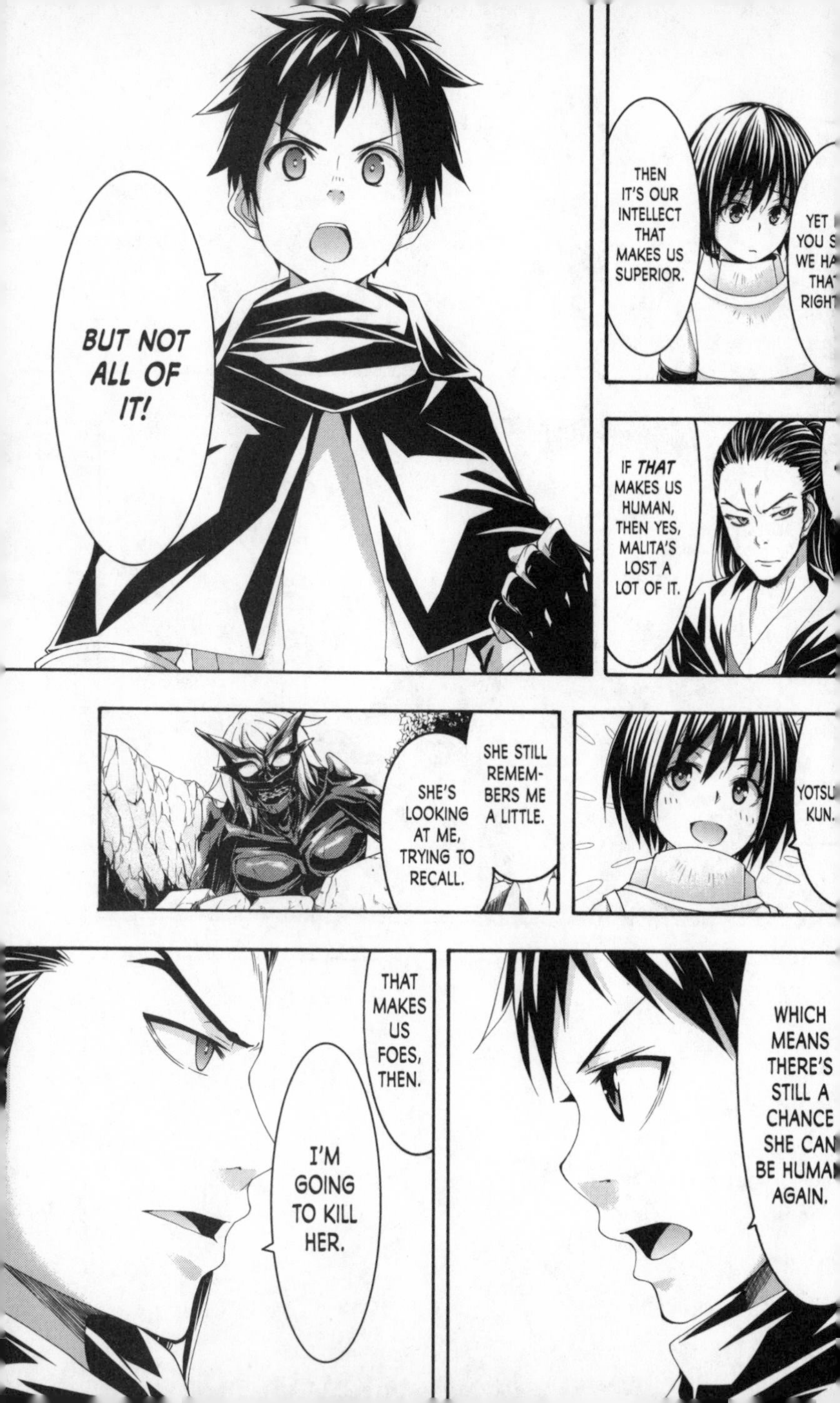
YET YOU S WE HA THA RIGHT
THEN IT'S OUR INTELLECT THAT MAKES US SUPERIOR.
IF *THAT* MAKES US HUMAN, THEN YES, MALITA'S LOST A LOT OF IT.
BUT NOT ALL OF IT!
YOTSU KUN.
SHE STILL REMEM-BERS ME A LITTLE.
SHE'S LOOKING AT ME, TRYING TO RECALL.
WHICH MEANS THERE'S STILL A CHANCE SHE CAN BE HUMA AGAIN.
THAT MAKES US FOES, THEN.
I'M GOING TO KILL HER.

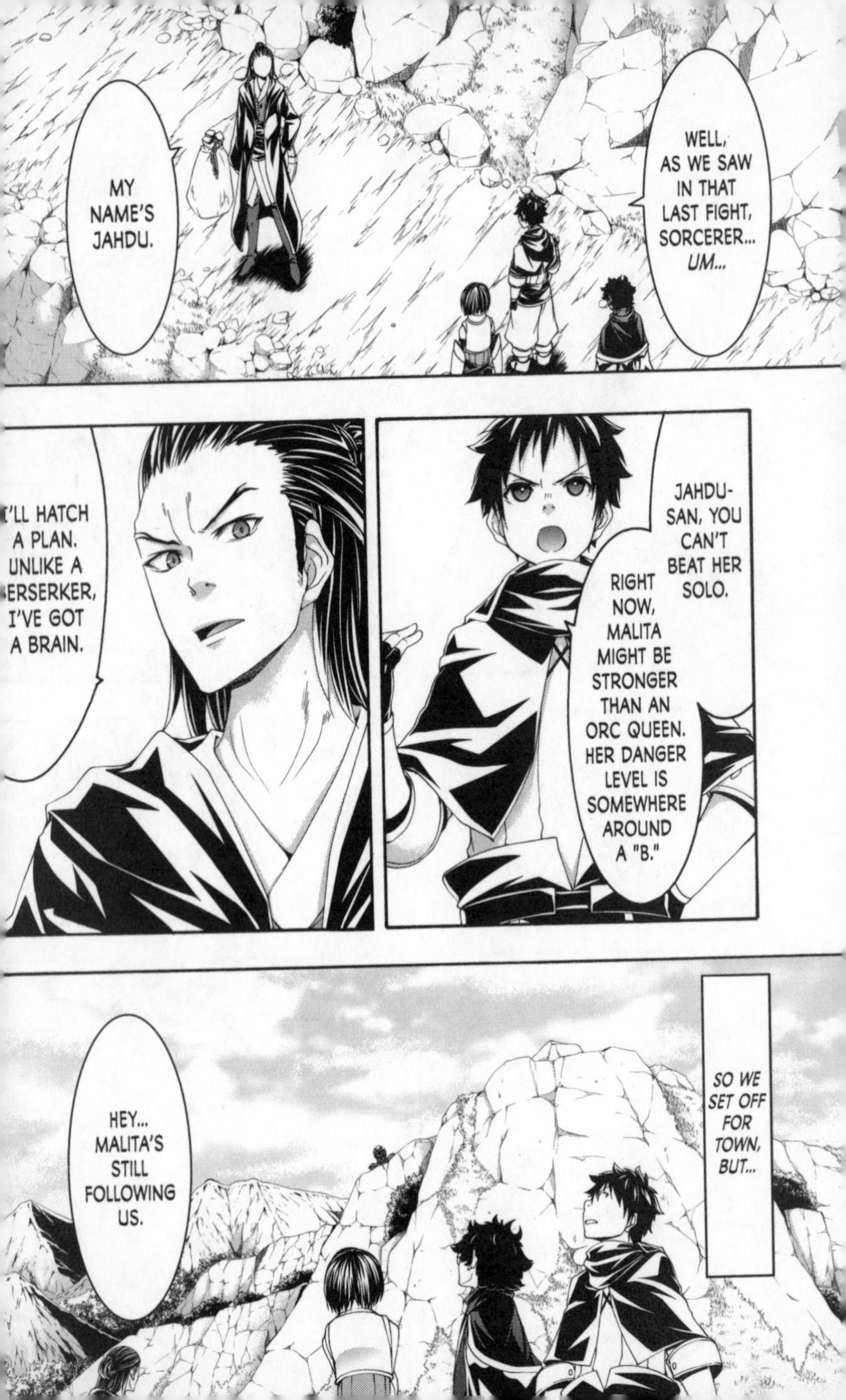
WELL, AS WE SAW IN THAT LAST FIGHT, SORCERER... UM...
MY NAME'S JAHDU.
JAHDU-SAN, YOU CAN'T BEAT HER SOLO.
RIGHT NOW, MALITA MIGHT BE STRONGER THAN AN ORC QUEEN. HER DANGER LEVEL IS SOMEWHERE AROUND A "B."
'LL HATCH A PLAN. UNLIKE A ERSERKER, I'VE GOT A BRAIN.
SO WE SET OFF FOR TOWN, BUT...
HEY... MALITA'S STILL FOLLOWING US.

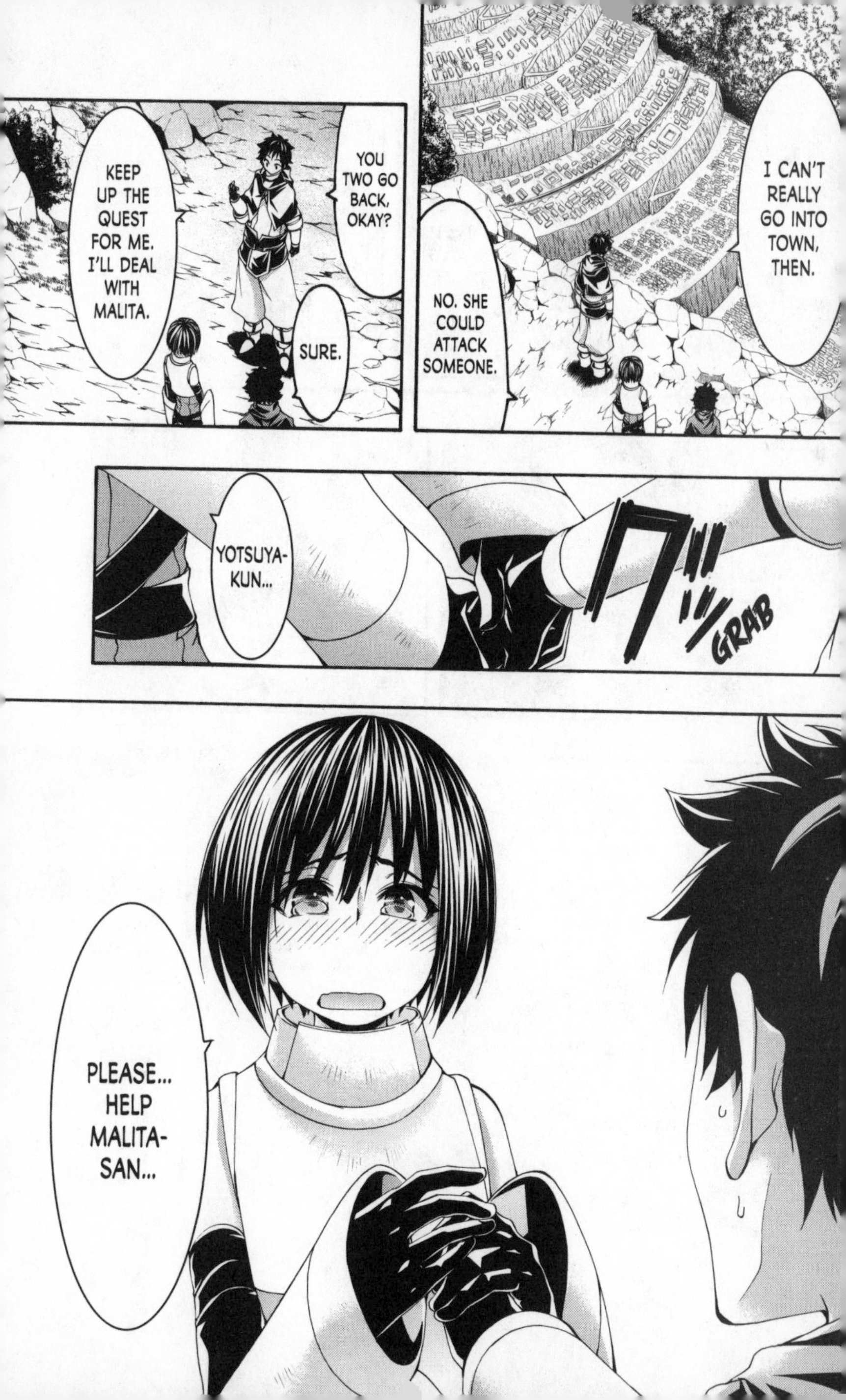
I CAN'T REALLY GO INTO TOWN, THEN.
NO. SHE COULD ATTACK SOMEONE.
YOU TWO GO BACK, OKAY?
KEEP UP THE QUEST FOR ME. I'LL DEAL WITH MALITA.
SURE.
グッ
GRAB
YOTSUYA-KUN...
PLEASE... HELP MALITA-SAN...

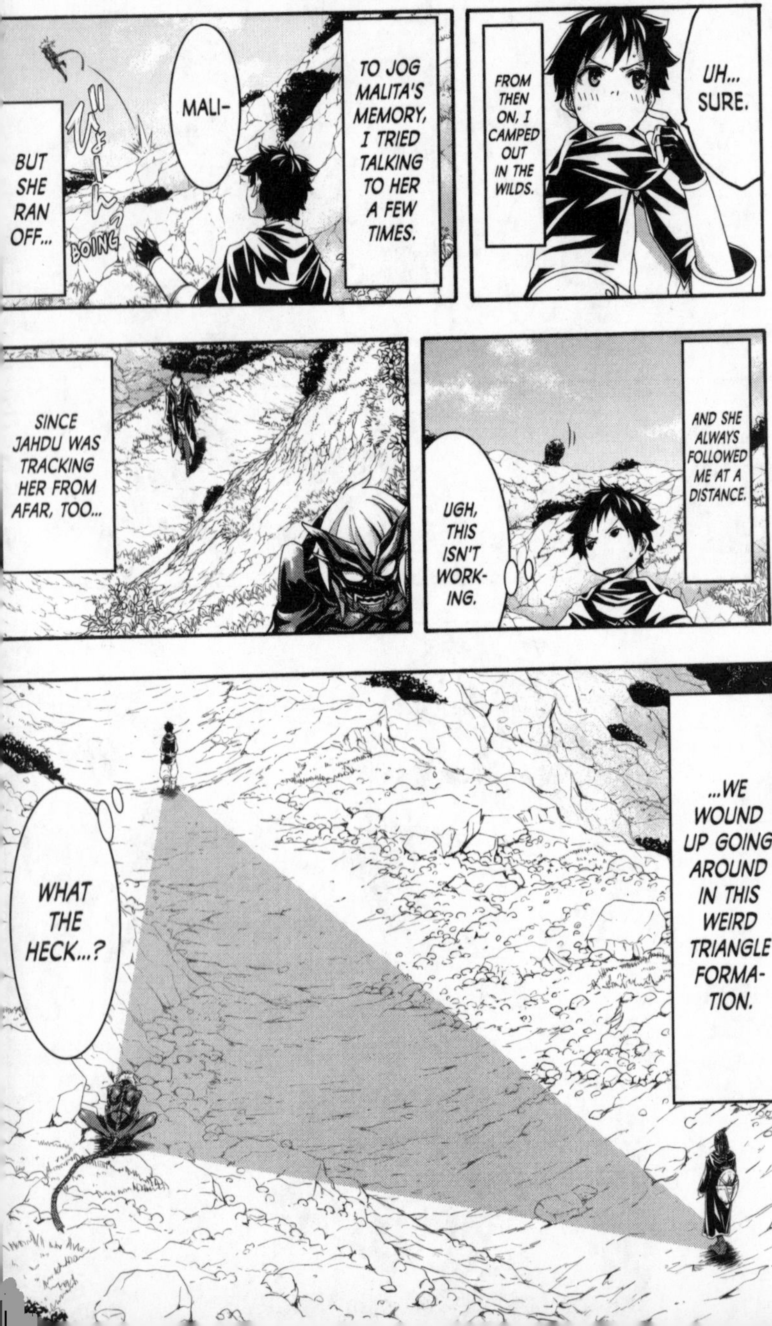
UH... SURE.
FROM THEN ON, I CAMPED OUT IN THE WILDS.
TO JOG MALITA'S MEMORY, I TRIED TALKING TO HER A FEW TIMES.
MALI-
びょーん
BOING
BUT SHE RAN OFF...
AND SHE ALWAYS FOLLOWED ME AT A DISTANCE.
UGH, THIS ISN'T WORKING.
SINCE JAHDU WAS TRACKING HER FROM AFAR, TOO...
...WE WOUND UP GOING AROUND IN THIS WEIRD TRIANGLE FORMATION.
WHAT THE HECK...?

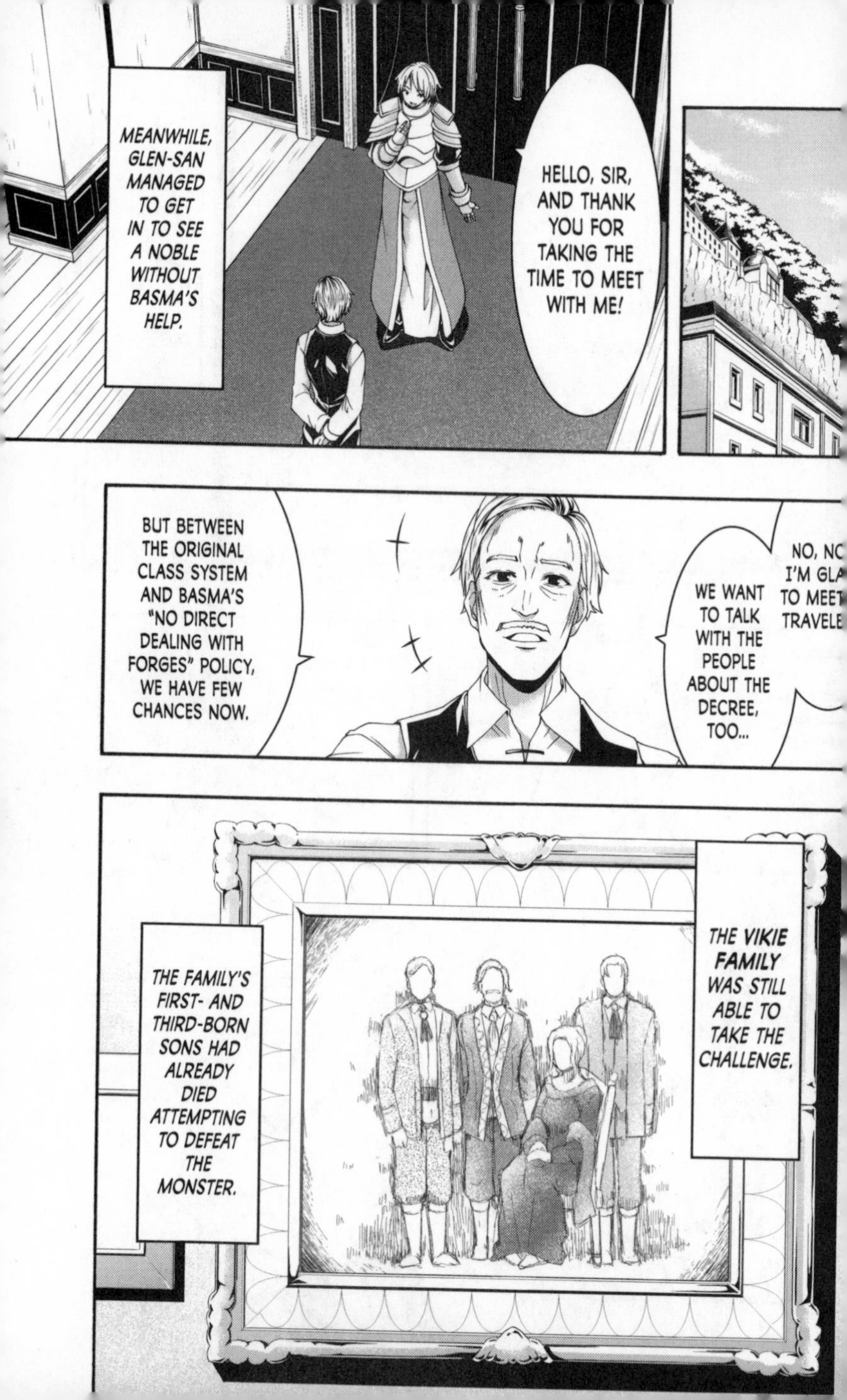
HELLO, SIR, AND THANK YOU FOR TAKING THE TIME TO MEET WITH ME!
MEANWHILE, GLEN-SAN MANAGED TO GET IN TO SEE A NOBLE WITHOUT BASMA'S HELP.
NO, NO I'M GLA TO MEET TRAVELE
WE WANT TO TALK WITH THE PEOPLE ABOUT THE DECREE, TOO...
BUT BETWEEN THE ORIGINAL CLASS SYSTEM AND BASMA'S "NO DIRECT DEALING WITH FORGES" POLICY, WE HAVE FEW CHANCES NOW.
THE VIKIE FAMILY WAS STILL ABLE TO TAKE THE CHALLENGE.
THE FAMILY'S FIRST- AND THIRD-BORN SONS HAD ALREADY DIED ATTEMPTING TO DEFEAT THE MONSTER.

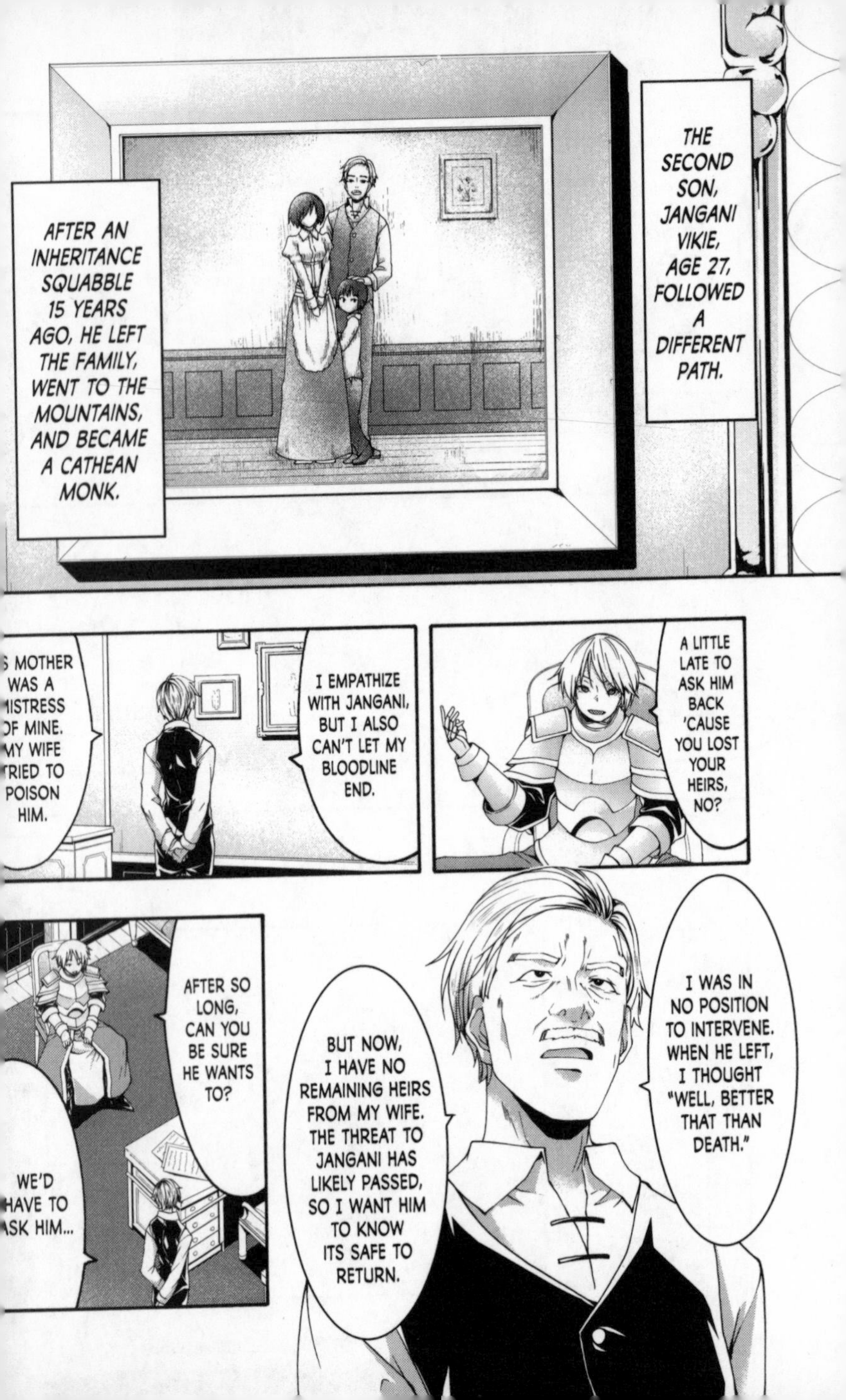
THE SECOND SON, JANGANI VIKIE, AGE 27, FOLLOWED A DIFFERENT PATH.
AFTER AN INHERITANCE SQUABBLE 15 YEARS AGO, HE LEFT THE FAMILY, WENT TO THE MOUNTAINS, AND BECAME A CATHEAN MONK.
A LITTLE LATE TO ASK HIM BACK 'CAUSE YOU LOST YOUR HEIRS, NO?
I EMPATHIZE WITH JANGANI, BUT I ALSO CAN'T LET MY BLOODLINE END.
S MOTHER WAS A ISTRESS OF MINE. Y WIFE RIED TO POISON HIM.
I WAS IN NO POSITION TO INTERVENE. WHEN HE LEFT, I THOUGHT "WELL, BETTER THAT THAN DEATH."
BUT NOW, I HAVE NO REMAINING HEIRS FROM MY WIFE. THE THREAT TO JANGANI HAS LIKELY PASSED, SO I WANT HIM TO KNOW ITS SAFE TO RETURN.
AFTER SO LONG, CAN YOU BE SURE HE WANTS TO?
WE'D HAVE TO SK HIM...

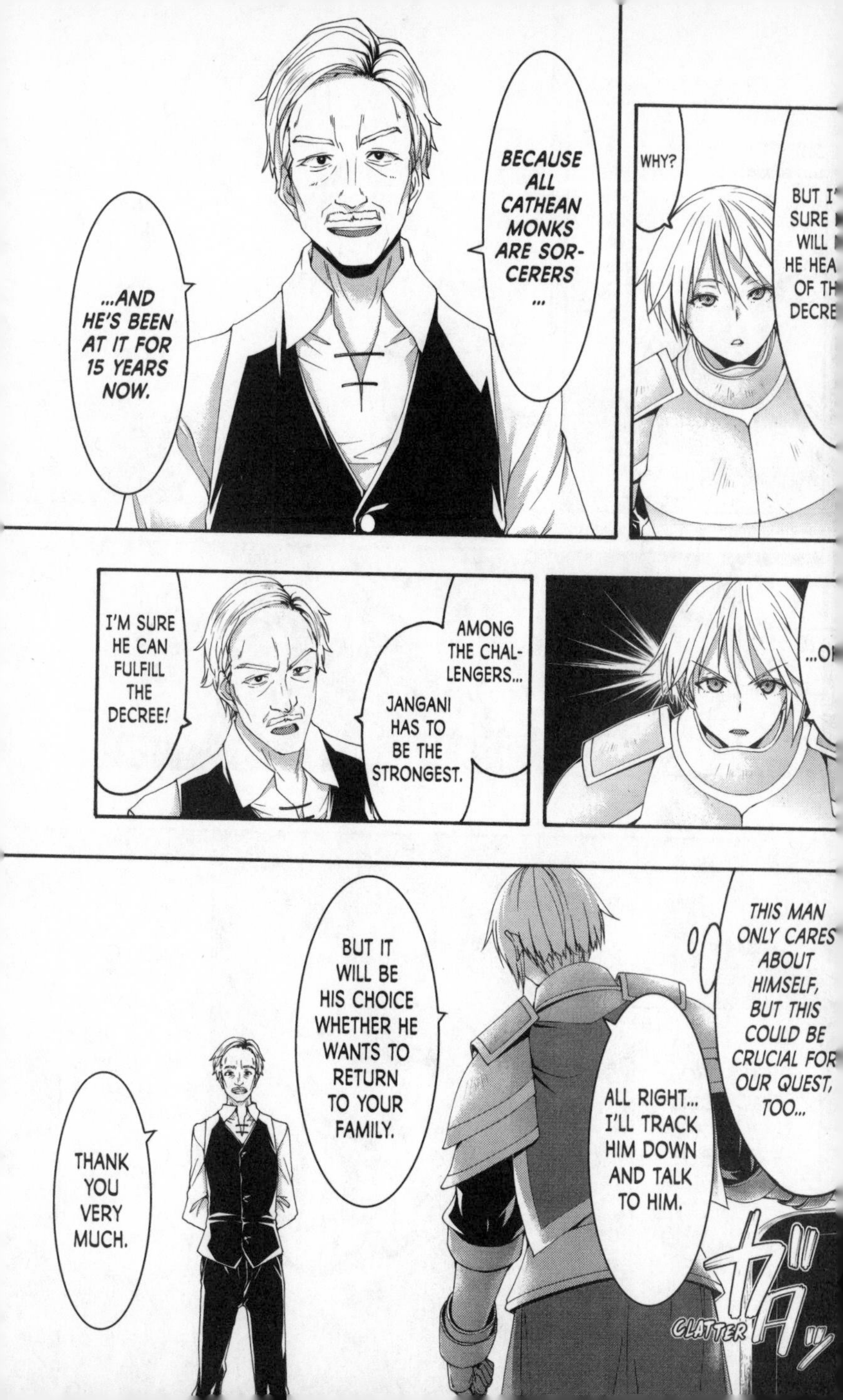

BUT I' SURE WILL HE HEA OF TH DECRE
WHY?
BECAUSE ALL CATHEAN MONKS ARE SORCERERS...
...AND HE'S BEEN AT IT FOR 15 YEARS NOW.
...OI
AMONG THE CHALLENGERS...
JANGANI HAS TO BE THE STRONGEST.
I'M SURE HE CAN FULFILL THE DECREE!
THIS MAN ONLY CARES ABOUT HIMSELF, BUT THIS COULD BE CRUCIAL FOR OUR QUEST, TOO...
ALL RIGHT... I'LL TRACK HIM DOWN AND TALK TO HIM.
CLATTER
BUT IT WILL BE HIS CHOICE WHETHER HE WANTS TO RETURN TO YOUR FAMILY.
THANK YOU VERY MUCH.

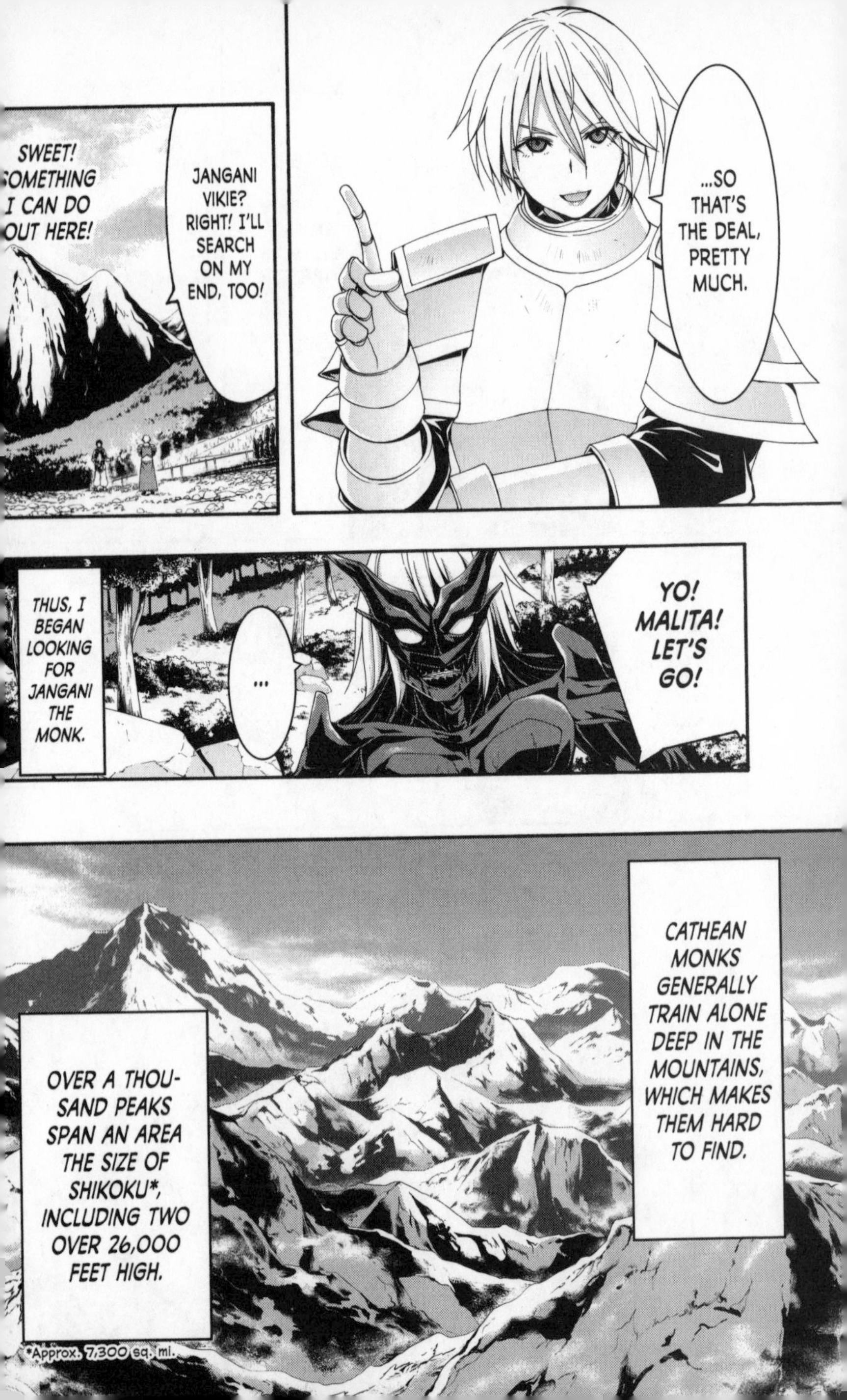
...SO THAT'S THE DEAL, PRETTY MUCH.
JANGANI VIKIE? RIGHT! I'LL SEARCH ON MY END, TOO!
SWEET! SOMETHING I CAN DO OUT HERE!
YO! MALITA! LET'S GO!
...
THUS, I BEGAN LOOKING FOR JANGANI THE MONK.
CATHEAN MONKS GENERALLY TRAIN ALONE DEEP IN THE MOUNTAINS, WHICH MAKES THEM HARD TO FIND.
OVER A THOU-SAND PEAKS SPAN AN AREA THE SIZE OF SHIKOKU*, INCLUDING TWO OVER 26,000 FEET HIGH.
*Approx. 7,300 sq. mi.

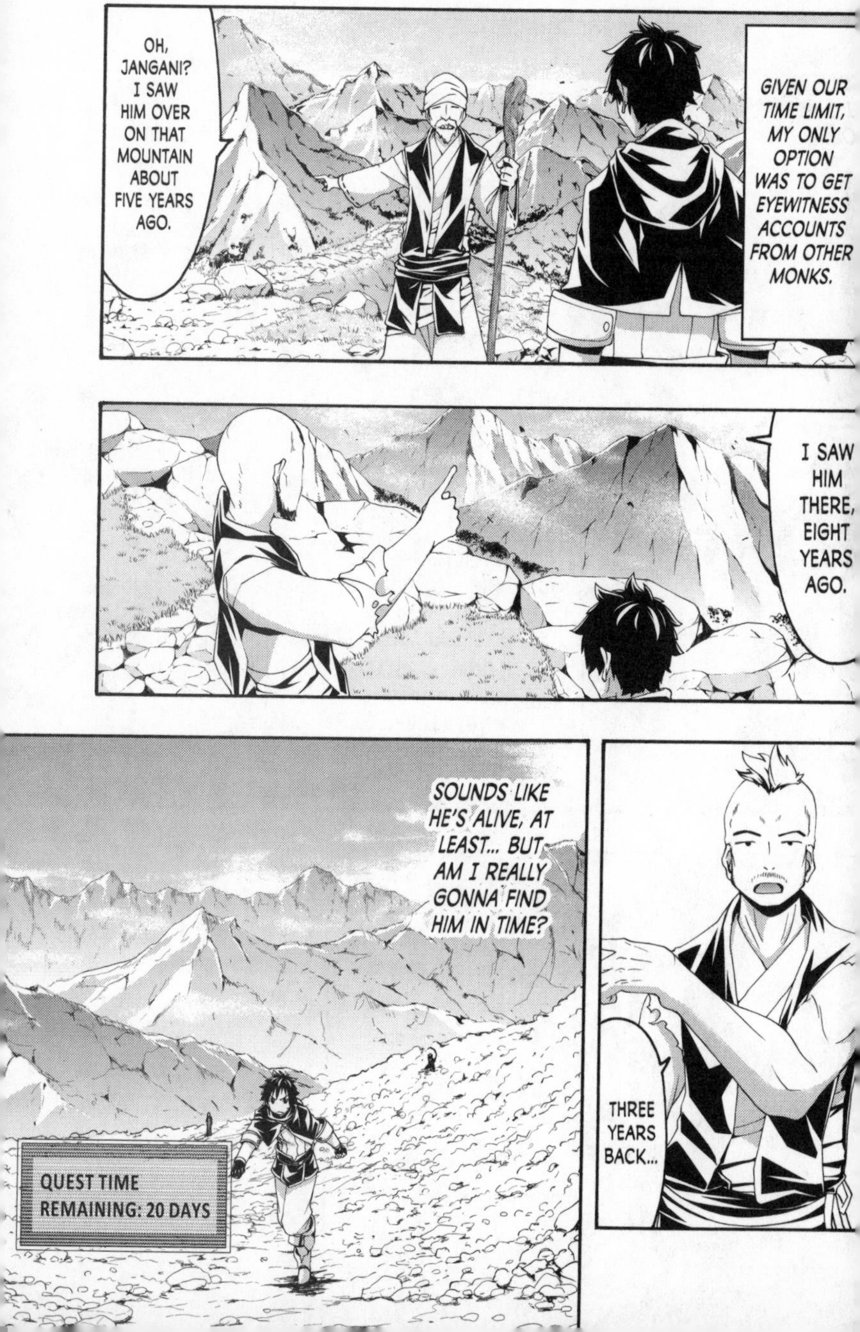
GIVEN OUR TIME LIMIT, MY ONLY OPTION WAS TO GET EYEWITNESS ACCOUNTS FROM OTHER MONKS.
OH, JANGANI? I SAW HIM OVER ON THAT MOUNTAIN ABOUT FIVE YEARS AGO.
I SAW HIM THERE, EIGHT YEARS AGO.
THREE YEARS BACK...
SOUNDS LIKE HE'S ALIVE, AT LEAST... BUT AM I REALLY GONNA FIND HIM IN TIME?
QUEST TIME REMAINING: 20 DAYS

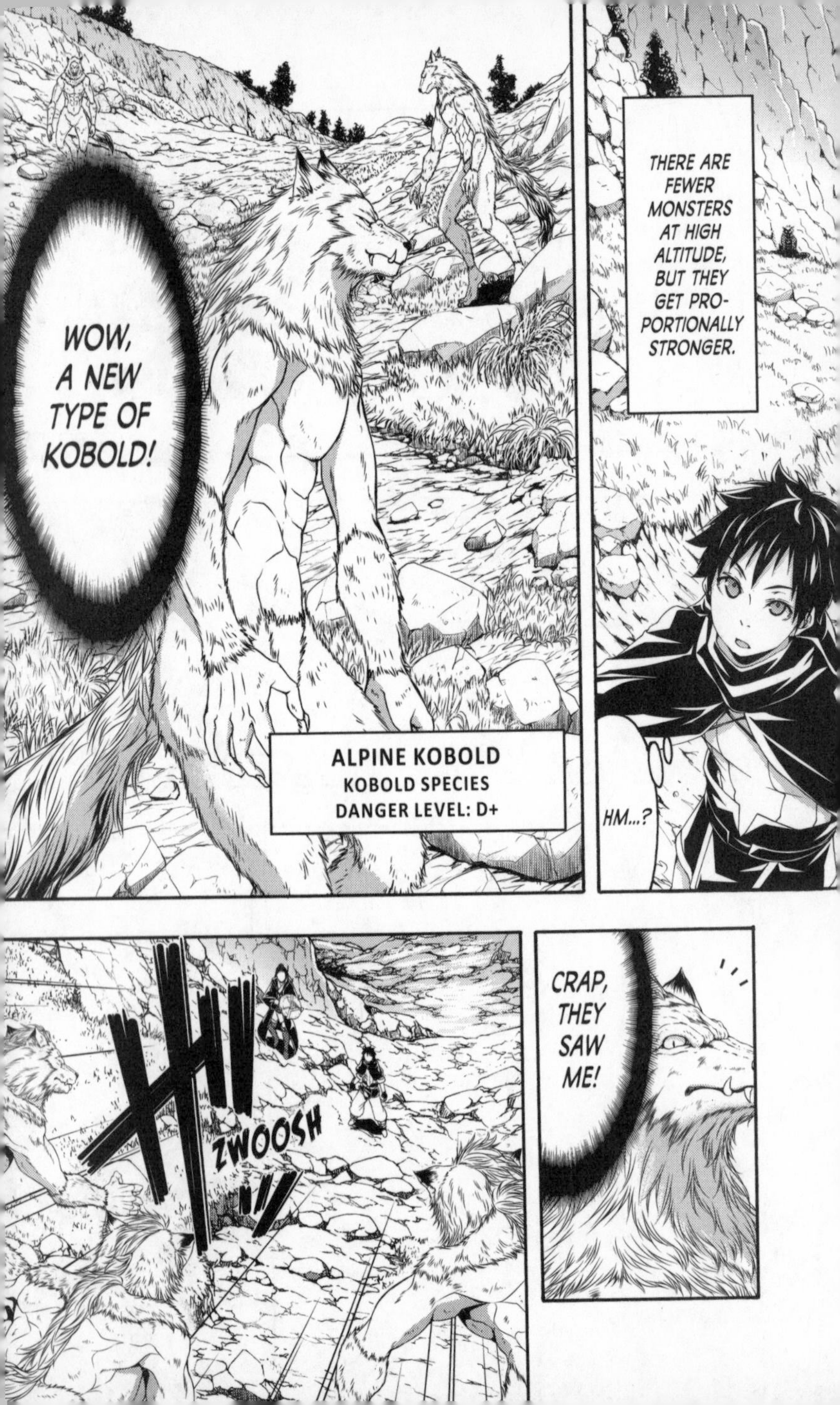
THERE ARE FEWER MONSTERS AT HIGH ALTITUDE, BUT THEY GET PRO-PORTIONALLY STRONGER.
HM...?
WOW, A NEW TYPE OF KOBOLD!
ALPINE KOBOLD
KOBOLD SPECIES
DANGER LEVEL: D+
CRAP, THEY SAW ME!
ZWOOSH

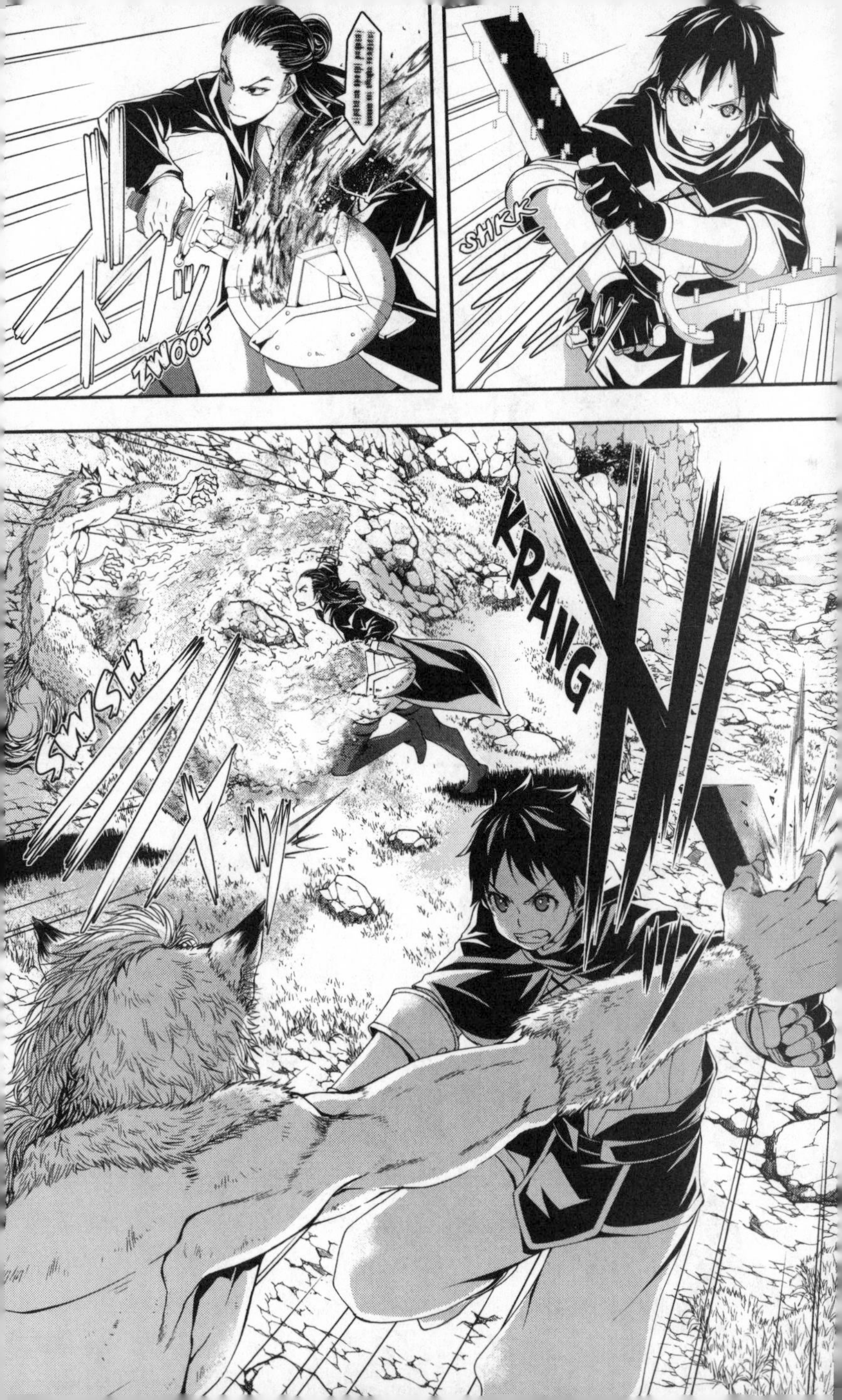
SHKK
ZWOOF
KRANG
SWSH

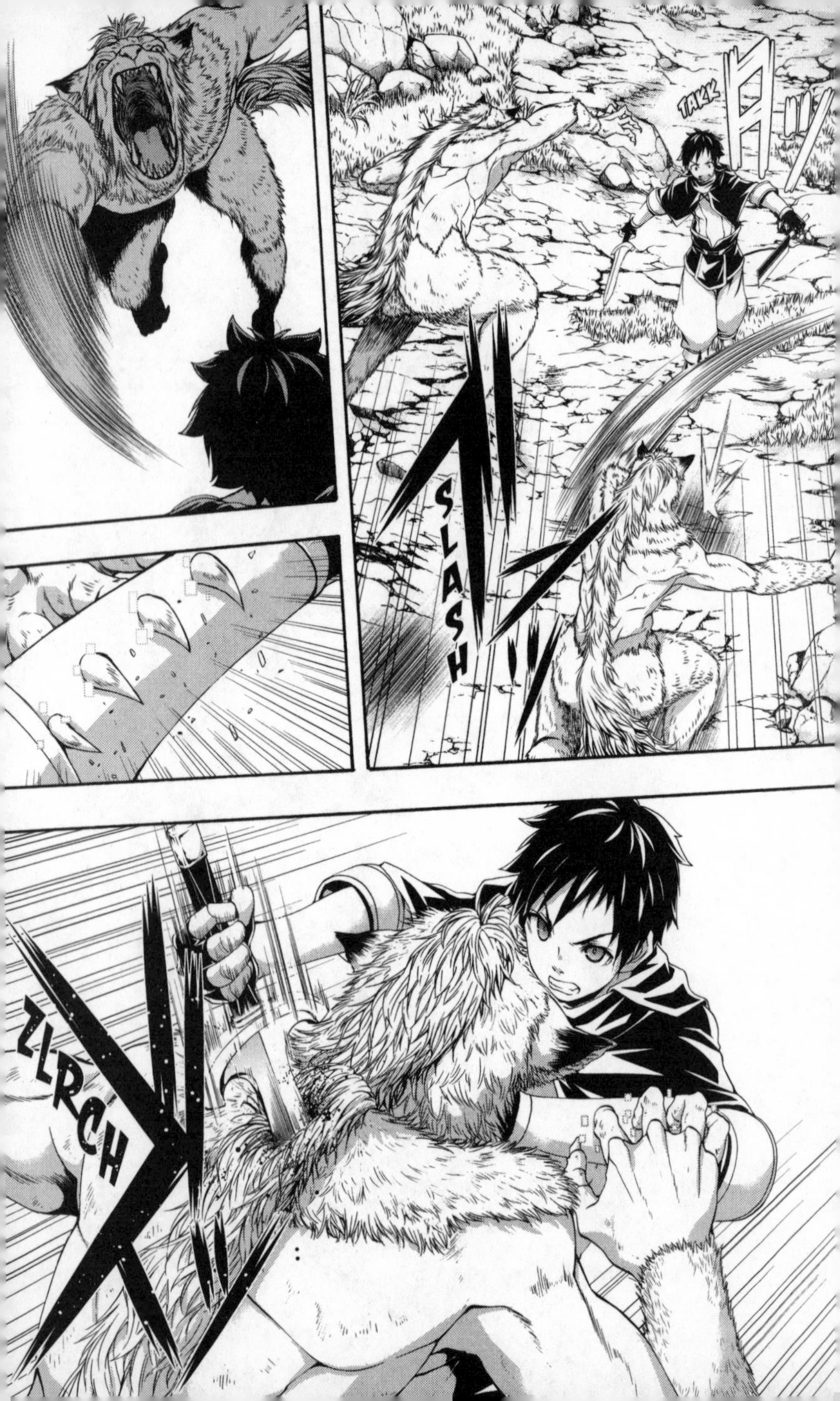
TAKK
SLASH
ZLRCH

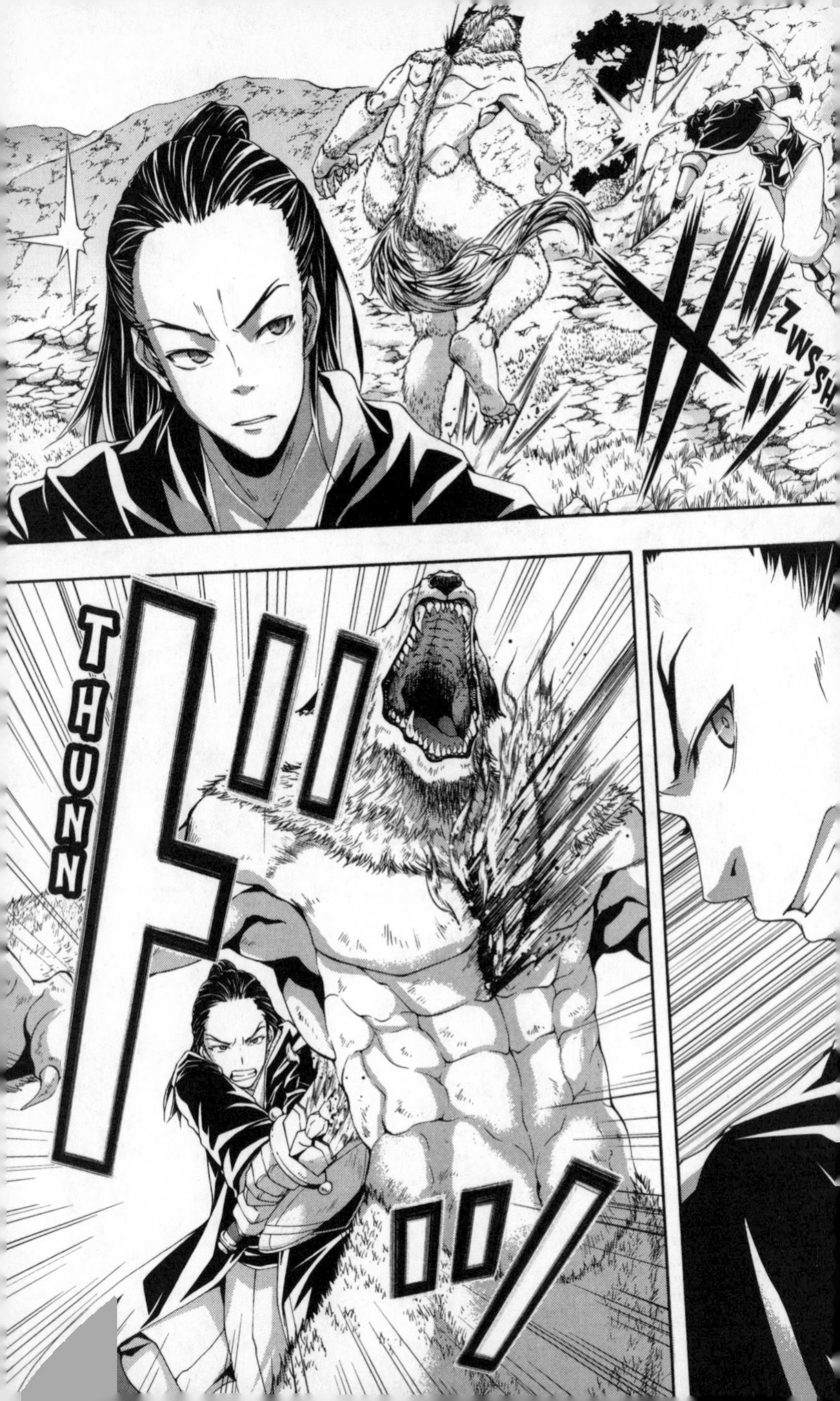
ZWSSH
THUNN

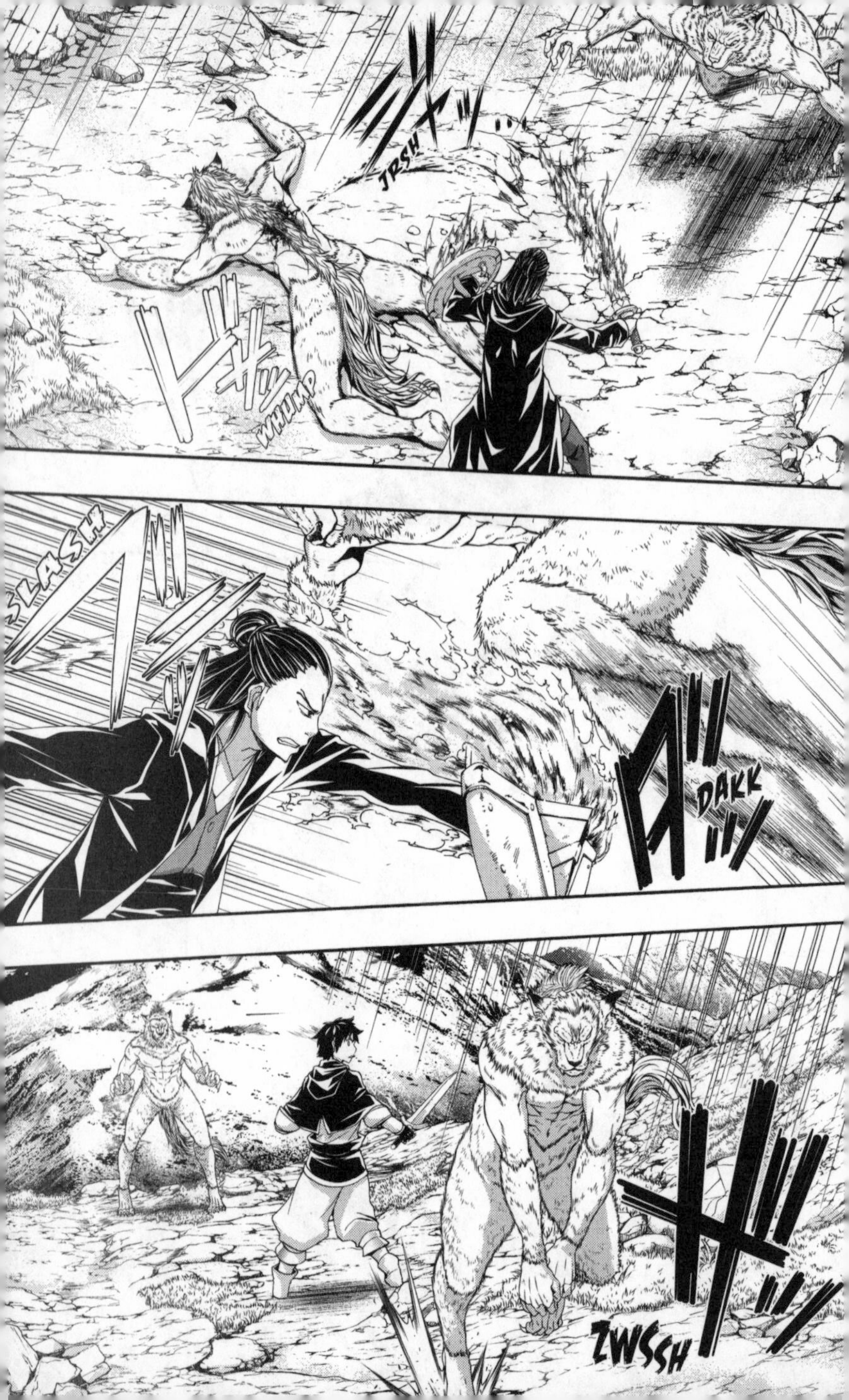
JRSH
WHUMP
DAKK
SLASH
ZWSSH

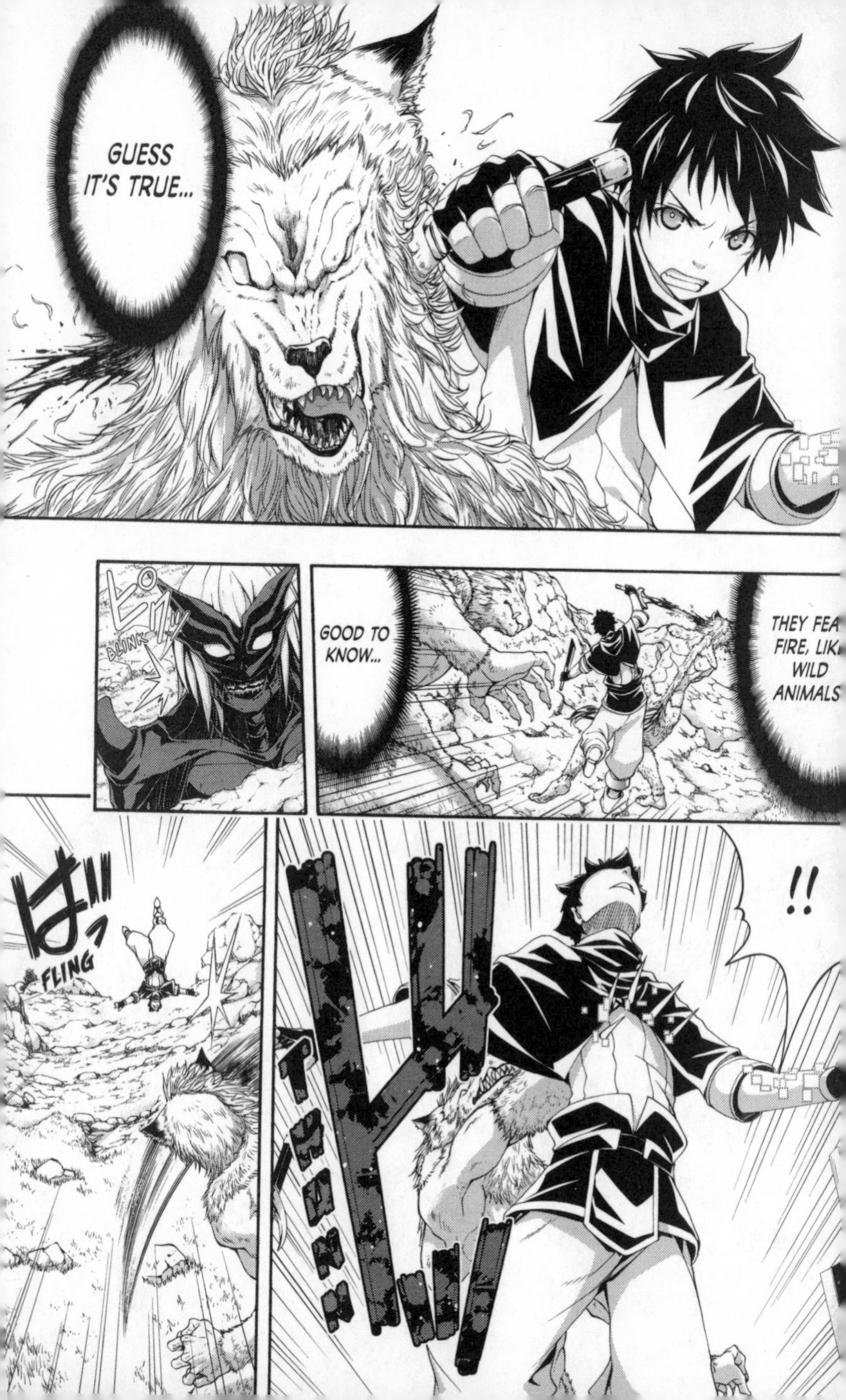
GUESS IT'S TRUE...
THEY FEA FIRE, LIK WILD ANIMALS
GOOD TO KNOW...
ピクッ
BLINK
!!
はっ
FLING

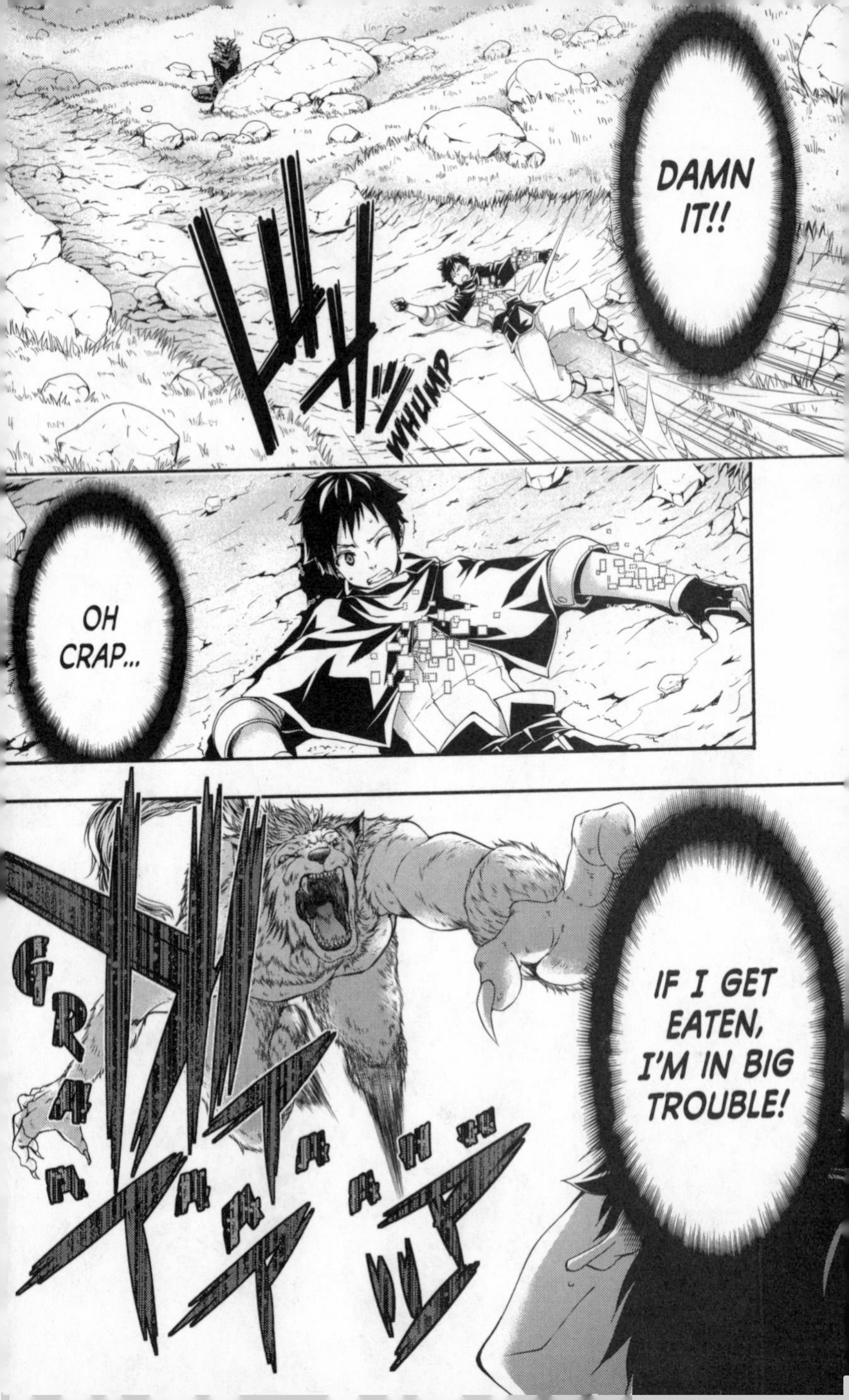
DAMN IT!!
WHUMP
OH CRAP...
IF I GET EATEN, I'M IN BIG TROUBLE!
GRRAAAAA

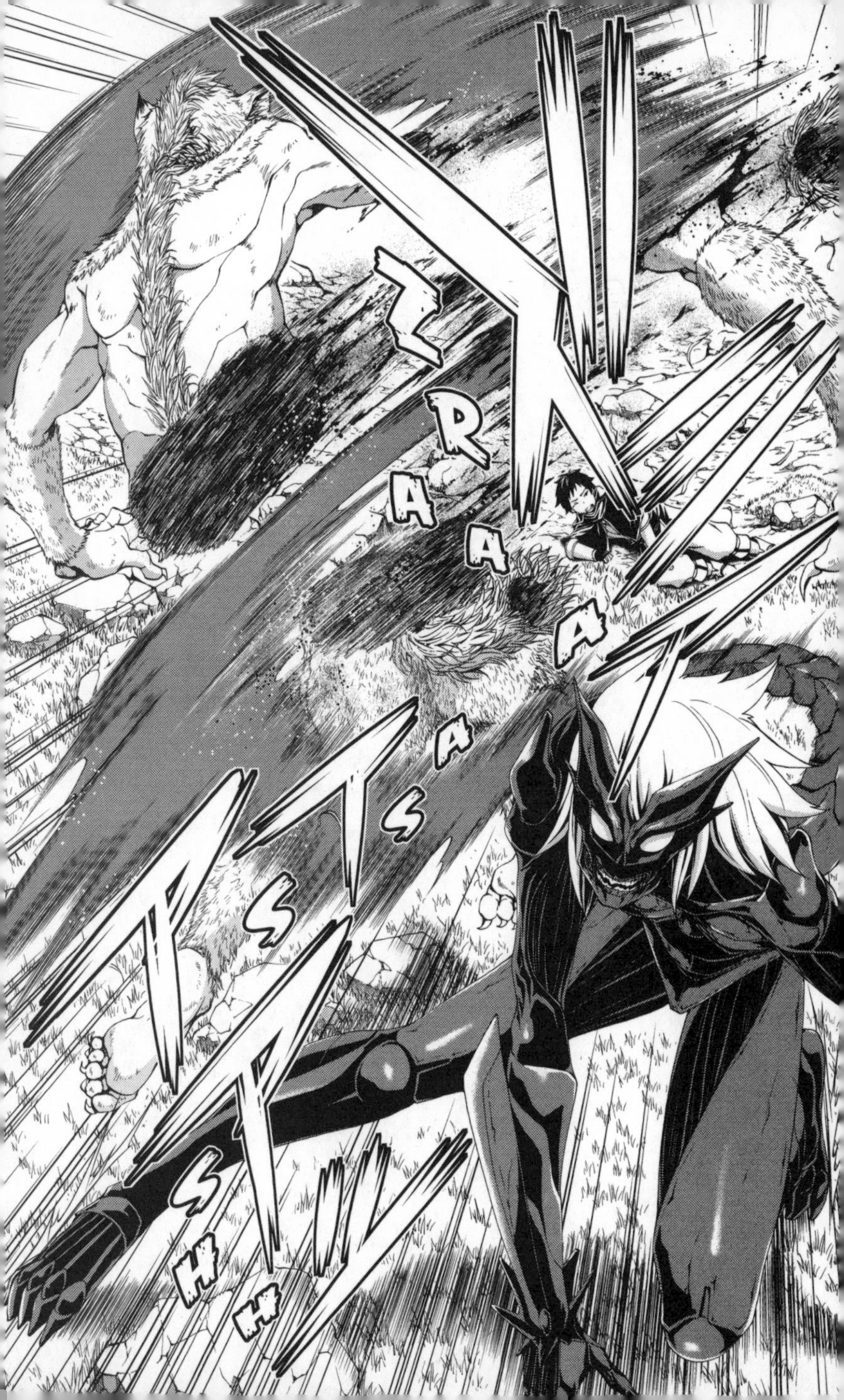
ZRAAA

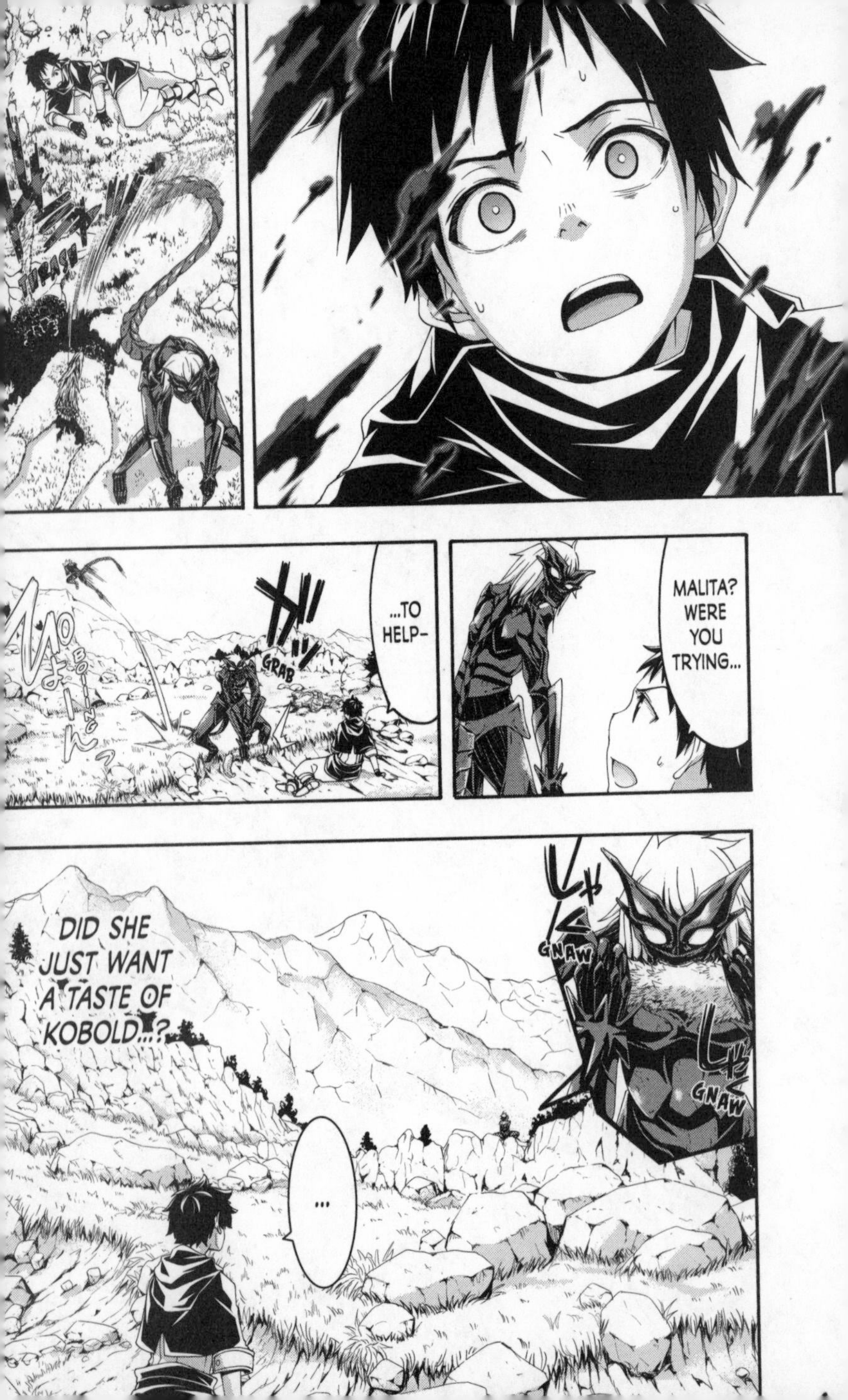
THRASH
MALITA? WERE YOU TRYING...
...TO HELP-
GRAB
BOING
GNAW
GNAW
DID SHE JUST WANT A TASTE OF KOBOLD...?
...

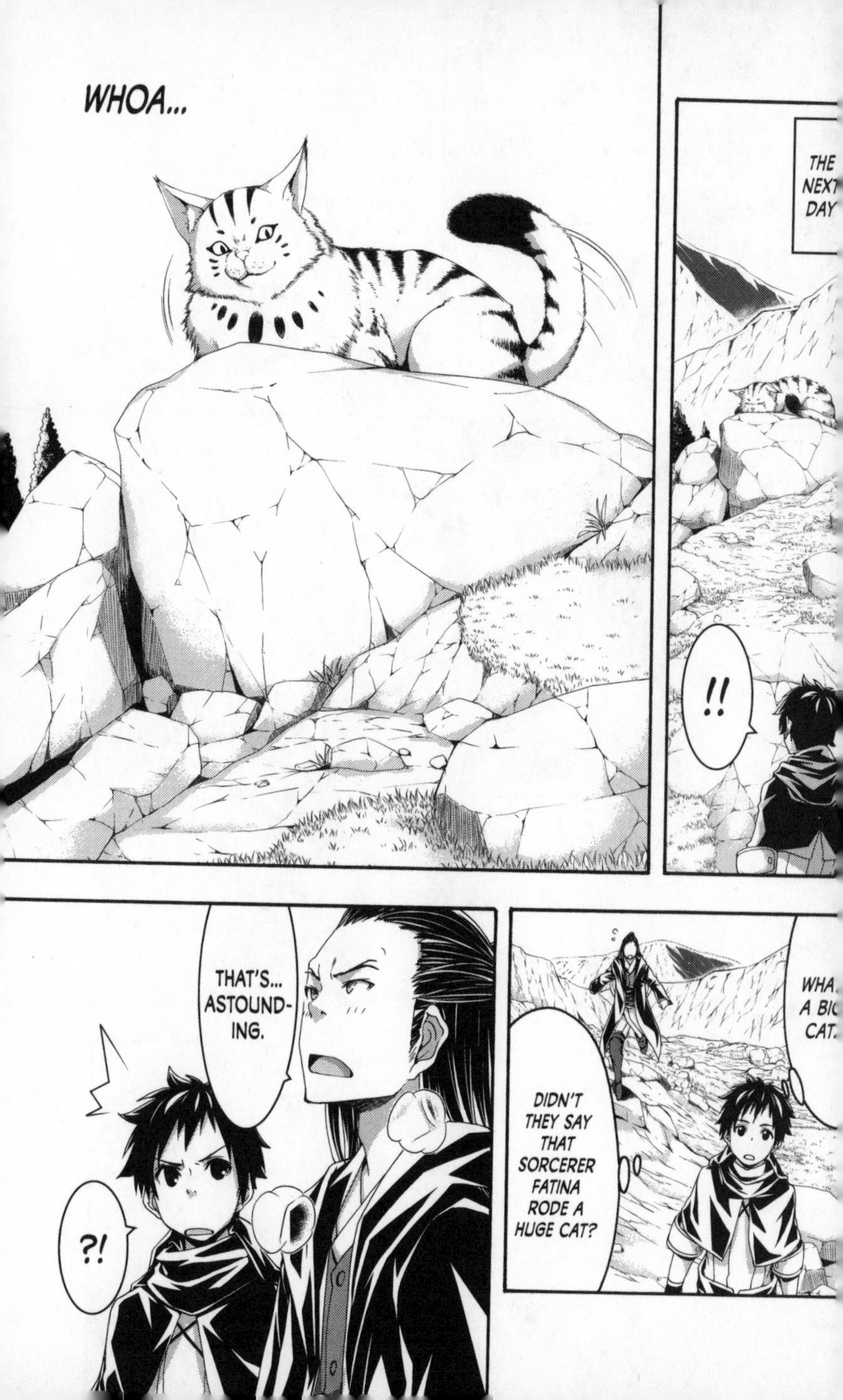
THE NEXT DAY
!!
WHOA...
WHA
A BI
CAT.
DIDN'T THEY SAY THAT SORCERER FATINA RODE A HUGE CAT?
THAT'S... ASTOUNDING.
?!

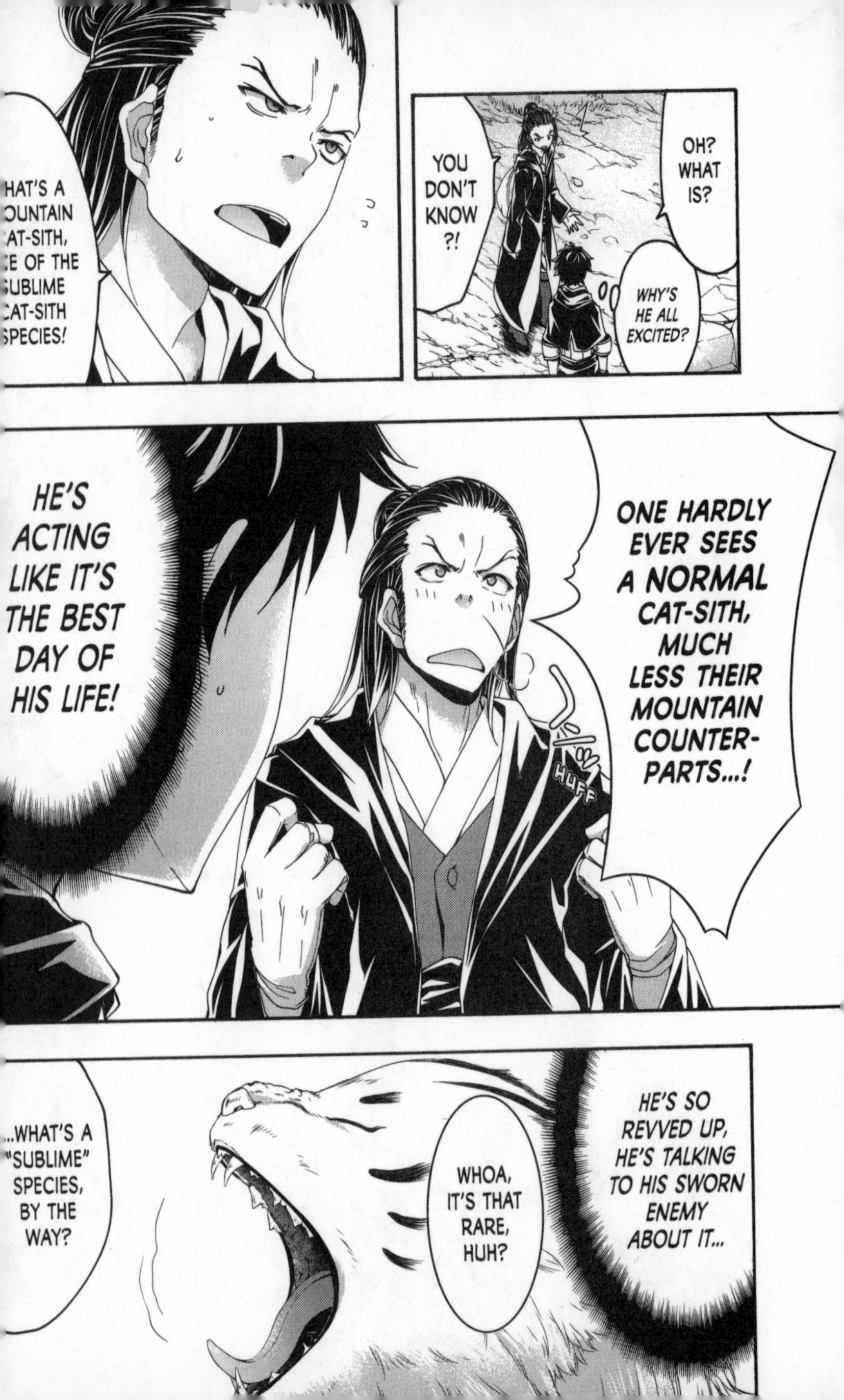
OH? WHAT IS?
WHY'S HE ALL EXCITED?
YOU DON'T KNOW?!
HAT'S A OUNTAIN AT-SITH, E OF THE UBLIME CAT-SITH PECIES!
ONE HARDLY EVER SEES A NORMAL CAT-SITH, MUCH LESS THEIR MOUNTAIN COUNTER-PARTS...!
HUFF
HE'S ACTING LIKE IT'S THE BEST DAY OF HIS LIFE!
HE'S SO REVVED UP, HE'S TALKING TO HIS SWORN ENEMY ABOUT IT...
WHOA, IT'S THAT RARE, HUH?
...WHAT'S A "SUBLIME" SPECIES, BY THE WAY?

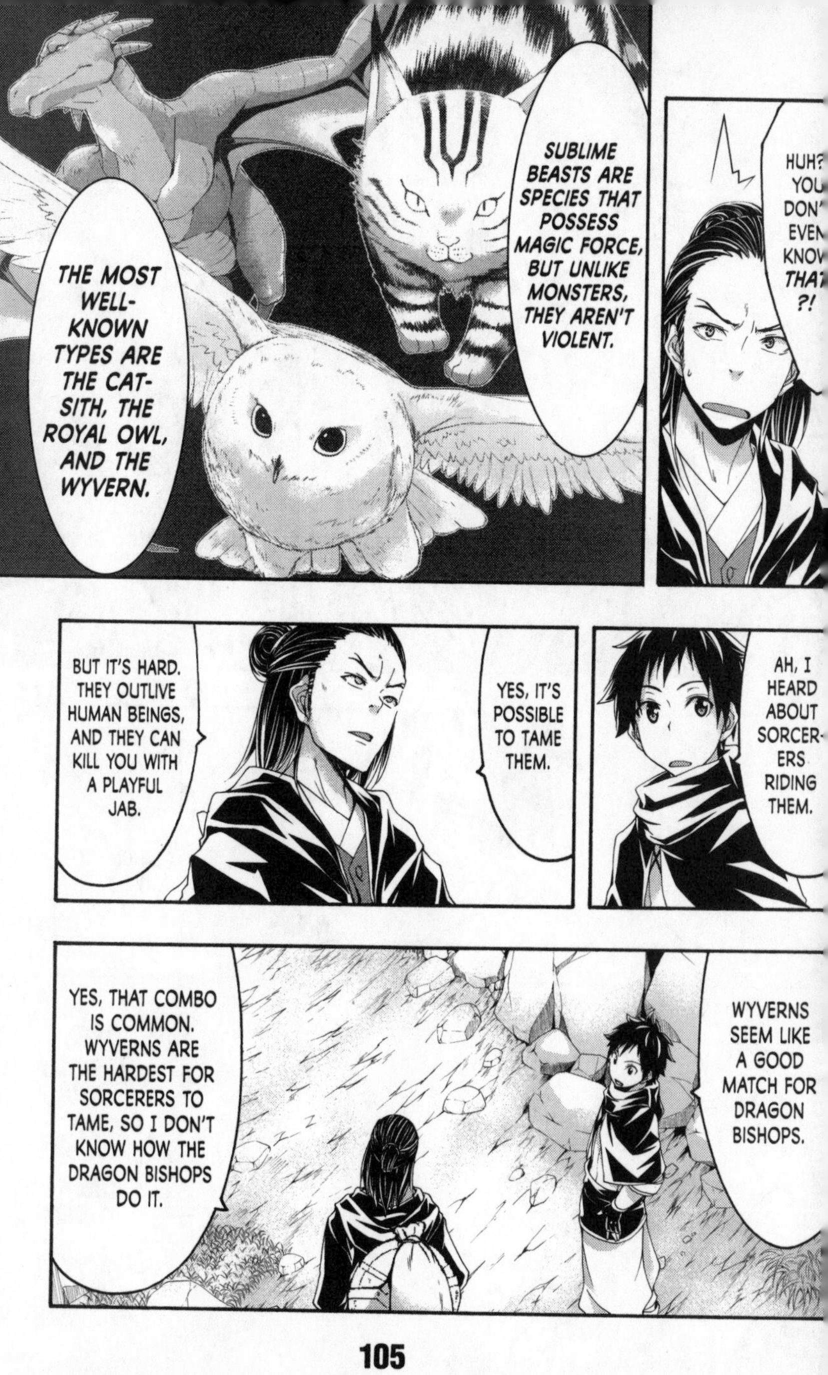
HUH? YOU DON' EVEN KNOW THA ?!
SUBLIME BEASTS ARE SPECIES THAT POSSESS MAGIC FORCE, BUT UNLIKE MONSTERS, THEY AREN'T VIOLENT.
THE MOST WELL-KNOWN TYPES ARE THE CAT-SITH, THE ROYAL OWL, AND THE WYVERN.
AH, I HEARD ABOUT SORCERERS RIDING THEM.
YES, IT'S POSSIBLE TO TAME THEM.
BUT IT'S HARD. THEY OUTLIVE HUMAN BEINGS, AND THEY CAN KILL YOU WITH A PLAYFUL JAB.
WYVERNS SEEM LIKE A GOOD MATCH FOR DRAGON BISHOPS.
YES, THAT COMBO IS COMMON. WYVERNS ARE THE HARDEST FOR SORCERERS TO TAME, SO I DON'T KNOW HOW THE DRAGON BISHOPS DO IT.

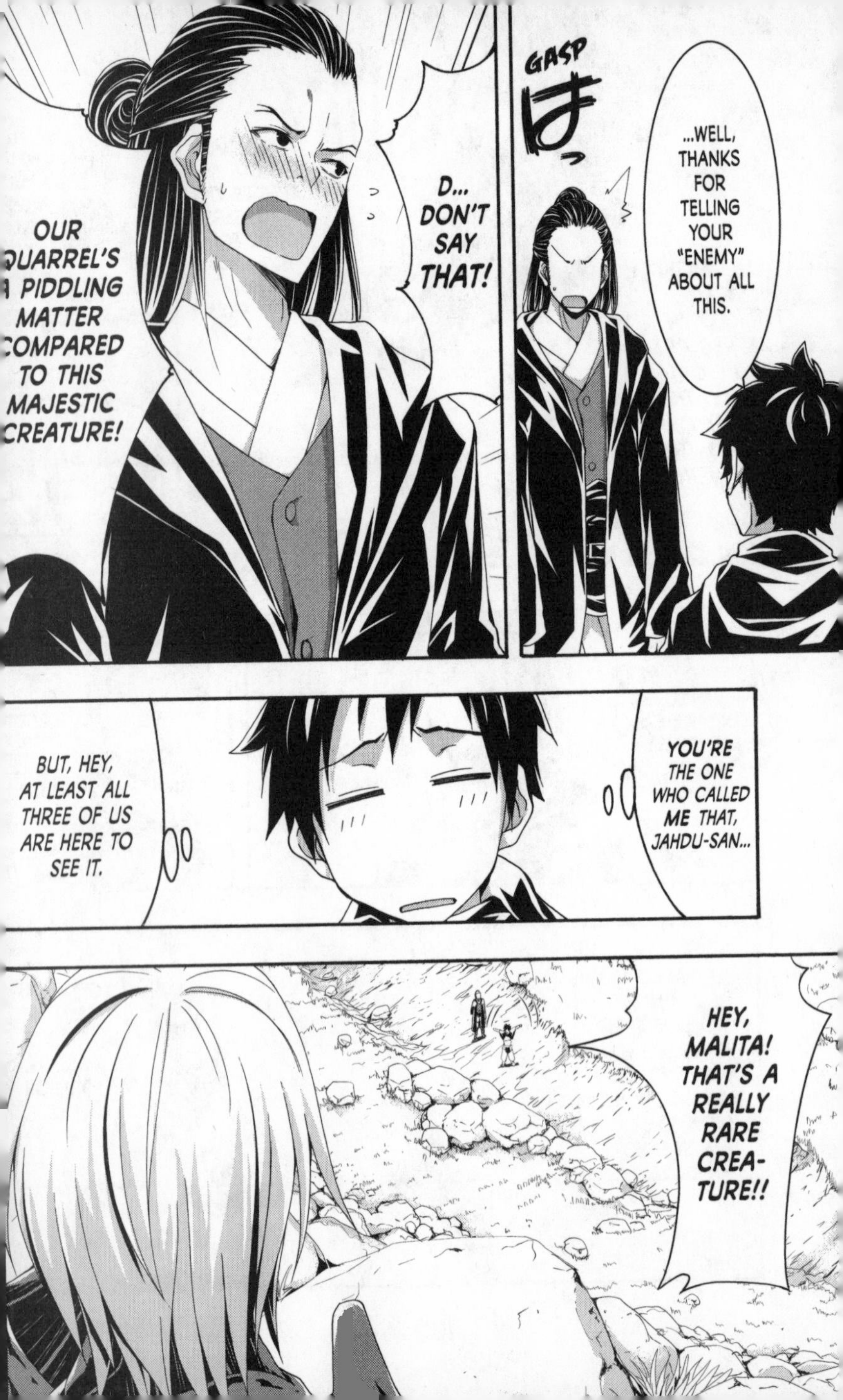
...WELL, THANKS FOR TELLING YOUR "ENEMY" ABOUT ALL THIS.
GASP
D... DON'T SAY THAT!
OUR QUARREL'S A PIDDLING MATTER COMPARED TO THIS MAJESTIC CREATURE!
YOU'RE THE ONE WHO CALLED ME THAT, JAHDU-SAN...
BUT, HEY, AT LEAST ALL THREE OF US ARE HERE TO SEE IT.
HEY, MALITA! THAT'S A REALLY RARE CREA-TURE!!

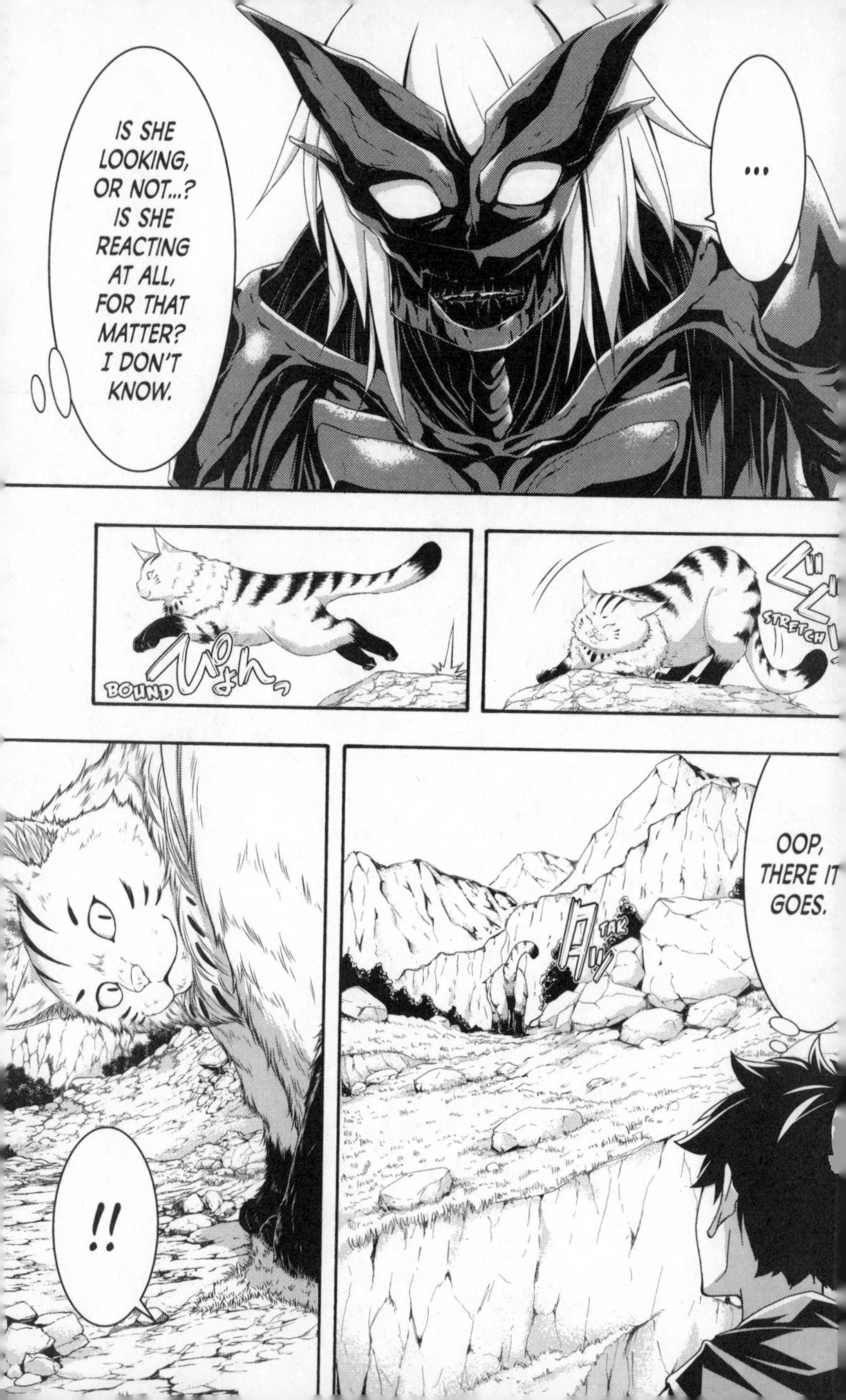
...
IS SHE LOOKING, OR NOT...? IS SHE REACTING AT ALL, FOR THAT MATTER? I DON'T KNOW.
STRETCH
BOUND
OOP, THERE IT GOES.
TAK
!!

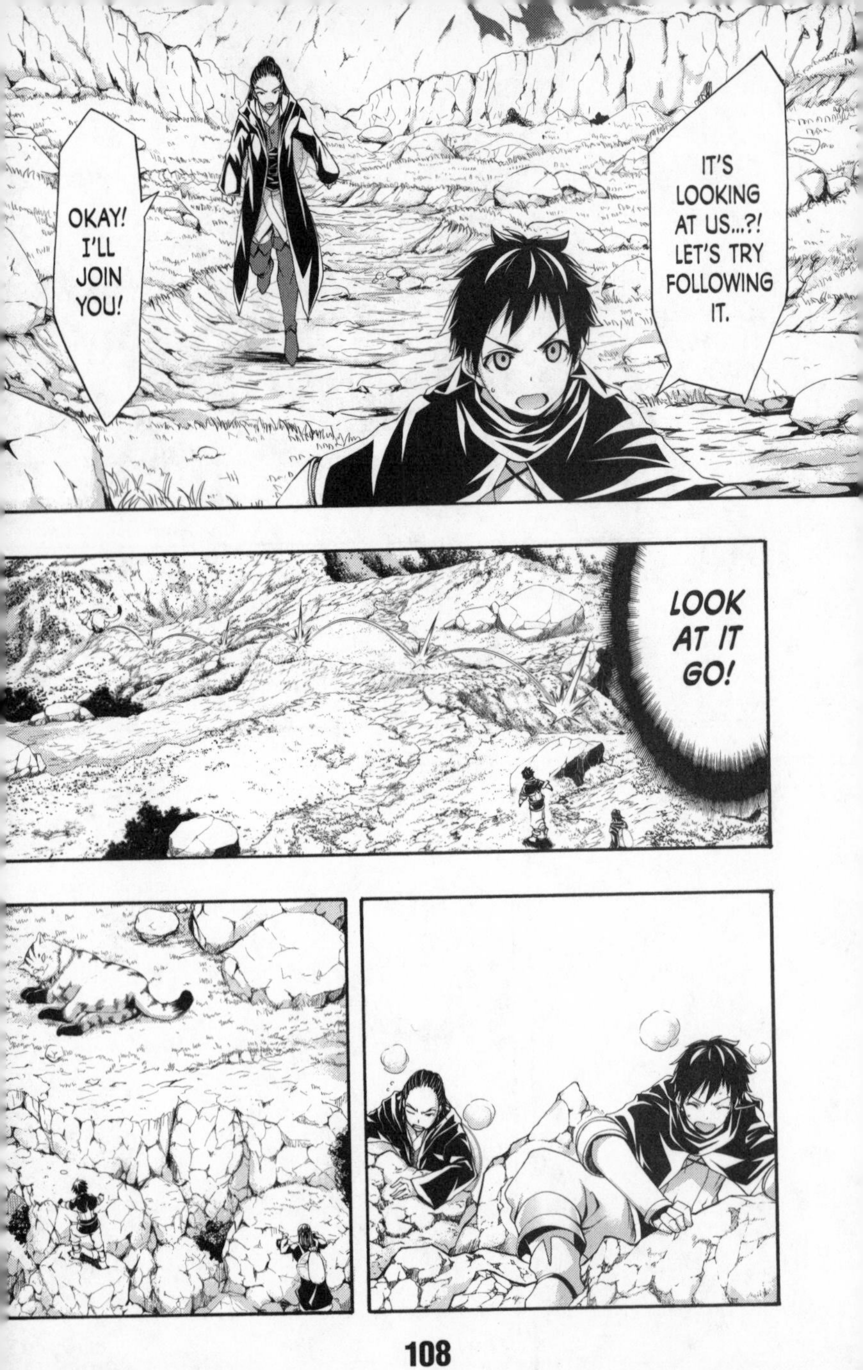
IT'S LOOKING AT US...?! LET'S TRY FOLLOWING IT.
OKAY! I'LL JOIN YOU!
LOOK AT IT GO!

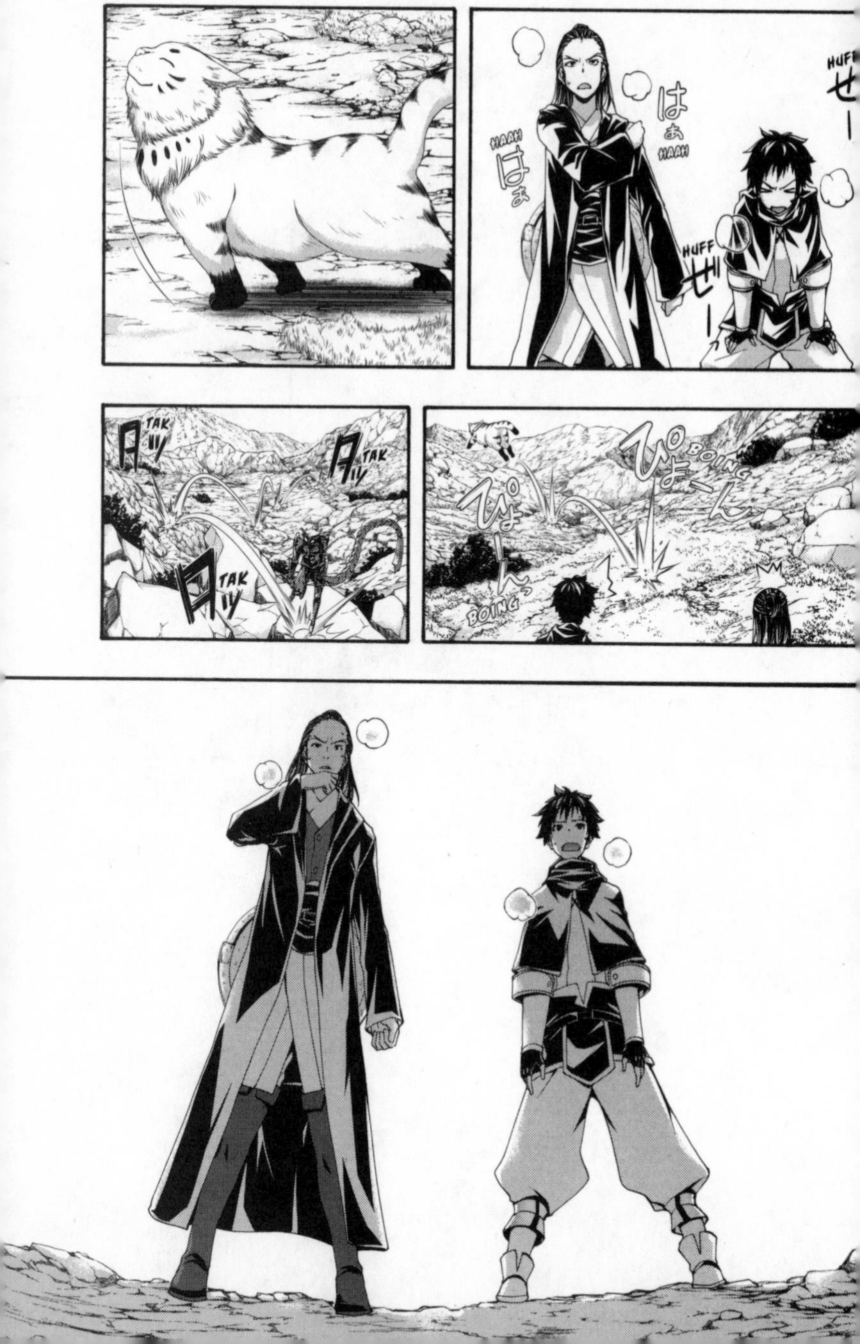

HUFF
ぜー
はぁ
HAAH
HAAH
はぁ
HUFF
ぜー
ぴょーん
BOING
ぴょーんっ
BOING
タッ
TAK
タッ
TAK
タッ
TAK

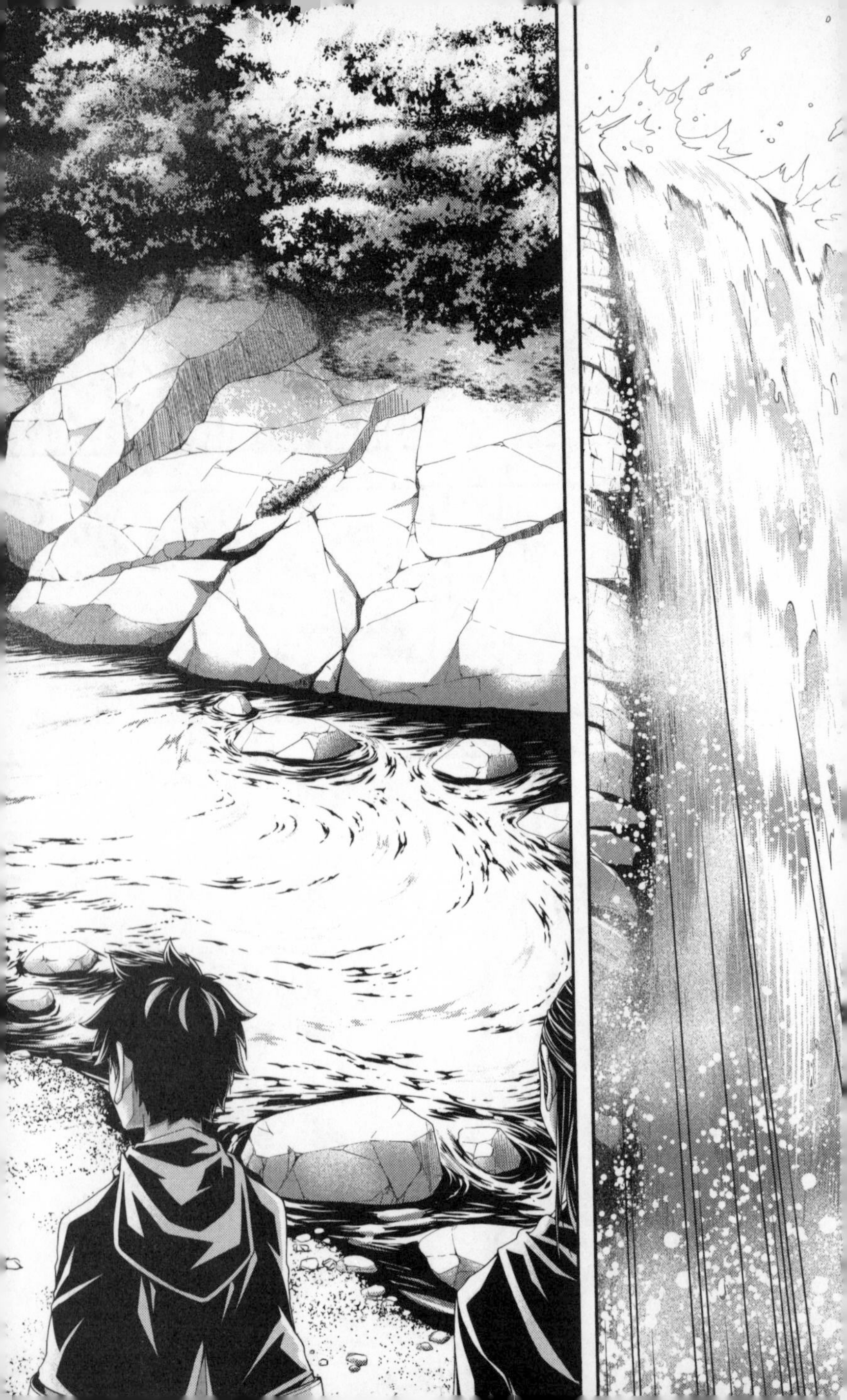

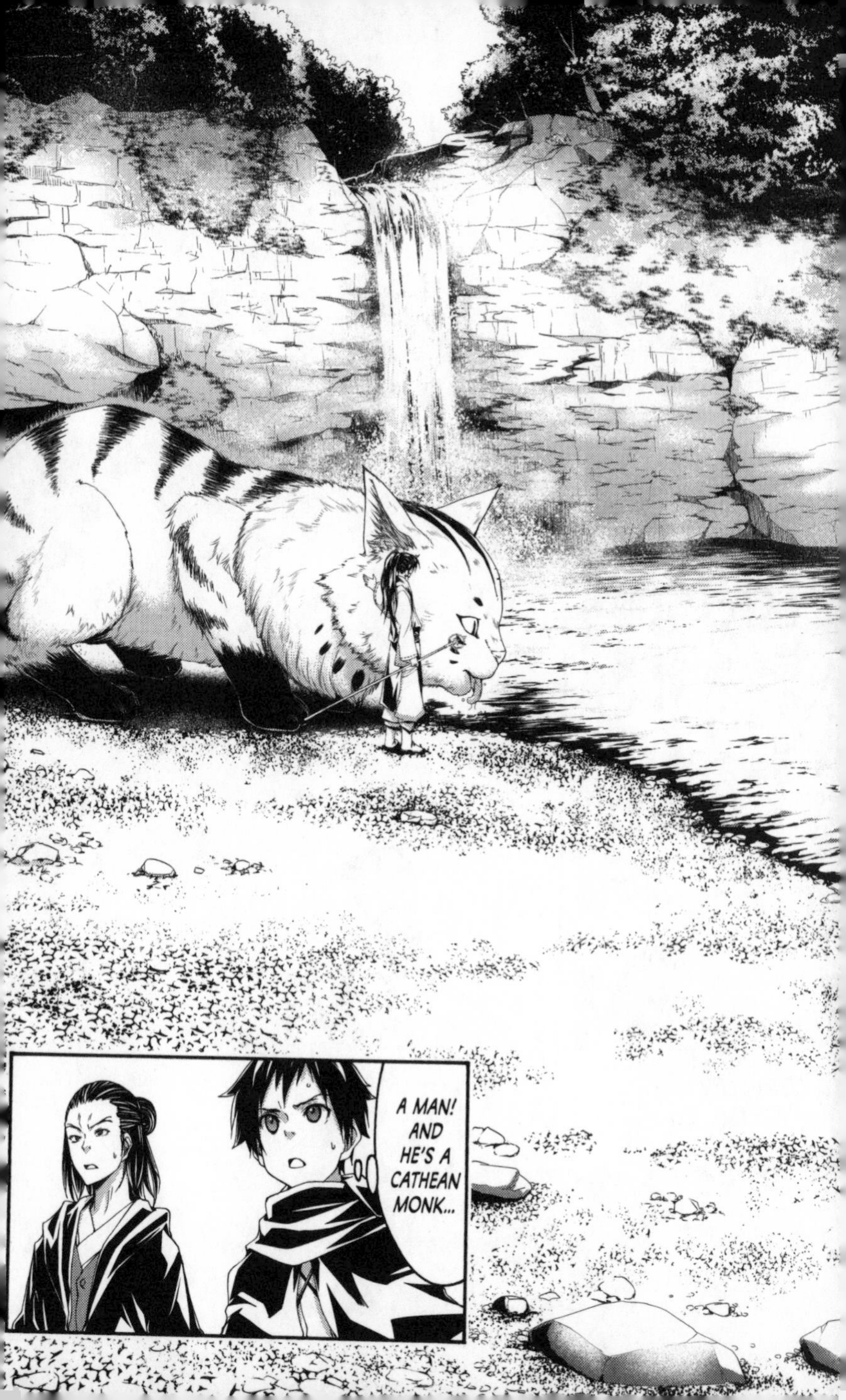
A MAN! AND HE'S A CATHEAN MONK...

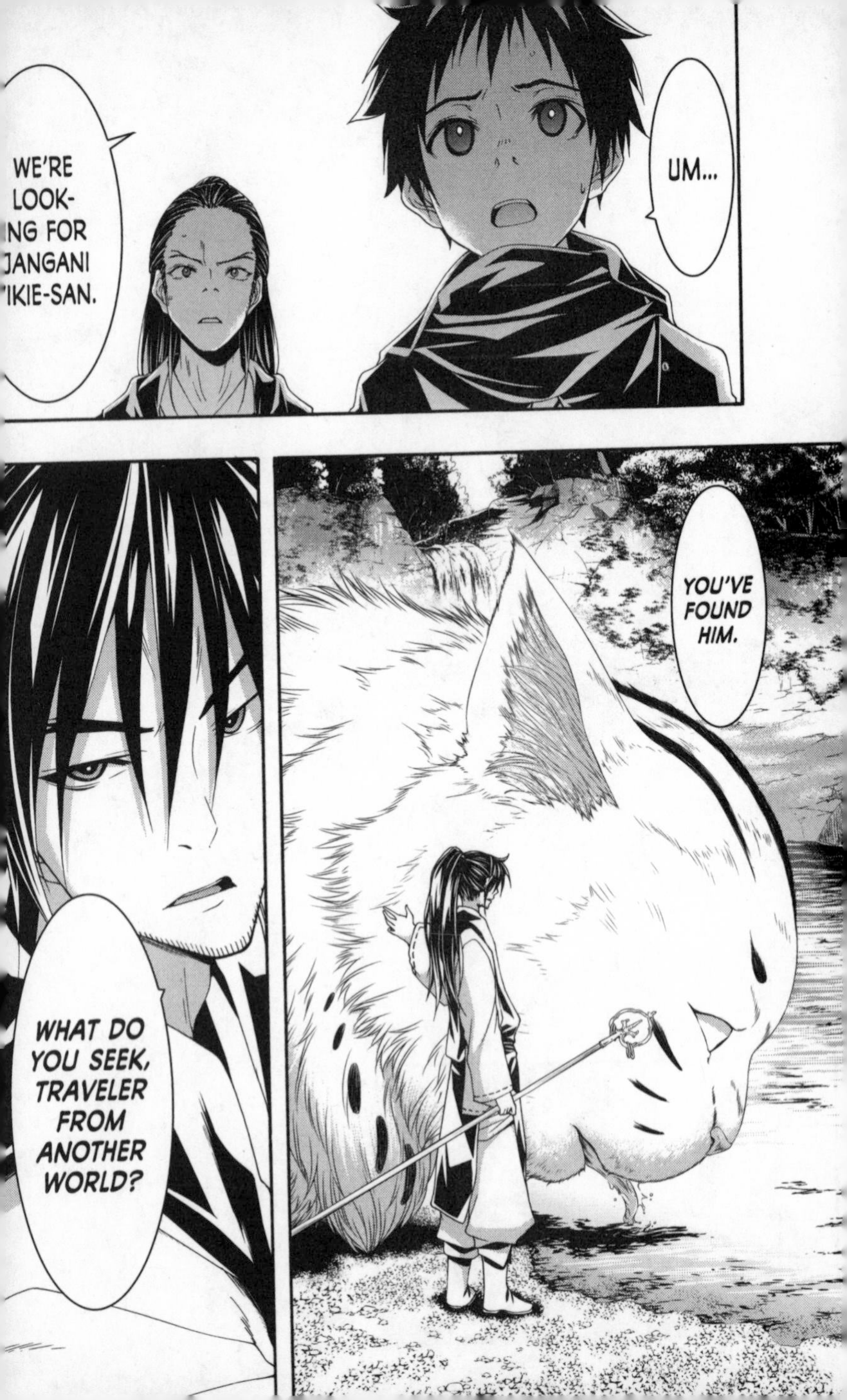
UM...
WE'RE LOOK-NG FOR JANGANI IKIE-SAN.
YOU'VE FOUND HIM.
WHAT DO YOU SEEK, TRAVELER FROM ANOTHER WORLD?

I'M STANDING ON
A MILLION LIVES

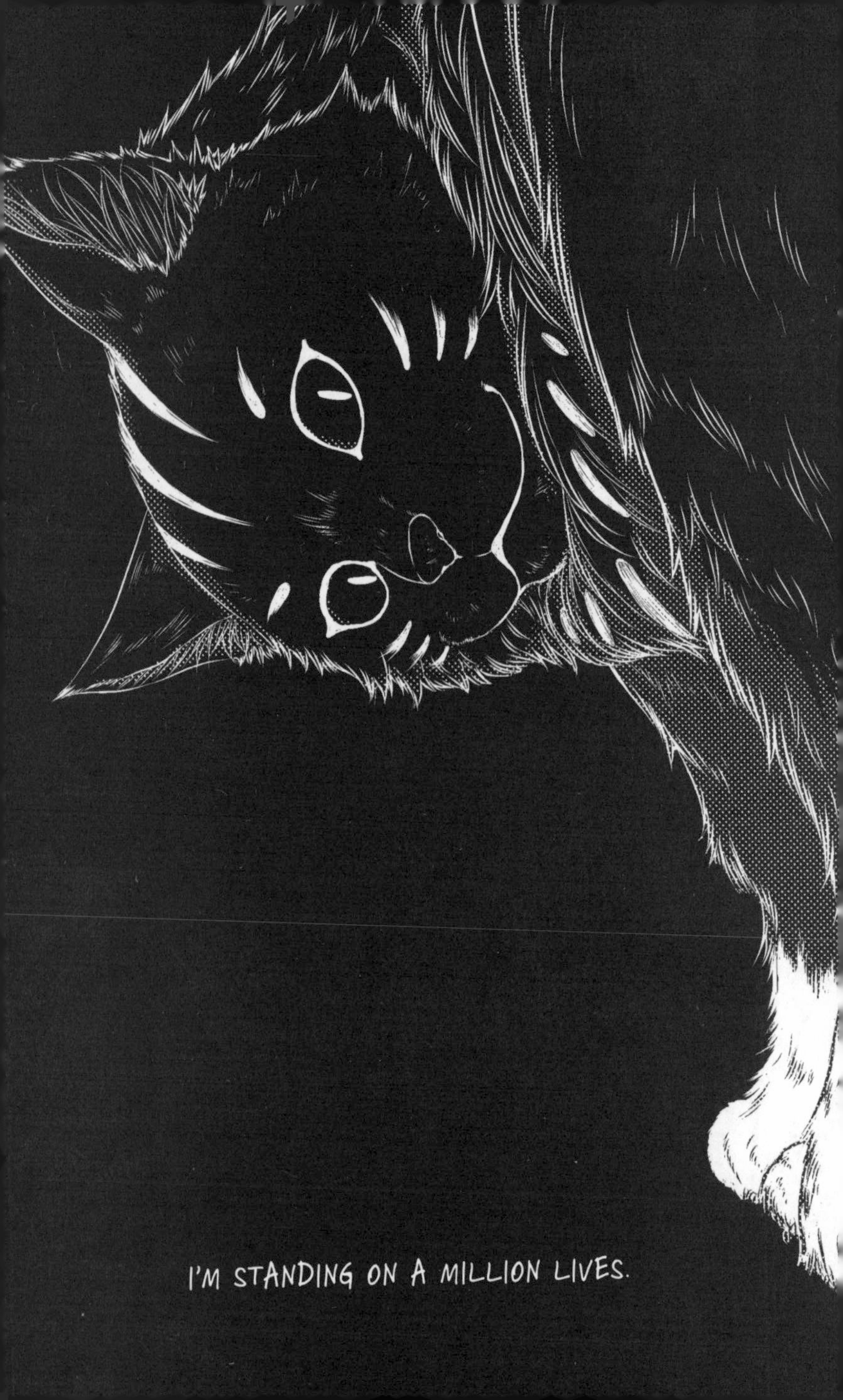
I'M STANDING ON A MILLION LIVES.

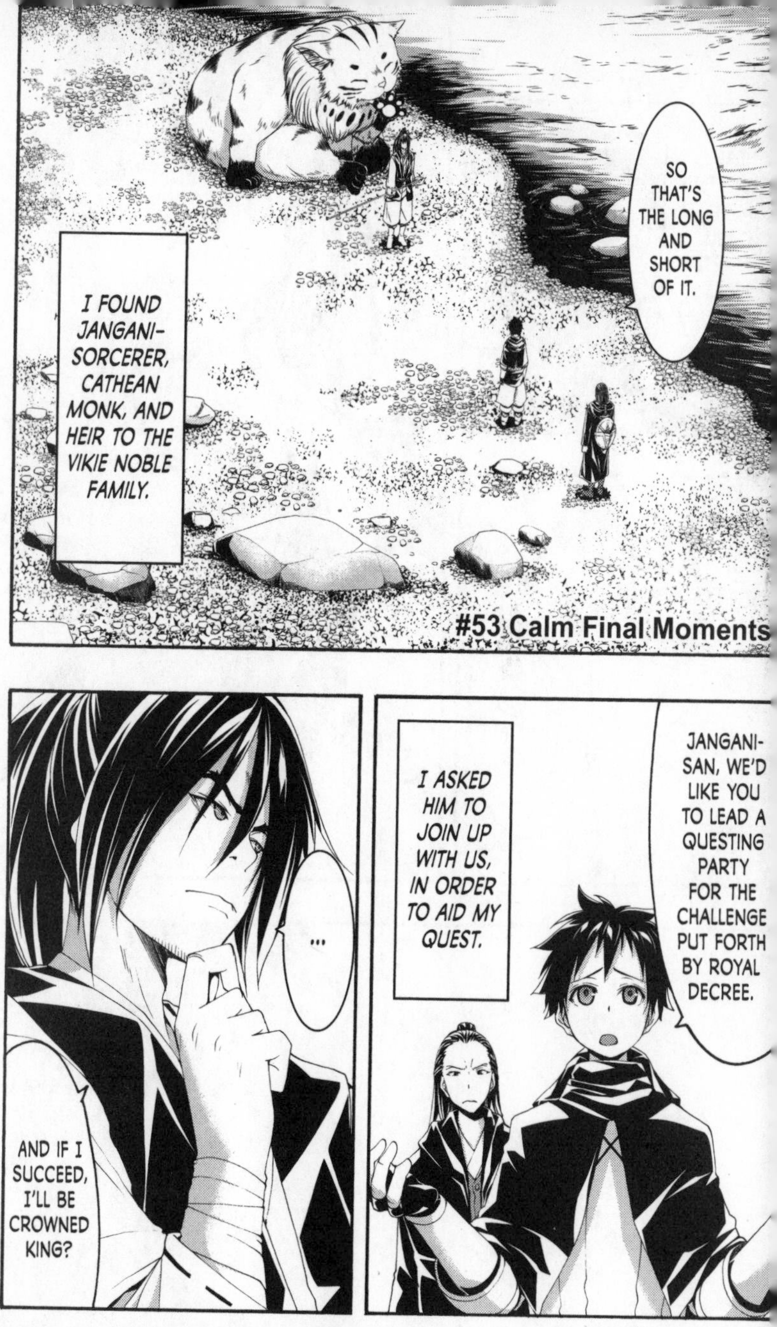
SO THAT'S THE LONG AND SHORT OF IT.
I FOUND JANGANI-SORCERER, CATHEAN MONK, AND HEIR TO THE VIKIE NOBLE FAMILY.
#53 Calm Final Moments
JANGANI-SAN, WE'D LIKE YOU TO LEAD A QUESTING PARTY FOR THE CHALLENGE PUT FORTH BY ROYAL DECREE.
I ASKED HIM TO JOIN UP WITH US, IN ORDER TO AID MY QUEST.
...
AND IF I SUCCEED, I'LL BE CROWNED KING?

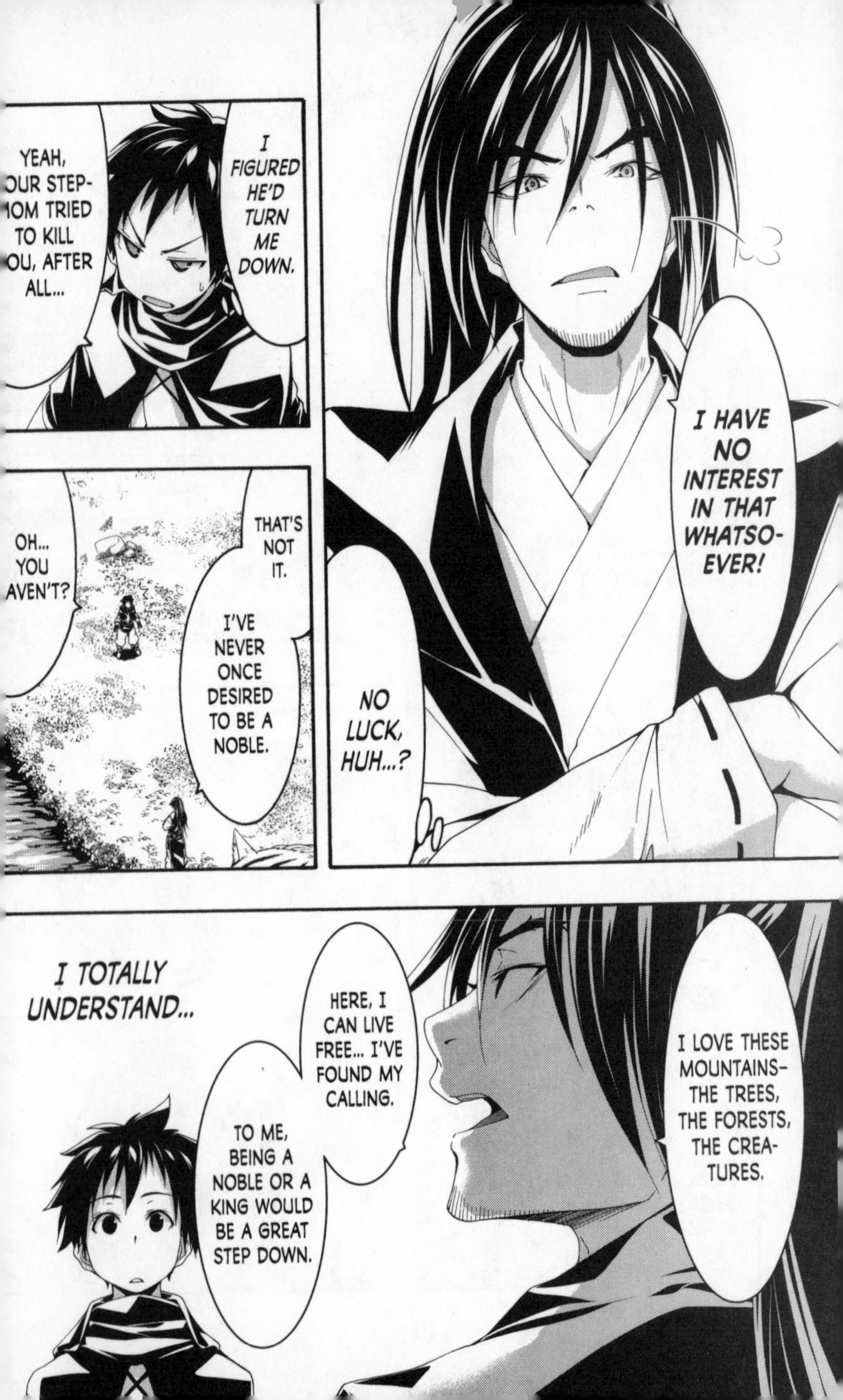
I HAVE NO INTEREST IN THAT WHATSOEVER!
NO LUCK, HUH...?
I FIGURED HE'D TURN ME DOWN.
YEAH, OUR STEP-MOM TRIED TO KILL YOU, AFTER ALL...
THAT'S NOT IT.
I'VE NEVER ONCE DESIRED TO BE A NOBLE.
OH... YOU HAVEN'T?
I LOVE THESE MOUNTAINS–THE TREES, THE FORESTS, THE CREATURES.
HERE, I CAN LIVE FREE... I'VE FOUND MY CALLING.
TO ME, BEING A NOBLE OR A KING WOULD BE A GREAT STEP DOWN.
I TOTALLY UNDERSTAND...

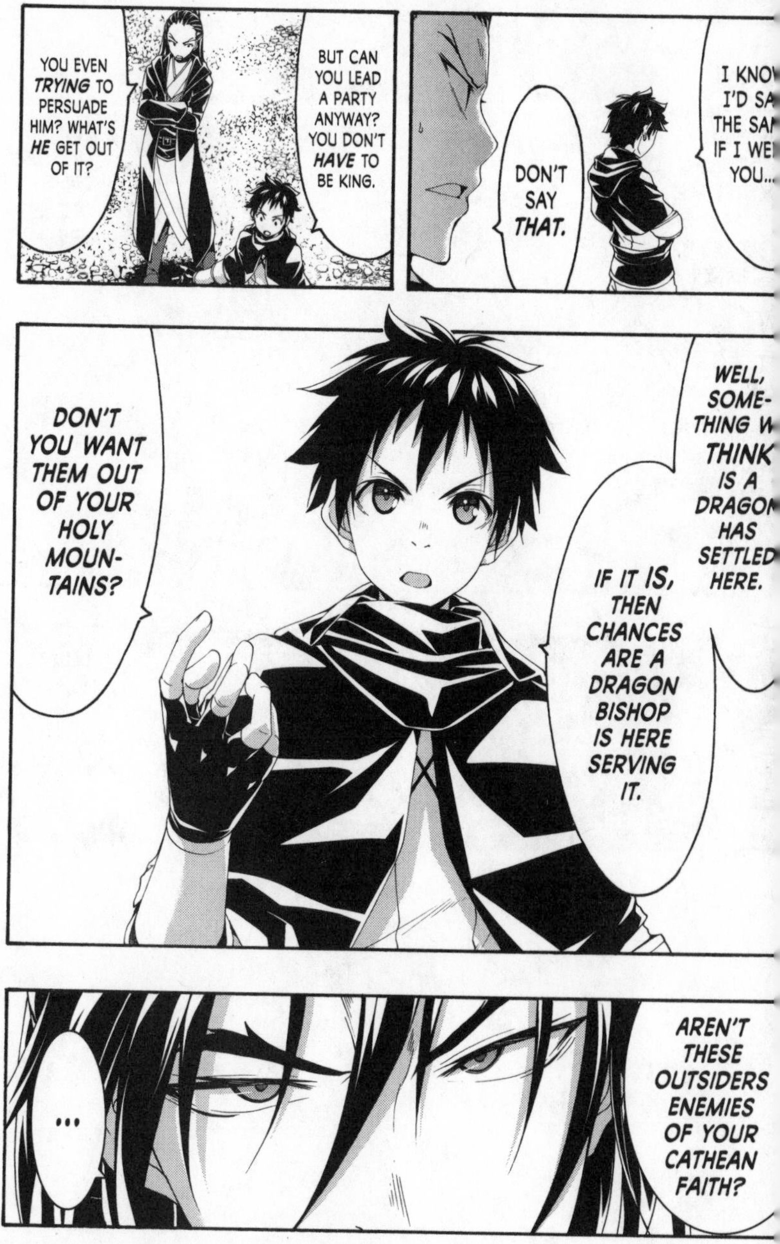
I KNOV I'D SA THE SAI IF I WE YOU...
DON'T SAY *THAT.*
BUT CAN YOU LEAD A PARTY ANYWAY? YOU DON'T *HAVE* TO BE KING.
YOU EVEN *TRYING* TO PERSUADE HIM? WHAT'S *HE* GET OUT OF IT?
WELL, SOME-THING W THINK IS A DRAGOI HAS SETTLED HERE.
IF IT IS, THEN CHANCES ARE A DRAGON BISHOP IS HERE SERVING IT.
DON'T YOU WANT THEM OUT OF YOUR HOLY MOUN-TAINS?
AREN'T THESE OUTSIDERS ENEMIES OF YOUR CATHEAN FAITH?
...

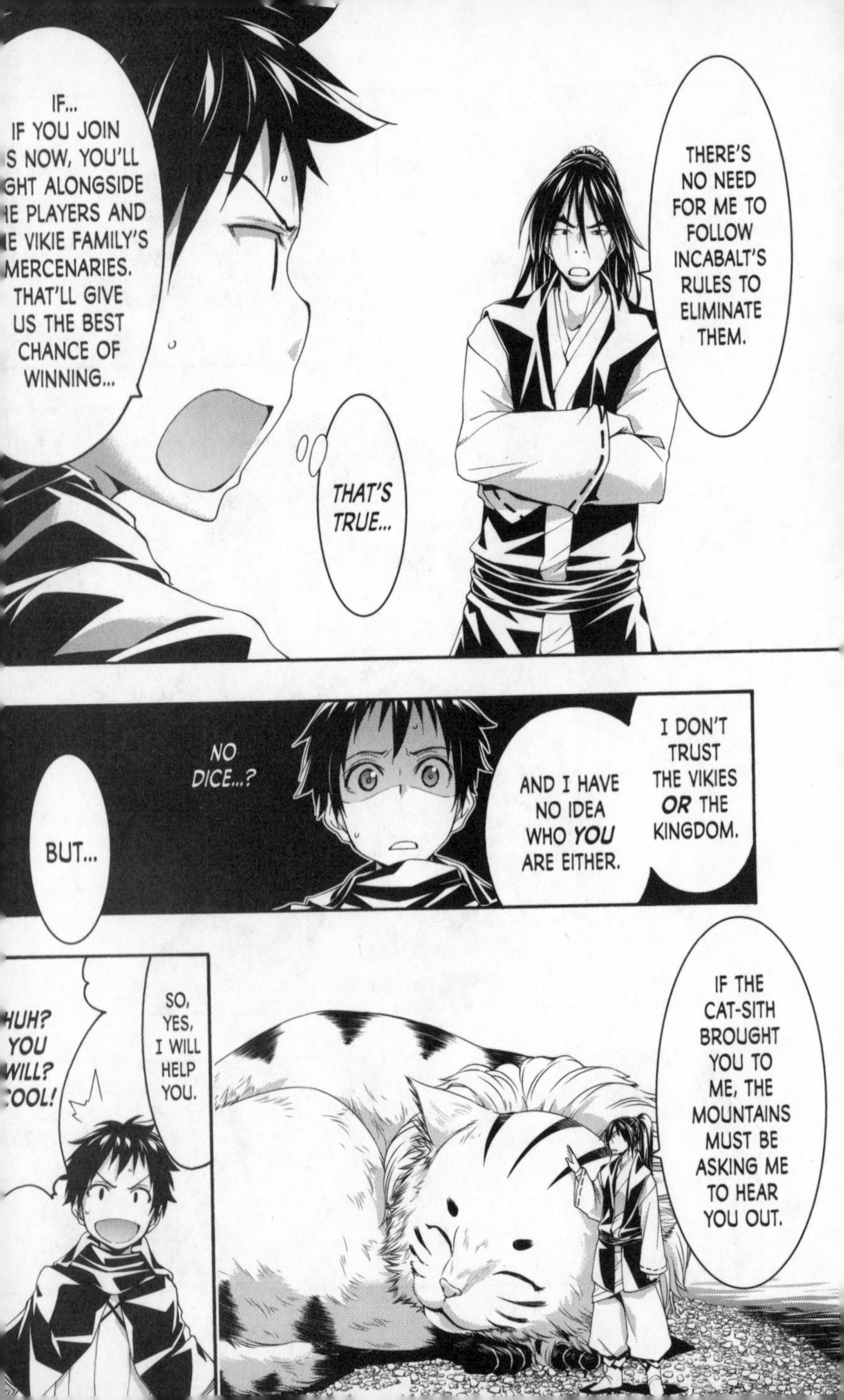
THERE'S NO NEED FOR ME TO FOLLOW INCABALT'S RULES TO ELIMINATE THEM.
IF... IF YOU JOIN S NOW, YOU'LL GHT ALONGSIDE IE PLAYERS AND IE VIKIE FAMILY'S MERCENARIES. THAT'LL GIVE US THE BEST CHANCE OF WINNING...
THAT'S TRUE...
I DON'T TRUST THE VIKIES OR THE KINGDOM.
AND I HAVE NO IDEA WHO YOU ARE EITHER.
NO DICE...?
BUT...
IF THE CAT-SITH BROUGHT YOU TO ME, THE MOUNTAINS MUST BE ASKING ME TO HEAR YOU OUT.
SO, YES, I WILL HELP YOU.
HUH? YOU WILL? COOL!

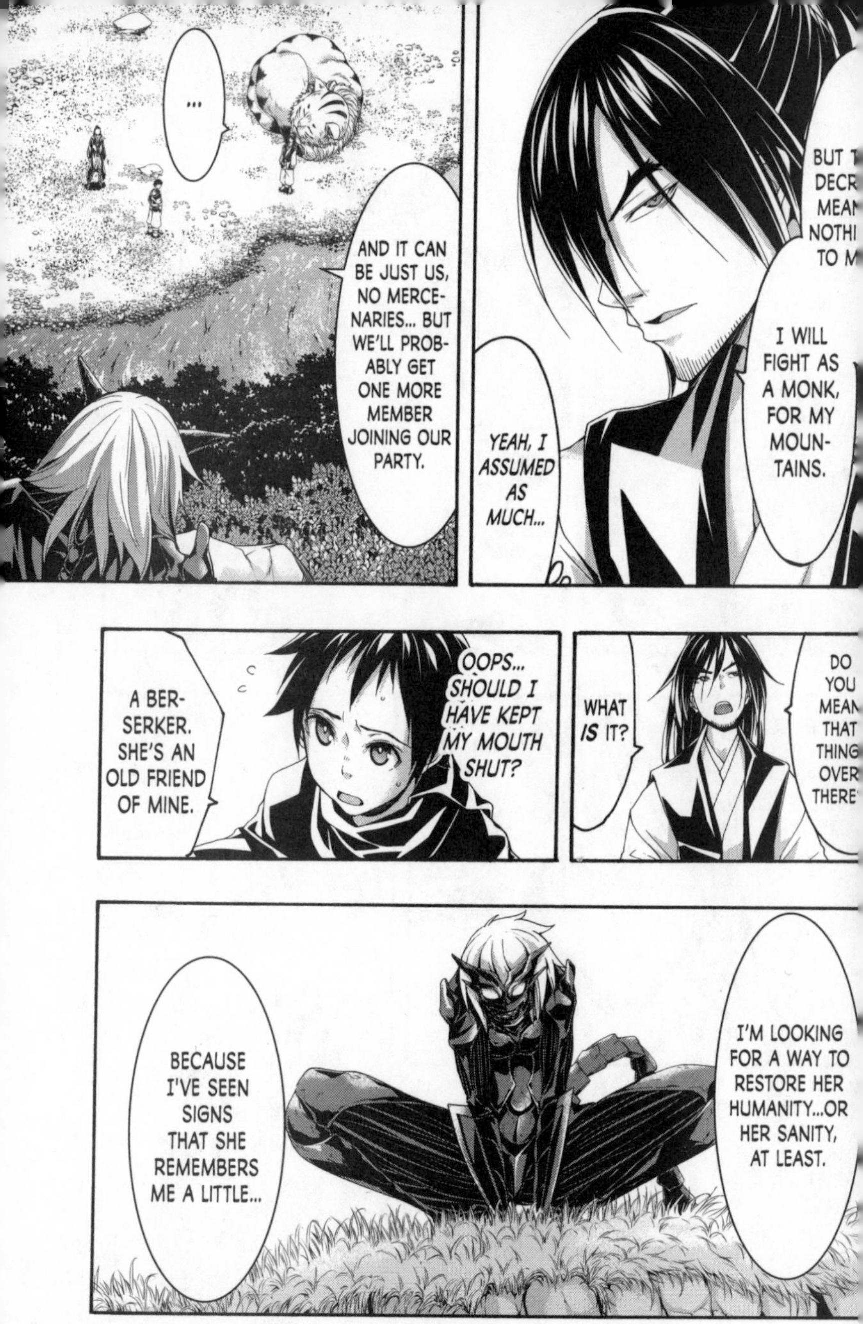
I WILL FIGHT AS A MONK, FOR MY MOUNTAINS.
YEAH, I ASSUMED AS MUCH...
...
AND IT CAN BE JUST US, NO MERCENARIES... BUT WE'LL PROBABLY GET ONE MORE MEMBER JOINING OUR PARTY.
DO YOU MEAN THAT THING OVER THERE
WHAT *IS* IT?
OOPS... SHOULD I HAVE KEPT MY MOUTH SHUT?
A BERSERKER. SHE'S AN OLD FRIEND OF MINE.
I'M LOOKING FOR A WAY TO RESTORE HER HUMANITY...OR HER SANITY, AT LEAST.
BECAUSE I'VE SEEN SIGNS THAT SHE REMEMBERS ME A LITTLE...

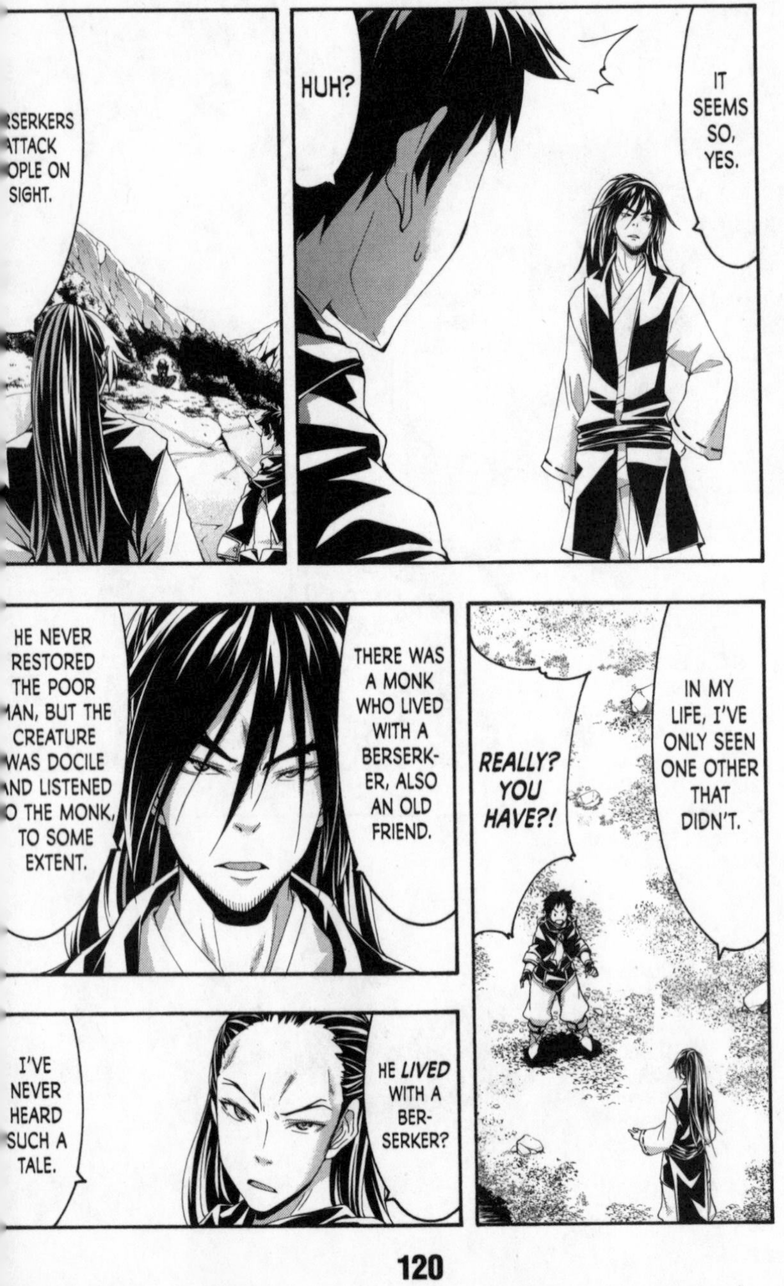
IT SEEMS SO, YES.
HUH?
RSERKERS ATTACK OPLE ON SIGHT.
IN MY LIFE, I'VE ONLY SEEN ONE OTHER THAT DIDN'T.
REALLY? YOU HAVE?!
THERE WAS A MONK WHO LIVED WITH A BERSERK-ER, ALSO AN OLD FRIEND.
HE NEVER RESTORED THE POOR IAN, BUT THE CREATURE WAS DOCILE ND LISTENED O THE MONK, TO SOME EXTENT.
HE *LIVED* WITH A BER-SERKER?
I'VE NEVER HEARD SUCH A TALE.

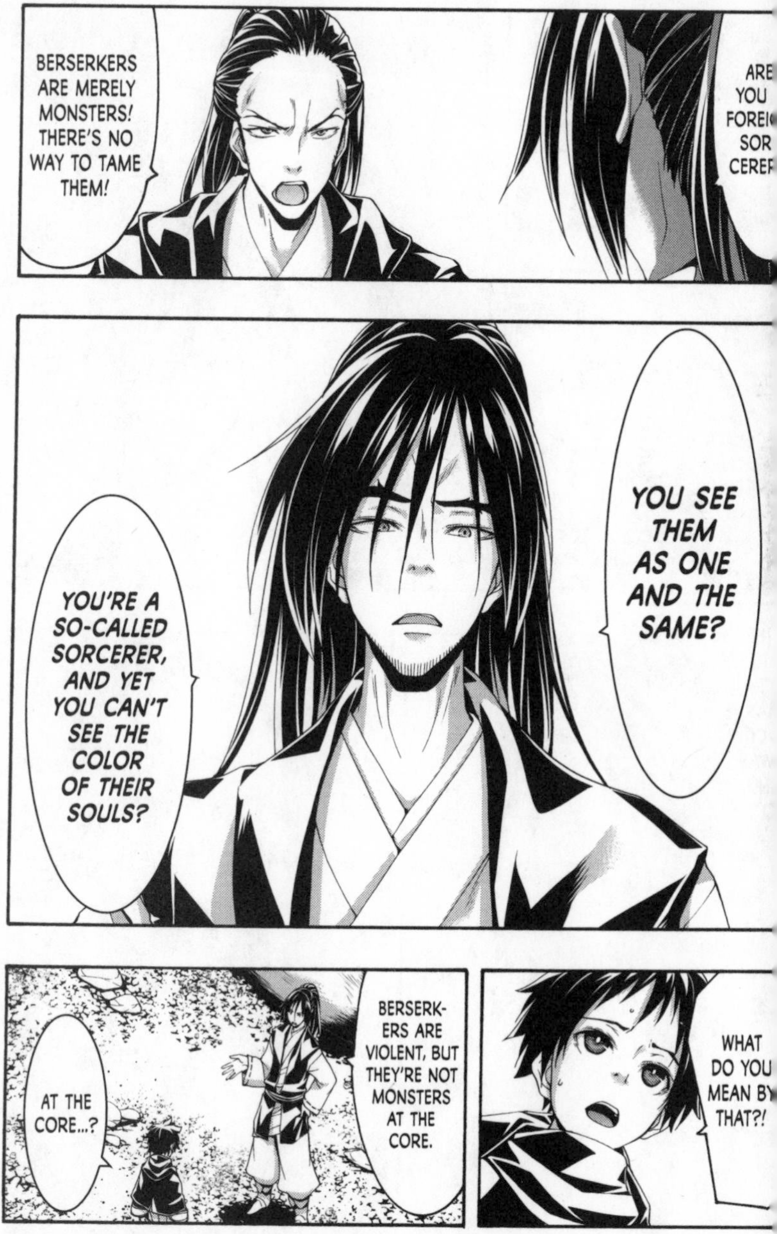
ARE YOU FOREI SORCERE
BERSERKERS ARE MERELY MONSTERS! THERE'S NO WAY TO TAME THEM!
YOU SEE THEM AS ONE AND THE SAME?
YOU'RE A SO-CALLED SORCERER, AND YET YOU CAN'T SEE THE COLOR OF THEIR SOULS?
WHAT DO YOU MEAN BY THAT?!
BERSERKERS ARE VIOLENT, BUT THEY'RE NOT MONSTERS AT THE CORE.
AT THE CORE...?

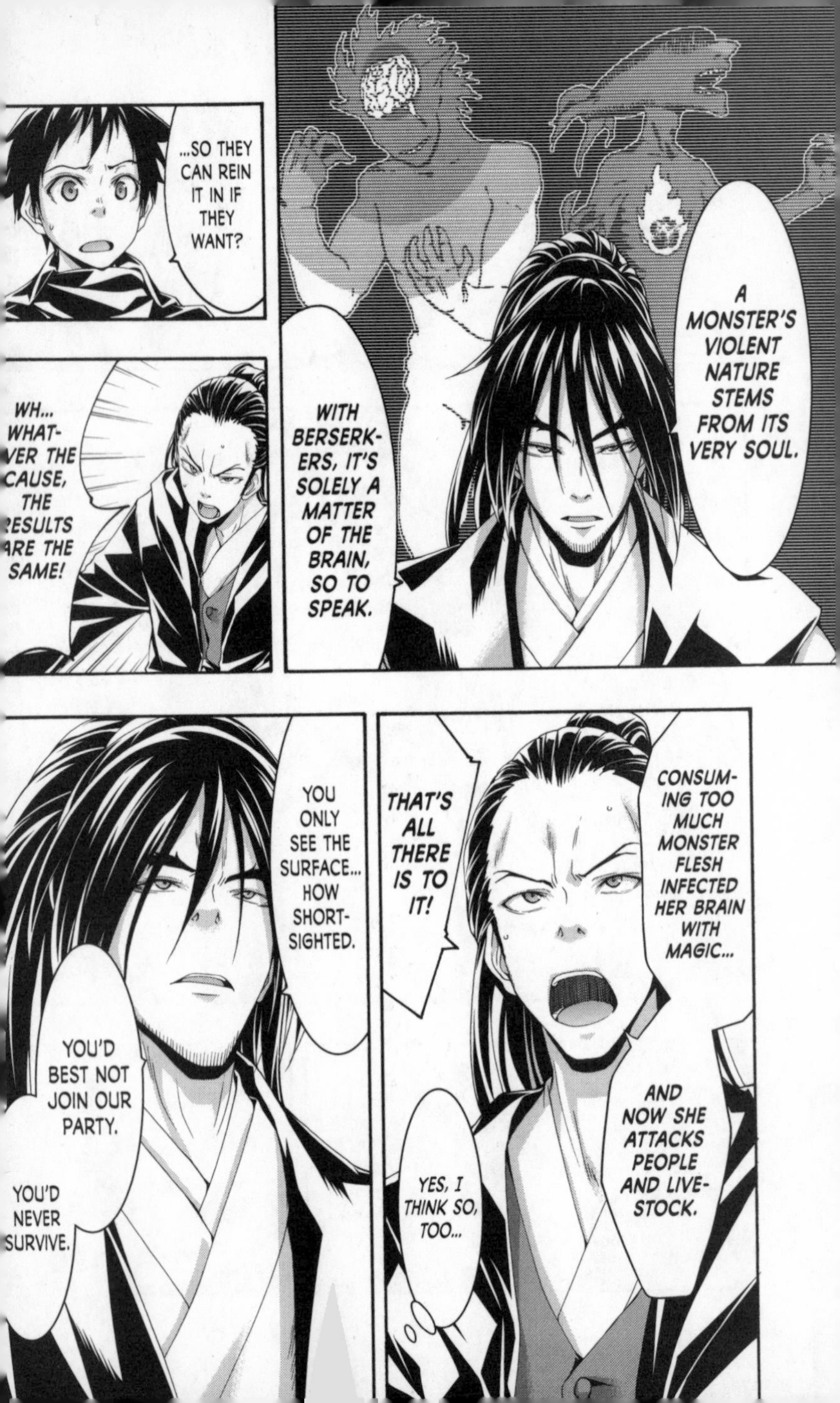
A MONSTER'S VIOLENT NATURE STEMS FROM ITS VERY SOUL.
WITH BERSERKERS, IT'S SOLELY A MATTER OF THE BRAIN, SO TO SPEAK.
...SO THEY CAN REIN IT IN IF THEY WANT?
WH... WHATEVER THE CAUSE, THE RESULTS ARE THE SAME!
CONSUMING TOO MUCH MONSTER FLESH INFECTED HER BRAIN WITH MAGIC...
AND NOW SHE ATTACKS PEOPLE AND LIVESTOCK.
THAT'S ALL THERE IS TO IT!
YES, I THINK SO, TOO...
YOU ONLY SEE THE SURFACE... HOW SHORTSIGHTED.
YOU'D BEST NOT JOIN OUR PARTY.
YOU'D NEVER SURVIVE.

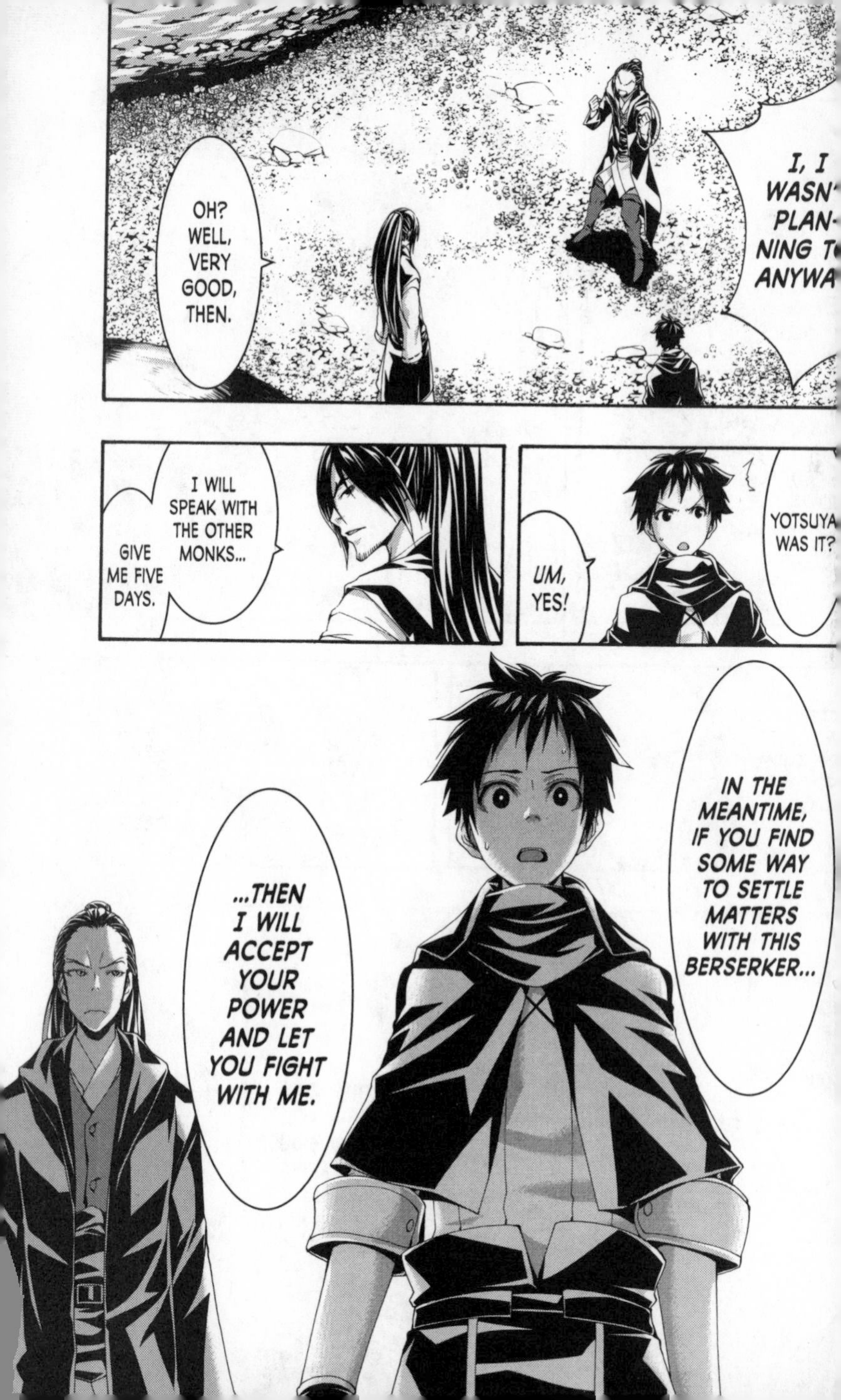

I, I WASN' PLAN-NING T ANYWA
OH? WELL, VERY GOOD, THEN.
YOTSUYA WAS IT?
UM, YES!
I WILL SPEAK WITH THE OTHER MONKS...
GIVE ME FIVE DAYS.
IN THE MEANTIME, IF YOU FIND SOME WAY TO SETTLE MATTERS WITH THIS BERSERKER...
...THEN I WILL ACCEPT YOUR POWER AND LET YOU FIGHT WITH ME.

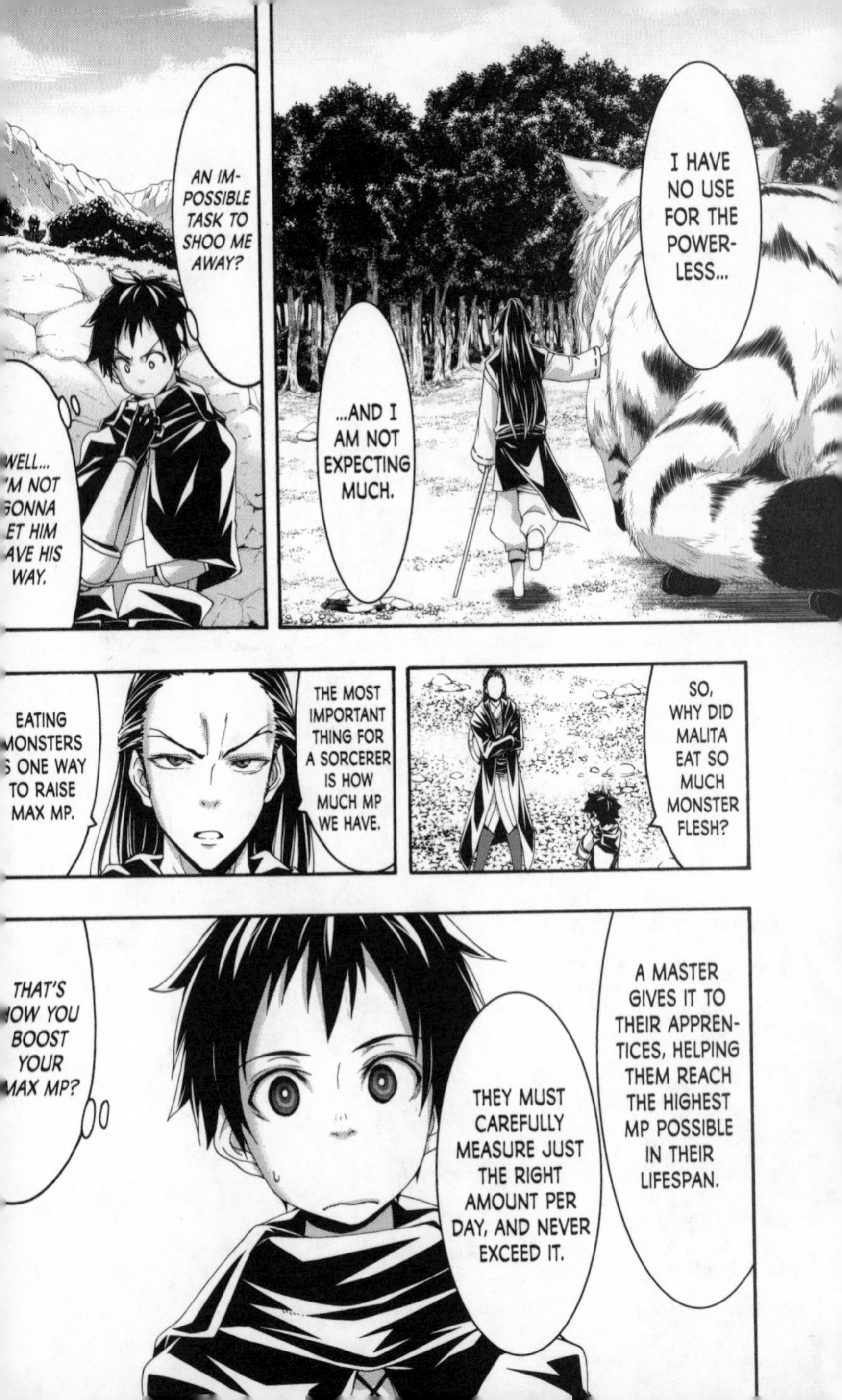

I HAVE NO USE FOR THE POWER-LESS...
...AND I AM NOT EXPECTING MUCH.
AN IM-POSSIBLE TASK TO SHOO ME AWAY?
WELL... 'M NOT GONNA ET HIM AVE HIS WAY.
SO, WHY DID MALITA EAT SO MUCH MONSTER FLESH?
THE MOST IMPORTANT THING FOR A SORCERER IS HOW MUCH MP WE HAVE.
EATING MONSTERS S ONE WAY TO RAISE MAX MP.
A MASTER GIVES IT TO THEIR APPREN-TICES, HELPING THEM REACH THE HIGHEST MP POSSIBLE IN THEIR LIFESPAN.
THEY MUST CAREFULLY MEASURE JUST THE RIGHT AMOUNT PER DAY, AND NEVER EXCEED IT.
THAT'S OW YOU BOOST YOUR AX MP?

SHE *WAS?* WHY?!

...BUT IN THIS CASE, SHE WAS SNEAKING MEAT ON THE SIDE.

SO IF *THIS* BEFALL AN AP PRENTI IT'S SE AS TH MASTER ERROR

...

ASK HER...

N IDE

...IF YOU TRULY THINK YOU *CAN.*

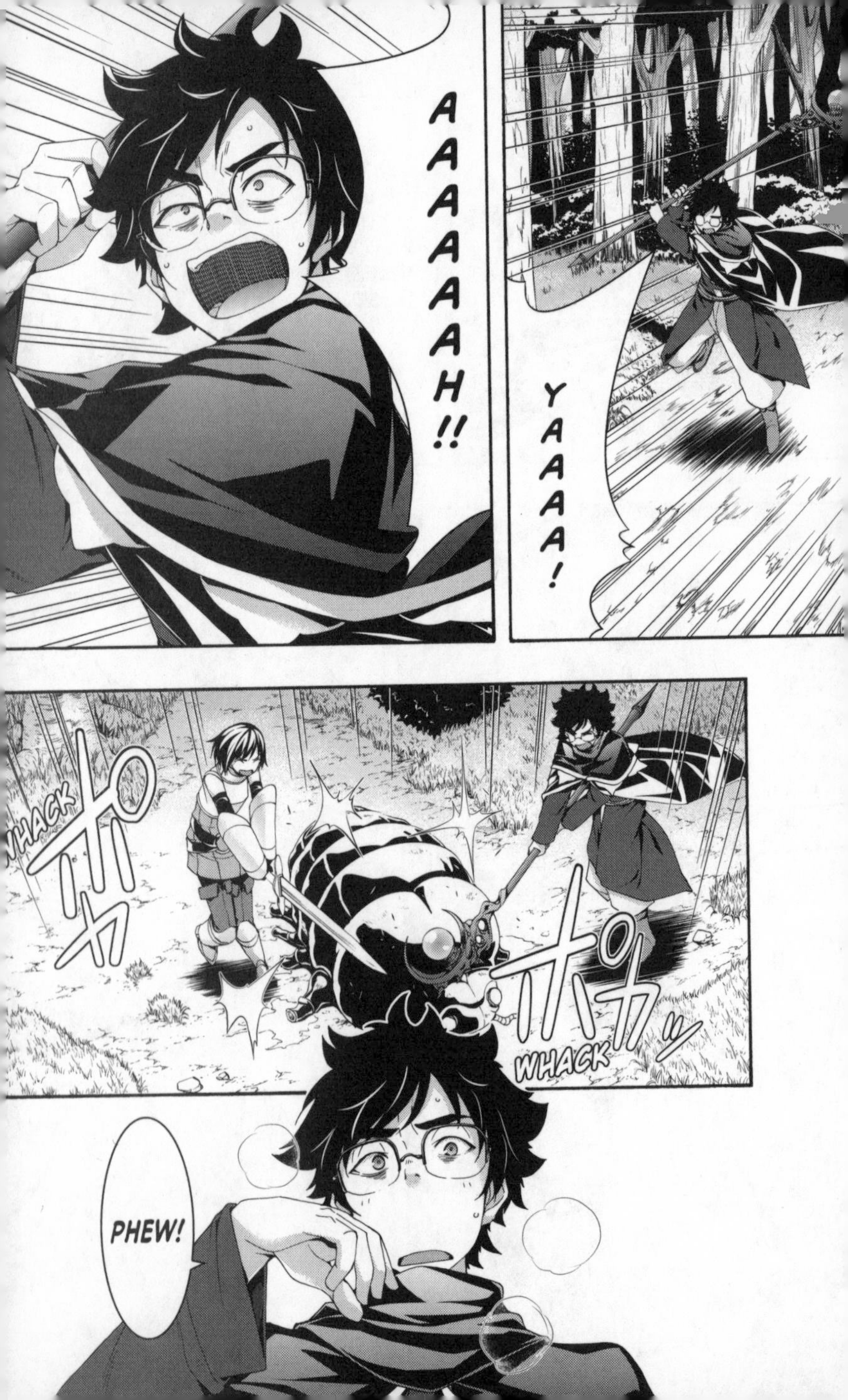
YAAAAA!
AAAAAAAH!!
WHACK
WHACK
PHEW!

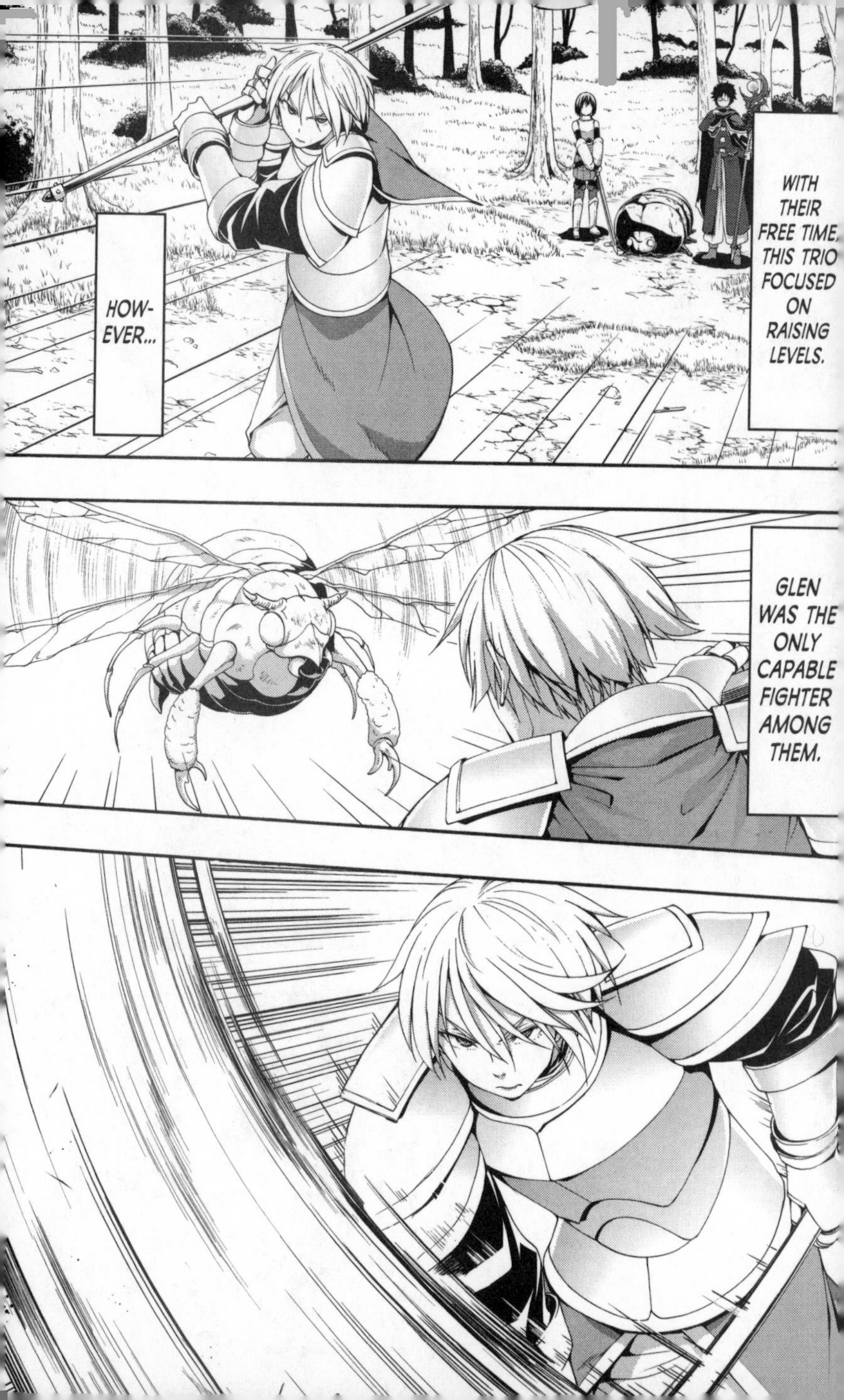
WITH THEIR FREE TIME, THIS TRIO FOCUSED ON RAISING LEVELS.
HOW-EVER...
GLEN WAS THE ONLY CAPABLE FIGHTER AMONG THEM.

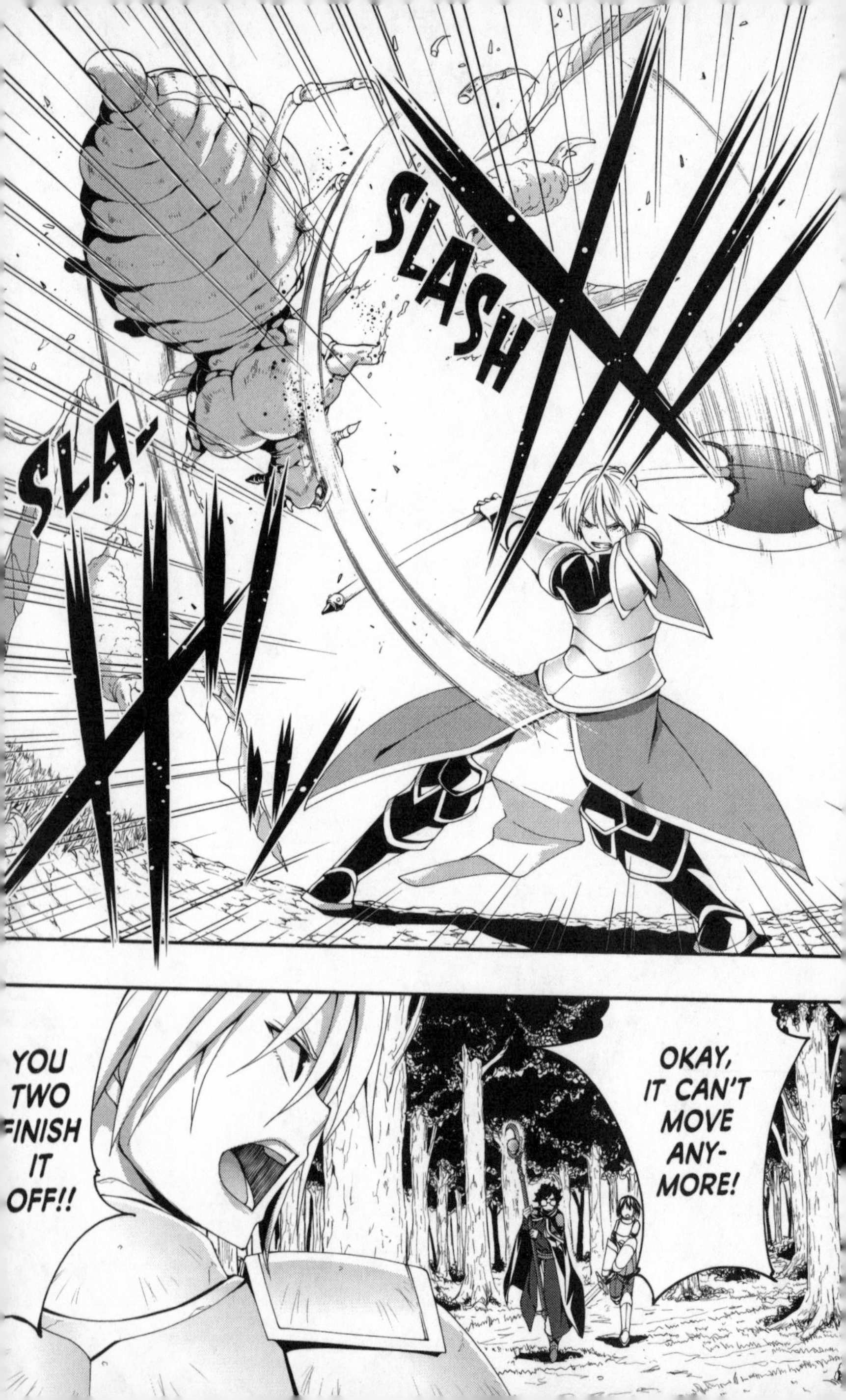
SLASH
SLA-
OKAY, IT CAN'T MOVE ANY-MORE!
YOU TWO FINISH IT OFF!!

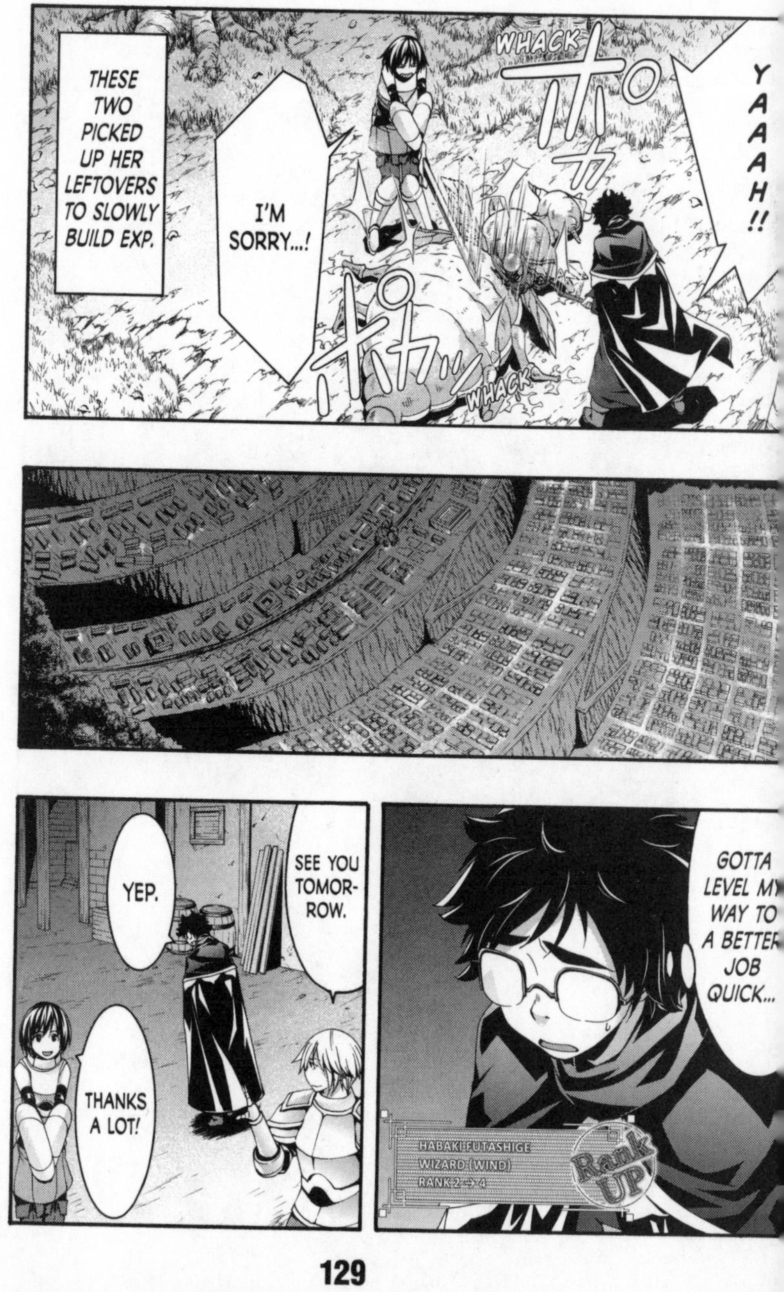
YAAAAH!!
WHACK
WHACK
I'M SORRY...!
THESE TWO PICKED UP HER LEFTOVERS TO SLOWLY BUILD EXP.
GOTTA LEVEL MY WAY TO A BETTER JOB QUICK...
HABAKI FUTASHIGE
WIZARD (WIND)
RANK 2 → 4
Rank UP
SEE YOU TOMOR-ROW.
YEP.
THANKS A LOT!

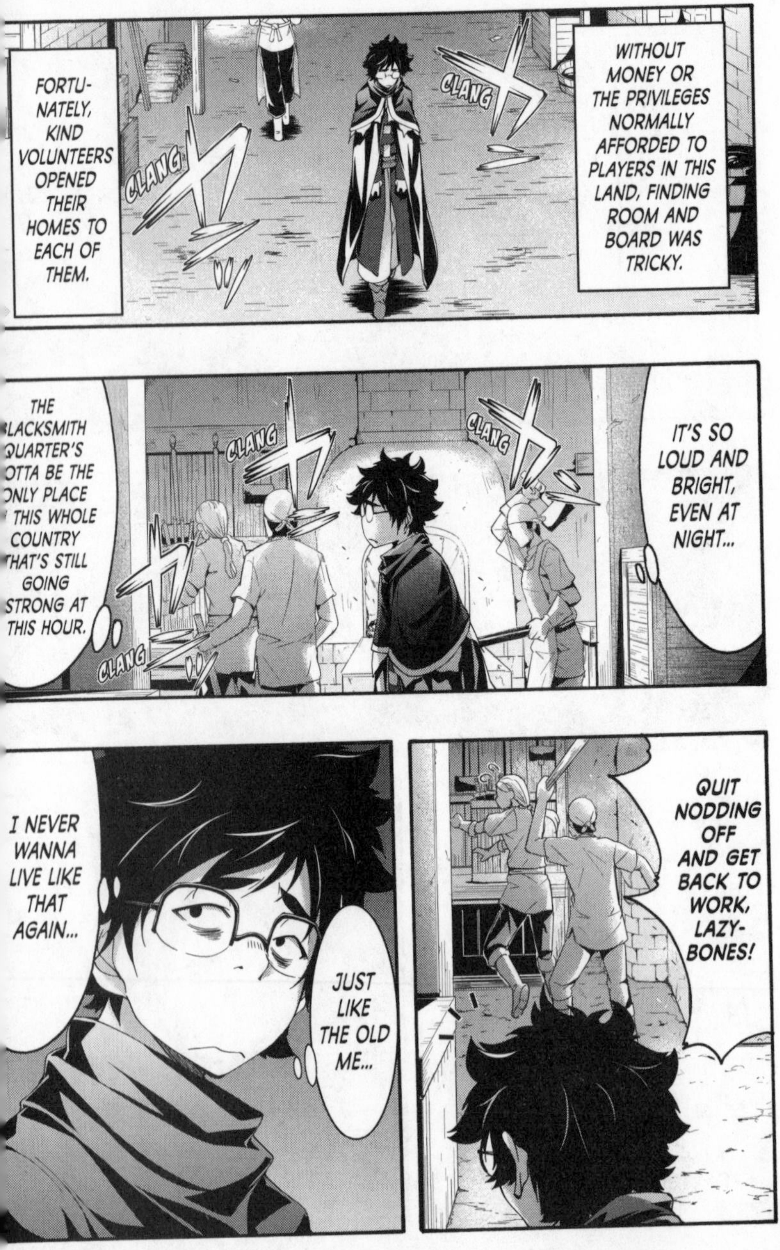
WITHOUT MONEY OR THE PRIVILEGES NORMALLY AFFORDED TO PLAYERS IN THIS LAND, FINDING ROOM AND BOARD WAS TRICKY.
CLANG
CLANG
FORTU-NATELY, KIND VOLUNTEERS OPENED THEIR HOMES TO EACH OF THEM.
IT'S SO LOUD AND BRIGHT, EVEN AT NIGHT...
CLANG
CLANG
CLANG
THE LACKSMITH QUARTER'S OTTA BE THE NLY PLACE THIS WHOLE COUNTRY HAT'S STILL GOING STRONG AT THIS HOUR.
QUIT NODDING OFF AND GET BACK TO WORK, LAZY-BONES!
JUST LIKE THE OLD ME...
I NEVER WANNA LIVE LIKE THAT AGAIN...

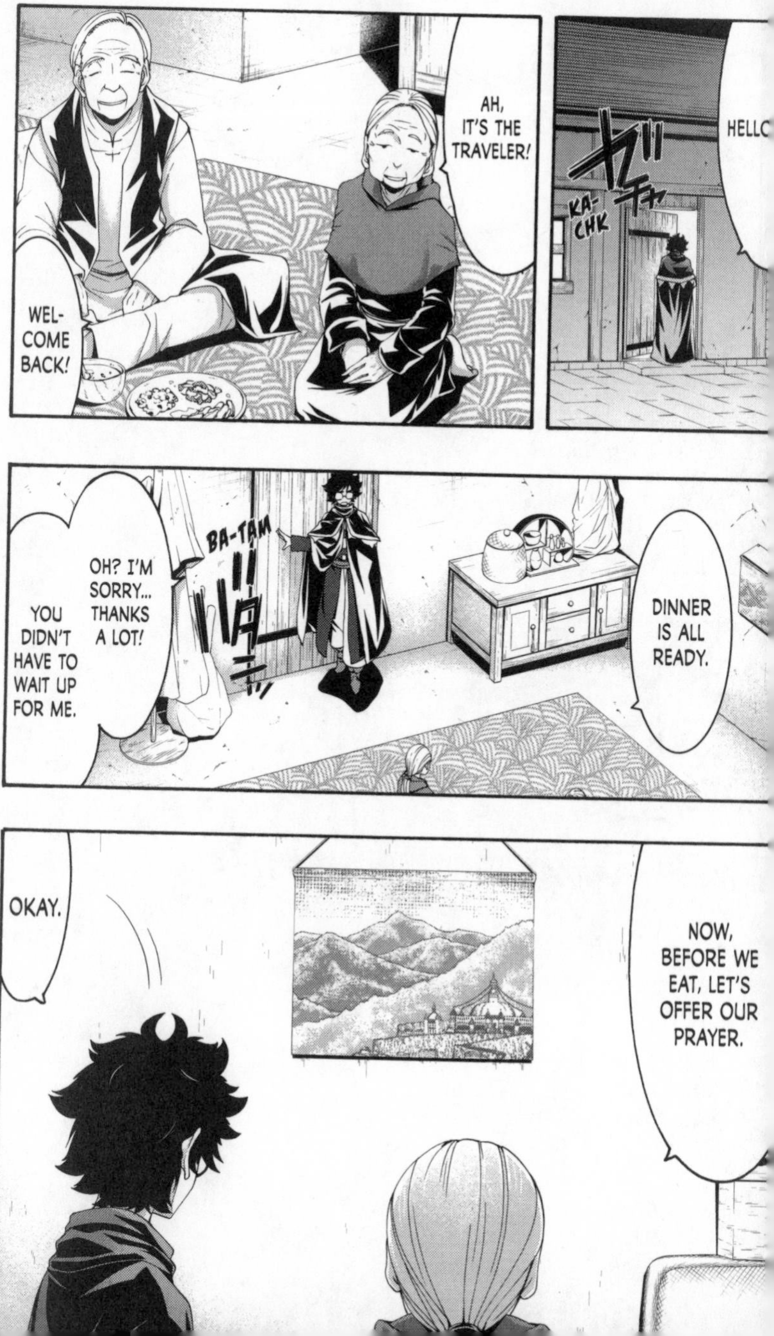
HELLO
KA-CHK
AH, IT'S THE TRAVELER!
WEL-COME BACK!
BA-TAM
DINNER IS ALL READY.
OH? I'M SORRY... THANKS A LOT!
YOU DIDN'T HAVE TO WAIT UP FOR ME.
NOW, BEFORE WE EAT, LET'S OFFER OUR PRAYER.
OKAY.

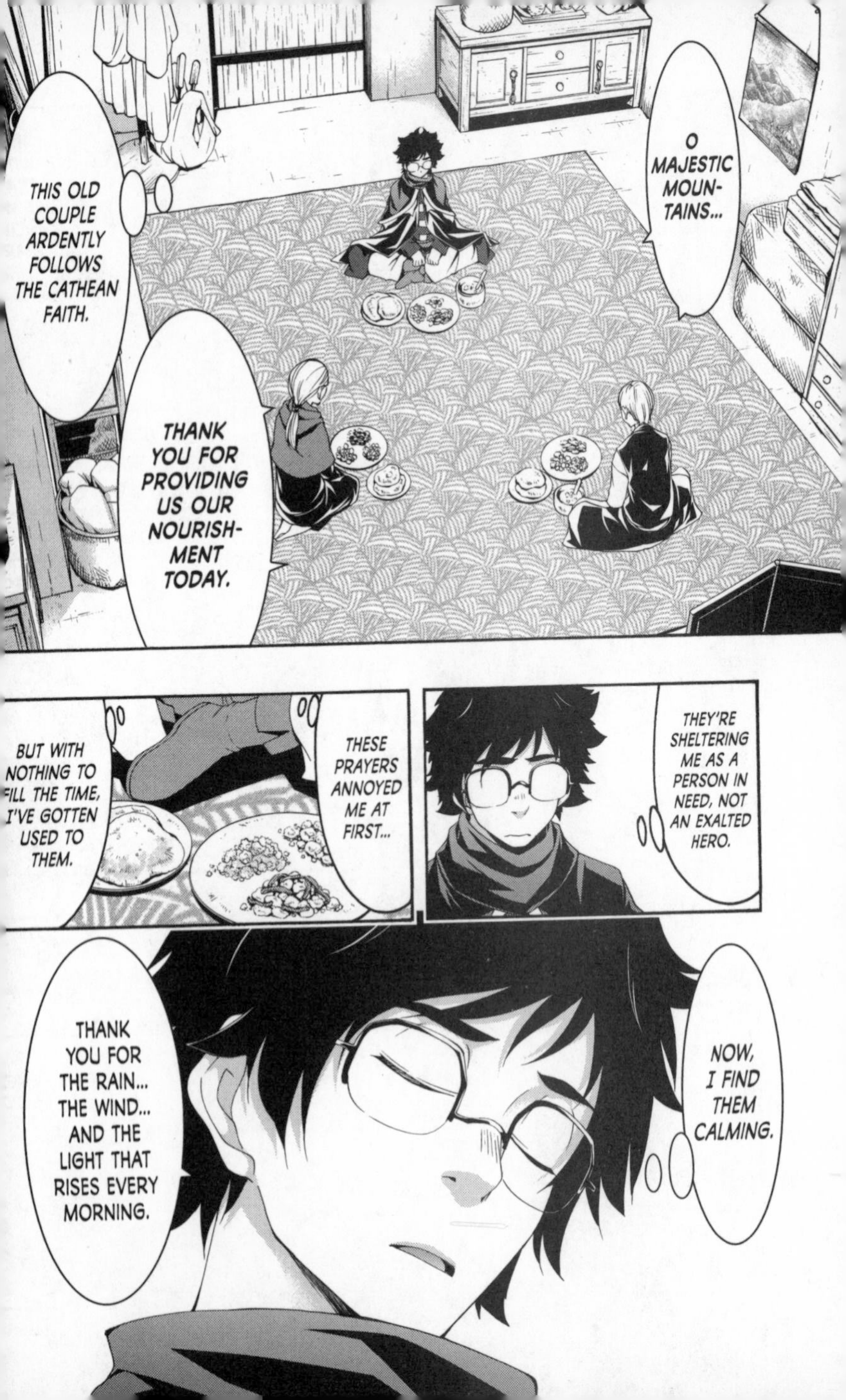
O MAJESTIC MOUNTAINS...
THANK YOU FOR PROVIDING US OUR NOURISHMENT TODAY.
THIS OLD COUPLE ARDENTLY FOLLOWS THE CATHEAN FAITH.
THEY'RE SHELTERING ME AS A PERSON IN NEED, NOT AN EXALTED HERO.
THESE PRAYERS ANNOYED ME AT FIRST...
BUT WITH NOTHING TO FILL THE TIME, I'VE GOTTEN USED TO THEM.
NOW, I FIND THEM CALMING.
THANK YOU FOR THE RAIN... THE WIND... AND THE LIGHT THAT RISES EVERY MORNING.

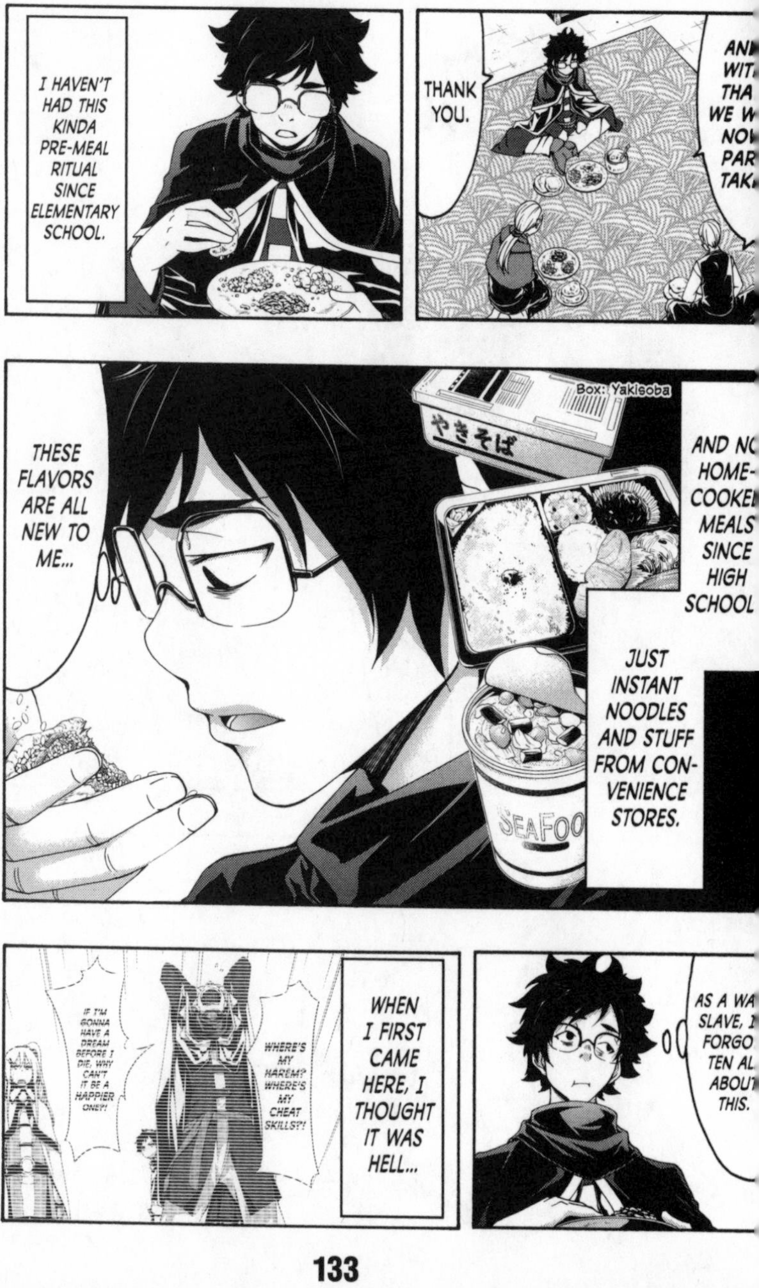
AN WIT THA WE W NO PAR TAK
THANK YOU.
I HAVEN'T HAD THIS KINDA PRE-MEAL RITUAL SINCE ELEMENTARY SCHOOL.
AND NO HOME-COOKE MEALS SINCE HIGH SCHOOL
JUST INSTANT NOODLES AND STUFF FROM CON-VENIENCE STORES.
Box: Yakisoba
やきそば
SEAFOO
THESE FLAVORS ARE ALL NEW TO ME...
AS A WA SLAVE, I FORGO TEN AL ABOUT THIS.
WHEN I FIRST CAME HERE, I THOUGHT IT WAS HELL...
WHERE'S MY HAREM? WHERE'S MY CHEAT SKILLS?!
IF I'M GONNA HAVE A DREAM BEFORE I DIE, WHY CAN'T IT BE A HAPPIER ONE?!

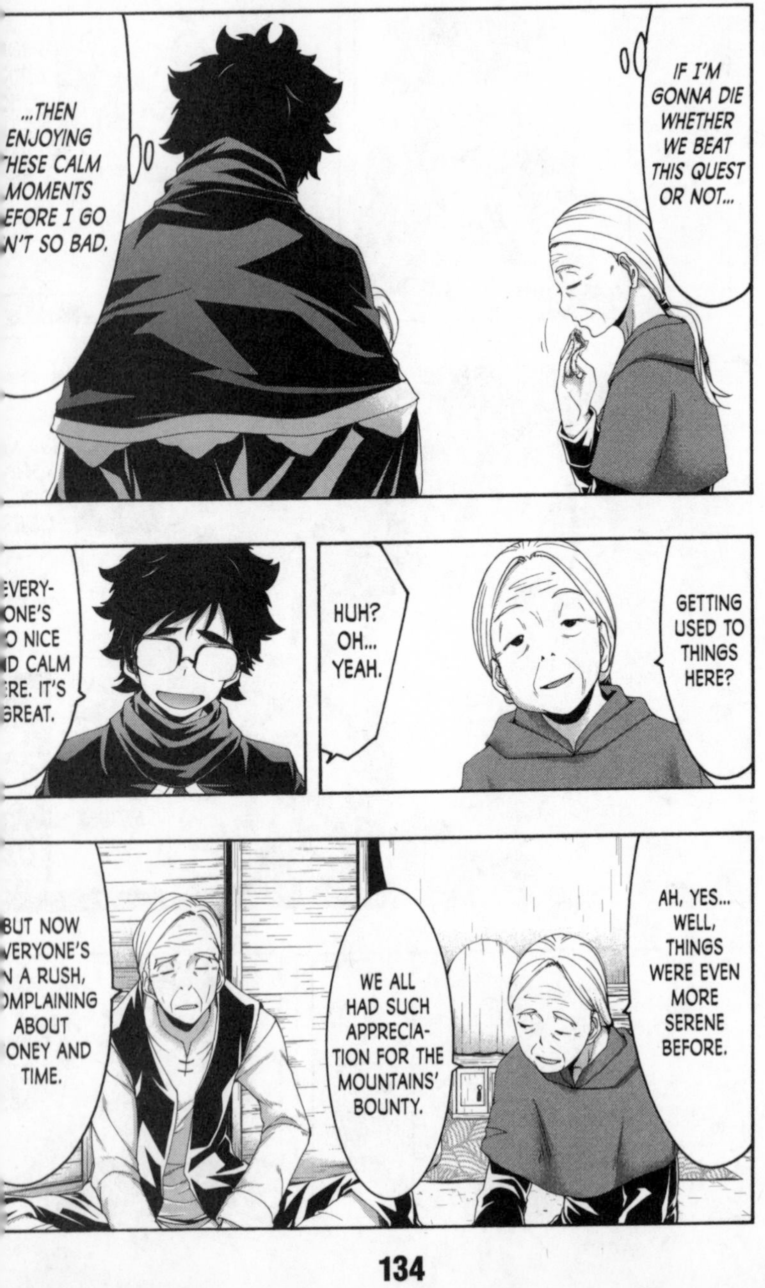
IF I'M GONNA DIE WHETHER WE BEAT THIS QUEST OR NOT...
...THEN ENJOYING 'HESE CALM MOMENTS EFORE I GO N'T SO BAD.
GETTING USED TO THINGS HERE?
HUH? OH... YEAH.
EVERY-ONE'S O NICE D CALM ERE. IT'S GREAT.
AH, YES... WELL, THINGS WERE EVEN MORE SERENE BEFORE.
WE ALL HAD SUCH APPRECIA-TION FOR THE MOUNTAINS' BOUNTY.
BUT NOW VERYONE'S N A RUSH, OMPLAINING ABOUT ONEY AND TIME.

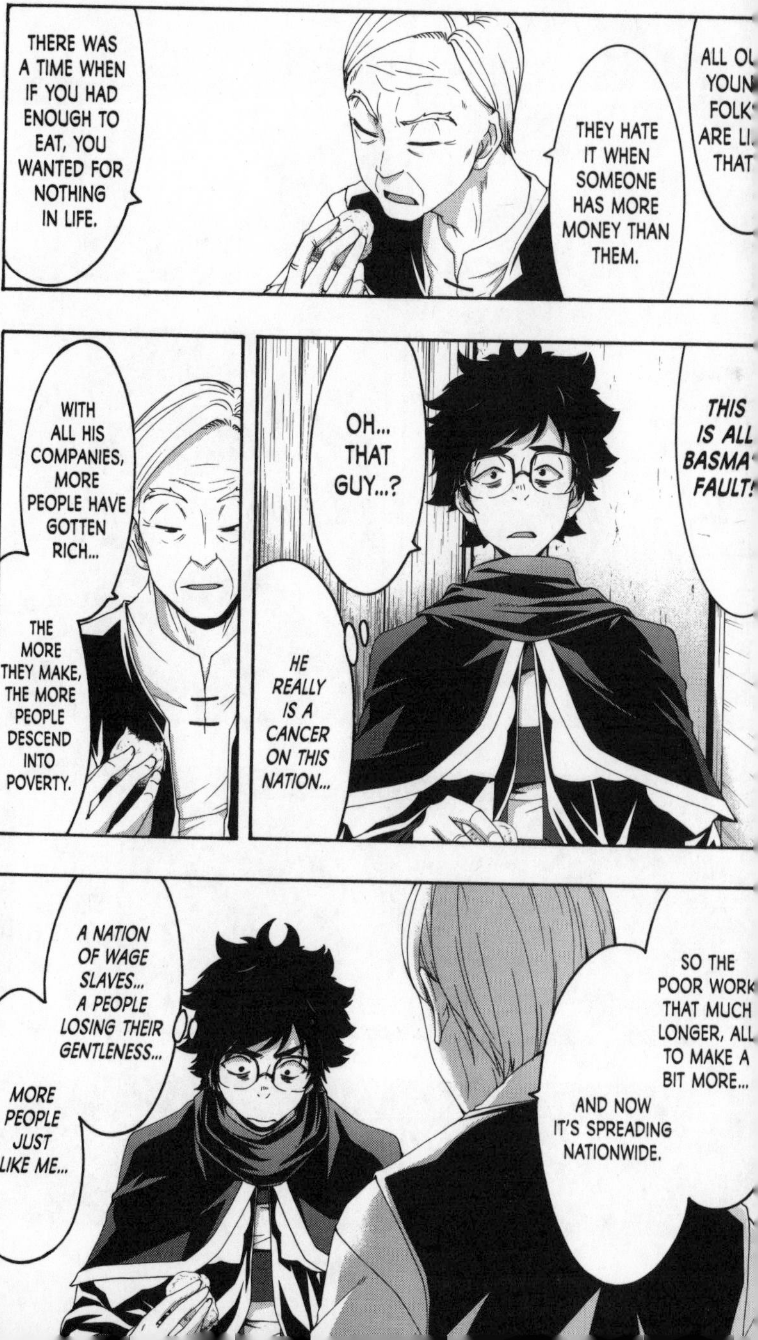
ALL OU YOUN FOLK ARE LI THAT
THEY HATE IT WHEN SOMEONE HAS MORE MONEY THAN THEM.
THERE WAS A TIME WHEN IF YOU HAD ENOUGH TO EAT, YOU WANTED FOR NOTHING IN LIFE.
THIS IS ALL BASMA FAULT!
OH... THAT GUY...?
HE REALLY IS A CANCER ON THIS NATION...
WITH ALL HIS COMPANIES, MORE PEOPLE HAVE GOTTEN RICH...
THE MORE THEY MAKE, THE MORE PEOPLE DESCEND INTO POVERTY.
SO THE POOR WORK THAT MUCH LONGER, ALL TO MAKE A BIT MORE...
AND NOW IT'S SPREADING NATIONWIDE.
A NATION OF WAGE SLAVES... A PEOPLE LOSING THEIR GENTLENESS...
MORE PEOPLE JUST LIKE ME...

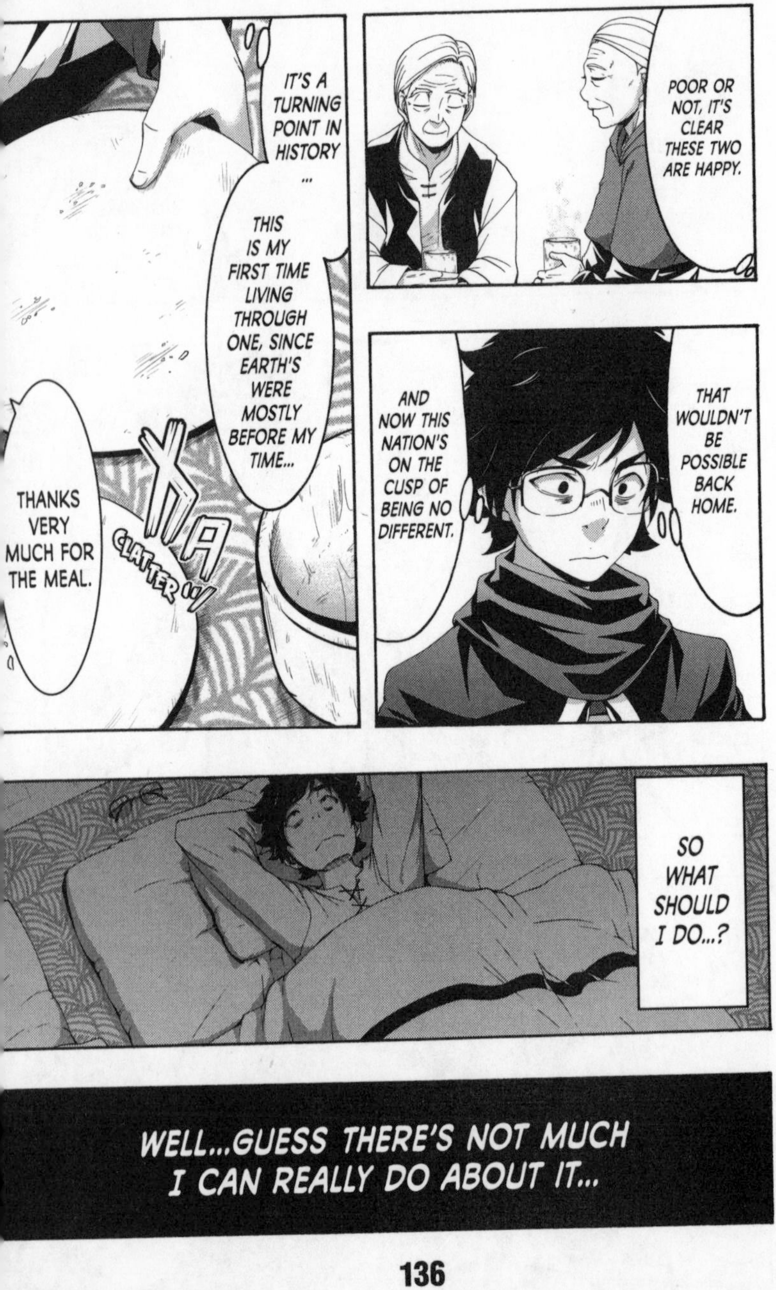
POOR OR NOT, IT'S CLEAR THESE TWO ARE HAPPY.
THAT WOULDN'T BE POSSIBLE BACK HOME.
AND NOW THIS NATION'S ON THE CUSP OF BEING NO DIFFERENT.
IT'S A TURNING POINT IN HISTORY ...
THIS IS MY FIRST TIME LIVING THROUGH ONE, SINCE EARTH'S WERE MOSTLY BEFORE MY TIME...
THANKS VERY MUCH FOR THE MEAL.
CLATTER
SO WHAT SHOULD I DO...?
WELL...GUESS THERE'S NOT MUCH I CAN REALLY DO ABOUT IT...

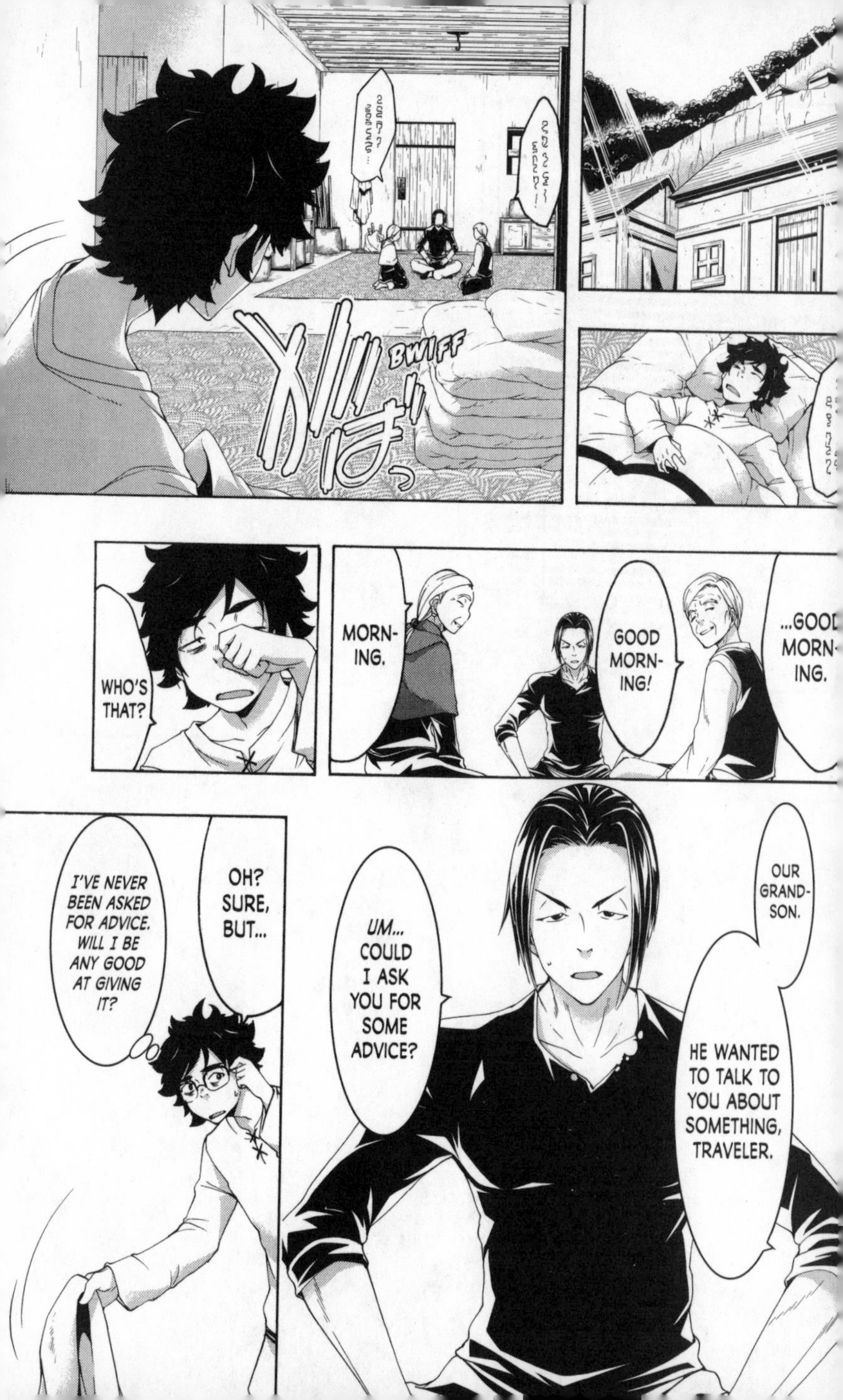

がばっ
BWIFF
...GOOD MORNING.
GOOD MORNING!
MORNING.
WHO'S THAT?
OUR GRANDSON.
HE WANTED TO TALK TO YOU ABOUT SOMETHING, TRAVELER.
UM... COULD I ASK YOU FOR SOME ADVICE?
OH? SURE, BUT...
I'VE NEVER BEEN ASKED FOR ADVICE. WILL I BE ANY GOOD AT GIVING IT?

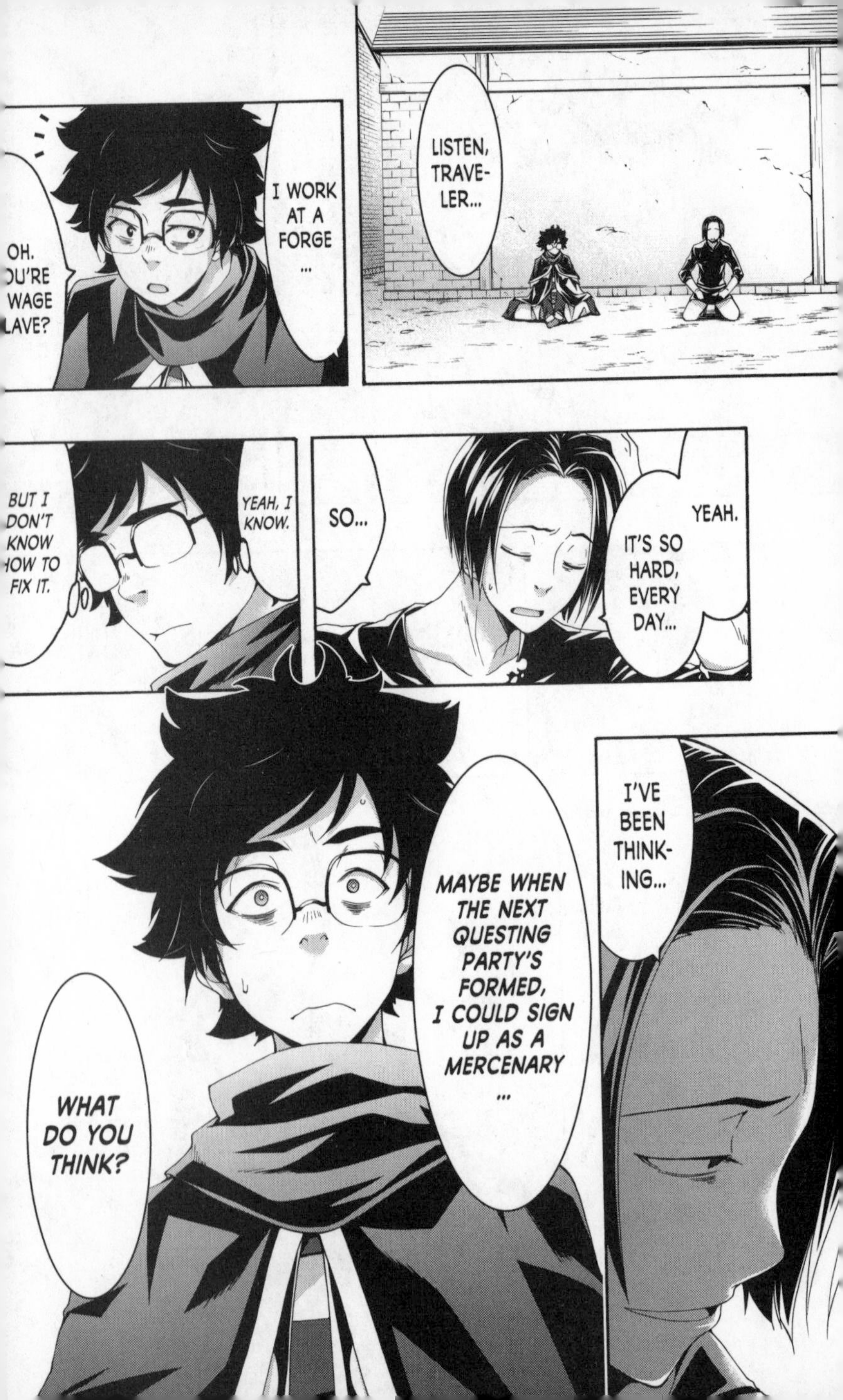
LISTEN, TRAVELER...
I WORK AT A FORGE...
OH. U'RE WAGE LAVE?
YEAH. IT'S SO HARD, EVERY DAY...
SO...
YEAH, I KNOW.
BUT I DON'T KNOW HOW TO FIX IT.
I'VE BEEN THINKING...
MAYBE WHEN THE NEXT QUESTING PARTY'S FORMED, I COULD SIGN UP AS A MERCENARY...
WHAT DO YOU THINK?

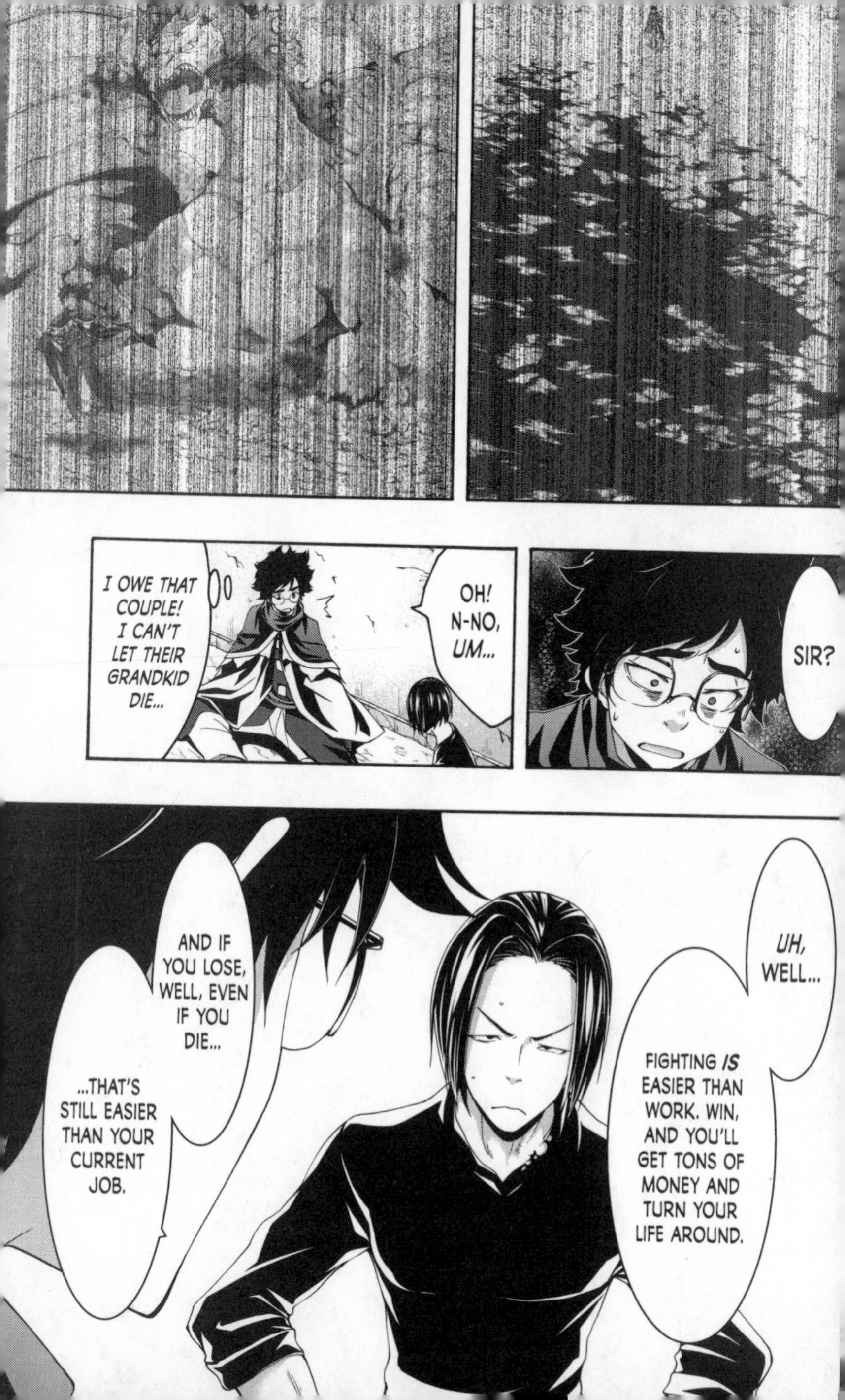
SIR?
OH! N-NO, UM...
I OWE THAT COUPLE! I CAN'T LET THEIR GRANDKID DIE...
UH, WELL...
FIGHTING IS EASIER THAN WORK. WIN, AND YOU'LL GET TONS OF MONEY AND TURN YOUR LIFE AROUND.
AND IF YOU LOSE, WELL, EVEN IF YOU DIE...
...THAT'S STILL EASIER THAN YOUR CURRENT JOB.

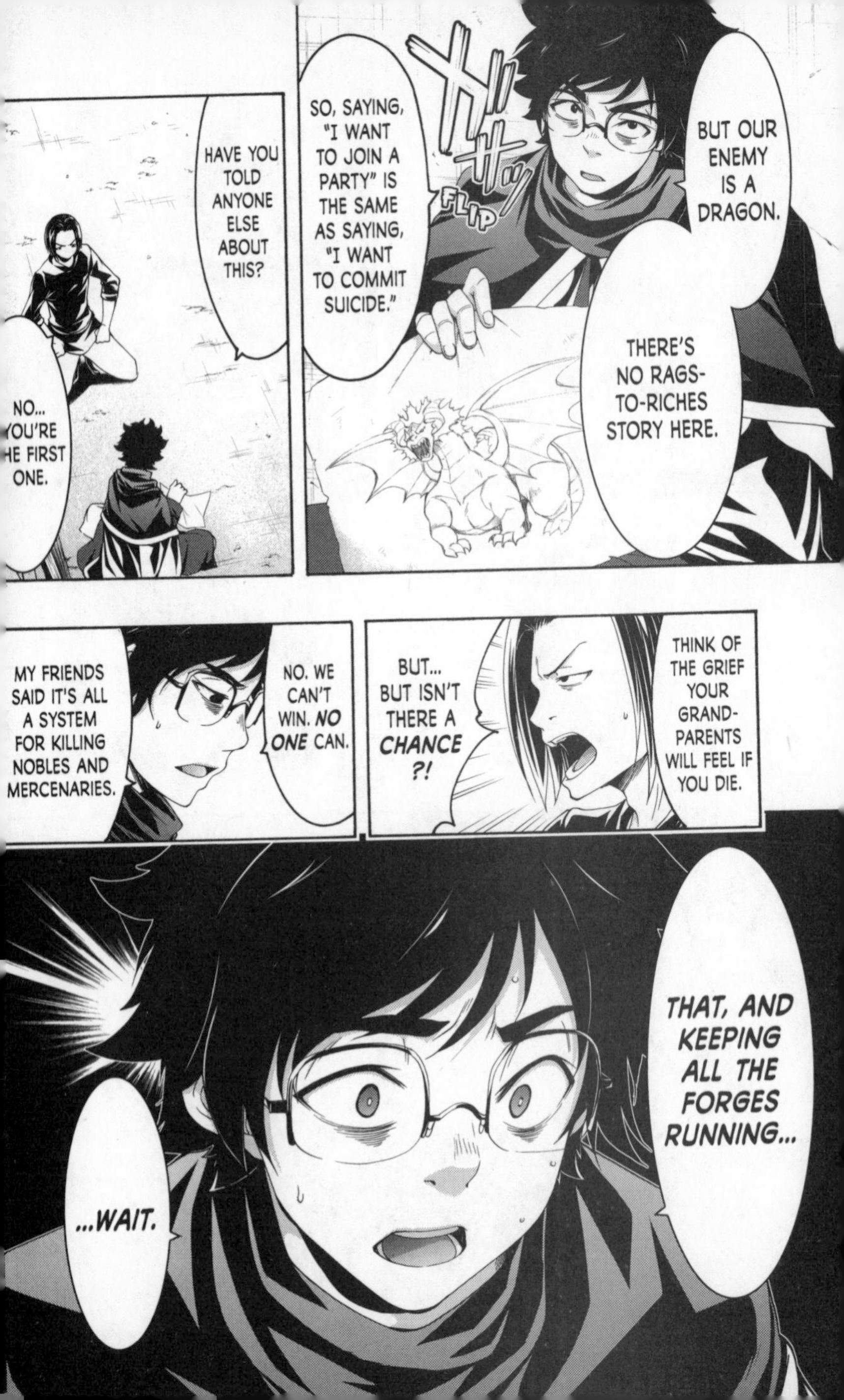
BUT OUR ENEMY IS A DRAGON.
FLIP
THERE'S NO RAGS-TO-RICHES STORY HERE.
SO, SAYING, "I WANT TO JOIN A PARTY" IS THE SAME AS SAYING, "I WANT TO COMMIT SUICIDE."
HAVE YOU TOLD ANYONE ELSE ABOUT THIS?
NO... YOU'RE HE FIRST ONE.
THINK OF THE GRIEF YOUR GRAND-PARENTS WILL FEEL IF YOU DIE.
BUT... BUT ISN'T THERE A *CHANCE* ?!
NO. WE CAN'T WIN. *NO ONE* CAN.
MY FRIENDS SAID IT'S ALL A SYSTEM FOR KILLING NOBLES AND MERCENARIES.
THAT, AND KEEPING ALL THE FORGES RUNNING...
...WAIT.

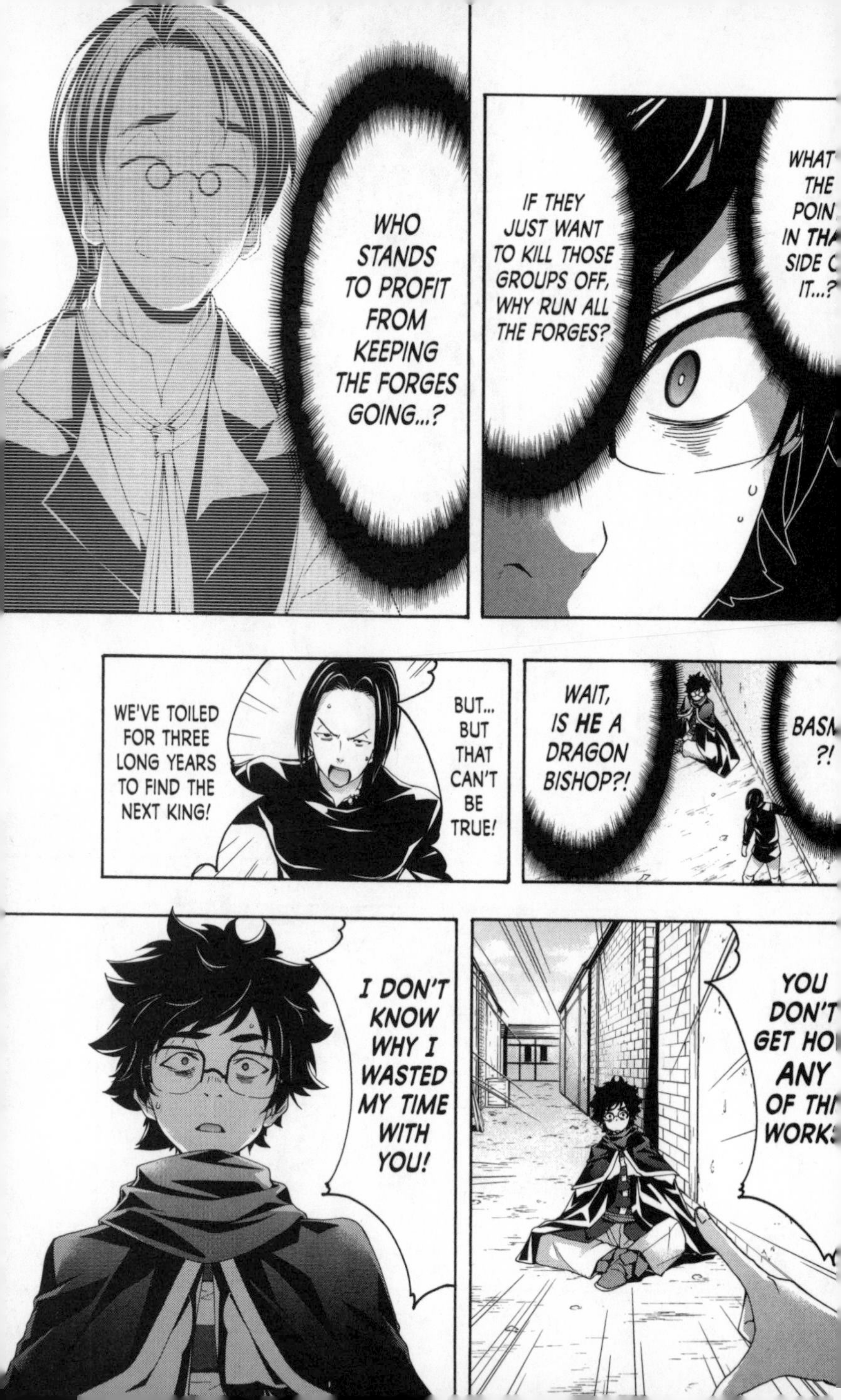
WHAT THE POIN IN THA SIDE C IT...?
IF THEY JUST WANT TO KILL THOSE GROUPS OFF, WHY RUN ALL THE FORGES?
WHO STANDS TO PROFIT FROM KEEPING THE FORGES GOING...?
BASM ?!
WAIT, IS HE A DRAGON BISHOP?!
BUT... BUT THAT CAN'T BE TRUE!
WE'VE TOILED FOR THREE LONG YEARS TO FIND THE NEXT KING!
YOU DON'T GET HO ANY OF THI WORKS
I DON'T KNOW WHY I WASTED MY TIME WITH YOU!

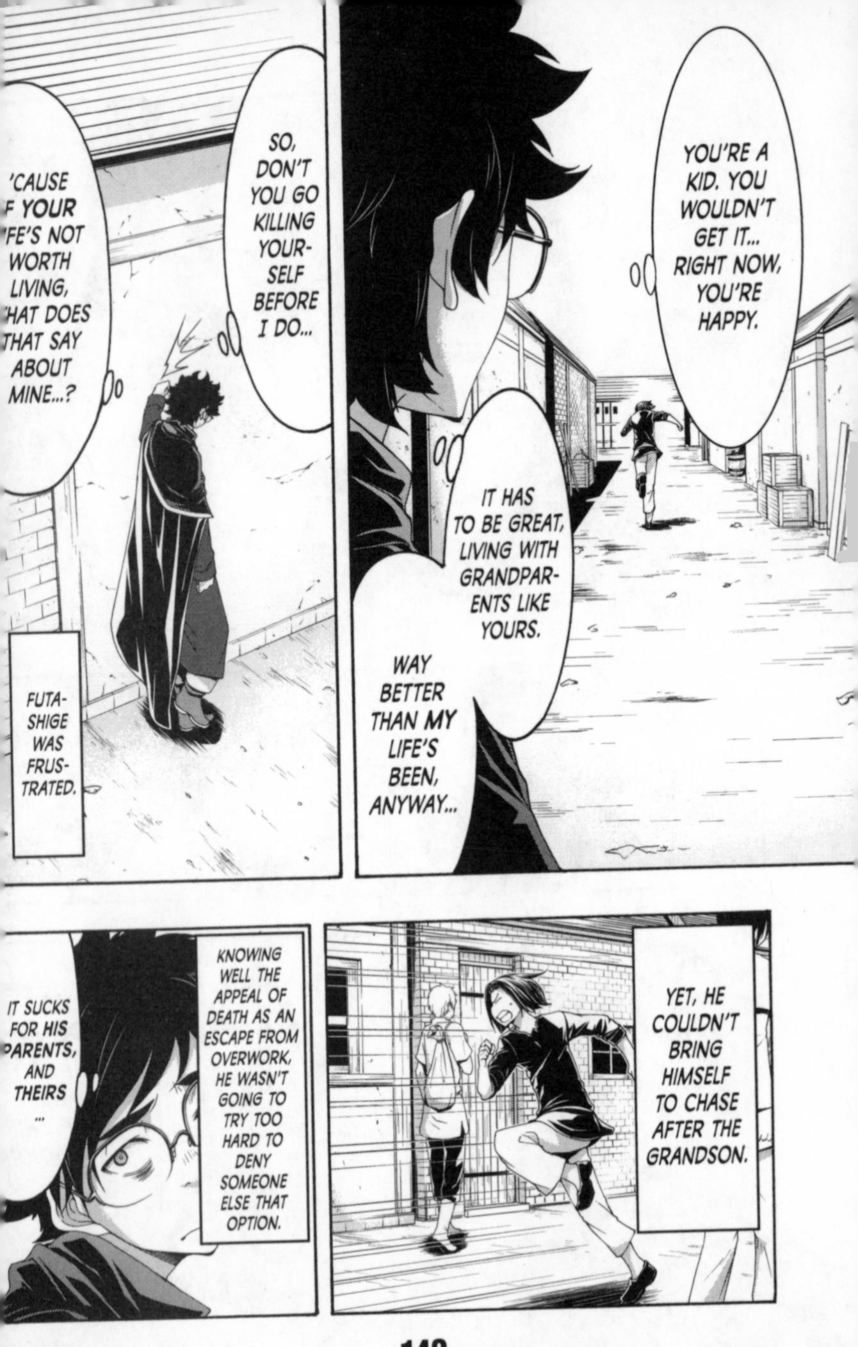
YOU'RE A KID. YOU WOULDN'T GET IT... RIGHT NOW, YOU'RE HAPPY.
IT HAS TO BE GREAT, LIVING WITH GRANDPAR-ENTS LIKE YOURS.
WAY BETTER THAN MY LIFE'S BEEN, ANYWAY...
SO, DON'T YOU GO KILLING YOUR-SELF BEFORE I DO...
'CAUSE F YOUR 'FE'S NOT WORTH LIVING, 'HAT DOES THAT SAY ABOUT MINE...?
FUTA-SHIGE WAS FRUS-TRATED.
YET, HE COULDN'T BRING HIMSELF TO CHASE AFTER THE GRANDSON.
KNOWING WELL THE APPEAL OF DEATH AS AN ESCAPE FROM OVERWORK, HE WASN'T GOING TO TRY TOO HARD TO DENY SOMEONE ELSE THAT OPTION.
IT SUCKS FOR HIS 'ARENTS, AND THEIRS ...

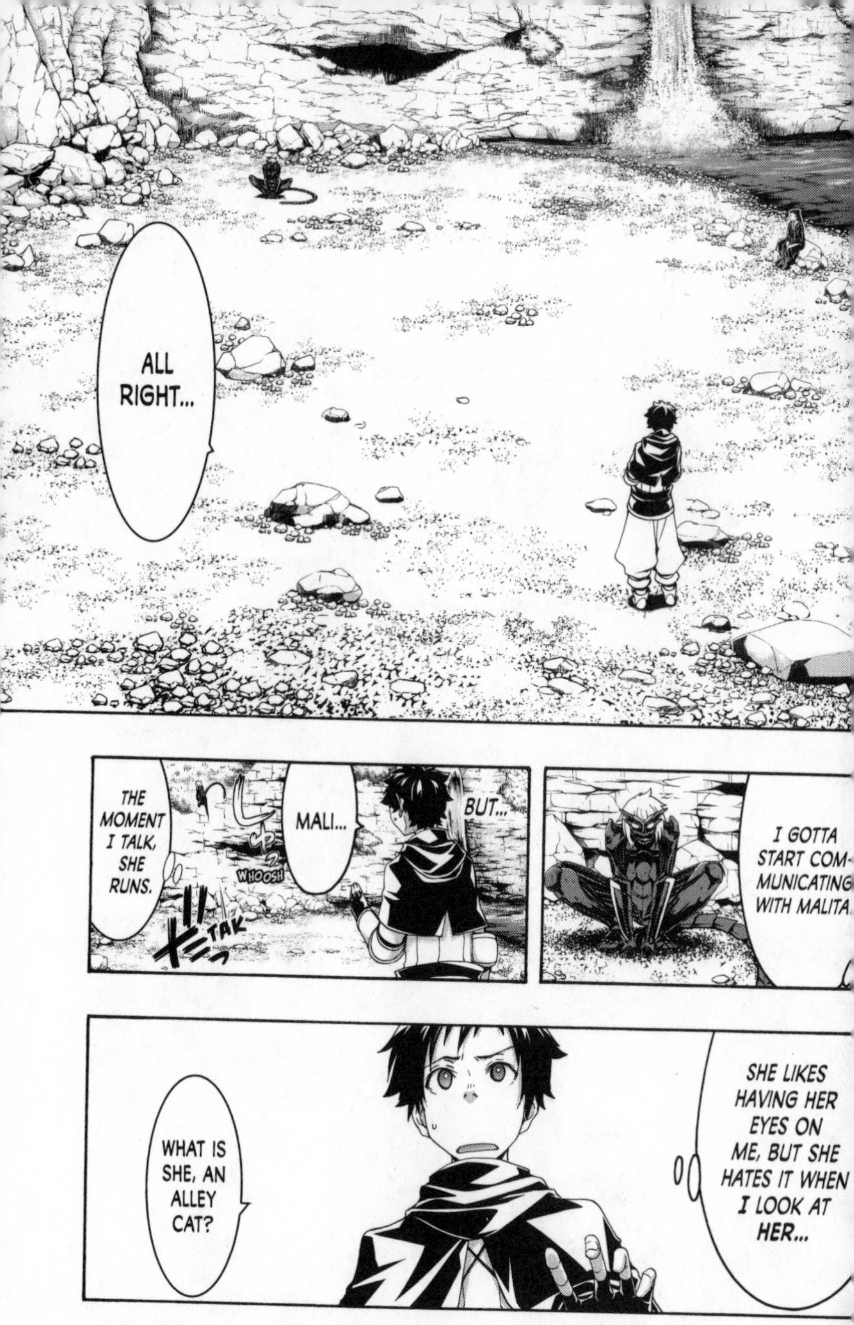
ALL RIGHT...
I GOTTA START COMMUNICATING WITH MALITA.
BUT...
MALI...
WHOOSH
THE MOMENT I TALK, SHE RUNS.
TAK
SHE LIKES HAVING HER EYES ON ME, BUT SHE HATES IT WHEN I LOOK AT HER...
WHAT IS SHE, AN ALLEY CAT?

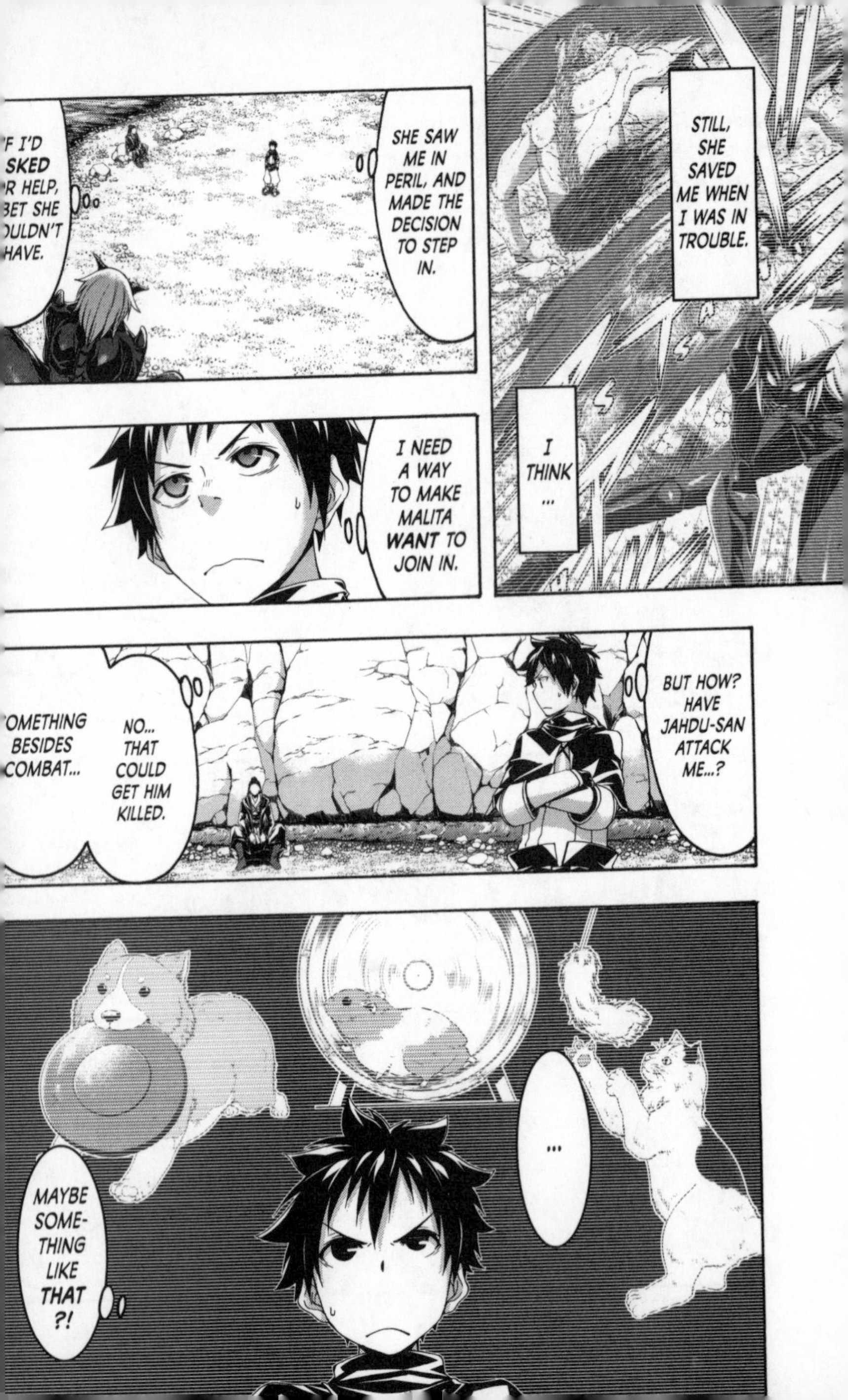
STILL, SHE SAVED ME WHEN I WAS IN TROUBLE.
I THINK...
SHE SAW ME IN PERIL, AND MADE THE DECISION TO STEP IN.
F I'D SKED R HELP, BET SHE ULDN'T HAVE.
I NEED A WAY TO MAKE MALITA WANT TO JOIN IN.
BUT HOW? HAVE JAHDU-SAN ATTACK ME...?
NO... THAT COULD GET HIM KILLED.
OMETHING BESIDES COMBAT...
...
MAYBE SOME-THING LIKE THAT?!

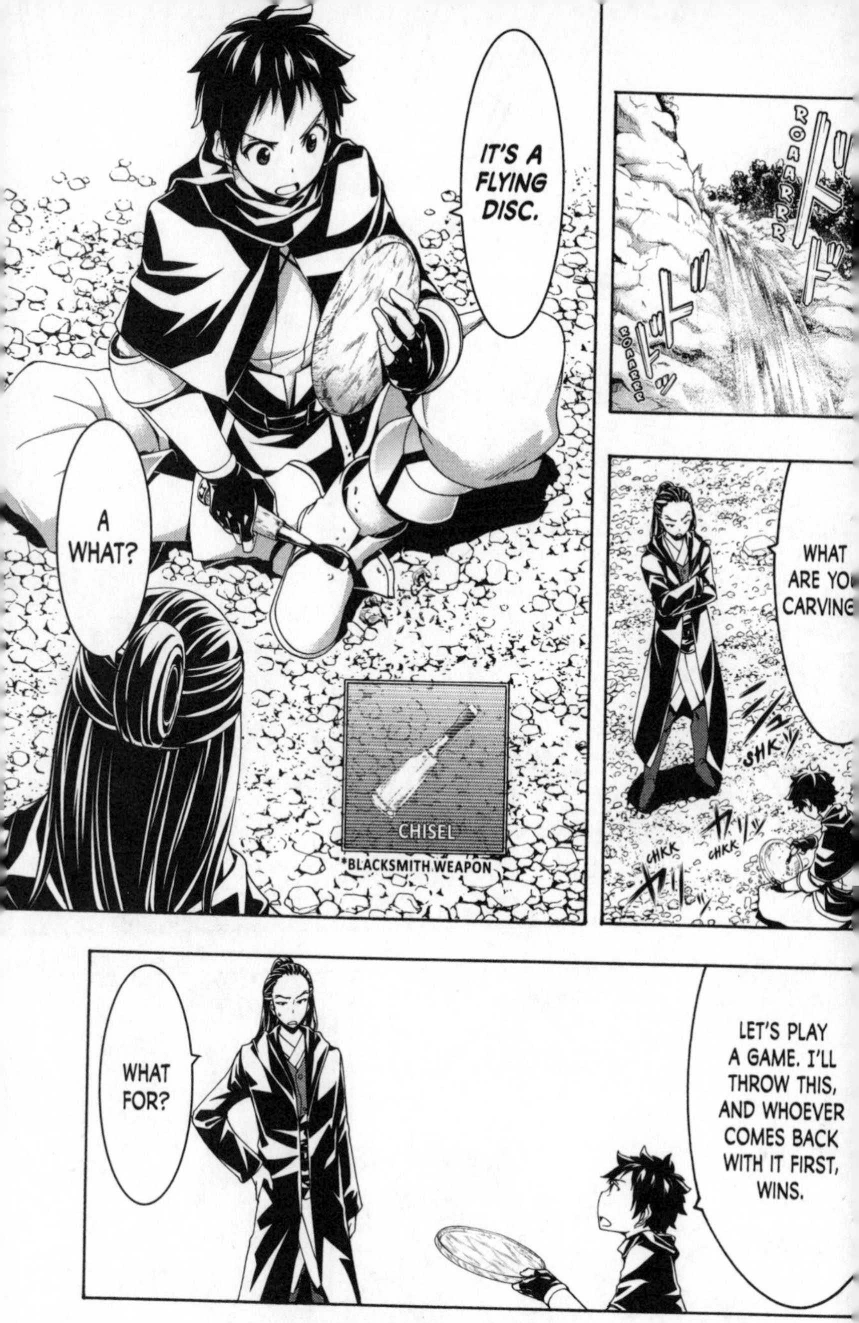
ROAARRR
ROAARRR
WHAT ARE YO CARVING
SHK
CHKK
CHKK
IT'S A FLYING DISC.
A WHAT?
CHISEL
*BLACKSMITH WEAPON
LET'S PLAY A GAME. I'LL THROW THIS, AND WHOEVER COMES BACK WITH IT FIRST, WINS.
WHAT FOR?

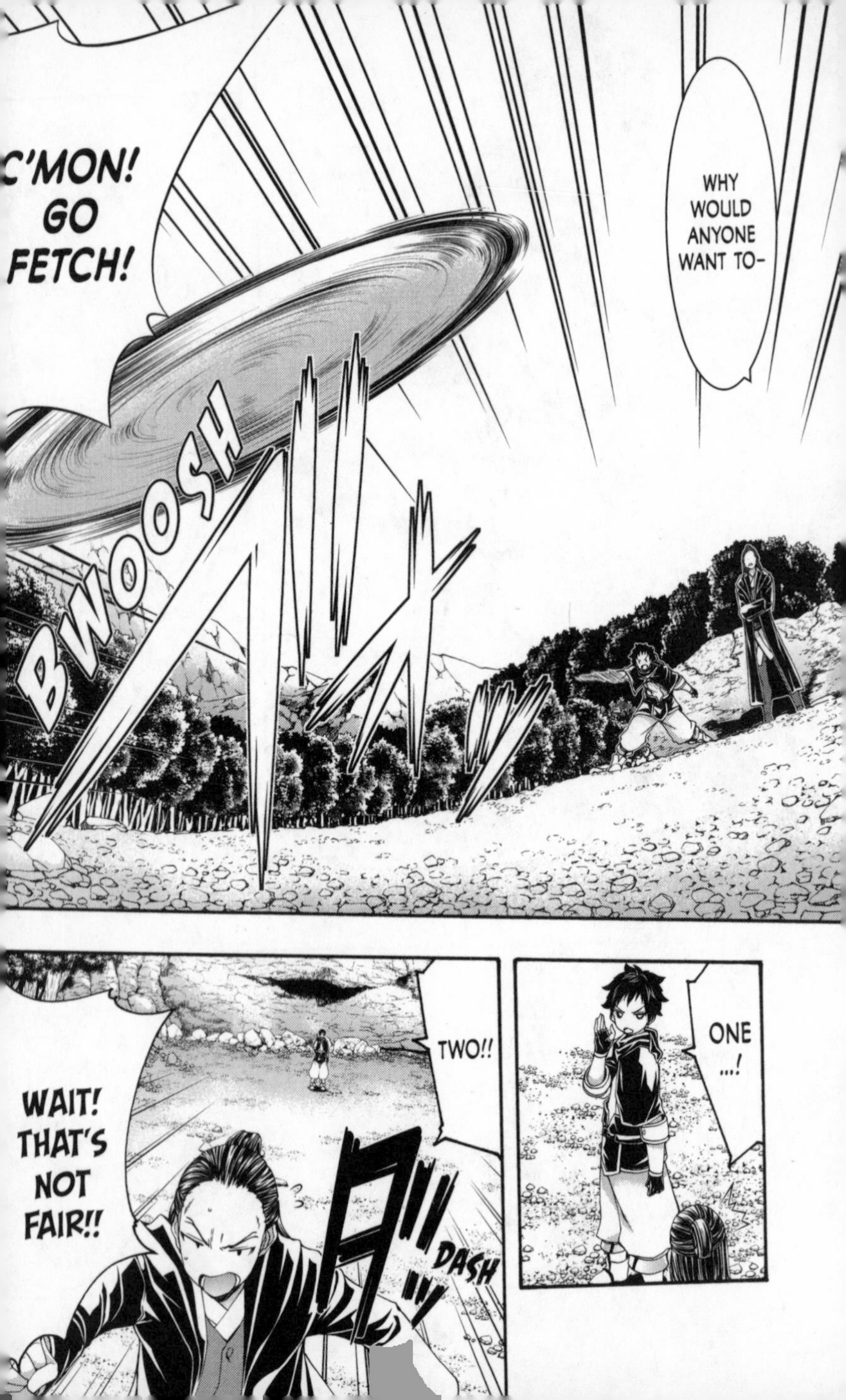

WHY WOULD ANYONE WANT TO-
C'MON! GO FETCH!
BWOOSH
ONE ...!
TWO!!
WAIT! THAT'S NOT FAIR!!
DASH

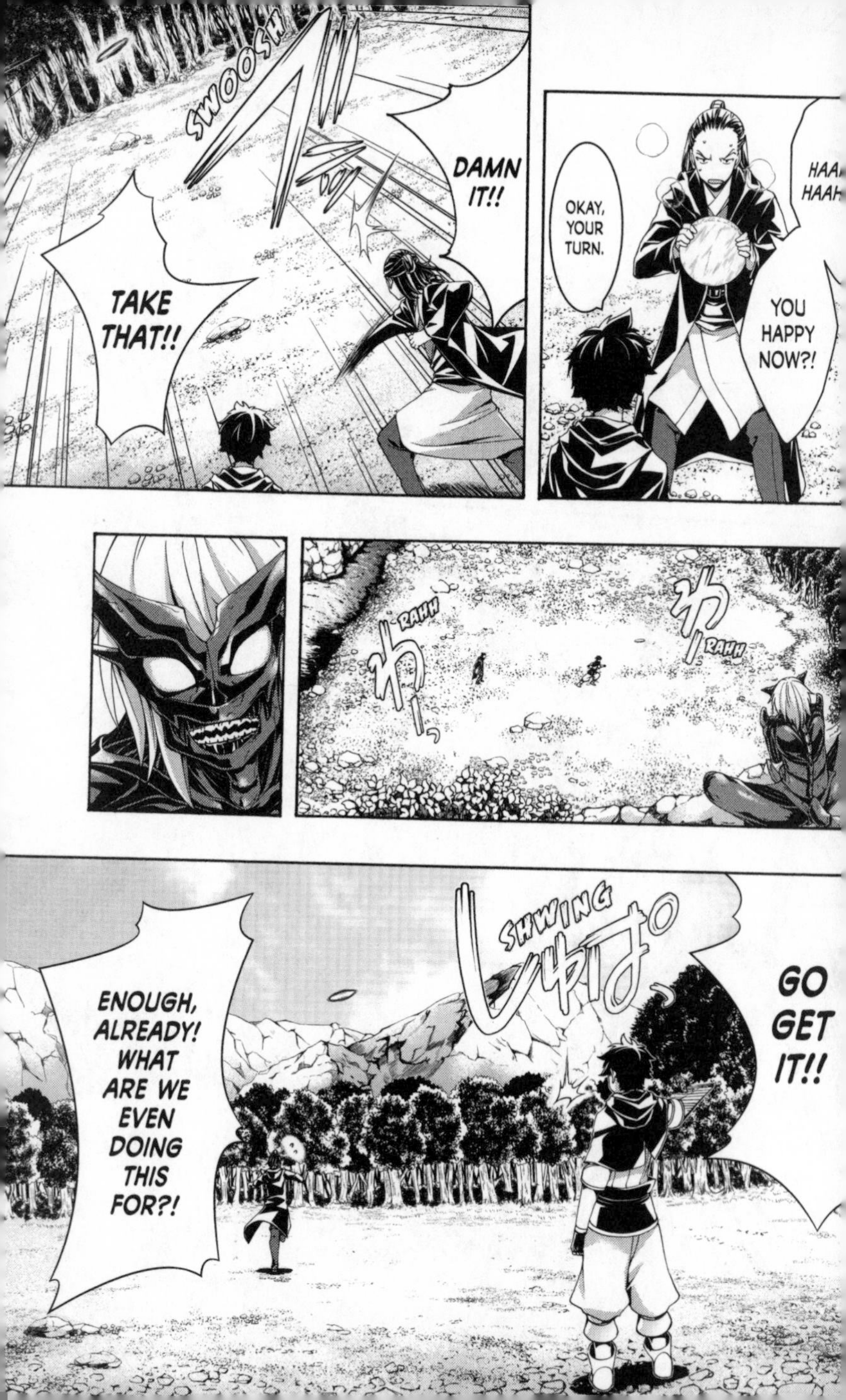
HAAH HAAH
YOU HAPPY NOW?!
OKAY, YOUR TURN.
DAMN IT!!
SWOOSH
TAKE THAT!!
RAHH
RAHH
GO GET IT!!
SHWING
ENOUGH, ALREADY! WHAT ARE WE EVEN DOING THIS FOR?!

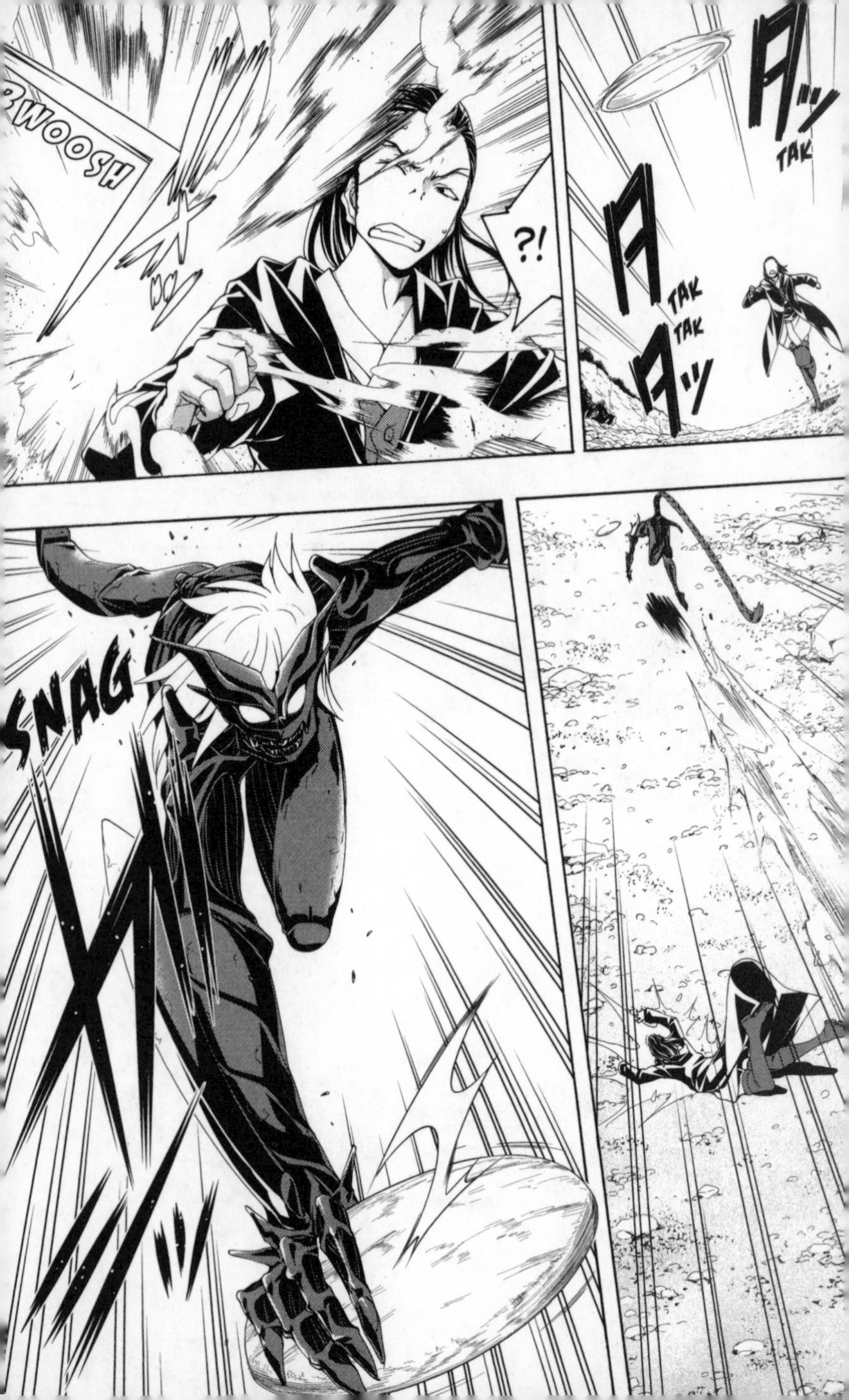

タッ
TAK
タ
TAK TAK
タッ
BWOOSH
?!
SNAG

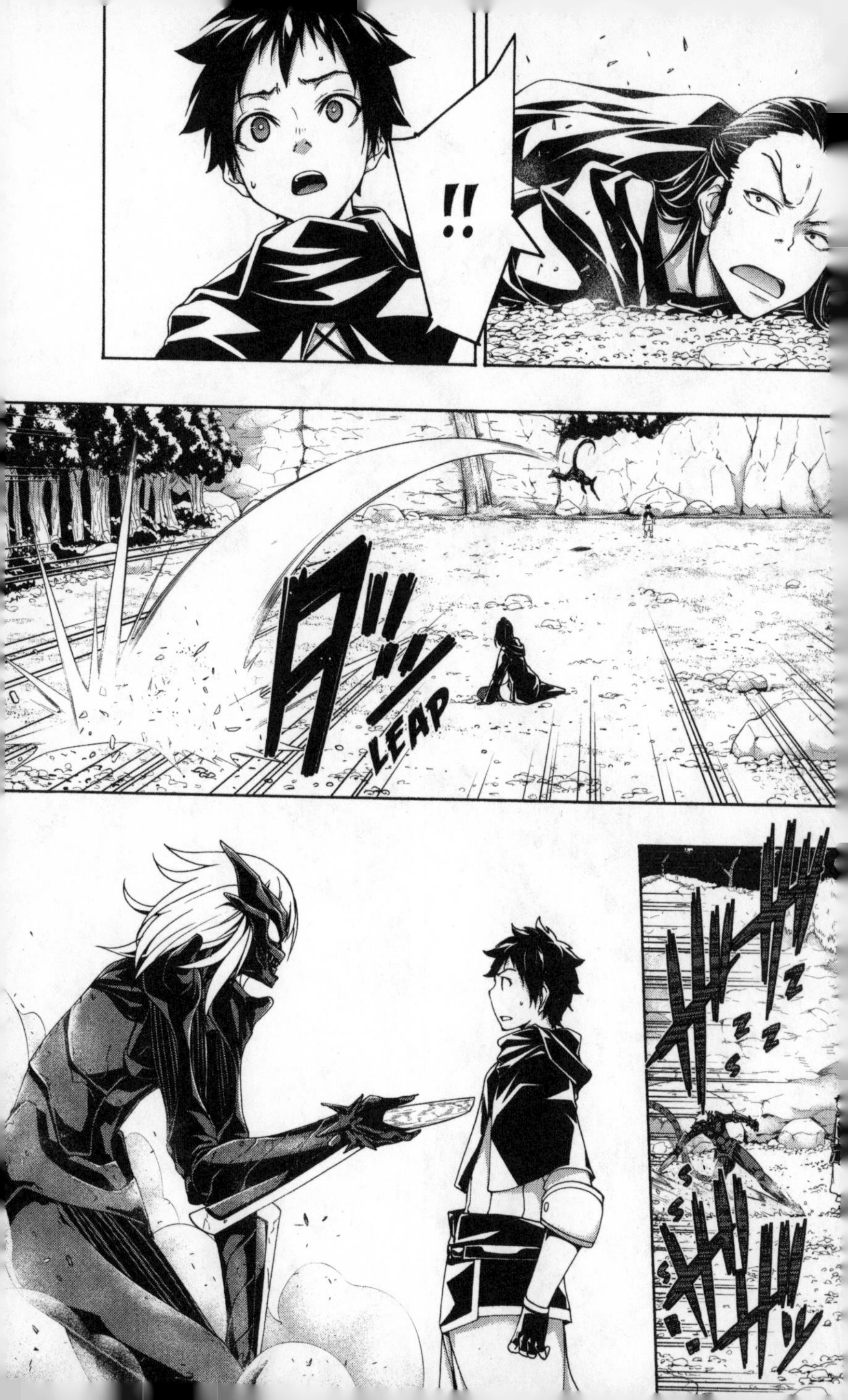
!!
LEAP

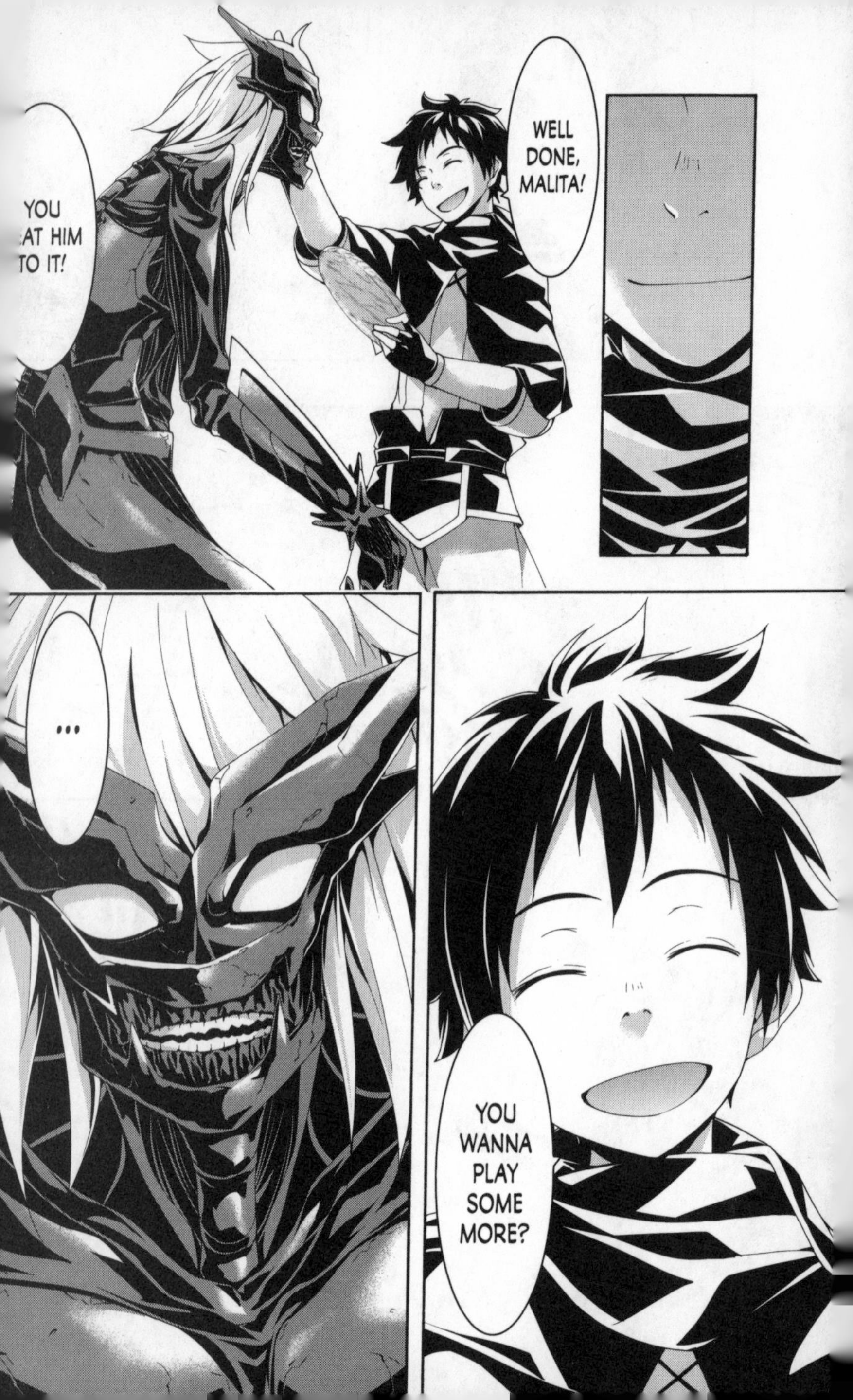
WELL DONE, MALITA!
YOU AT HIM TO IT!
YOU WANNA PLAY SOME MORE?
...

I'M STANDING ON A MILLION LIVES

I'M STANDING ON A MILLION LIVES.

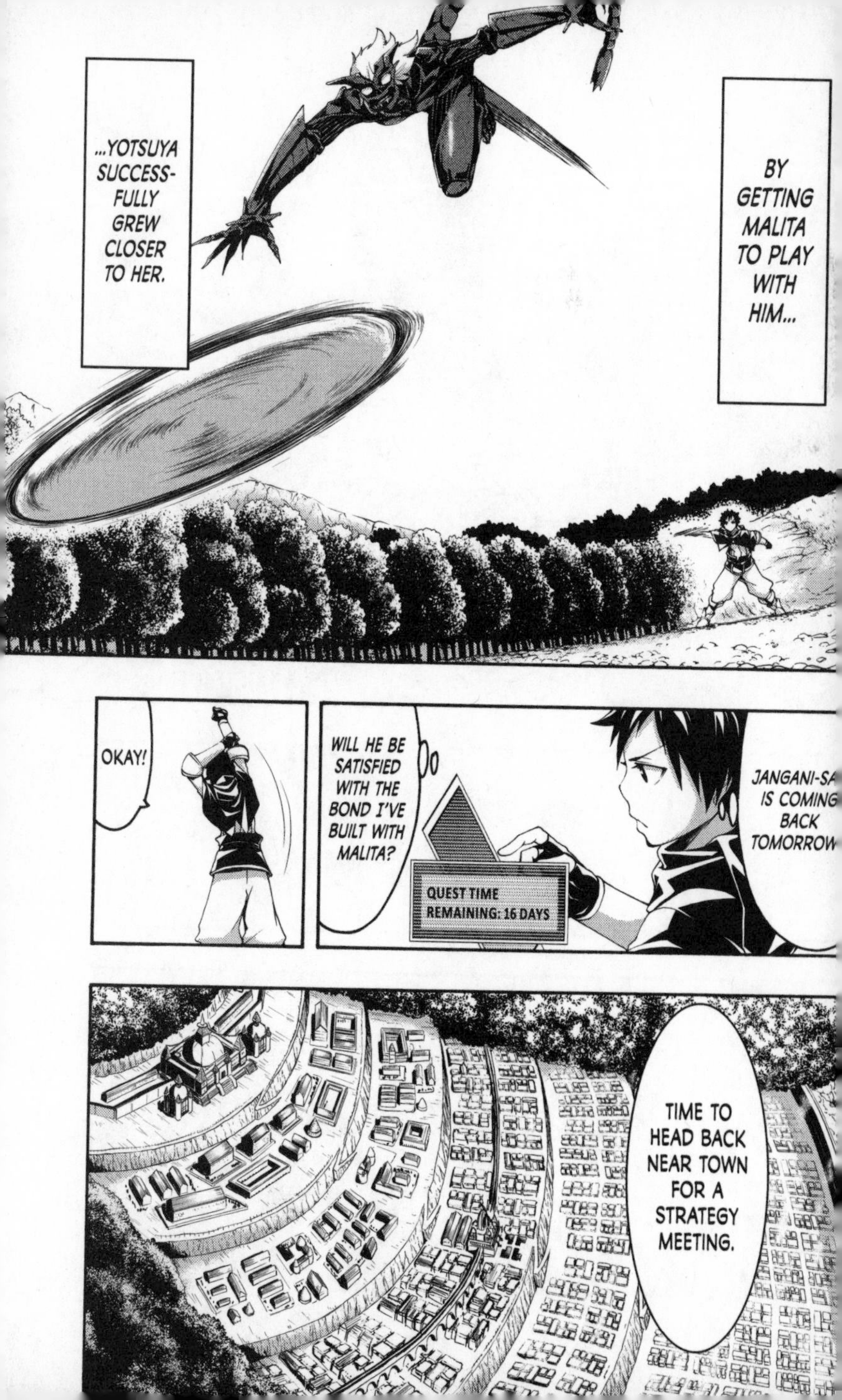
BY GETTING MALITA TO PLAY WITH HIM...
...YOTSUYA SUCCESS-FULLY GREW CLOSER TO HER.
JANGANI-SA IS COMING BACK TOMORROW
WILL HE BE SATISFIED WITH THE BOND I'VE BUILT WITH MALITA?
QUEST TIME REMAINING: 16 DAYS
OKAY!
TIME TO HEAD BACK NEAR TOWN FOR A STRATEGY MEETING.

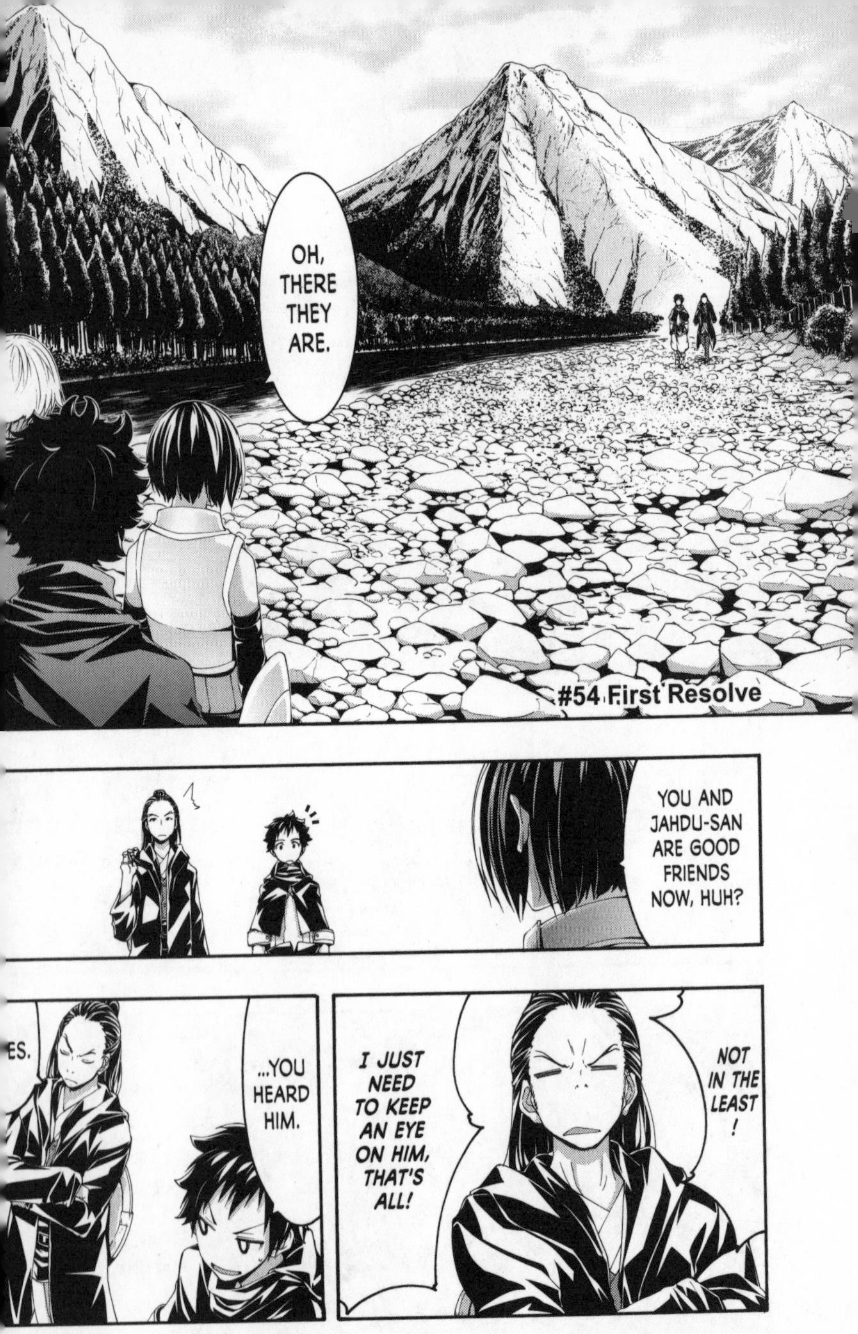
OH, THERE THEY ARE.
#54 First Resolve
YOU AND JAHDU-SAN ARE GOOD FRIENDS NOW, HUH?
NOT IN THE LEAST!
I JUST NEED TO KEEP AN EYE ON HIM, THAT'S ALL!
...YOU HEARD HIM.
ES.

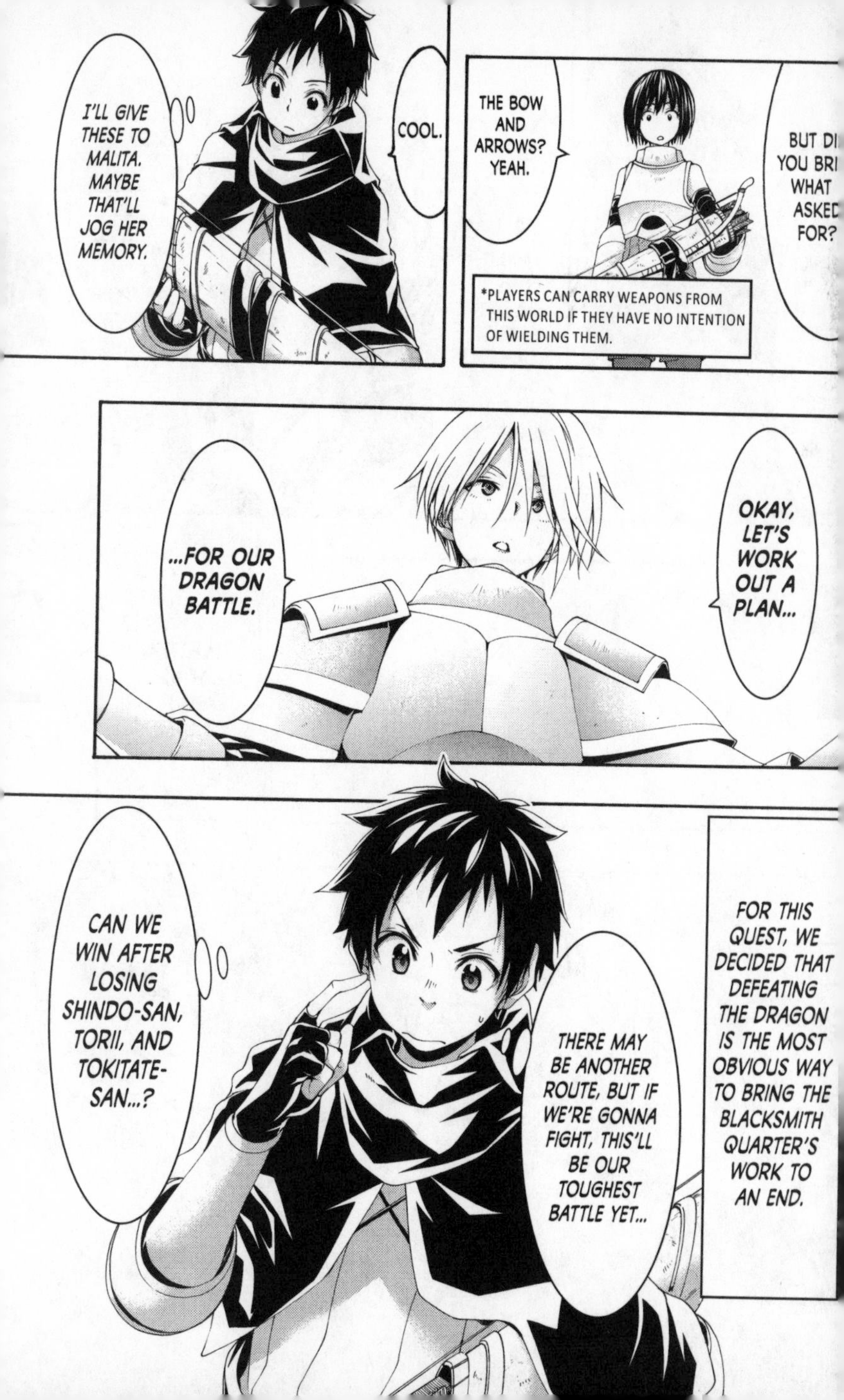

BUT DI YOU BRI WHAT ASKED FOR?
THE BOW AND ARROWS? YEAH.
*PLAYERS CAN CARRY WEAPONS FROM THIS WORLD IF THEY HAVE NO INTENTION OF WIELDING THEM.
COOL.
I'LL GIVE THESE TO MALITA. MAYBE THAT'LL JOG HER MEMORY.
OKAY, LET'S WORK OUT A PLAN...
...FOR OUR DRAGON BATTLE.
FOR THIS QUEST, WE DECIDED THAT DEFEATING THE DRAGON IS THE MOST OBVIOUS WAY TO BRING THE BLACKSMITH QUARTER'S WORK TO AN END.
THERE MAY BE ANOTHER ROUTE, BUT IF WE'RE GONNA FIGHT, THIS'LL BE OUR TOUGHEST BATTLE YET...
CAN WE WIN AFTER LOSING SHINDO-SAN, TORII, AND TOKITATE-SAN...?

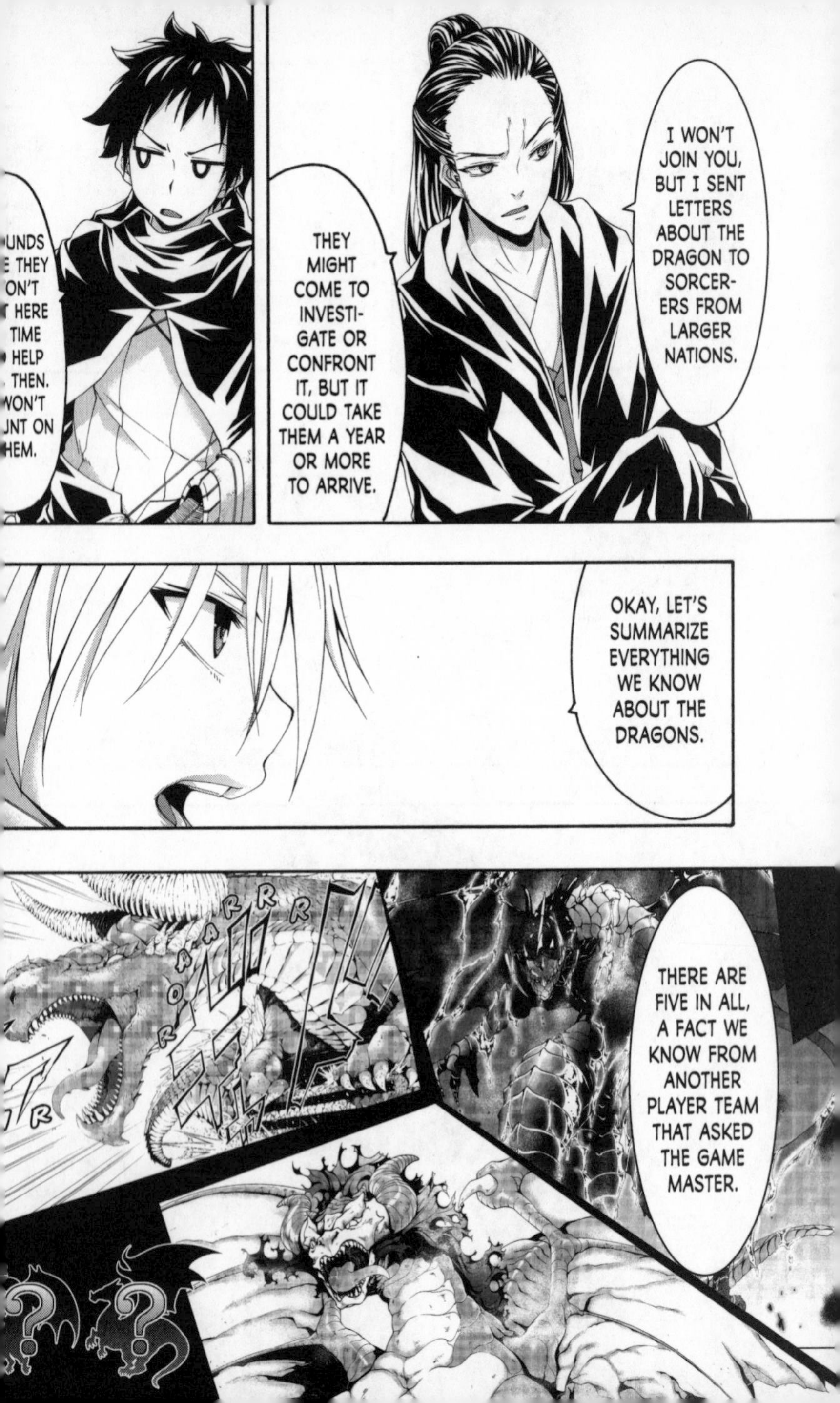
I WON'T JOIN YOU, BUT I SENT LETTERS ABOUT THE DRAGON TO SORCER-ERS FROM LARGER NATIONS.
THEY MIGHT COME TO INVESTI-GATE OR CONFRONT IT, BUT IT COULD TAKE THEM A YEAR OR MORE TO ARRIVE.
OKAY, LET'S SUMMARIZE EVERYTHING WE KNOW ABOUT THE DRAGONS.
THERE ARE FIVE IN ALL, A FACT WE KNOW FROM ANOTHER PLAYER TEAM THAT ASKED THE GAME MASTER.
ROAARRR

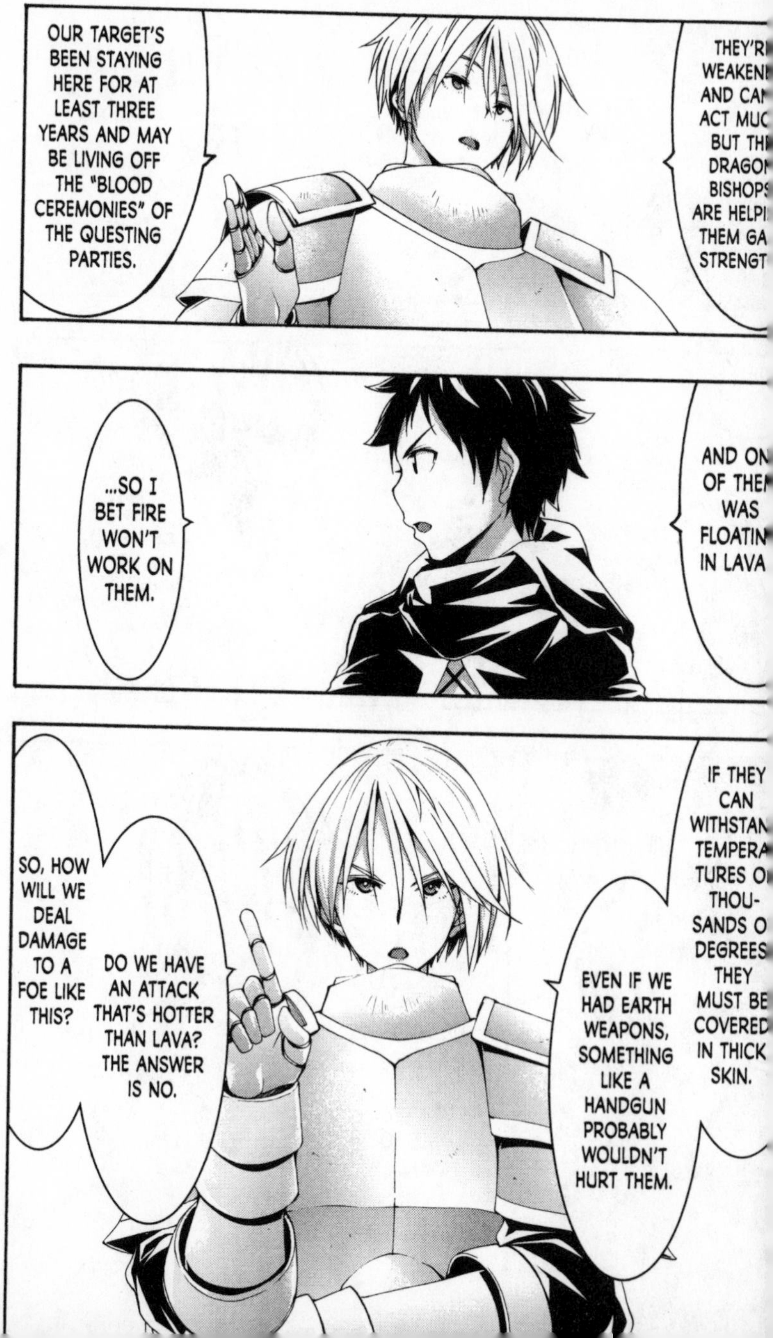
THEY'R WEAKEN AND CA ACT MUC BUT TH DRAGO BISHOP ARE HELPI THEM GA STRENGT
OUR TARGET'S BEEN STAYING HERE FOR AT LEAST THREE YEARS AND MAY BE LIVING OFF THE "BLOOD CEREMONIES" OF THE QUESTING PARTIES.
AND ON OF THE WAS FLOATIN IN LAVA
...SO I BET FIRE WON'T WORK ON THEM.
IF THEY CAN WITHSTAN TEMPERA TURES O THOU- SANDS O DEGREES THEY MUST BE COVERED IN THICK SKIN.
EVEN IF WE HAD EARTH WEAPONS, SOMETHING LIKE A HANDGUN PROBABLY WOULDN'T HURT THEM.
DO WE HAVE AN ATTACK THAT'S HOTTER THAN LAVA? THE ANSWER IS NO.
SO, HOW WILL WE DEAL DAMAGE TO A FOE LIKE THIS?

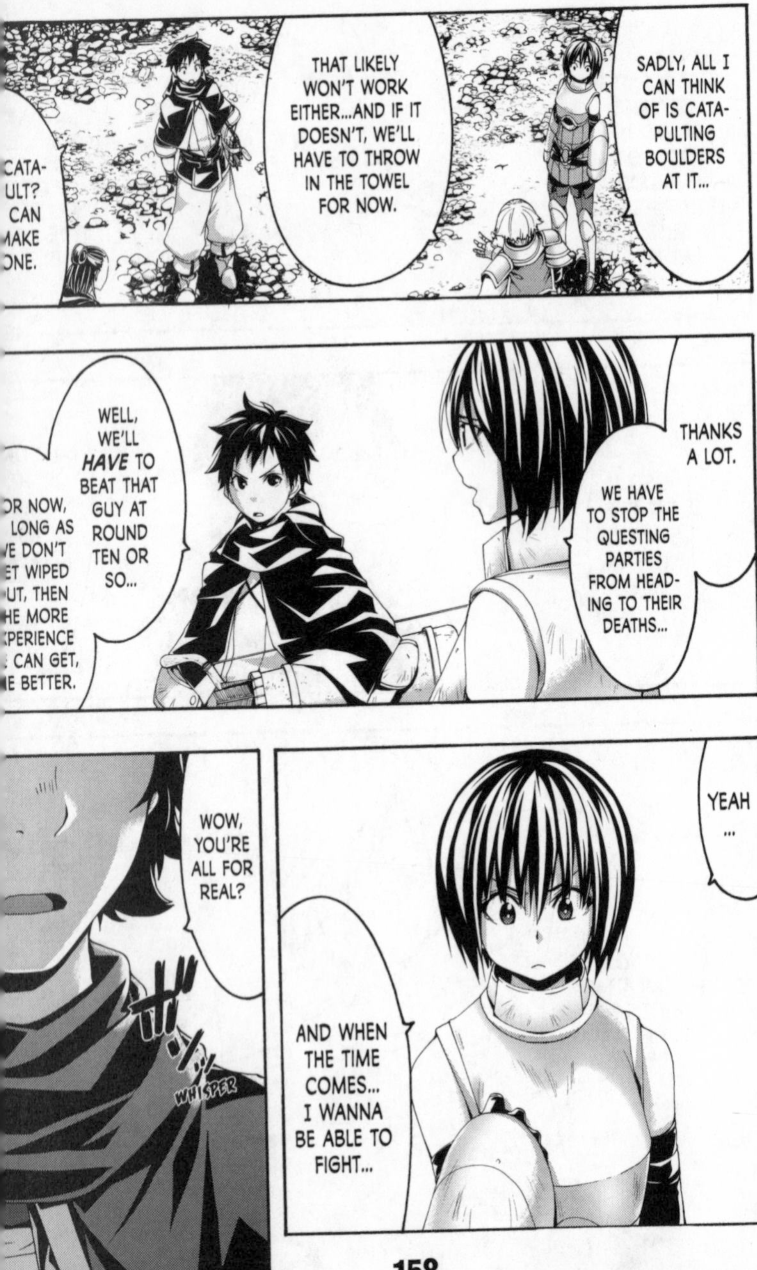
SADLY, ALL I CAN THINK OF IS CATA-PULTING BOULDERS AT IT...
THAT LIKELY WON'T WORK EITHER...AND IF IT DOESN'T, WE'LL HAVE TO THROW IN THE TOWEL FOR NOW.
CATA-ULT? CAN MAKE ONE.
THANKS A LOT.
WE HAVE TO STOP THE QUESTING PARTIES FROM HEAD-ING TO THEIR DEATHS...
WELL, WE'LL HAVE TO BEAT THAT GUY AT ROUND TEN OR SO...
OR NOW, LONG AS VE DON'T ET WIPED UT, THEN HE MORE PERIENCE CAN GET, E BETTER.
YEAH ...
AND WHEN THE TIME COMES... I WANNA BE ABLE TO FIGHT...
WOW, YOU'RE ALL FOR REAL?
WHISPER

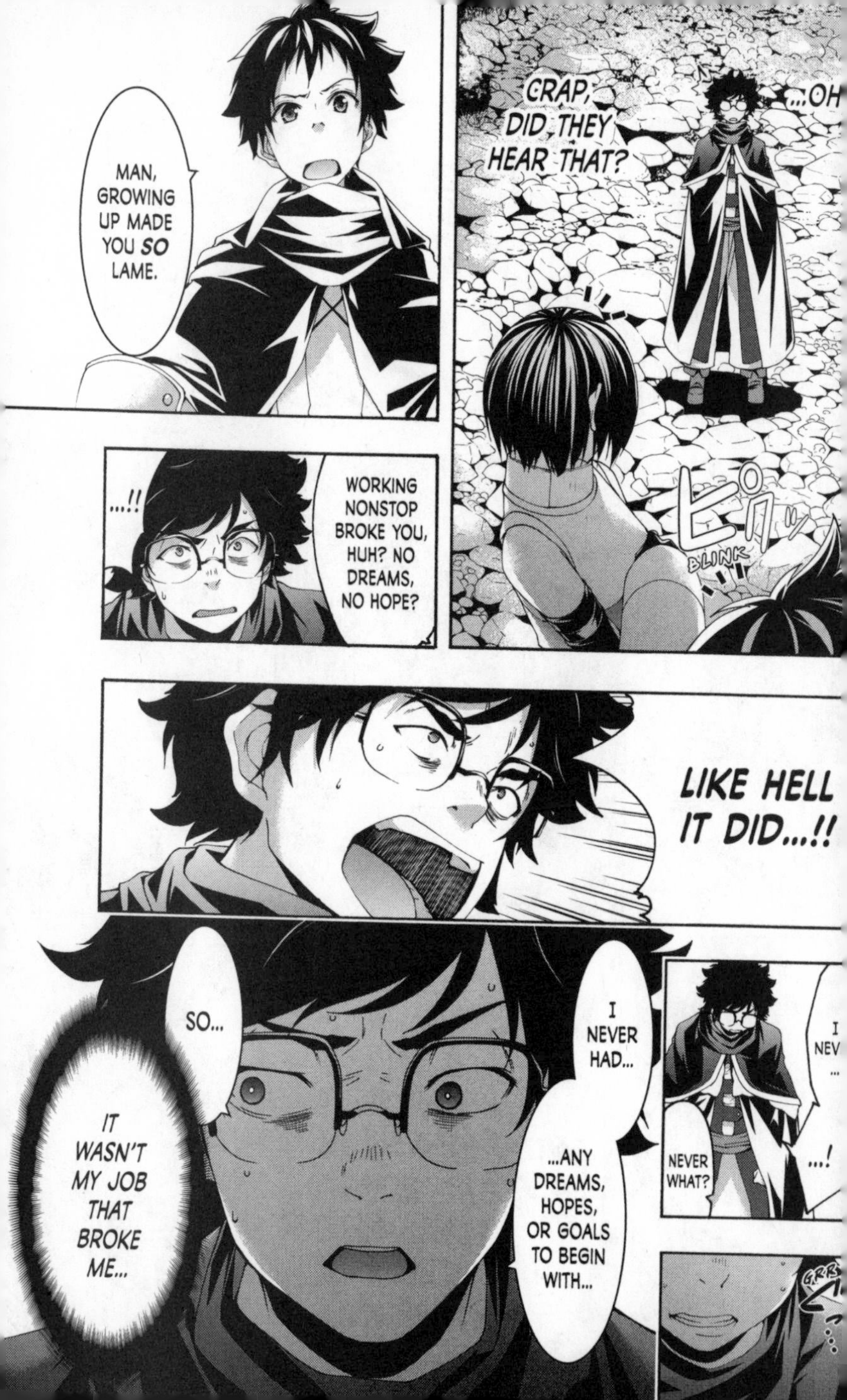
...OH
CRAP, DID THEY HEAR THAT?
ピクッ
BLINK
MAN, GROWING UP MADE YOU *SO* LAME.
...!!
WORKING NONSTOP BROKE YOU, HUH? NO DREAMS, NO HOPE?
LIKE HELL IT DID...!!
I NEV ...
...!
NEVER WHAT?
GRR
I NEVER HAD...
...ANY DREAMS, HOPES, OR GOALS TO BEGIN WITH...
SO...
IT WASN'T MY JOB THAT BROKE ME...

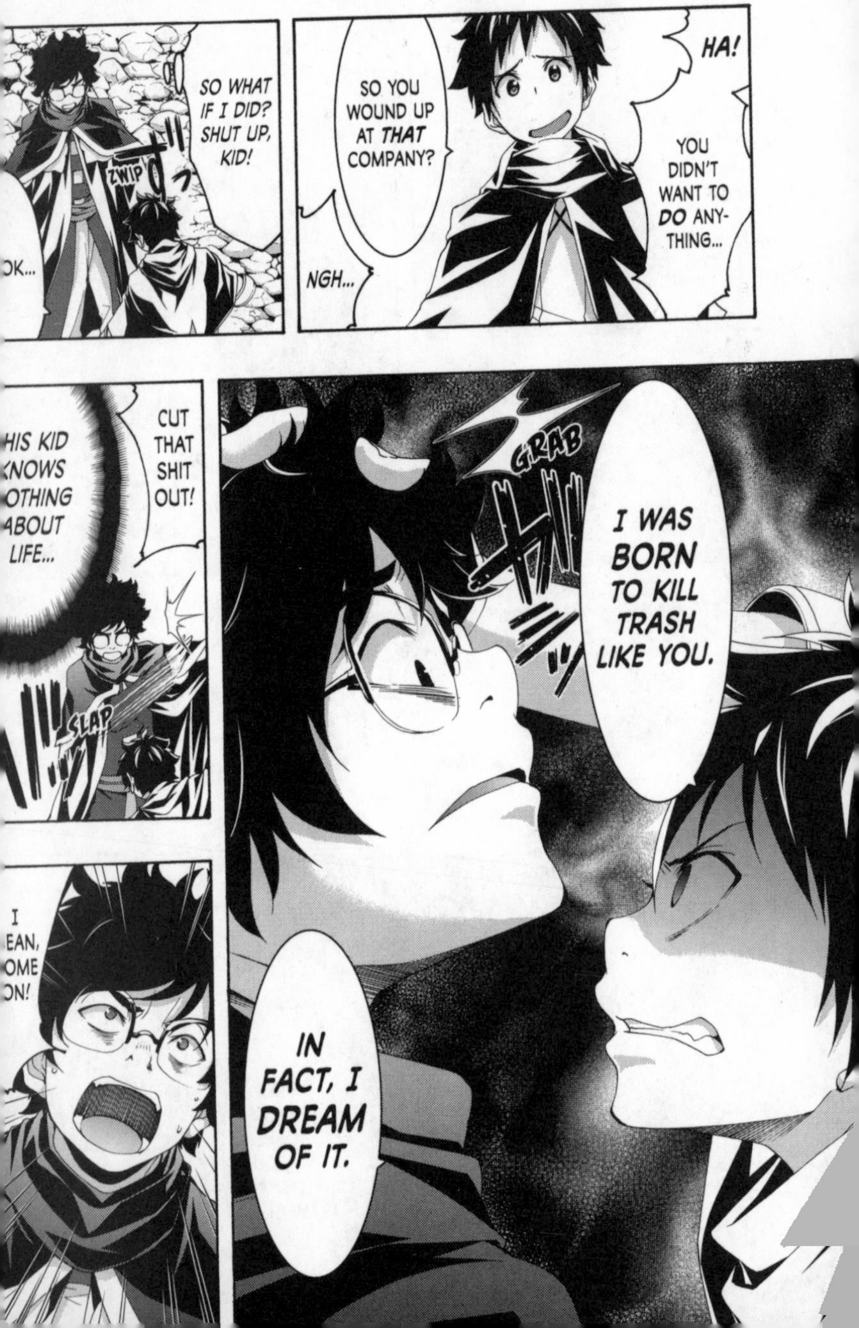
HA!
YOU DIDN'T WANT TO DO ANYTHING...
SO YOU WOUND UP AT THAT COMPANY?
NGH...
SO WHAT IF I DID? SHUT UP, KID!
ZWIP
OK...
GRAB
I WAS BORN TO KILL TRASH LIKE YOU.
IN FACT, I DREAM OF IT.
CUT THAT SHIT OUT!
HIS KID KNOWS OTHING ABOUT LIFE...
SLAP
I EAN, OME ON!

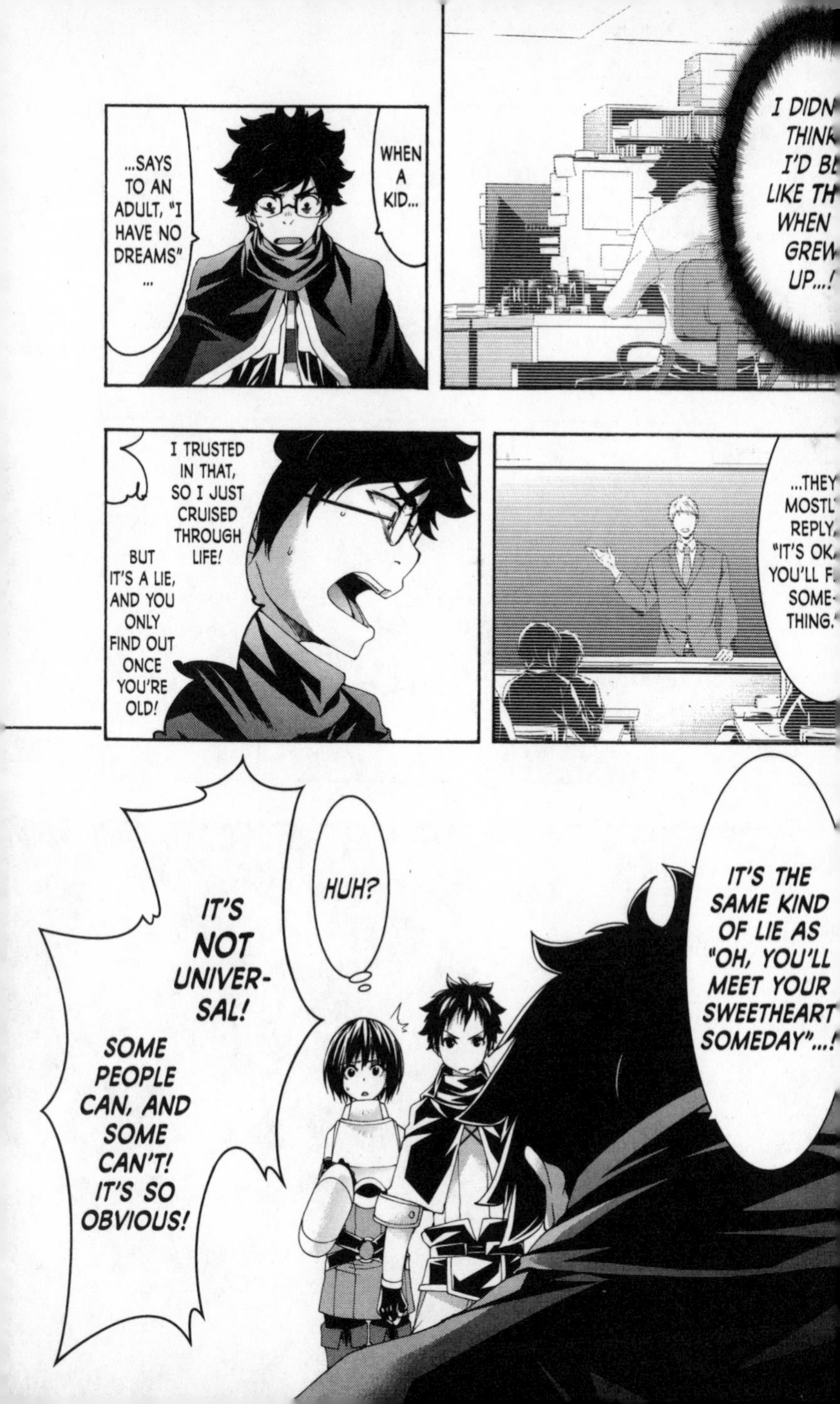
I DIDN THINK I'D BE LIKE TH WHEN GREW UP...!
WHEN A KID...
...SAYS TO AN ADULT, "I HAVE NO DREAMS" ...
...THEY MOSTL REPLY, "IT'S OK YOU'LL F SOME-THING."
I TRUSTED IN THAT, SO I JUST CRUISED THROUGH LIFE!
BUT IT'S A LIE, AND YOU ONLY FIND OUT ONCE YOU'RE OLD!
IT'S THE SAME KIND OF LIE AS "OH, YOU'LL MEET YOUR SWEETHEART SOMEDAY"...!
HUH?
IT'S NOT UNIVER-SAL!
SOME PEOPLE CAN, AND SOME CAN'T! IT'S SO OBVIOUS!

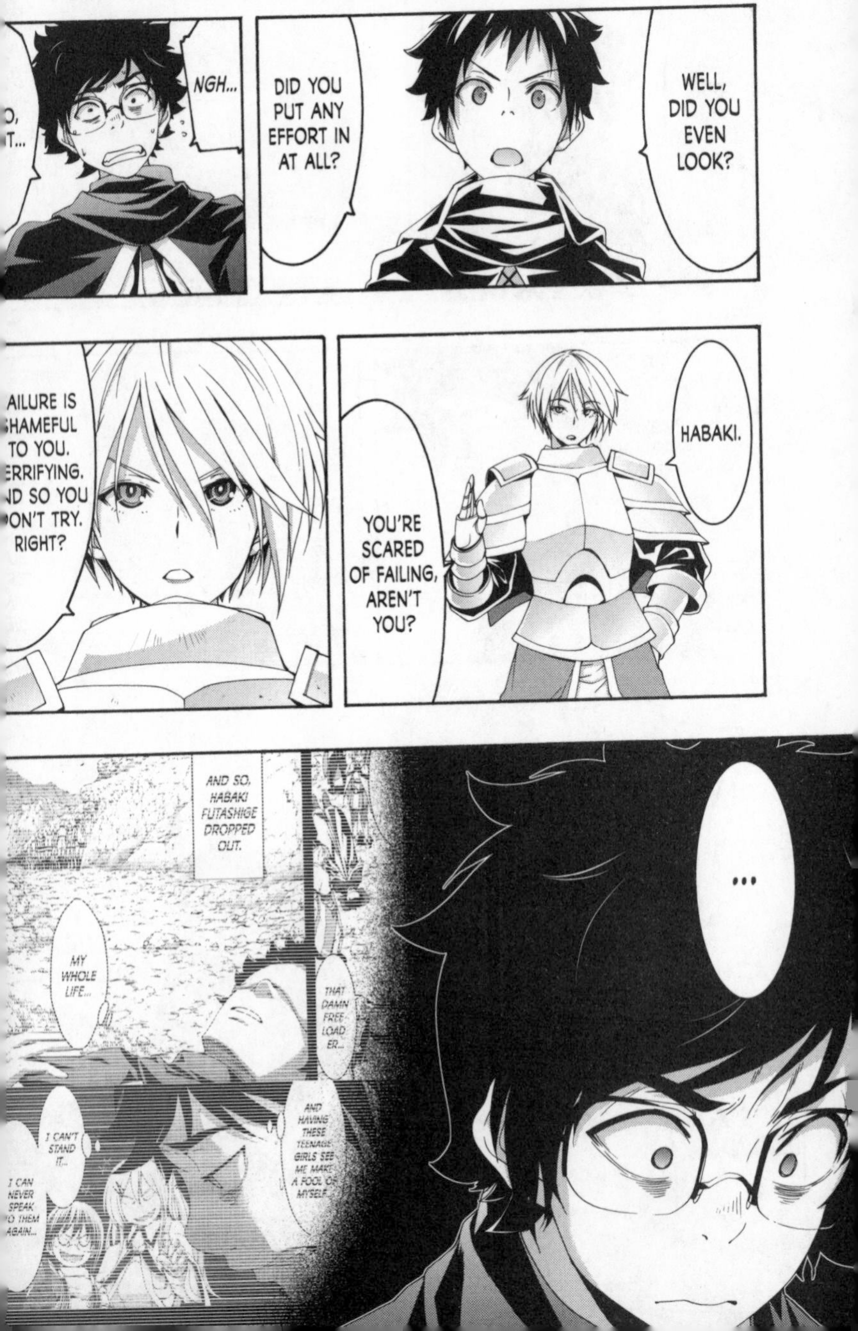
WELL, DID YOU EVEN LOOK?
DID YOU PUT ANY EFFORT IN AT ALL?
NGH...
HABAKI.
YOU'RE SCARED OF FAILING, AREN'T YOU?
AILURE IS SHAMEFUL TO YOU. ERRIFYING. ND SO YOU ON'T TRY. RIGHT?
...
AND SO, HABAKI FUTASHIGE DROPPED OUT.
THAT DAMN FREE LOAD ER...
MY WHOLE LIFE...
AND HAVING THESE TEENAGE GIRLS SEE ME MAKE A FOOL OF MYSELF...
I CAN'T STAND IT...
I CAN NEVER SPEAK TO THEM AGAIN...

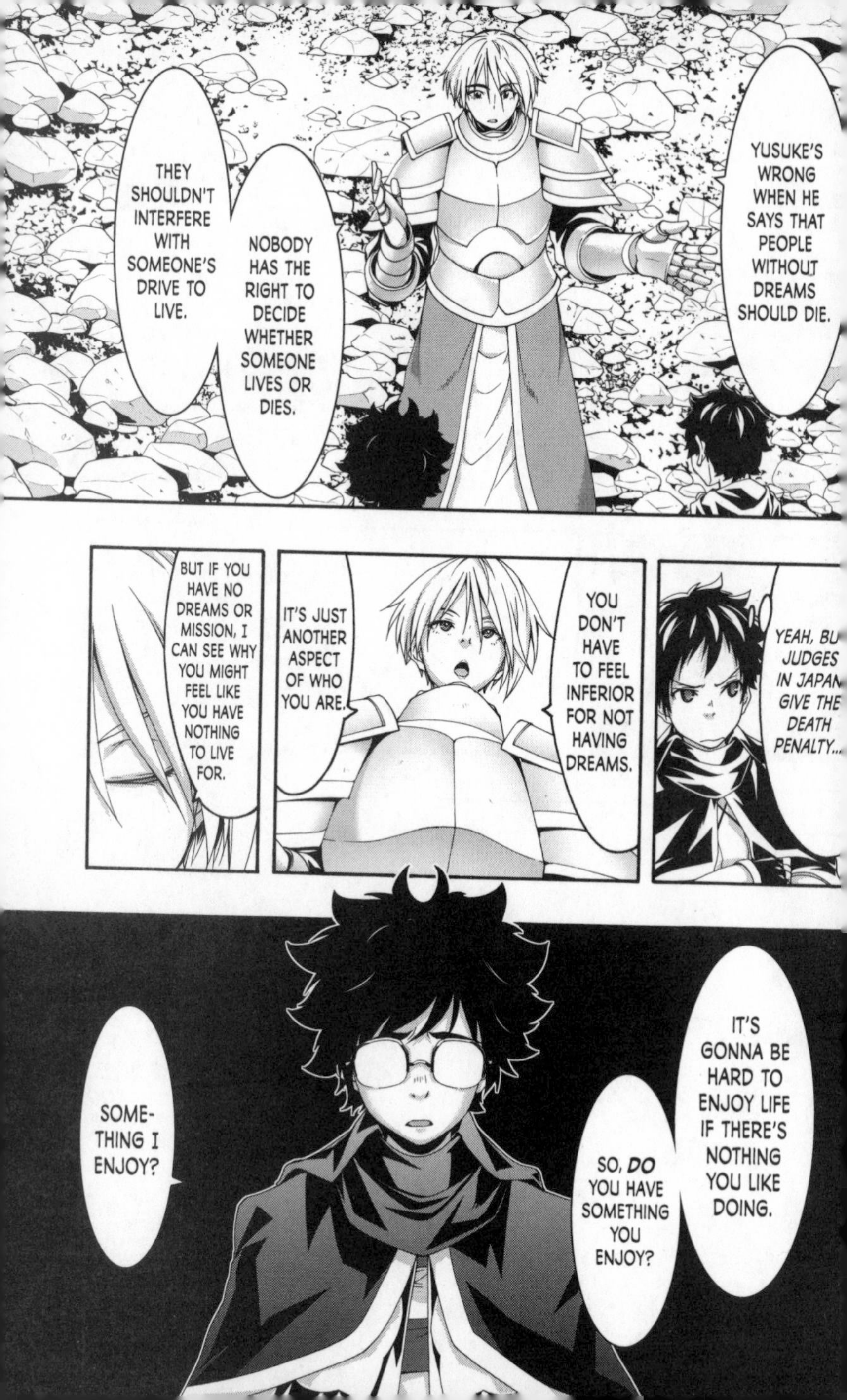
YUSUKE'S WRONG WHEN HE SAYS THAT PEOPLE WITHOUT DREAMS SHOULD DIE.
NOBODY HAS THE RIGHT TO DECIDE WHETHER SOMEONE LIVES OR DIES.
THEY SHOULDN'T INTERFERE WITH SOMEONE'S DRIVE TO LIVE.
YEAH, BU JUDGES IN JAPAN GIVE THE DEATH PENALTY...
YOU DON'T HAVE TO FEEL INFERIOR FOR NOT HAVING DREAMS.
IT'S JUST ANOTHER ASPECT OF WHO YOU ARE.
BUT IF YOU HAVE NO DREAMS OR MISSION, I CAN SEE WHY YOU MIGHT FEEL LIKE YOU HAVE NOTHING TO LIVE FOR.
IT'S GONNA BE HARD TO ENJOY LIFE IF THERE'S NOTHING YOU LIKE DOING.
SO, *DO* YOU HAVE SOMETHING YOU ENJOY?
SOME-THING I ENJOY?

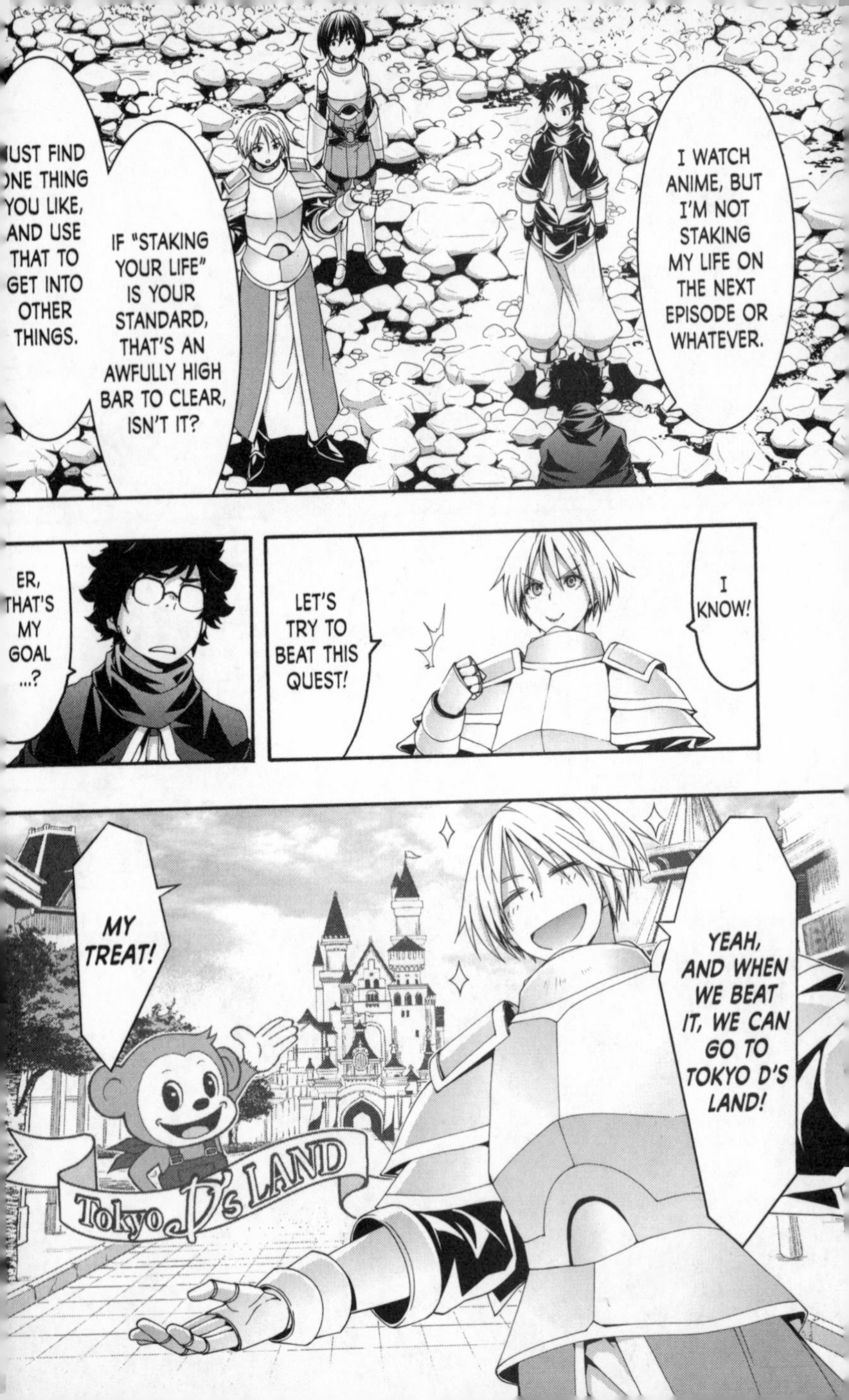
I WATCH ANIME, BUT I'M NOT STAKING MY LIFE ON THE NEXT EPISODE OR WHATEVER.
IF "STAKING YOUR LIFE" IS YOUR STANDARD, THAT'S AN AWFULLY HIGH BAR TO CLEAR, ISN'T IT?
JUST FIND ONE THING YOU LIKE, AND USE THAT TO GET INTO OTHER THINGS.
I KNOW!
LET'S TRY TO BEAT THIS QUEST!
ER, THAT'S MY GOAL ...?
YEAH, AND WHEN WE BEAT IT, WE CAN GO TO TOKYO D'S LAND!
MY TREAT!
Tokyo D's LAND

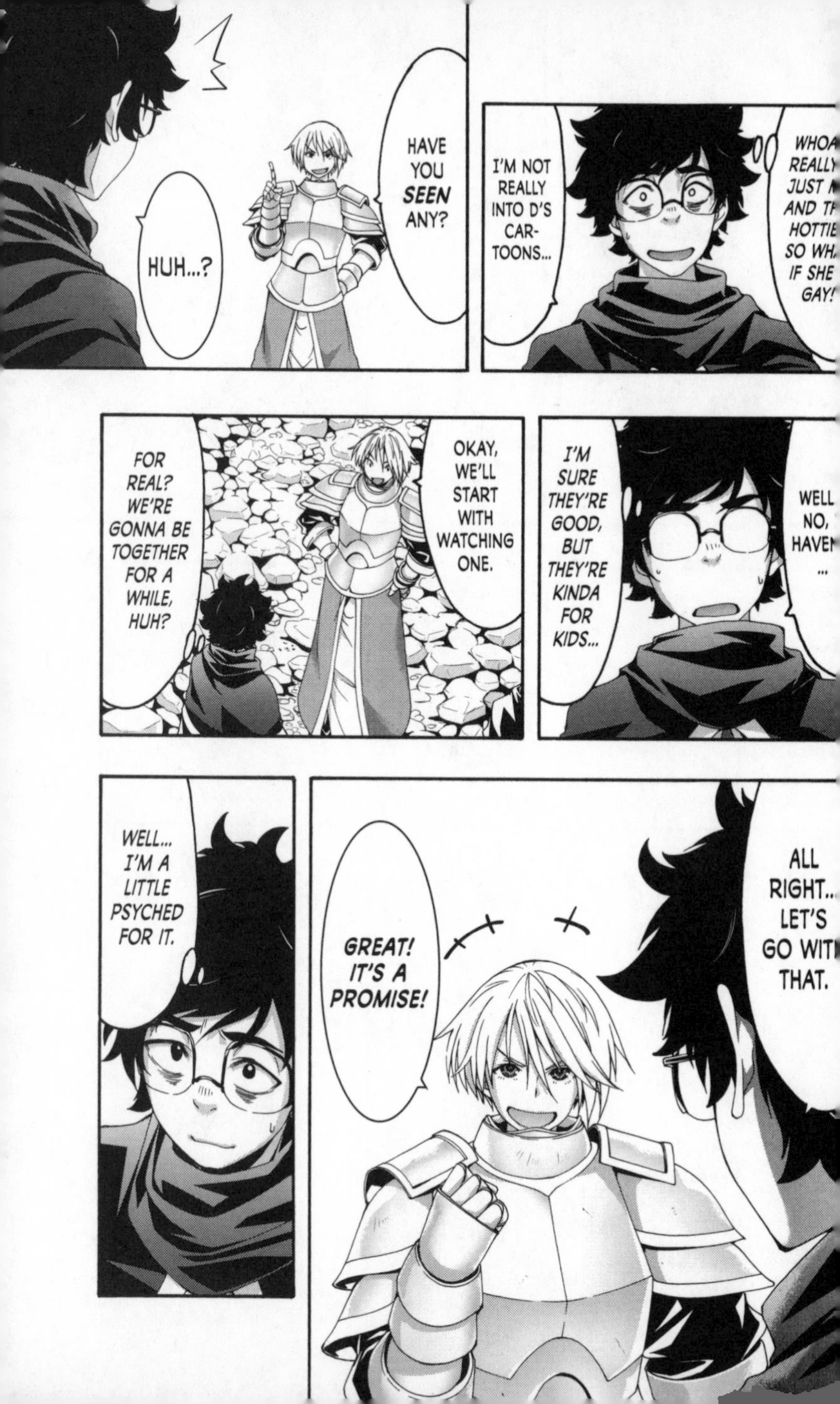
WHOA REALLY JUST M AND TH HOTTIE SO WHA IF SHE GAY!
I'M NOT REALLY INTO D'S CAR-TOONS...
HAVE YOU SEEN ANY?
HUH...?
WELL NO, HAVEN ...
I'M SURE THEY'RE GOOD, BUT THEY'RE KINDA FOR KIDS...
OKAY, WE'LL START WITH WATCHING ONE.
FOR REAL? WE'RE GONNA BE TOGETHER FOR A WHILE, HUH?
ALL RIGHT... LET'S GO WIT THAT.
GREAT! IT'S A PROMISE!
WELL... I'M A LITTLE PSYCHED FOR IT.

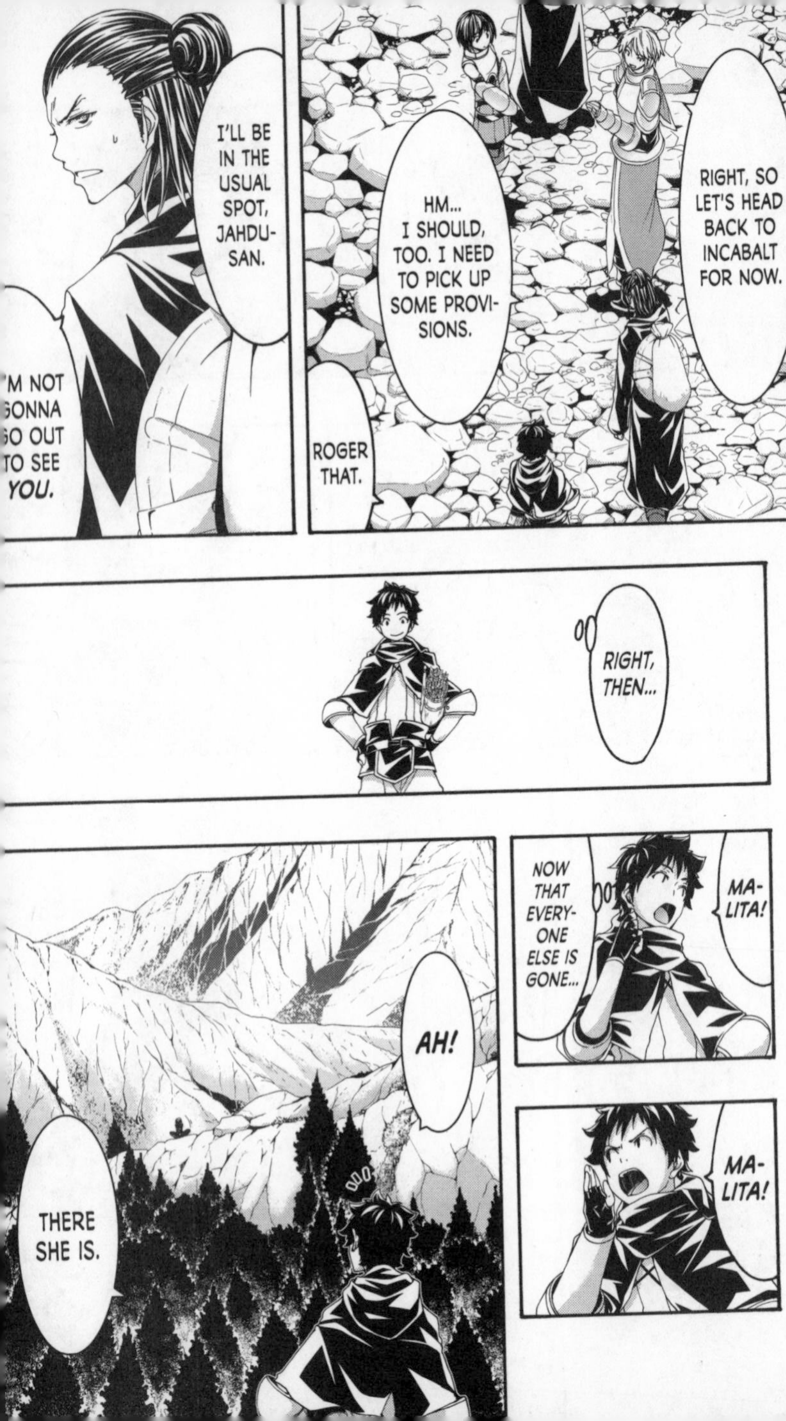
RIGHT, SO LET'S HEAD BACK TO INCABALT FOR NOW.
HM... I SHOULD, TOO. I NEED TO PICK UP SOME PROVISIONS.
ROGER THAT.
I'LL BE IN THE USUAL SPOT, JAHDU-SAN.
'M NOT GONNA GO OUT TO SEE *YOU.*
RIGHT, THEN...
MA-LITA!
NOW THAT EVERYONE ELSE IS GONE...
MA-LITA!
AH!
THERE SHE IS.

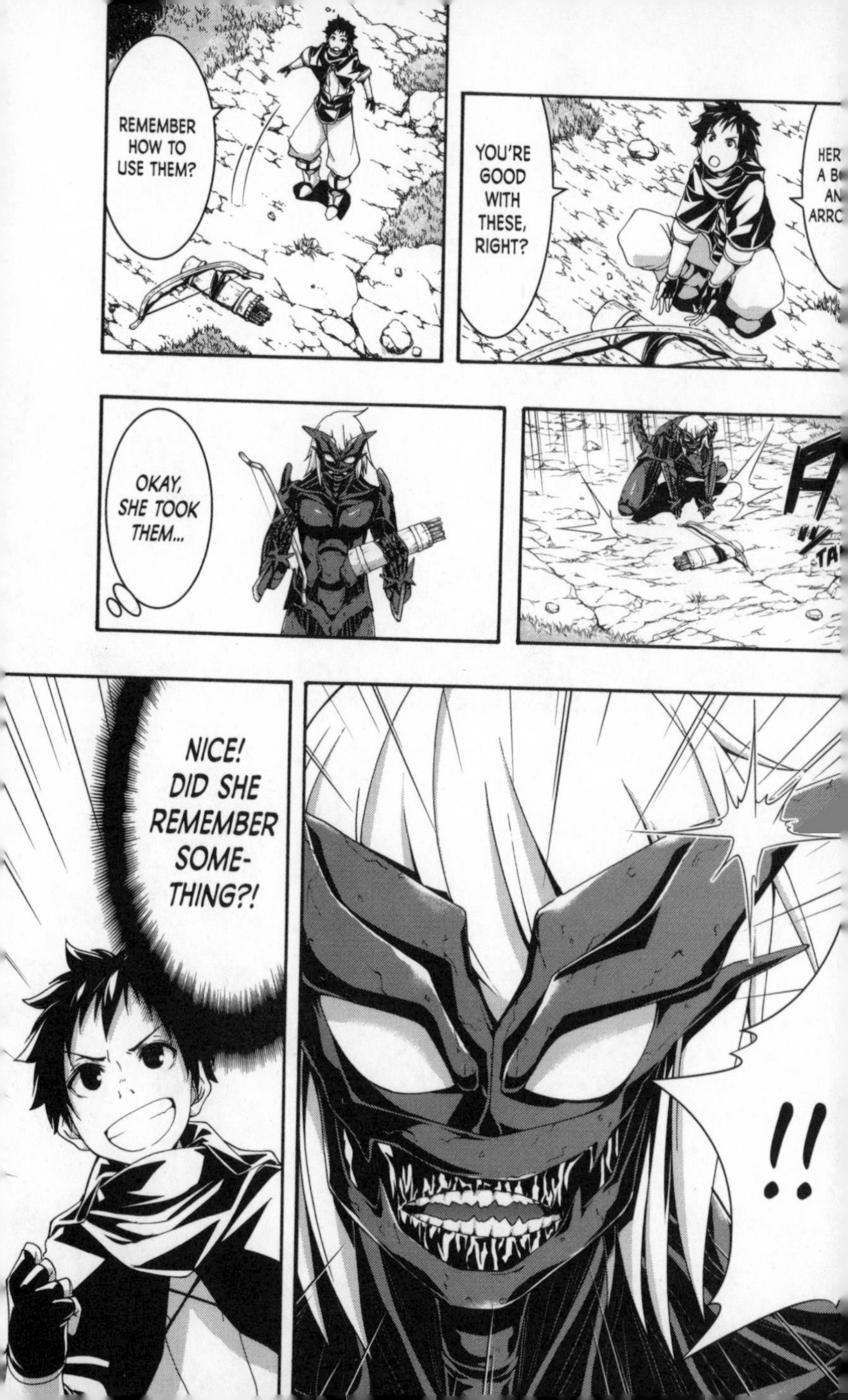
YOU'RE GOOD WITH THESE, RIGHT?
REMEMBER HOW TO USE THEM?
OKAY, SHE TOOK THEM...
!!
NICE! DID SHE REMEMBER SOME-THING?!

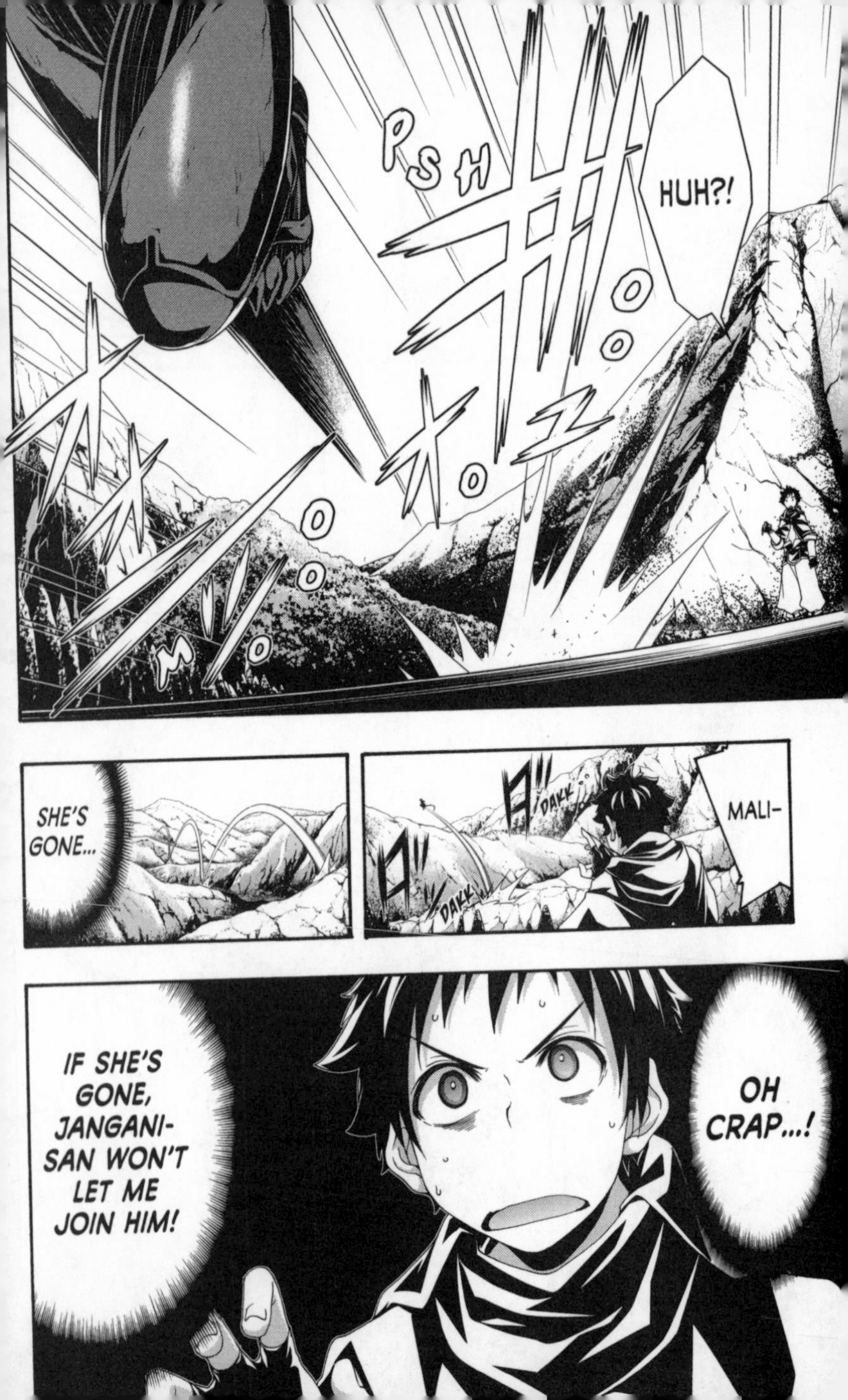
HUH?!
PSH
MALI-
DAKK
DAKK
SHE'S GONE...
OH CRAP...!
IF SHE'S GONE, JANGANI-SAN WON'T LET ME JOIN HIM!

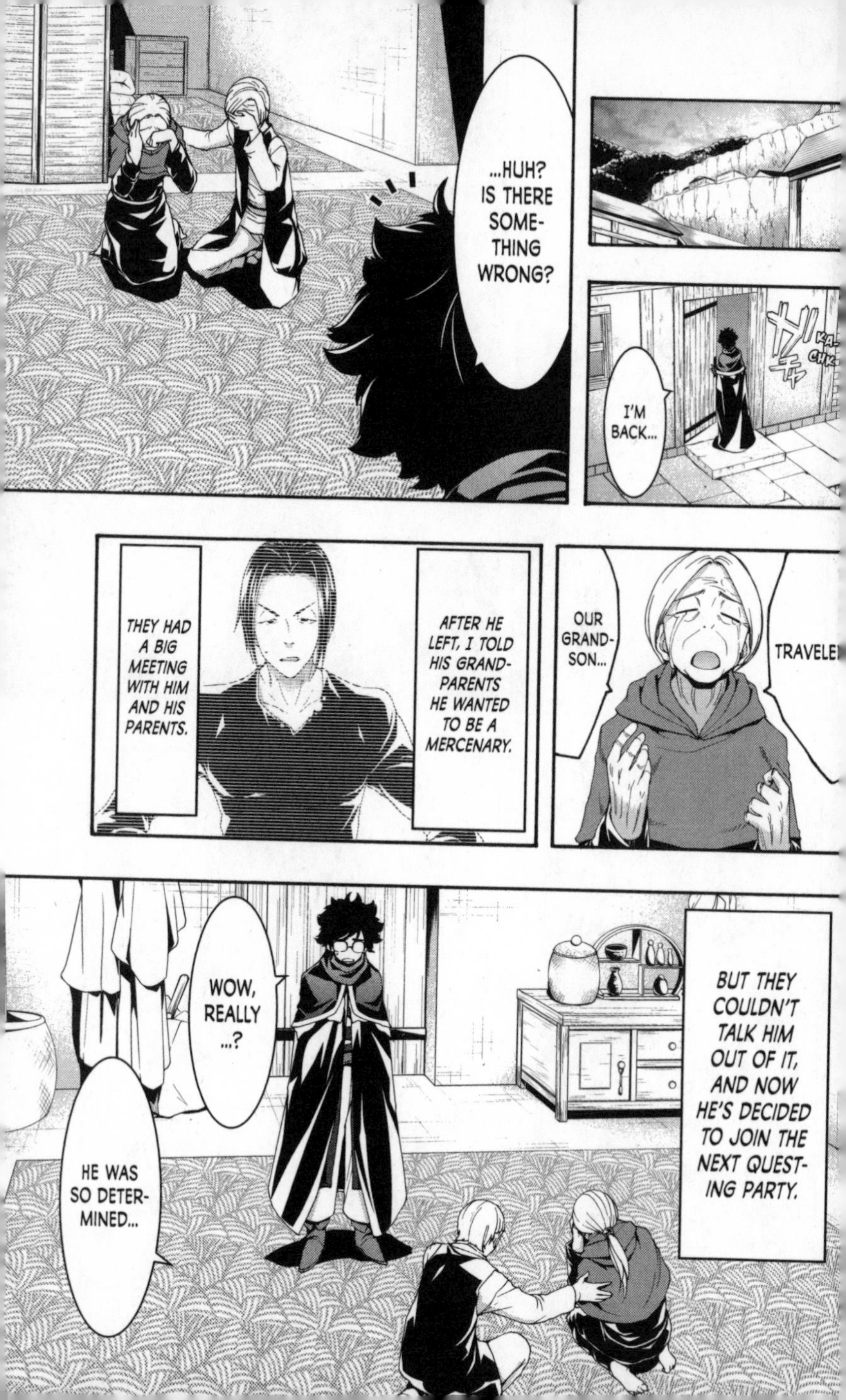
KA-CHK
I'M BACK...
...HUH? IS THERE SOME-THING WRONG?
TRAVELE
OUR GRAND-SON...
AFTER HE LEFT, I TOLD HIS GRAND-PARENTS HE WANTED TO BE A MERCENARY.
THEY HAD A BIG MEETING WITH HIM AND HIS PARENTS.
BUT THEY COULDN'T TALK HIM OUT OF IT, AND NOW HE'S DECIDED TO JOIN THE NEXT QUEST-ING PARTY.
WOW, REALLY ...?
HE WAS SO DETER-MINED...

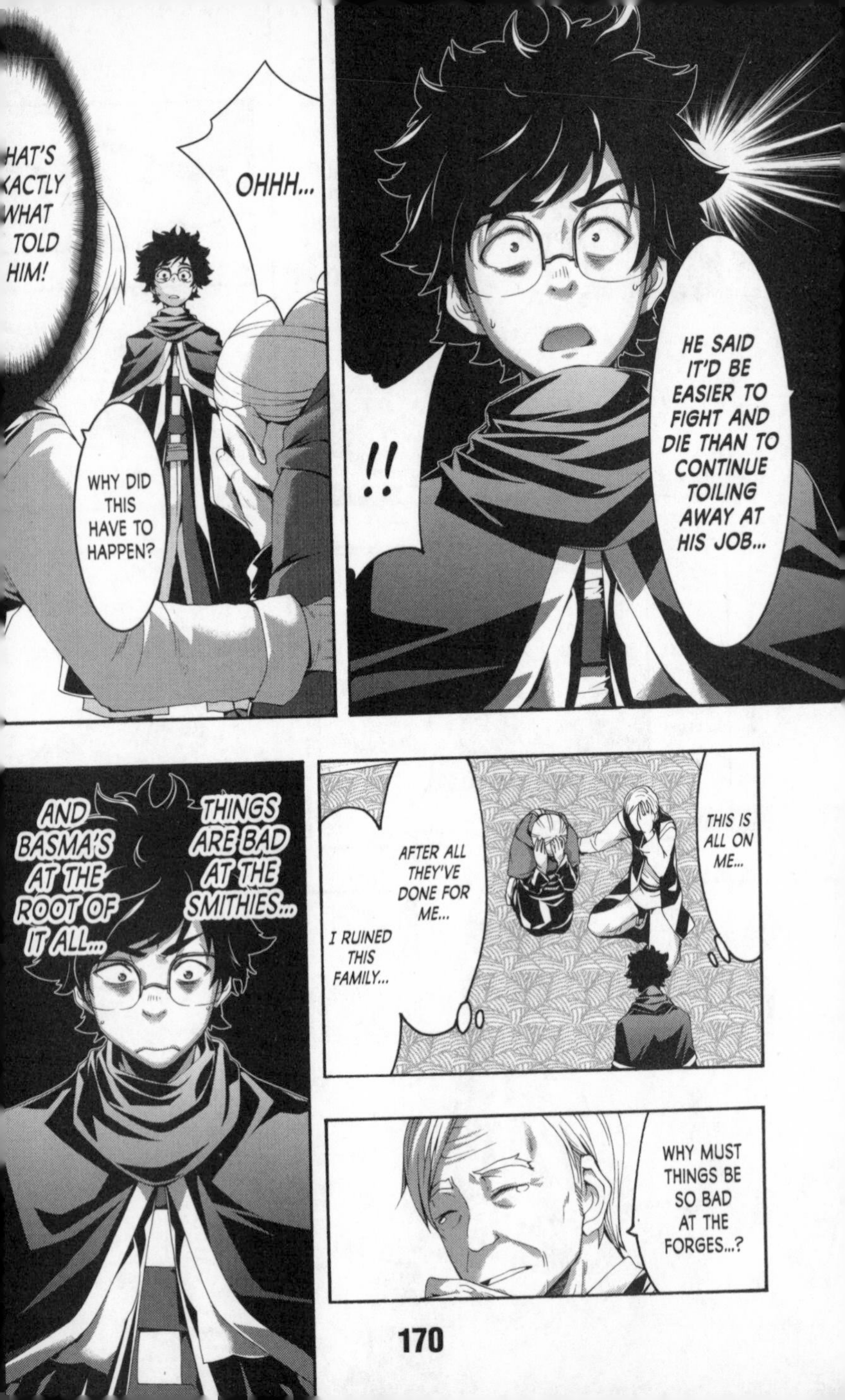
HE SAID IT'D BE EASIER TO FIGHT AND DIE THAN TO CONTINUE TOILING AWAY AT HIS JOB...
!!
OHHH...
HAT'S ACTLY WHAT TOLD HIM!
WHY DID THIS HAVE TO HAPPEN?
THIS IS ALL ON ME...
AFTER ALL THEY'VE DONE FOR ME...
I RUINED THIS FAMILY...
WHY MUST THINGS BE SO BAD AT THE FORGES...?
THINGS ARE BAD AT THE SMITHIES...
AND BASMA'S AT THE ROOT OF IT ALL...

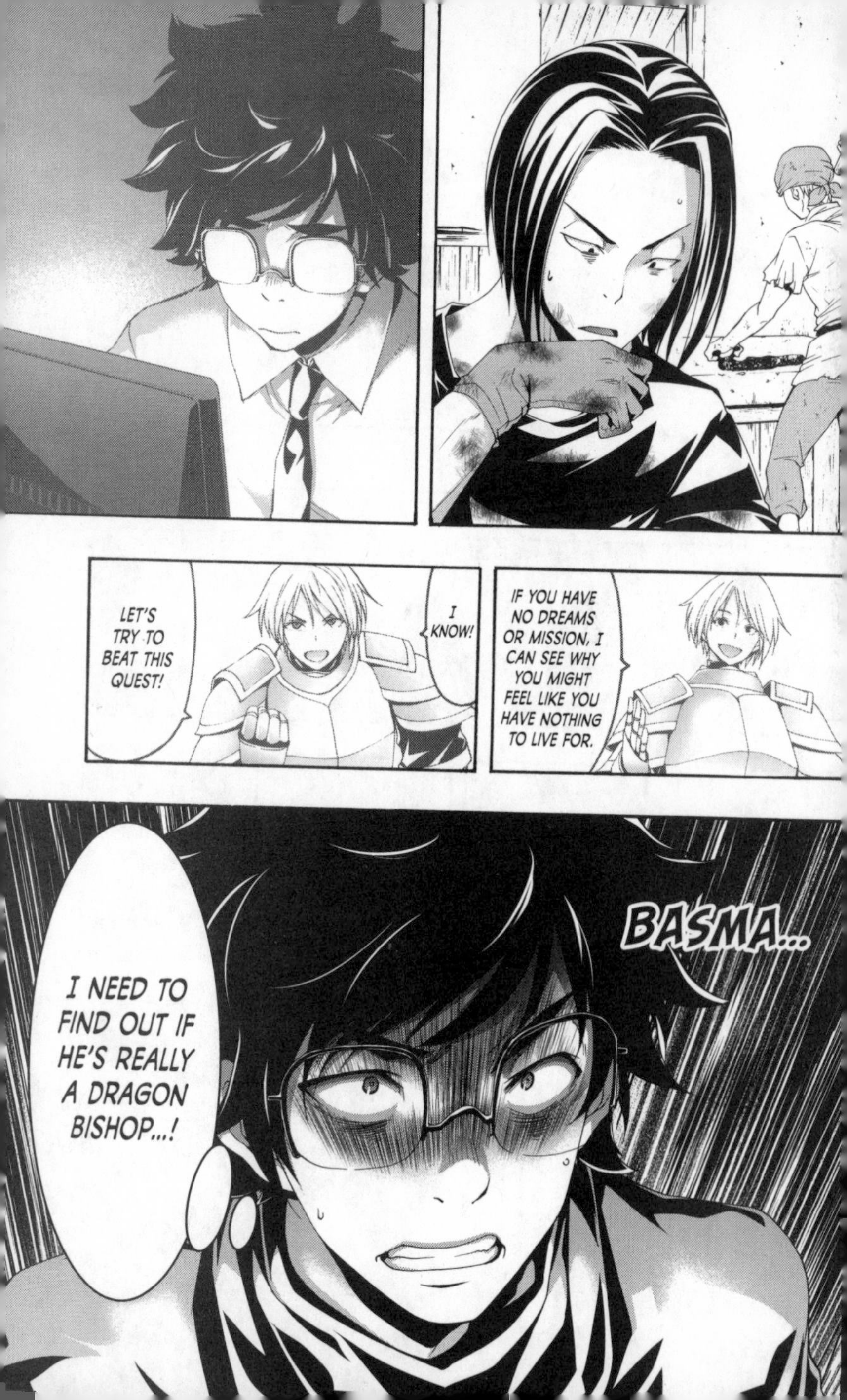
IF YOU HAVE NO DREAMS OR MISSION, I CAN SEE WHY YOU MIGHT FEEL LIKE YOU HAVE NOTHING TO LIVE FOR.
I KNOW!
LET'S TRY TO BEAT THIS QUEST!
BASMA...
I NEED TO FIND OUT IF HE'S REALLY A DRAGON BISHOP...!

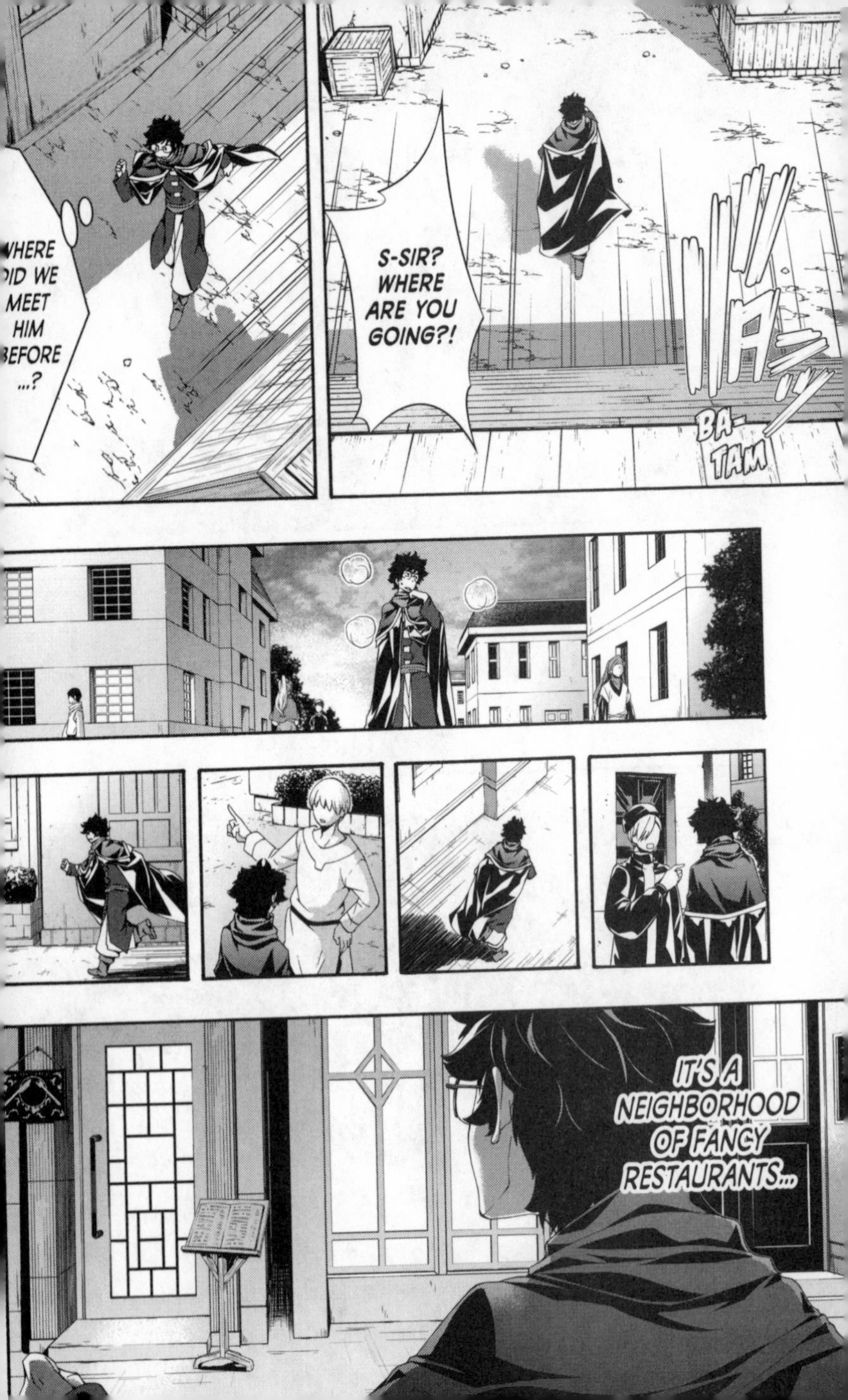
S-SIR? WHERE ARE YOU GOING?!
BA-TAM
WHERE DID WE MEET HIM BEFORE ...?
IT'S A NEIGHBORHOOD OF FANCY RESTAURANTS...

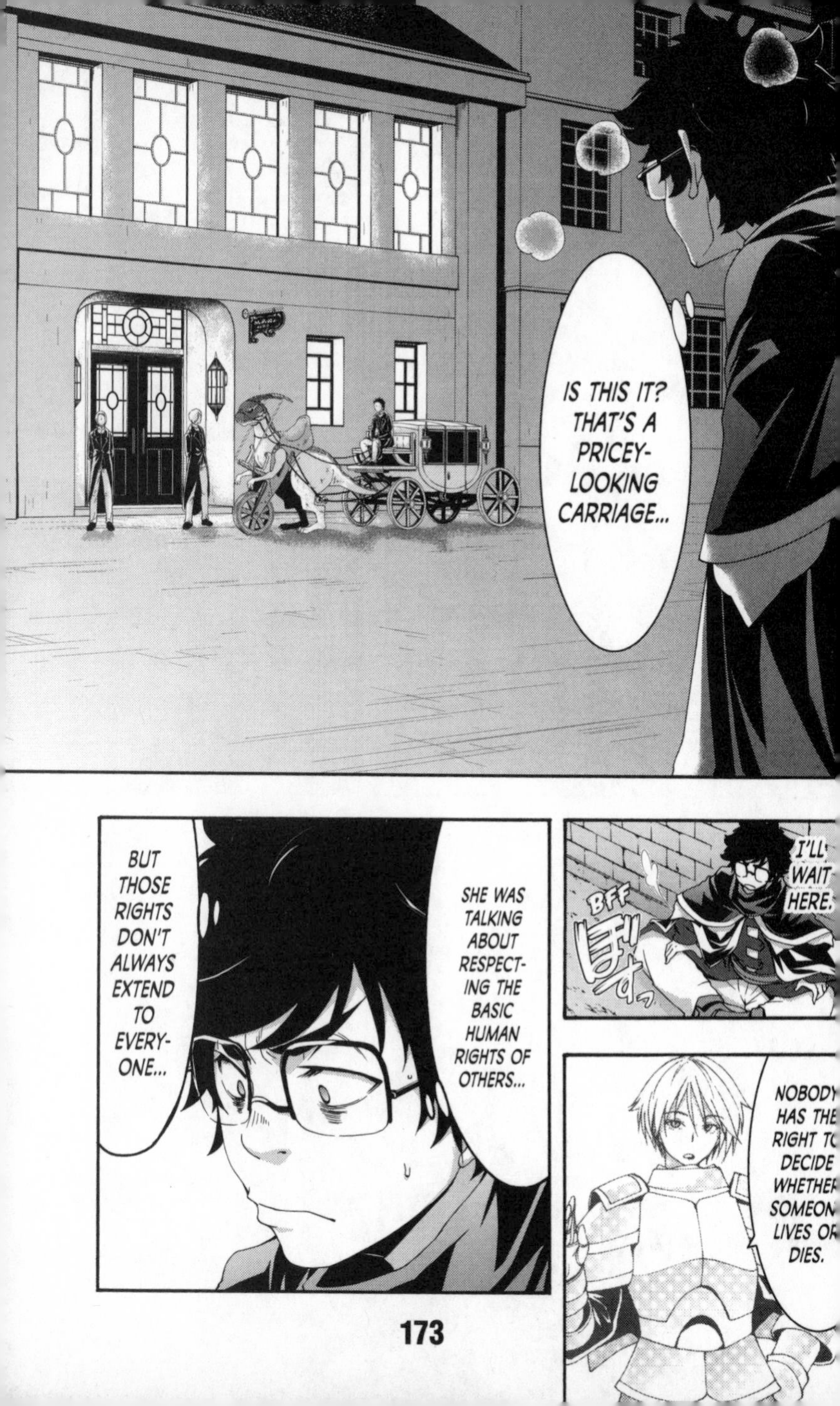

IS THIS IT? THAT'S A PRICEY-LOOKING CARRIAGE...
I'LL WAIT HERE.
BFF
NOBODY HAS THE RIGHT TO DECIDE WHETHER SOMEONE LIVES OR DIES.
SHE WAS TALKING ABOUT RESPECTING THE BASIC HUMAN RIGHTS OF OTHERS...
BUT THOSE RIGHTS DON'T ALWAYS EXTEND TO EVERYONE...

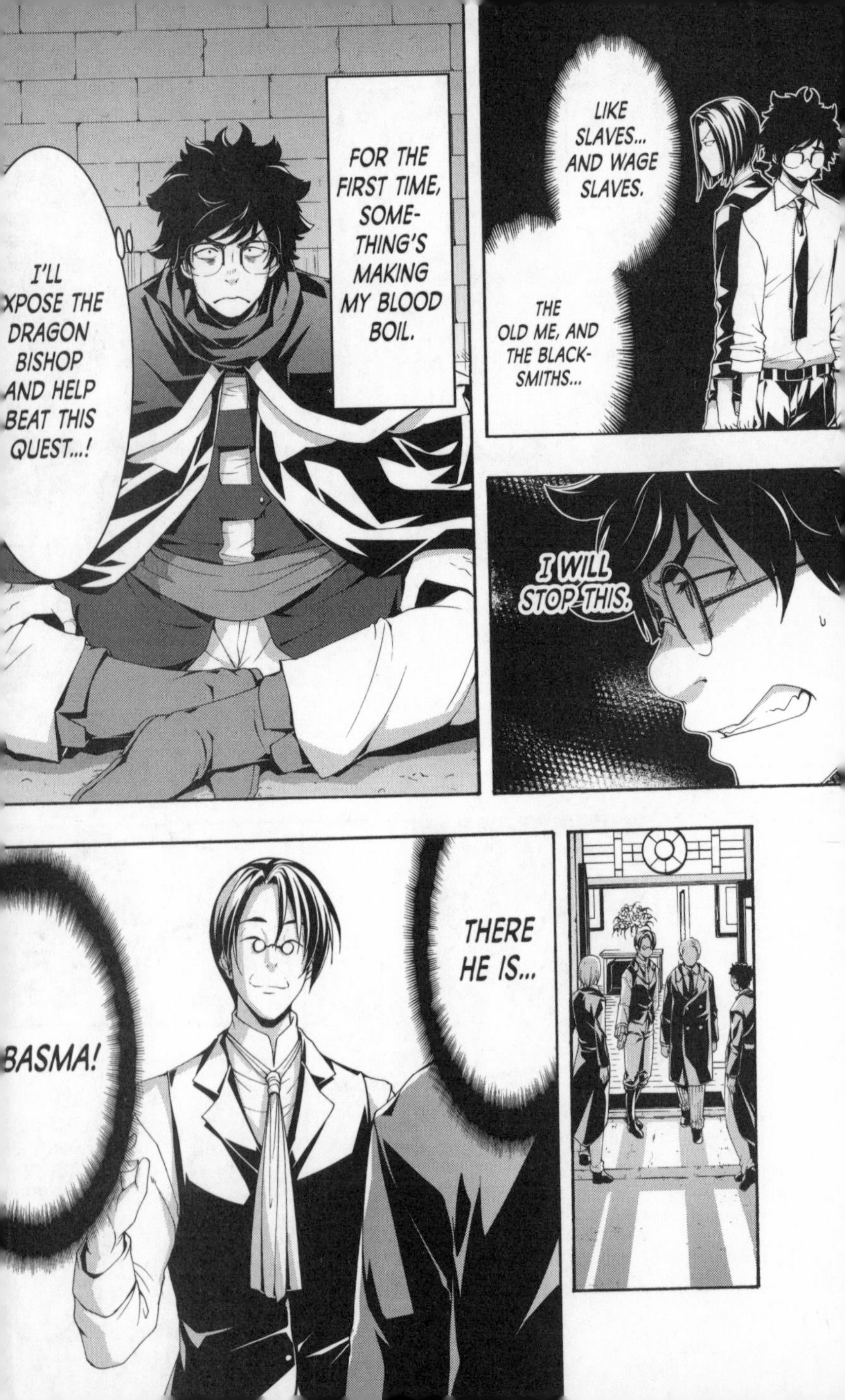

LIKE SLAVES... AND WAGE SLAVES.
THE OLD ME, AND THE BLACKSMITHS...
I WILL STOP THIS.
FOR THE FIRST TIME, SOMETHING'S MAKING MY BLOOD BOIL.
I'LL XPOSE THE DRAGON BISHOP AND HELP BEAT THIS QUEST...!
THERE HE IS...
BASMA!

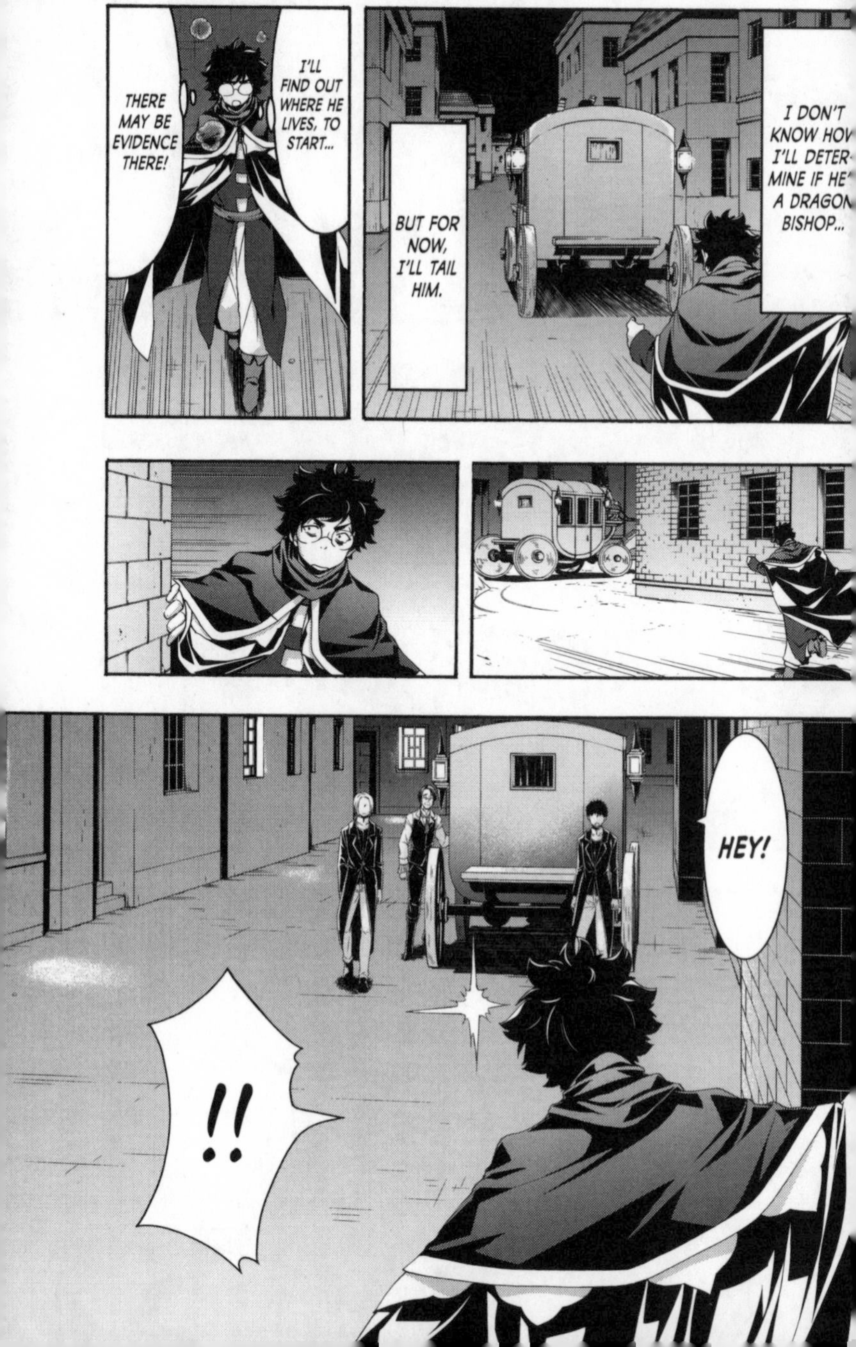
I DON'T KNOW HOV I'LL DETER-MINE IF HE' A DRAGON BISHOP...
BUT FOR NOW, I'LL TAIL HIM.
I'LL FIND OUT WHERE HE LIVES, TO START...
THERE MAY BE EVIDENCE THERE!
HEY!
!!

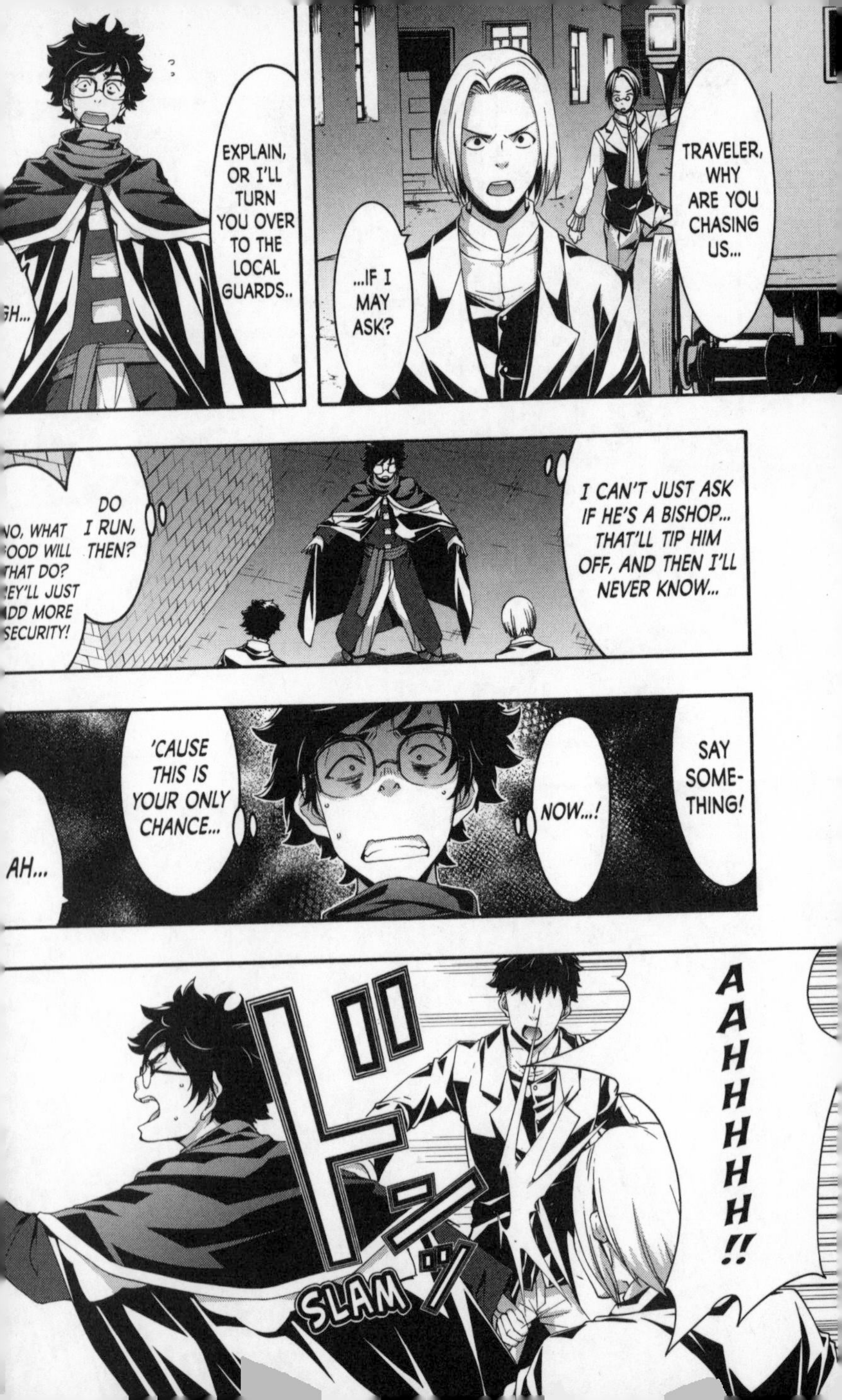

TRAVELER, WHY ARE YOU CHASING US...
...IF I MAY ASK?
EXPLAIN, OR I'LL TURN YOU OVER TO THE LOCAL GUARDS..
GH...
I CAN'T JUST ASK IF HE'S A BISHOP... THAT'LL TIP HIM OFF, AND THEN I'LL NEVER KNOW...
DO I RUN, THEN?
NO, WHAT OOD WILL THAT DO? EY'LL JUST DD MORE SECURITY!
SAY SOME-THING!
NOW...!
'CAUSE THIS IS YOUR ONLY CHANCE...
AH...
AAHHHHHH!!
SLAM

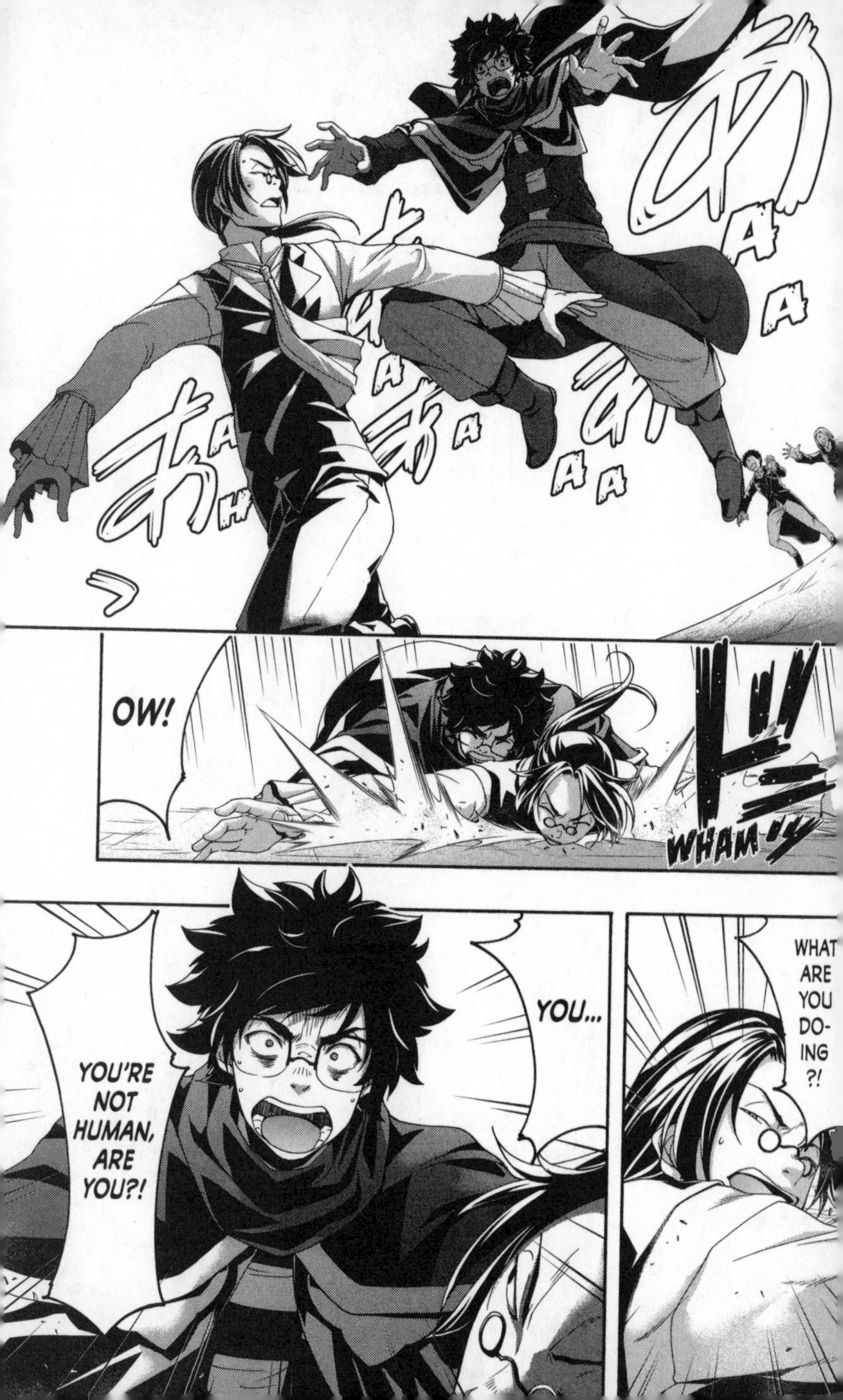

OW!
WHAM
WHAT ARE YOU DO-ING?!
YOU...
YOU'RE NOT HUMAN, ARE YOU?!

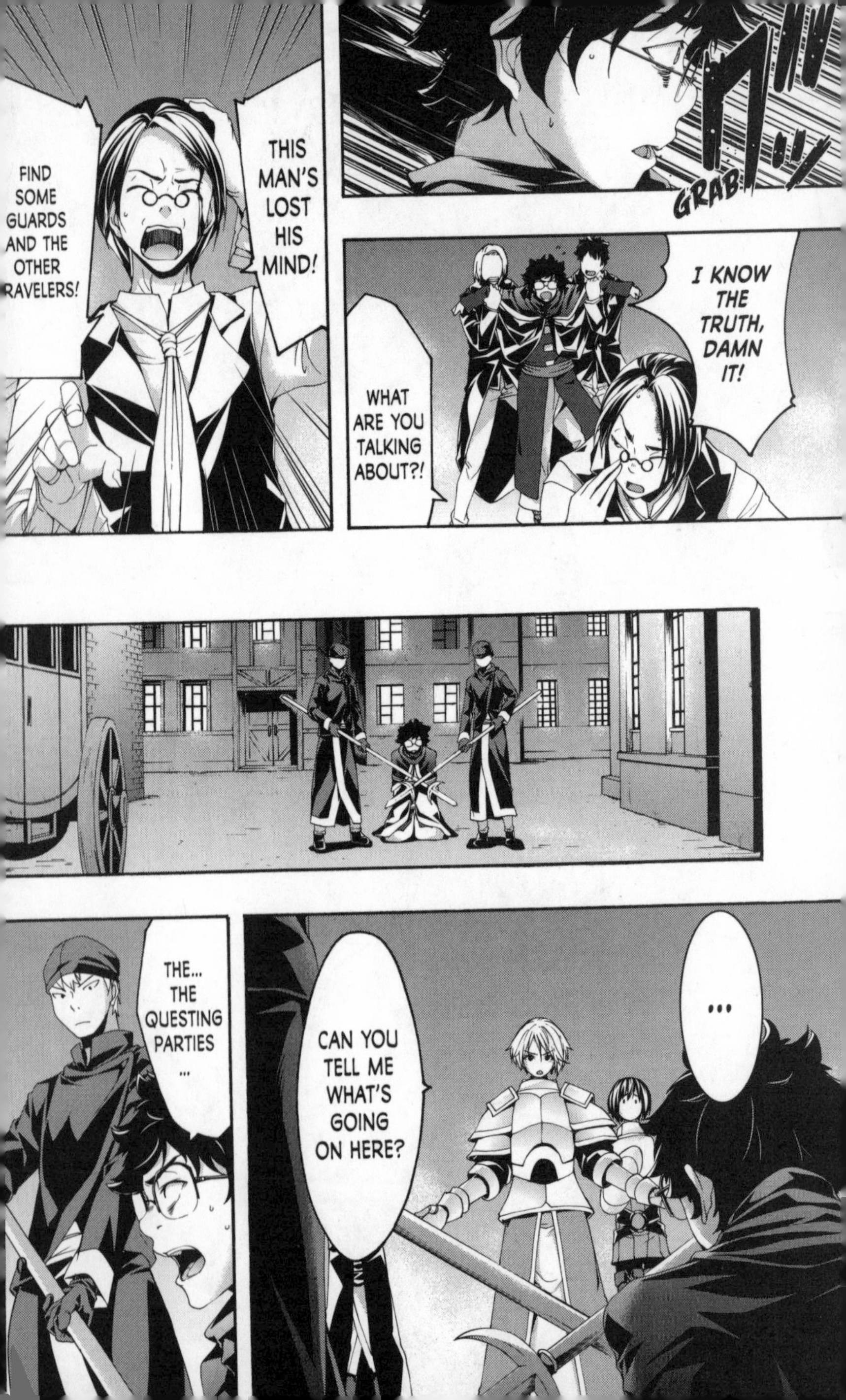
GRAB
I KNOW THE TRUTH, DAMN IT!
WHAT ARE YOU TALKING ABOUT?!
THIS MAN'S LOST HIS MIND!
FIND SOME GUARDS AND THE OTHER RAVELERS!
...
CAN YOU TELL ME WHAT'S GOING ON HERE?
THE... THE QUESTING PARTIES ...

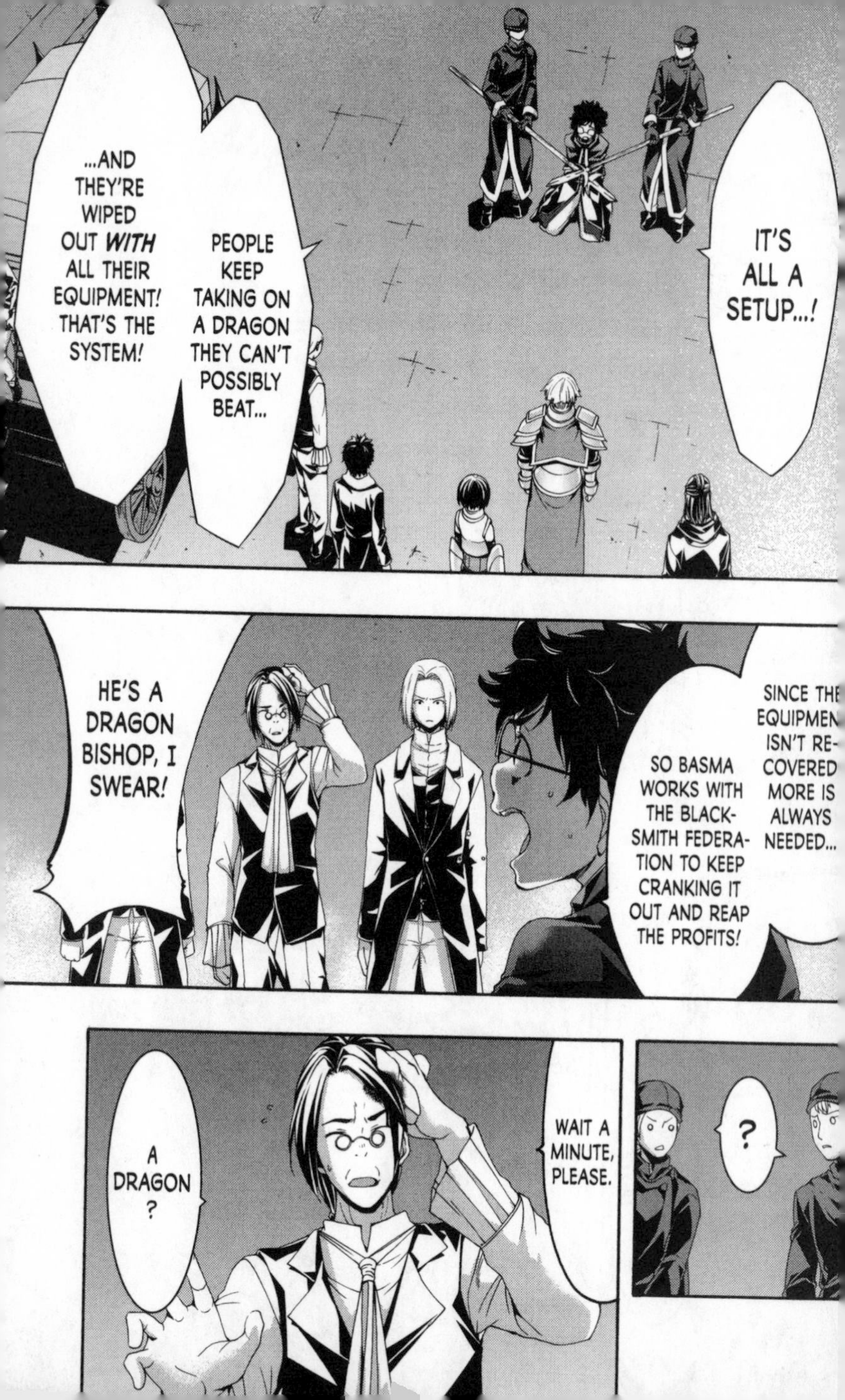
IT'S ALL A SETUP...!
PEOPLE KEEP TAKING ON A DRAGON THEY CAN'T POSSIBLY BEAT...
...AND THEY'RE WIPED OUT *WITH* ALL THEIR EQUIPMENT! THAT'S THE SYSTEM!
SINCE THE EQUIPMEN ISN'T RECOVERED MORE IS ALWAYS NEEDED...
SO BASMA WORKS WITH THE BLACKSMITH FEDERATION TO KEEP CRANKING IT OUT AND REAP THE PROFITS!
HE'S A DRAGON BISHOP, I SWEAR!
?
WAIT A MINUTE, PLEASE.
A DRAGON?

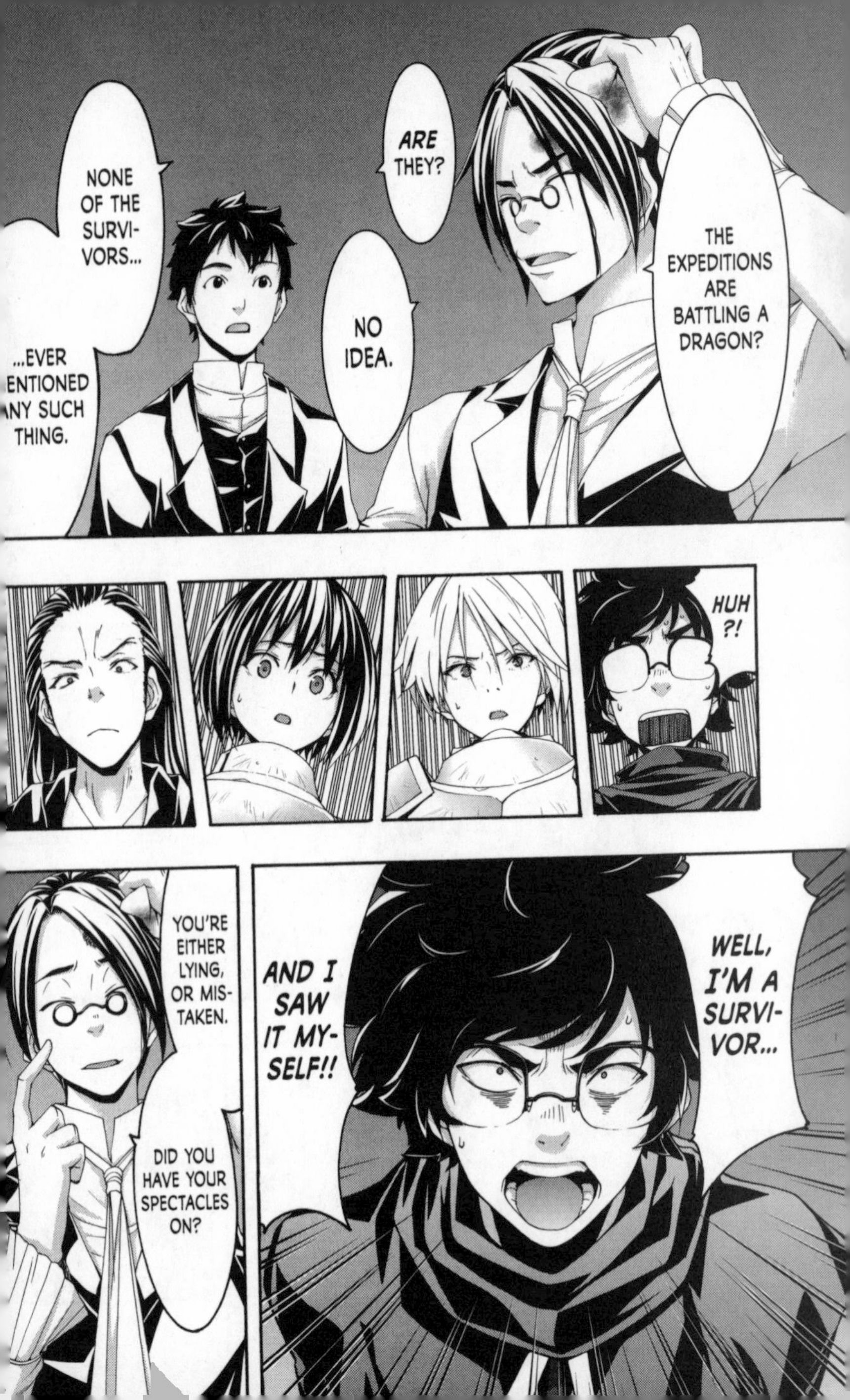
THE EXPEDITIONS ARE BATTLING A DRAGON?
ARE THEY?
NO IDEA.
NONE OF THE SURVIVORS...
...EVER ENTIONED NY SUCH THING.
HUH ?!
WELL, I'M A SURVIVOR...
AND I SAW IT MYSELF!!
YOU'RE EITHER LYING, OR MISTAKEN.
DID YOU HAVE YOUR SPECTACLES ON?

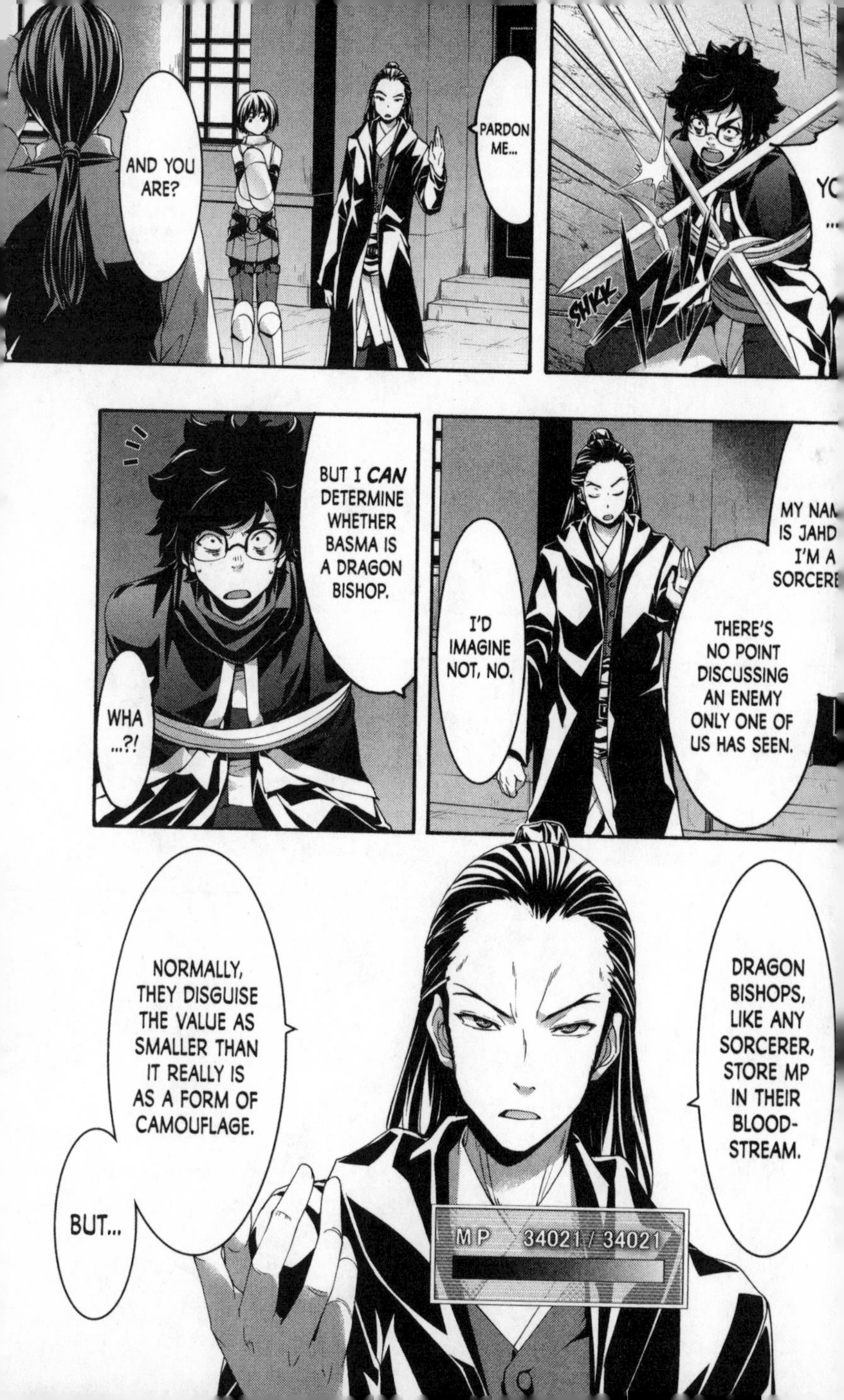
YC ...
SHKK
PARDON ME...
AND YOU ARE?
MY NAM IS JAHD I'M A SORCERE
THERE'S NO POINT DISCUSSING AN ENEMY ONLY ONE OF US HAS SEEN.
I'D IMAGINE NOT, NO.
BUT I *CAN* DETERMINE WHETHER BASMA IS A DRAGON BISHOP.
WHA ...?!
DRAGON BISHOPS, LIKE ANY SORCERER, STORE MP IN THEIR BLOOD-STREAM.
NORMALLY, THEY DISGUISE THE VALUE AS SMALLER THAN IT REALLY IS AS A FORM OF CAMOUFLAGE.
BUT...
MP 34021 / 34021

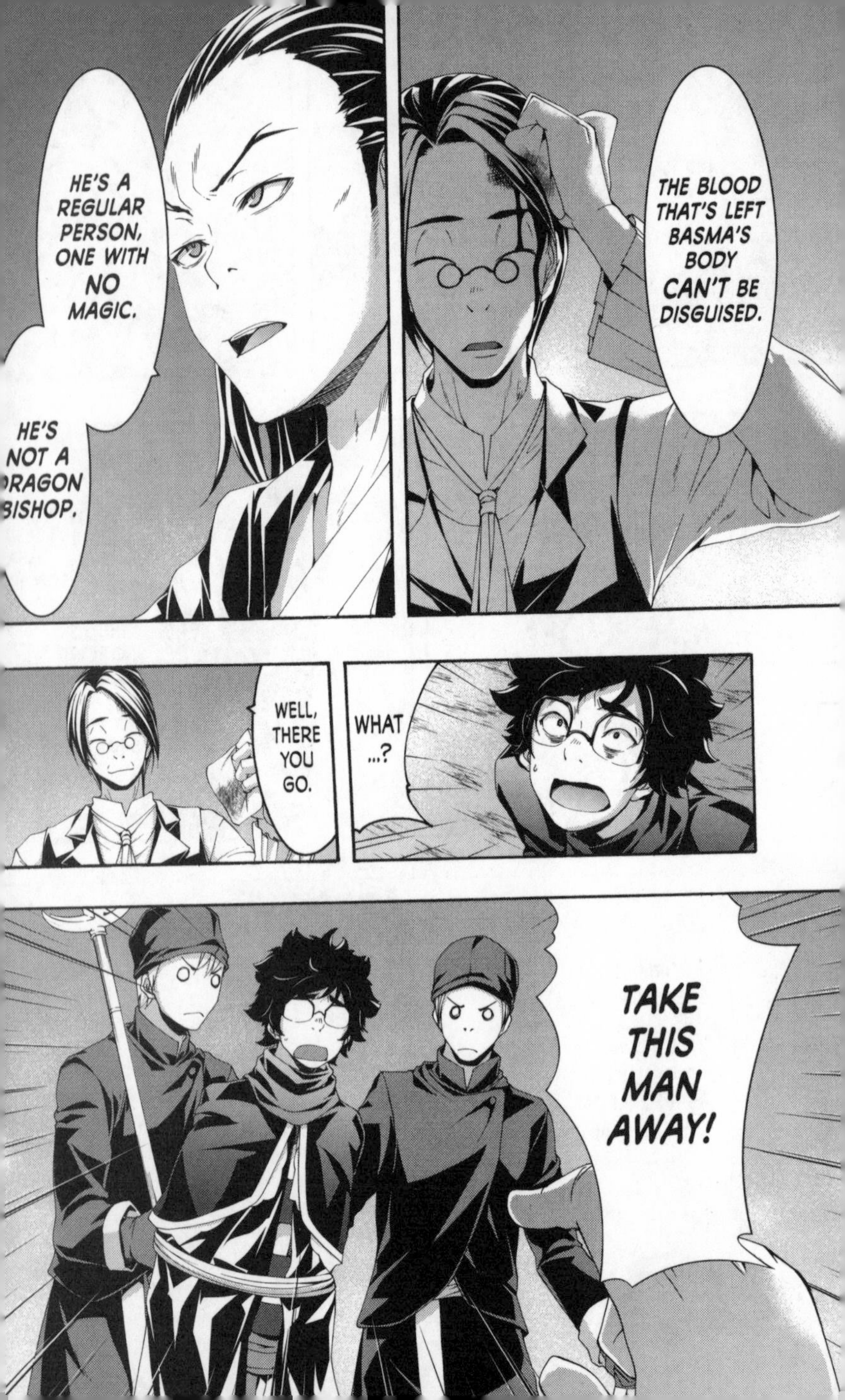
THE BLOOD THAT'S LEFT BASMA'S BODY CAN'T BE DISGUISED.
HE'S A REGULAR PERSON, ONE WITH NO MAGIC.
HE'S NOT A RAGON ISHOP.
WHAT ...?
WELL, THERE YOU GO.
TAKE THIS MAN AWAY!

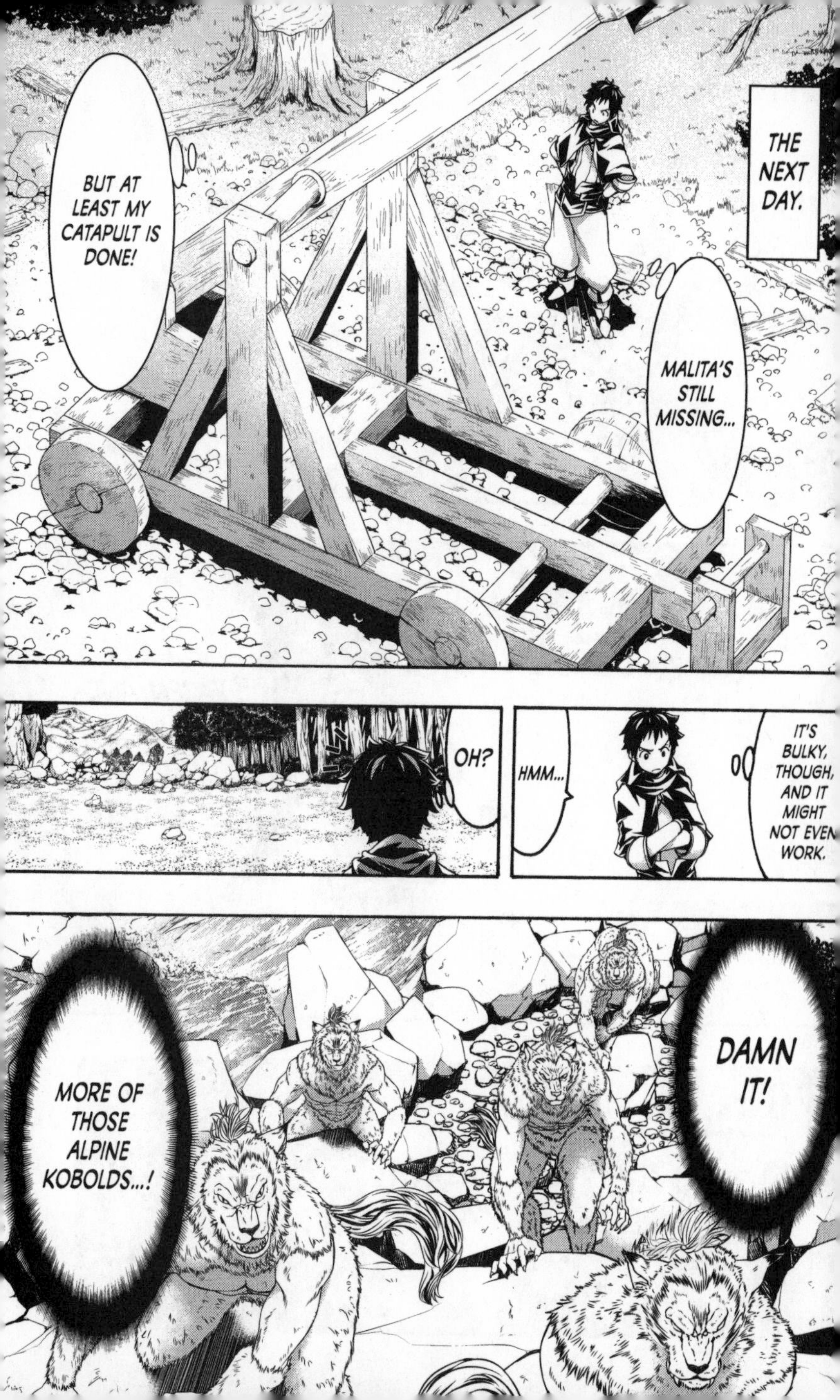
THE NEXT DAY.
MALITA'S STILL MISSING...
BUT AT LEAST MY CATAPULT IS DONE!
IT'S BULKY, THOUGH, AND IT MIGHT NOT EVEN WORK.
HMM...
OH?
DAMN IT!
MORE OF THOSE ALPINE KOBOLDS...!

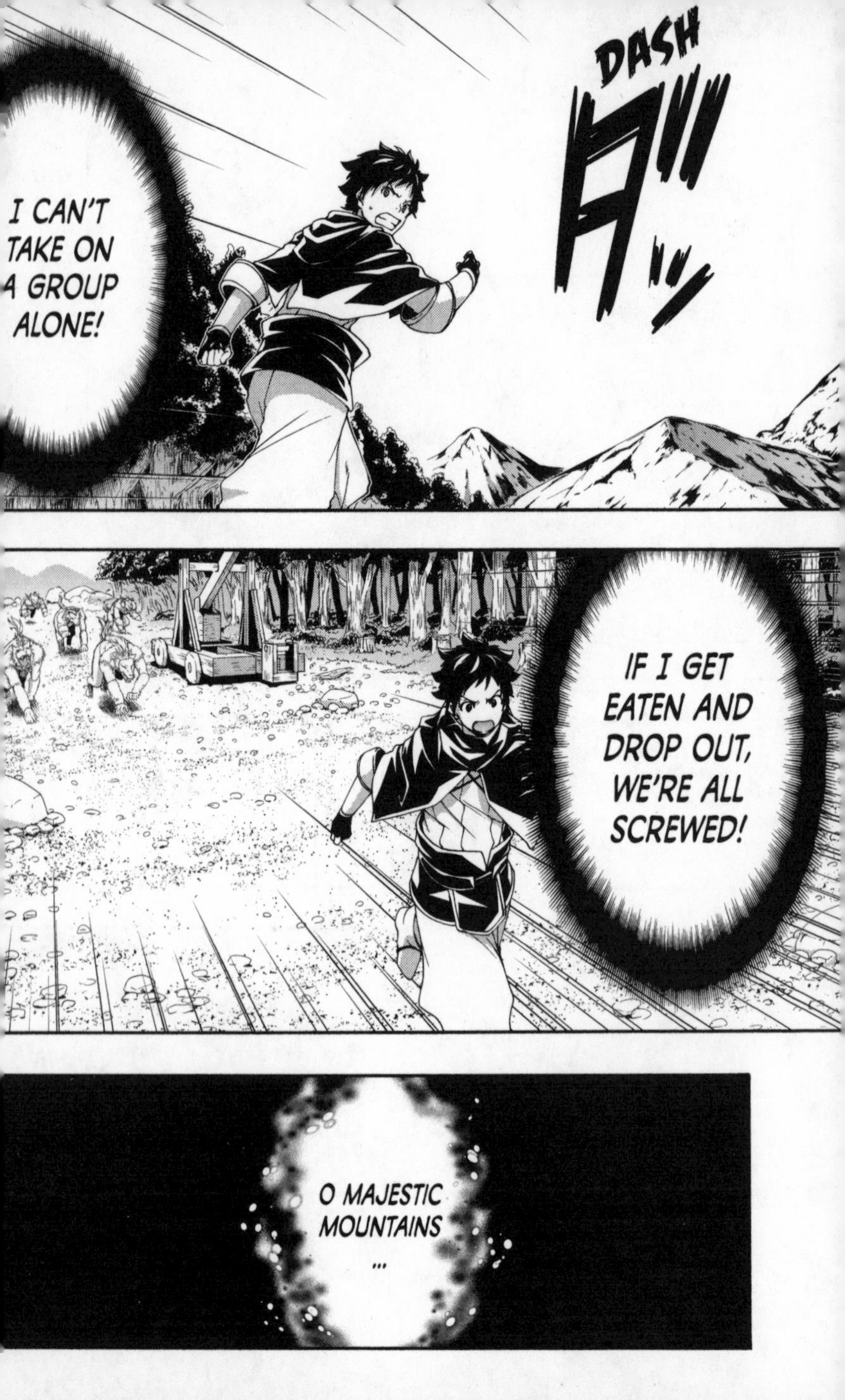
DASH
I CAN'T TAKE ON A GROUP ALONE!
IF I GET EATEN AND DROP OUT, WE'RE ALL SCREWED!
O MAJESTIC MOUNTAINS ...

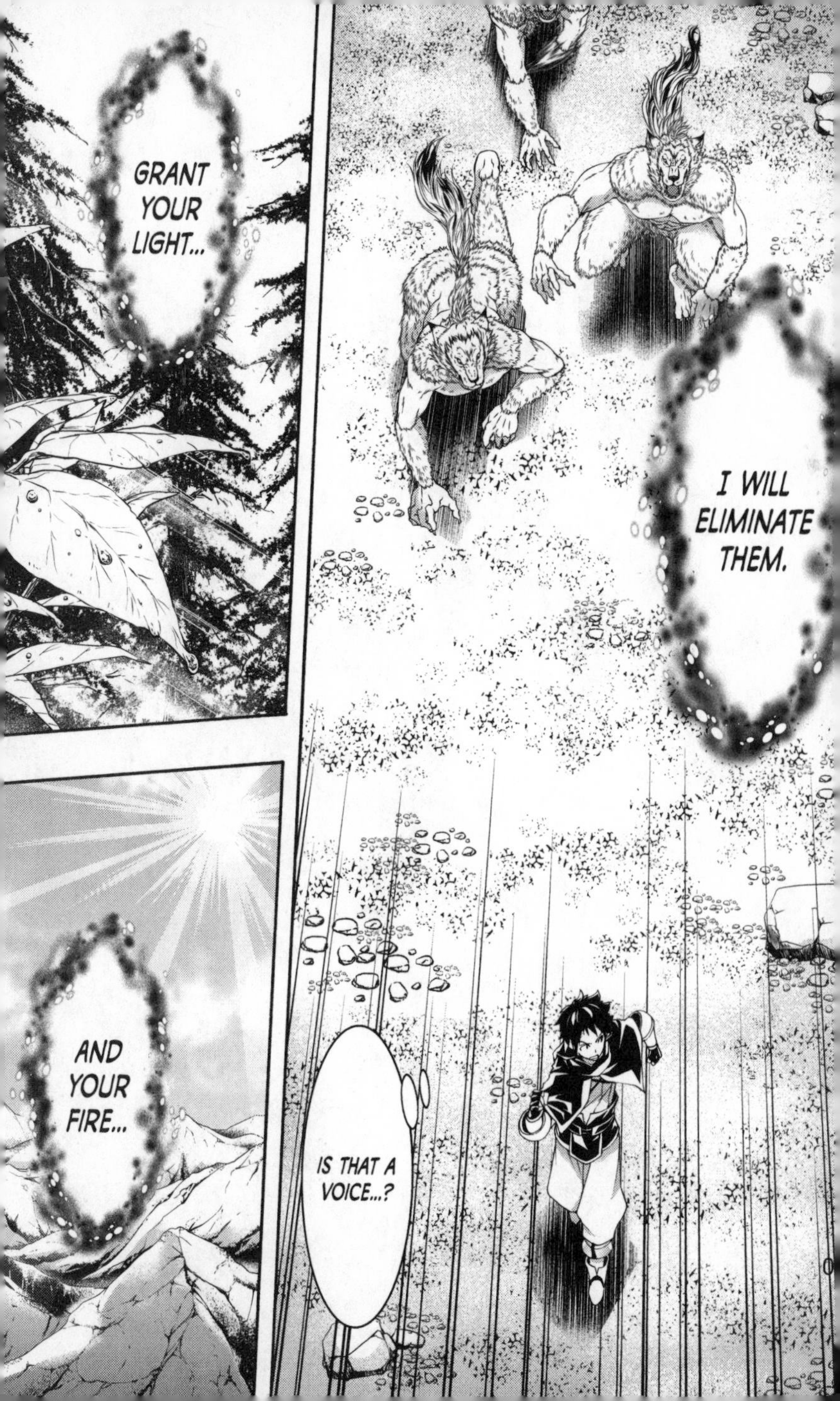
I WILL ELIMINATE THEM.
IS THAT A VOICE...?
GRANT YOUR LIGHT...
AND YOUR FIRE...

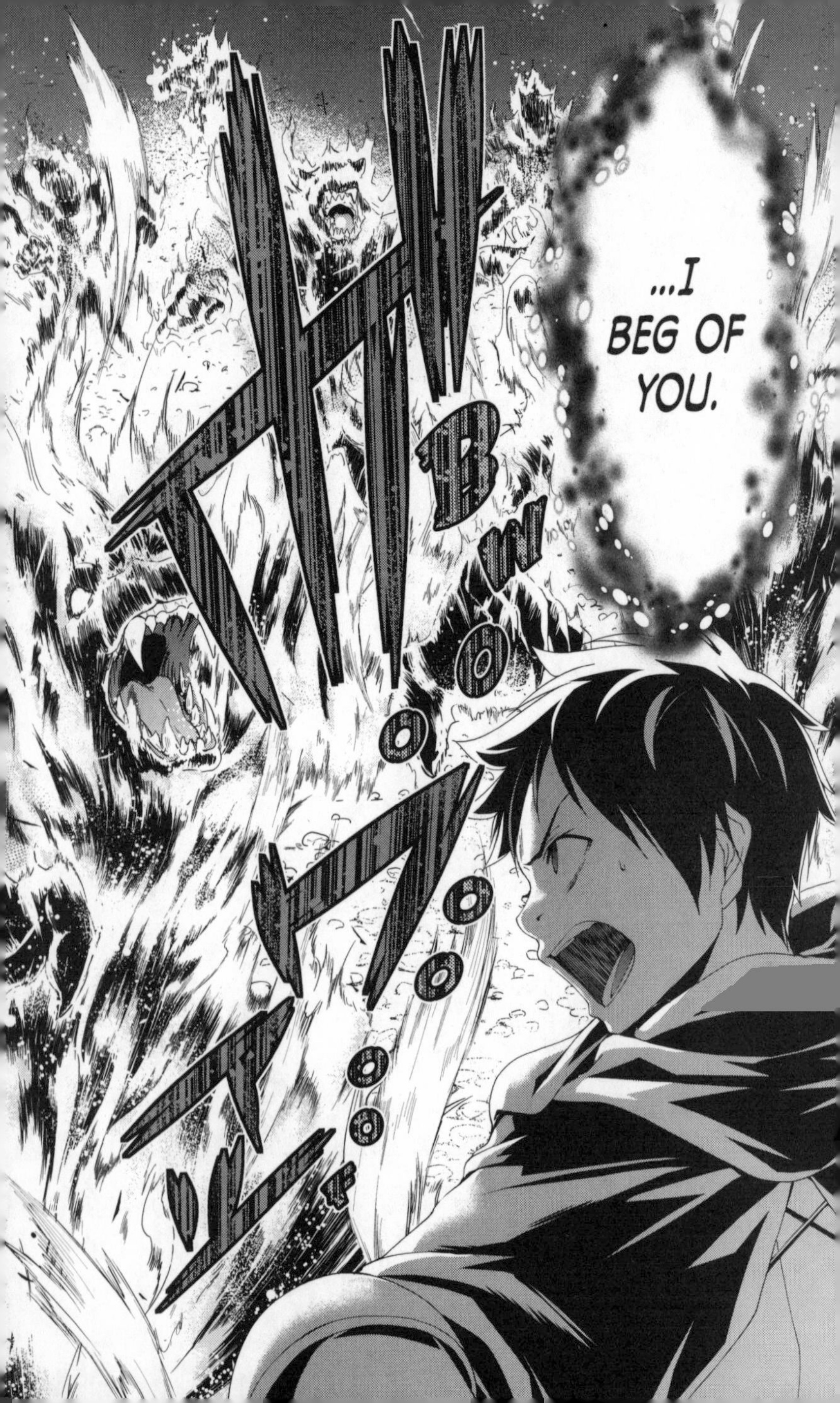
...I BEG OF YOU.

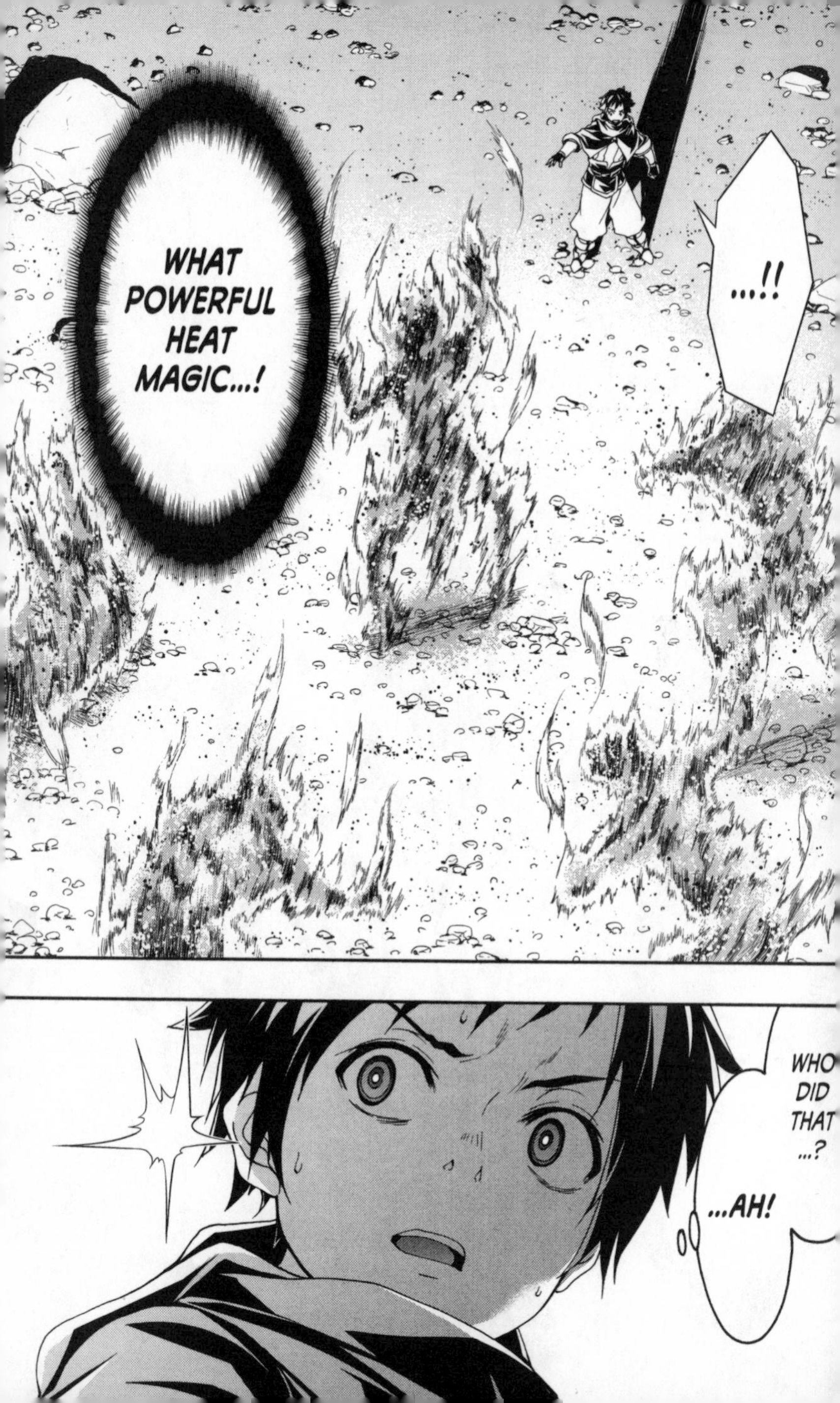

...!!
WHAT POWERFUL HEAT MAGIC...!
WHO DID THAT ...?
...AH!

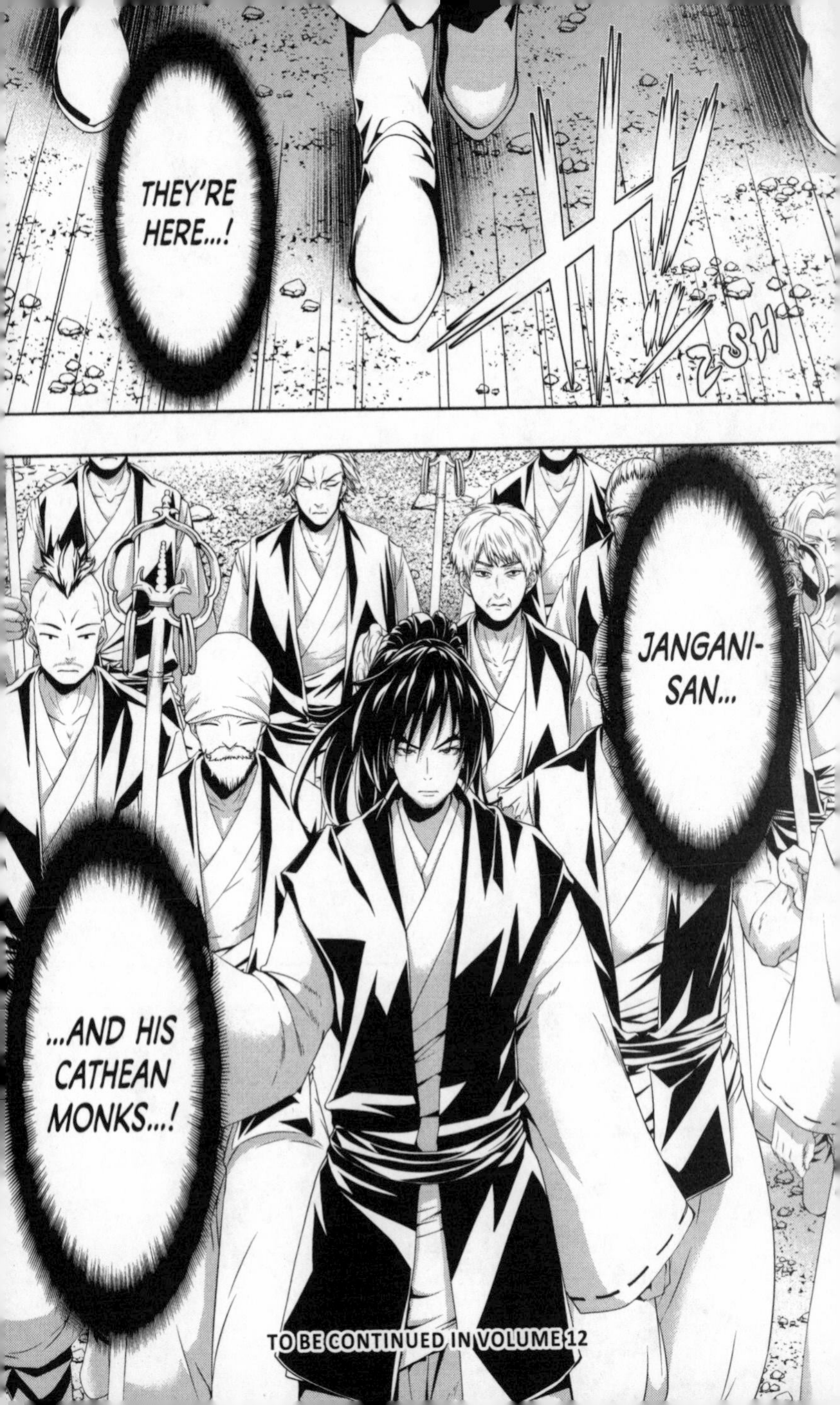
THEY'RE HERE...!
ZSH
JANGANI-SAN...
...AND HIS CATHEAN MONKS...!
TO BE CONTINUED IN VOLUME 12

Young characters and steampunk setting, like *Howl's Moving Castle* and *Battle Angel Alita*

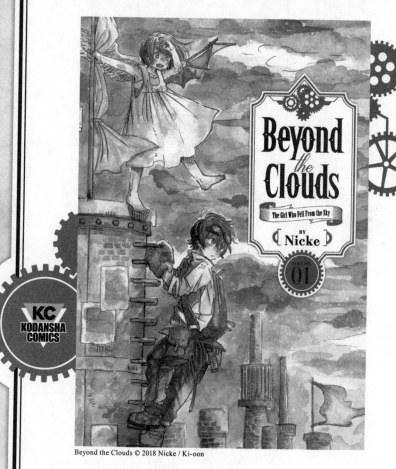

Beyond the Clouds © 2018 Nicke / Ki-oon

A boy with a talent for machines and a mysterious girl whose wings he's fixed will take you beyond the clouds! In the tradition of the high-flying, resonant adventure stories of Studio Ghibli comes a gorgeous tale about the longing of young hearts for adventure and friendship!

Knight of the Ice ©Yayoi Oga...

Yayoi Oga...

SKATING THRILLS AND ICY CHILLS WITH THIS NEW TINGLY ROMANCE SERIES!

A rom-com on ice, perfect for fans of *Princess Jellyfish* and *Wotakoi*.

Kokoro is the talk of the figure-skating world, winning trophies and hearts. But little do they know... he's actually a huge nerd! From the beloved creator of *You're My Pet* (*Tramps Like Us*).

Chitose is a serious young woman, working for the health magazine *SASSO*. Or at least, she would be, if she wasn't constantly getting distracted by her childhood friend, international figure skating star Kokoro Kijinami! In the public eye and on the ice, Kokoro is a gallant, flawless knight, but behind his glittery costumes and breathtaking spins lies a secret: He's actually a hopelessly romantic otaku, who can only land his quad jumps when Chitose is on hand to recite a spell from his favorite magical girl anime!

KC
KODANSHA
COMICS